Stained Glass

A Novel

Patsy Ann Odom

ISBN-13: 978-0998194967
ISBN-10: 0998194964

UNIVERSITY
PRESS

St. Andrews University Press

St. Andrews University
(A Branch of Webber International University)
1700 Dogwood Mile
Laurinburg, NC 28352
press@sa.edu
(910) 277-5310

For my children:

The light of my life
Pam, Dwayne, and Kim

and my grandchildren:
Carrie, Jeff, Ashleigh, Adam, Matt, Daniel, and David

Acknowledgments

To write a book has been my lifelong wish. But I procrastinated. I wrote in journals, created vignettes, played with poems, and dropped them all into a box that gathered dust. One day at Scotland High (Laurinburg) we English teachers formed a writers' club. We wrote, read aloud, listened, and responded with our ideas. From their encouragement I started writing all the time with a new belief in myself. In time the club dwindled, my writing waned, papers filled the old box. No one to share with. Yet that encouragement prevailed.

I am deeply grateful for the continuing faith from my friends, colleagues, and family. They believed in me when I doubted myself. There are too many names to list.

Now I have my own book on a shelf.

I cannot thank my editor, Dr. Ted Wojtasik, enough for sending it out to others. Ted, without you my novel would not exist. Heartfelt thanks go to you for your incredible expertise and patience. You never seemed to mind that I changed the chapter rewrites at least three or four times after they were done. You always listened to me intently and came up with logical answers. I am grateful for your keen insight into the story and your ideas. Thank you for giving me new perspectives, keeping me focused, and moving the pieces into shape. But most of all, thank you for believing in me and becoming a friend.

Many thanks go to Gwyn Harris and Kate Blackburn as my first readers and their enthusiasm for my stories. I appreciate their proofreading, feedback, ideas, and hours of talking. And Kate, thanks for turning a mess into concise prose. To Sarah McIntyre Watson, thank you so much for your help along the way: your interest, your listening and sharing of ideas, the information about Bird Island, your loyal support, and many kindnesses. The life-long friendships we all shared are priceless.

To my more recent weekly writing group that's lasted for years I give my heartfelt gratitude to Nancy Barrineau and Sue Fidler. What would I have done without you? I doubt that I would have finished a book. Thank you for reading hundreds of pages, giving feedback for rewrites of numerous drafts, copy-editing, fine-tuning characters, and scrutinizing the narrative voice. And most of all, thank you for your continuing support, inspiration, and friendship. You've helped me understand my own novel. And you never gave up on me. Love to you.

To Carol Whitehead, thank you so much for all your enthusiasm and joy in living that has kept me going. On the days I found myself under a big writer's block, I knew all I had to do was call you—and you'd knock it off. I love you for that. I appreciate all the hours you've listened to me. And to Barbara Edwards Dunn, many thanks for your continuing support and zeal in spreading the news about my book among your friends and acquaintances in Pinehurst and Southern Pines, and in your book club. I love having you as my friend. To my artist friend Cathy Adams, a tremendous thank you for the beautiful art on the book's cover. You knew exactly how to paint symbols of heart-felt moments.

To the ladies in my three book clubs—the Thursday Afternoon Book Club, the Bookmark Club, and the Wild Women—I appreciate very much the interest and support you have shown me. I hope you'll enjoy reading my novel.

A lot of gratitude goes to the Weymouth Center in Southern Pines for giving me weeks to escape into another world to write and converse with other published writers. Many thanks to Dr. Shelby Stephenson, North Carolina Poet Laureate (2015-2018), former creative writing professor, and editor of *Pembroke Magazine* at the University of North Carolina at Pembroke. I'm deeply grateful to you for publishing my personal essay "Of Ghosts and Time" in *Pembroke Magazine,* a small part of which appears in my book.

Finally, my family. I love you all for what you do and say. During my writing journey you accepted my disappearances into a make-believe world. Thank you for understanding and allowing me space. Your patience has been remarkable and your content input wise. Thank you tremendously for your support in more ways than I can say. I give special thanks to my daughters Kim and Pam for their technical assistance. And to my son Dwayne, along with his sisters, a heartfelt thank you for believing in me.

Prologue

I dream of our old house being torn down, ripped apart, bit by bit, each piece pulled away by workmen who hurl the shingles and rafters, the window frames and doors, the front steps and the back steps, into mighty rushing winds. The mantel swooshes through empty rooms, vanishes. I push back the old mahogany chifforobe: it topples from the wall and turns to paper, thin sheets torn, caught up in the wind, swirling and swirling, like a child's pinwheel that starts to whistle like a train in the distance. The stained glass windows from the unfinished third floor, my childhood place of magic, comfort, and seclusion, crack and splinter into a magnificent kaleidoscope of colors that spreads and scatters bright shards of glass, caught by the mighty rushing winds, swirling and swirling, all about me as I try to catch the fragments that cut and slice my fingers and hands, bleeding and bleeding as the pinwheel starts to whistle like a train in the distance to whisper words of midnight dreams that come with the train sounds, rumbling and clanking, and become rushing winds, swirling and swirling, and the whistling intermingles with bright shards of stained glass and magic vibrates a primeval hum, low, long, its bellow reverberating over and over, roaring a shrill cry of pain or ecstasy that merges with the rushing winds, swirling and swirling, rumbling on and on and on, fading out down the track that leads me back to that other time ... healing.

Chapter 1

In January 1977, the phone rings at 3:30 and interrupts the English Department meeting. We jump as if reacting to a car's backfire or to a gunshot. The call is for me. Brennan, my son, 15 years old, enunciates each word equally, "Mama, come home."

He does not blurt out his typical "Mama, when're you coming home? I'm starving." No. My heart thumps. Something is wrong. His tone of voice is different—low, controlled, stripped, emphatic. Then his voice breaks. Brennan does not get emotional. He does not cry. I motion to Martha Sue, the department chair, and hurry from the room.

Outside an icy wind whips around the corner of Oakland High School, nearly pushing me over, and blows dirty snow across the parking lot, banking it tight against the cars. For weeks now this winter anomaly has shocked the Sandhills region and swept havoc across the South—a blizzard in North Carolina?

When I pull out onto 74 West a police car, blue lights flashing, speeds past Sam's Pit-Cooked Barbeque, swings around the Shell Station on the corner, and races down the exit to 401. I know where the car's headed. I flick on my lights and step on it, emulating the cop's lane changing amid slosh and ice. Keeping pace with the police car holds most of my focus. But horrendous questions dart at me: Where's Kayleigh? Is she all right? What about Annie Mae? If something happened to Alex, wouldn't her college have notified me by now? Mama? Oh, my God, what has she done?

It's strange when trauma happens. I can do whatever I have to do calmly and rationally without being present because I have already left my body and am floating somewhere nearby, carried by a force pushing me along to watch the other me—I listen and watch and feel.

And I see a blur of images: the police car's blue lights flashing in our driveway, neighbors milling around in the street, people waiting in our yard—watching our house. Everywhere. And Kayleigh, my 13-year-old daughter, dashes down the front steps, screaming and sobbing, and rushes across the street to her friend's house. Brennan hugs me and says, "Mama, don't go in there."

Preston, the sheriff, holds me tight in his arms as I smell that familiar whiff of Old Spice and cigar smoke. I feel completely safe, and then I lean back and look into his dark brown eyes that tell me what I haven't asked. With his arm around my shoulder, Preston leads me up the porch steps into the foyer and says in his low drawl, "Don't go any further, Erin. Just wait in the living room. The other room has to be cleaned."

Brennan steps forward and holds me, determined that I not go any closer. Shadows of people keep moving in and out. More police? More deputies? Then the coroner: his tall, thin figure in an all-black suit floats through the crowd. Over Brennan's shoulder, from the hallway, I see the end of a green sheet draped over a stretcher held by men leaving the den to go out the kitchen door. A policeman follows with a shotgun, one hand on the handle and another holding up the barrel—Brennan's shotgun that he got for Christmas, a month before.

I did not want to buy the shotgun. For a couple of years now Brennan has hunted with his buddies and their older brothers or dads and even the sheriff himself. He begged me for his own gun and promised to be careful and responsible. Preston, a long-time family friend, knew about my anxieties but convinced me to buy the shotgun. Brennan kept it unloaded on a high shelf in his closet. The buckshot shells were also there in a box.

A neighbor's husband immediately drives through record snow to Lees-McRae College to get my daughter Alex and to break the news to her gently. Another neighbor washes the bloody door leading to Brennan's room, closes off the room, and makes the den presentable.

I listen to the coroner in a low monotonous voice questioning and questioning my son and then me. I am shaking all over and freezing from the cold air that rushes in through doors, opening and closing, and I am horror-struck at Brennan's answers.

"After school," he says, "me and my buddy stop in the drive and see Kayleigh running down the front steps and screaming something about Grandma's dead and blood's on the floor. We run into the house and find Grandma's body on the floor in my bedroom. Her head's half gone and bloody. One eye hangs down. There's stuff everywhere. All over the ceilings and walls. Looks like an explosion. When I hear Kayleigh come back inside, I run out to keep her from seeing anything more than a body. I call the sheriff and then I call Mama."

I talk to the coroner, but I don't want to go back to the place where I was this morning—to see Mama's face at the window, staring at me, eyes empty, watching me leave. I tell him how earlier she'd followed me from room to room, wringing her hands while I rushed to gather books, purse, and coat to get to school on time with Brennan and Kayleigh already waiting in the car. "Erin Rose," Mama pleads, "don't leave me. Please don't leave. Tell me. What can I do today?" I'm running late. I'm empty of answers. "Mama, I don't know!" I answer as I shut the door in her face. Standing at the car I look back and see her eyes through the glass pane.

The local radio station announces Mama's death, and the food starts pouring in. Sweet potato pie is first. Then I can't believe the stream of visitors and food: fried chicken, field peas with okra, pecan pie, speckled butter beans, country-ham biscuits, apple pie, and more. Where am I to put it all? We have enough pies to start a bakery. And all my neighbors and friends offer to help, to hug, and to pray.

I pick up the phone to call Aunt Agatha, Mama's younger sister and my favorite relative. Is there any soft way to tell her?

When she answers, my voice is calm, emotionless— my heart racing, my insides trembling.

"Aunt Agatha, Mama shot herself."

There is silence and a long pause. She catches her breath. "Oh, Erin Rose ... my goodness, Honey. What are you saying? Oh, dear Lord, what has she done? How is she?"

"She's dead, Aunt Agatha." I sound like a little girl with a tiny voice.

"Oh, no-o-o. I'm on my way."

The police have gone to visit Annie Mae, a dear friend, a black woman, our maid-cook-nanny, who has worked for us every weekday since Kayleigh was five years old. She stays in the house until I get home from school. Now that Alex is in college, and Kayleigh and Brennan are in school until 3:00, Annie Mae works in the mornings and stays with Mama until 1:00. The police put Annie Mae through a detailed inquisition until they are satisfied that Mama took down the gun after Annie Mae left that afternoon.

Mama is gone, I keep assuring myself, as I sit on the sofa in the living room. However, I still feel her presence in the air around me, her eyes staring, following me wherever I walk like the eyes of a framed portrait in an art gallery.

Kayleigh has returned home from her friend's house.

"Mama," she says and hugs me. She lays her head on my chest. My arm goes around her, and I lean over to kiss the top of her head.

"Mama, something strange happened to me today."

"Do you want to tell me about it, Honey?"

"I knew about it, Mama. The minute the school bus stopped at our house and I stepped down in our yard. It was snowing. I looked up at our house and I was scared. I couldn't stop shaking. I felt something terrible had happened. I screamed, 'What's wrong?' I knew it was Grandma. She'd done something awful. I dropped my book sack and ran."

Now it is night. Ghostly quiet. Everyone is gone. Kayleigh and Brennan are asleep upstairs, and I wait for Alex to come home from the Appalachian Mountains through the flurry of snow. I pray for my dear friend who went after her.

This is the first time today my dry tears turn wet. I had felt so alone. I didn't know I had any real friends in this town. Even though Oak Glen is my hometown, my old home is gone, my family gone, my school friends gone. I never thought my acquaintances and colleagues were real friends. I had visualized my children and me in our own world, different from others—no father, no husband. My mother in her world of depression and addiction.

In the living room I sit with a pile of books around me. I crave these books: I can talk to myself, but I need someone to talk to me. Books talk to me. And I want to find poetry that will be fitting for Mama's funeral.

Exhausted, I fall into a deep sleep on the sofa. I hear a sound—a voice like a call from a deep well. I bolt up straight, startled, and look around. Its echo becomes louder and louder and clearer. First, the voice sounds surprised, then shocked, finally panicky. It's Mama, speaking my name: *"Erin Rose?—Erin Rose!—Er-in R-o-s-e ..."*

I am terrified. Such a helpless, hopeless cry. I feel that if I reach out, I will touch her, for Mama, in whatever form, appears there—lost. And I cannot dismiss this feeling or disclaim this voice. It is Mama's.

I sit, staring into the unknown edge of night, paralyzed in fear. I hear my own voice plead barely above a whisper, *"Mama, go back! Please go back."* My heart thumps so fast—my entire body shivers. I am too afraid to move my eyes around the room, but I dare not close them. I plead, *"Mama, please go away! Go back to wherever dead people go! You don't belong here now."* My voice cracks, and I start crying, hardly able to catch my breath. The light is still on, but darkness engulfs me. *"Oh, God, help me!"*

Time passes. But time like this cannot be measured.

The local domestic cleaning service has already cleaned Brennan's bedroom and part of the den twice, washing and scraping down the walls and ceiling and shampooing the carpet, but stains and the smell of death remain. *Is that why you're here, Mama? To find the missing parts of your head?*

The sound of crunching comes from the driveway. I jump. Boots stomp on the front porch, and the door opens.

"Mama?" Alex calls softly.

Thank God, she's home. She sees me beside a stack of books, frozen like a statue and staring into space.

She runs into the living room, snow still clinging to her coat and scarf, and reaches for me. "Oh, Mama!"

I move finally. We stand, holding each other tight as if afraid the other one will slip away. As I hug Alex I can still hear the Sheriff's explanation. Somehow, Mama climbed up on a chair, took the shotgun down, and loaded it with buckshot. She knew all about guns. She had worked as the sheriff's secretary and was even sworn in as an office deputy. The sheriff assumed she then dragged the chair into the bedroom, set the shotgun on the floor, got on her knees on the chair, pushed her mouth on the barrel, and pulled the trigger.

Chapter 2

In the morning I hear Kayleigh scream. She rushes from the den, and I catch her in the foyer before she runs from the house. In the bathroom the commode flushes. I hold her tight in my arms when Brennan and Alex appear. Kayleigh shivers all over and stammers so that I barely understand her words. Brennan slowly shakes his head as he walks toward us. His eyes lock with mine.

Kayleigh shouts, "It was Grandma! It was Grandma!" She bursts into uncontrollable, hysterical crying.

Brennan speaks low and emphatic. "Kayleigh, it was just a piece of trash. Just trash. A piece of trash on the floor. That's all, Kayleigh. I flushed it down the toilet."

"No. No. I picked up a piece of skull! Grandma's skull with her gray hair sticking out! I held it in my hand!" Kayleigh screams. She begins shaking again and pushes out of my arms and runs outside.

"It got caught in the rug, Mom," Brennan explains. "A little piece about an inch square with some hair. Almost under the sofa. Must've fallen from that sheet when they took her out ... who knows."

That is the moment the creepy feeling begins for my daughters—when they avoid walking into the den. Brennan remains stoic, seemingly unaffected by his grandmother's death, and insists on sleeping in his own room—*the death room*, we call it.

But, Mama, I still feel you in the air around me—in the air I breathe! Are you stalking me, trying to scare me to death because *I can't save you now?* And, Mama, why did you make life so hard for my children. Your grandchildren? To punish me?

Many days after school, they found you in your nightgown, sitting in the den smoking and staring blankly at the TV. You held your cigarette between fingers, then dropped your hand onto your nylon gown and sat in a daze, the cigarette burning a hole in the gown, scorching your skin. *And you didn't feel the burn?*

And that wasn't all, Mama. Kayleigh was often the first one home and found you drunk, sometimes sitting in a puddle of pee in your bathroom where you'd slipped down and couldn't get up. Kayleigh helped you up, put you in the tub, bathed you, dressed you, and mopped the floor before I got home. *I hated you for that!*

From deep in my gut such anger rolls up, a lump of raw rage. If only I could spit out that bile, I could swallow in peace. How could you have brought such unspeakable behavior to our home? I've tried so hard to protect my children from the stain of a "broken home" and the ache of having no real father; I've tried so hard to provide a loving home, a happy place for them to grow up, free of indignities. *How dare you shoot yourself here!* Leaving your body parts on walls and furniture for *them* to see? Where we have to look and live and remember every single day!

I sit on the hard pew in the middle of my three children and Annie Mae, who is probably the first black person to sit here in the front row. I insisted that she come with us in the limousine for the service in the funeral home chapel, and now she shares our pew. I hold hands with Brennan and Alex, who sit on each side of me. Kayleigh sits between Alex and Annie Mae, who places her strong arm around Kayleigh, who rests her head in Annie Mae's generous bosom and sobs uncontrollably.

I look at the coffin near the front of the chapel. I wonder what's she wearing. I don't remember. Just a corpse hiding its horror.

Behind the podium sit two men and a woman: the minister of the Methodist Church (where we go), the minister of the First Baptist Church (where Mama never went), and Rebecca, a long-time friend and Bible teacher (who's paid by private citizens to teach the Bible in public schools, a unique system in the South). I'm conscious of the ministers speaking something about redemption and rising with Christ, but my mind wanders. I can't follow doctrine anyway and certainly not now.

I glance at Rebecca, who plays her role well. No makeup, long hair, a prim dress (pants are disapproved of by the Fundamentalists). And I can see her at the same time in slacks or shorts at the beach talking and laughing freely with me and our Jewish friend.

Rebecca speaks, her voice soft and eloquent. "I am going to read poetry that Erin Rose selected for her mother."

I searched for the right passages. Neither her life nor her death bore witness to the established life in Oak Glen, North Carolina. Neither would her funeral.

I close my eyes and hear the soul of Robert Frost: "I have been one acquainted with the night, / I have walked out in rain—and back in rain, / I have out-walked the furthest city light ..." I lose myself in the language and Rebecca's melodious voice. I feel the mood of Mama's last days.

Rebecca recites the words of Kahlil Gibran from the "The Farewell," the last chapter of his book *The Prophet*: "To judge you by your failures is to cast blame upon the seasons for their inconstancy. / Ay, you are like an ocean, / And though heavy-grounded ships await the tide upon your shores, yet, even like an ocean, you cannot hasten your tides. / And like the seasons you are also, / And though in your winter you deny your spring, / Yet spring, reposing within you, smiles in her drowsiness and is not offended."

I am oblivious to the congregation. I am immersed in sound and in the touch of skin of hands I hold and the images Rebecca conjures up of water and mist, of cold winds and the bright sun. She continues: "Forget not that I shall come back to you. / A little while, and my longing shall gather dust and foam for another body. / A little while, a moment of rest upon the wind, and another woman shall bear me."

And I think of Kahlil Gibran, this dark, heavily-mustached Arab, a non-Christian and pantheistic poet, who writes of the transmigration of souls and reincarnation, and suddenly I smother an impulse to laugh at the ludicrous situation I have created, but no one seems to notice.

Mama, I've gotcha covered.

And, Mama, leading the procession out is your lover. Your lover of 25 years—the county sheriff, a deacon of the Presbyterian Church and past president of Kiwanis. Your loyal and upstanding lover who kept you stocked with liquor and promised to marry you when his wife died (she had been dying for years supposedly).

Yes, Mama, I've gotcha covered.

The winter of '77 is record-breaking cold, with blustering winds and snow. I sit at the gravesite and watch the dark coffin lowered into fake turf and hear the clang of the metal frame. Inside I visualize your half-face, with one remaining eye staring up at black dirt soon to rain down. And you, a half-headless mother, I see rising soundlessly from the grave, searching frantically for the rest of your parts. My tears are not of grief but of guilt at feeling no grief. Just a relief, Mama, that you're gone.

In recent years I wanted to be rid of you. Every minute you were demanding my attention: walking closely in my steps, expecting me to tell you how to live your life. I replied: learn rug-making, do needlepoint, start a jigsaw puzzle, read a novel, take a walk. When I was home from school during the summer, I took you to an occupational therapy workshop. You piddled with arts and crafts for a while but worried all the time about having the correct change for the Coke machine. Late one night you insisted that I make change for you. You would not hear of waiting until morning. To avoid your hysteria and my angry retorts, I threw a raincoat over my pajamas and drove to the nearest convenience store to change a fifty-cent coin into two quarters. So I gave up the therapy idea; you let go of "coin stress."

Chapter 3

The scent of blood—that is my first awareness when I open the door today after the funeral. No one else notices the smell, but to me the odor of blood gets stronger every day. Has my perception of *smell* gone haywire, too? That continual whiff of musk and tarnished copper? I crave fresh air, but for *this* January open windows and doors wouldn't do.

At least the funeral is over, the people gone, the food put away—enough to last a week—and my children are seeking solace with friends. In the living room the fire no longer crackles but burns low as glowing embers smolder and wood crumbles to ashes. Ashes to ashes. Matter cannot be destroyed; it changes form. I learned that in high school biology.

On the sofa I sit and stare at the dying fire, lost in the embers that fall hot red and turn golden. That's the moment when she comes: when my mind is blank and focusing on something—the fire in the fireplace, the edge of lace on a side table, a tea cup on the kitchen counter. She also comes when I sleep.

Mama comes in and sits beside me. She's in the air; I sense her by my heartbeats even before I feel her. Close. I am almost getting used to it by now, but this sense of terror that she creates stays.

Now I don't sit there thinking about it. I just feel her presence—the same way when you walk into a room and people quickly stop their argument but you sense something unpleasant has happened. You just feel tension in the air.

Souls, we are told, never die. Then aren't they around us, not in some Netherland up in the sky, but matter changed into another dimension here close by? Could their undying energy—vibration—make them tangible? I am horrified I will hallucinate.

Often I think of someone all day, and when the phone rings, I sense who it is before I pick up the phone. Occasionally, I have a strong need for specific communication: then the phone rings, a letter arrives, an unexpected check comes in the mail, or a friend knocks at my door. Are these mere coincidences?

A few days after the funeral Annie Mae and I start cleaning Mama's bedroom and bath. We clear the walk-in closet and pack her clothes neatly in boxes to give away to local charities. We find a dozen empty vodka bottles between the mattress and box springs. We throw out the pee-soaked mattress. We empty the medicine cabinet of bottles and bottles of Valium, a tranquilizer prescribed for everything and everyone in the '70s.

I drop all her personal letters and cards, both recent and old, into a huge garbage bag that I'll sort through later. The shoebox of photos I will add to my own. I will buy a new mattress and a bright-flowered bedspread. I will paint the walls a soft blue. I will polish the antique gate table and rocker with Old English, leaving them in their natural state. And I will paint the old mahogany bed white. For some unknown reason I want to sleep in it. After all, the bed is the one I was born in. And for a finishing touch I will arrange a cut-glass vase with magnolia leaves and put it on the table by the bay window.

Then I realize my biggest loss—Mama's diamond. Annie Mae and I search carefully through leftover junk in the dresser drawers: there are two lipsticks minus their tops, an inch-long eyebrow pencil, dried-up rouge, a tarnished necklace, an empty perfume bottle, and a beautiful rose mother-of-pearl hand mirror with a long crack. And there are piles and piles of little slips of paper with scribbles in someone else's handwriting, enough to fill an entire drawer. Love notes, I surmise by a quick glimpse at one or two "I love you's" written on scraps of paper torn from official forms.

My eyes begin to fill. Is this all? Is this all she has left? The treasure of a lifetime? Scraps? I read over bills, trashing most of them, and find that she's stopped paying her life insurance premiums. But where is her diamond? It is nowhere to be found. I call the funeral home, but they assure me the body had no jewelry on it.

That is when I cry. That is when I sit down at her dresser. As a little girl I loved trying on Mama's ring. I would sit at this dresser, putting on her rouge and lipstick, drawing black crescents over my brows like Joan Crawford, whom Mama liked to imitate, and then place the diamond on my finger, reaching out toward the mirror, seeing if I looked like Mama. The ring was white gold with delicate filigree wrapped around the diamond solitaire—a ring like hers could no longer be found in jewelry stores, but possibly at expensive antique shops or estate auctions. She had said that I could have it someday: her engagement ring from Daddy.

I want to move into her room that night, but I don't. The air feels chilled like the inside of a mausoleum. In late afternoon when the sun sets, a heaviness settles in empty spaces, like in an old vacant house that stands waiting for a new family or the wrecking ball. No. I don't want her room with her used-up makeup, a garbage bag of love-notes from her lover, and the empty space in the drawer where her ring should've been. I pull over the garbage bag, sit on the floor, and start digging out the scraps of paper with "I love you." In ten minutes I'm drowning in tears. I have never received a love note in my life.

I return home one afternoon after a teachers' meeting. It's been over a week since the funeral. In the kitchen Kayleigh is helping Brennan write a paper for his history class, and the two of them have nearly finished a box of Little Debbie cakes. Brennan has put the typewriter on the kitchen table because Kayleigh won't step a foot into the den anymore.

Blood is always there for me, seeping up at the end of each thought, spreading over every photograph. I live in a nightmare. When I sleep, surreal images exhaust me. I awake from dreams with Mama's eyes staring at me. She surrounds me like a shroud. I fear I'll become Electra in Eugene O'Neill's play—the daughter left in the house after her mother's death, mourning, and *becoming* her mother.

I walk into the den. "Ugh! What's that smell? It's like fermenting fruit!"

"We don't have any of that, Mama."

"Blood. It's the blood."

"Oh, no, Mama. Don't start that again," Brennan pleads.

I run upstairs, change my clothes, and return to the kitchen to get a knife. At first, my children ignore me. Then Brennan calls in alarm, "Mom, what are you doing? Stop it!"

I'm on my hands and knees, crawling through rooms, sniffing like a dog nearing its prey. "I have to find the blood."

Brennan tries to pull me up. "Mama, you're scaring me! You've got to get over this. *Please.*"

I push him away. "The carpet. I keep smelling blood on this carpet." When I approach Brennan's room, I smell a strong metallic scent that's nauseating. I dig in my nails to find the carpet seam. "I've got to find the blood!"

I start clawing and pulling and finally ripping the carpet up from the doorframe seam. By now Kayleigh is pleading with her brother to "do something!" They both try to pull me away. I yank again at the carpet. "My God! There it is—blood!" In front of me is a dark-red blood-soaked padding spread under the bedroom carpet.

I stand and find myself clenching my hands like Lady Macbeth and thinking "who would have thought she'd have so much blood in her!" Brennan jerks, twists, and uproots parts of the rug backing.

I call the carpet cleaner for emergency work. They rip up all the carpet to clean the floor underneath.

Did you know that wood soaked in blood for a number of days, a week, still retains the smell of blood? Even after scrubbing and sanding the surface? The blood seeps through and becomes a part of the very fiber of the wood.

"This is the best we can do, Ma'am. No way to clean this wood. To get rid of that blood, you'd have to cut out this part—probably the whole bedroom floor," one workman tells me.

I call a carpenter to cut up the floor and get rid of all the stain. Finally, a large portion is sawed off from the rest of the room. New wood is nailed in place, the walls and ceiling are painted blue, and a new sand-colored rug is installed. Am I foolish to think this is all?

Eyes pop out in the blue walls days after the painters leave. At first there're only a few splotches. Then, overnight, three walls are stained with bright eyespots wide open, staring—like the eyes of a peacock's tail—and I can hear their unearthly cries. And the eyes follow me with my movements. Kayleigh and Brennan see stained spots; I see peacock eyes. I call the painters. "Something is wrong with the paint!"

They come promptly. "There's nothing we can do. Not much you can do to cover up where blood's been," they say. "Just like egg stains. You can't cover up where the white of an egg's been. The albumin makes grease spots. Always comes through."

"But the cleaning service washed the walls twice," I reply.

"And we've painted twice, Ma'am," they say.

Momentarily, I think of wallpaper. Why didn't they tell me about the problem of painting these damaged walls? Would wallpaper have spotted, too? Quickly I dismiss the idea. What can I do?

Exhausted, I go to bed early. For a long and restless time I lie awake, my head filled with images of the day— faces of people, sounds of words. Then sleep falls thinly, heavily studded with large eyes protruding at me—peacock blue and amber.

The following morning, I focus on the furniture in my son's room. All of it needs polish; maybe a new wood stain? After stripping off the bed cover, I hold my breath. A residue of skin and tissue sticks between and around the spools in both the Jenny Lynn head-and-footboards. I put on gloves and scrape and scrape around the wood; then I sand and sand and refinish the walnut wood with a maple stain. I avoid looking at the wall and manage to finish in a couple of days.

At last I look up at my grandmother's antique mirror across from the bed. There is something stuck on it. I lift the mirror from the wall. The same fleshy "stuff," hard now like Super Glue, has spattered in the grooves of the carved wood and the corners. Again I take the paring knife and try to cut out the mess on the wood, but some of the hardened parts will not budge. I glance at the mirror ... and a look of desperation meets me. My God! Mama? No. No. Is that me?

I stare at my gloved hands soiled with Mama's residue. My hands start shaking, my mouth and throat are dry, and with great effort I take short gasps of air. My heart beats so fast it leaves a pain in the center of my chest. I drop the knife and rush to the garage, holding the mirror. I pour varnish into the corners and the grooves and then brush around the frame, sealing in skin particles—in my grandmother's mirror I've sealed up Mama.

Chapter 4

I grow up alone—most of the time. I have no brothers or sisters and no children nearby to play with. Daddy works 20 miles away in Bennettsville, South Carolina. Since I've never had playmates around—until Ruby Jean—I don't even know that I should miss them. I have the people in my books who never leave; they wait for me to come inside. The house, though, is often my comrade-in-arms in which I roam, share secrets, escape the world of strangers I don't understand.

Our house is plush, compared to many in the '40s. In the living room antique Queen Anne upholstered furniture, rose and green, faces a small blackened fireplace. A heavy black iron grate holds coal and heats the house in winter. Green ceramic tiles cover the wall around the fireplace and extend out to form a hearth where mahogany columns rise on each side to support the mantel and large backdrop. In the center of the mantel hangs a large oval mirror embedded with carved rose petals. A brass chandelier hangs in the center of the room, and on the west side a bay window looks out on the porch. Across the room the late afternoon sun shoots fire on the brass like a lit candle. Under the chandelier the faded Persian rug, a soft purple, lies in shadows. White French doors open to the dining room and also to the long hall that remains dark because of the mahogany wainscoting. But Mama hates every piece of it.

All the time I hear her say, "I'm living in a tomb! In a tomb of the O'Donovan's ancestry!"

Once, while puttering around in the upper dark rooms of our house, I find a hidden panel that opens to another dimension. It's just a loose panel I can push, and the opening is large enough for me to crawl through. At first I see nothing but black space, but when my eyes adjust to the dimness, a new world emerges. I crouch low under the roof's slanted beams until I realize I can stand up in a vast open space—the unfinished third floor of the house. It's as though this world is my own. Stained-glass windows in the turrets reflect a soft shaft of gold to me over the horizontal wood beams. It seems like the morning sun has just risen. I *know* ... *I know* if I keep staring at the light and don't look at my feet, I can balance myself on the wood beams. I pretend I'm a ballerina on a high wire and dance over the downstairs rooms. I've brought in my music box, which plays *Swan Lake*. When the music goes off, it plays in my head. I focus my eyes on the stained glass and the now-bright streaks of sun dust; I dare not glance even once at the darkness below because, for certain, I would fall through the ceiling.

Soon my golden path stops at a small platform with steps directly under the center of the roof. Above is a flat door, a secret doorway leading to another perspective of the world. I push open the door to the sky and climb out onto the roof top. And here I can touch the wind before it blows. From here I can see everything. As far as I can see, treetops stretch green—from the rose garden in the backyard to the top of the courthouse and the water tank and the train depot. I can spot the train before it gets to town. I stretch out my arms like the wings of a dove ready to fly.

I slip back to my magic place inside with the stained-glass windows. Straddling a beam and leaning against a post, I start writing in my new white leather journal.

My mind, a kaleidoscope, shifts bits and pieces of remembered colors, sounds, touches, scents: fire crackling in a woodstove, heat rising, the clanking and knocking in pipes that run to the water heater, the smell of Octagon soap, cedar chips. On a washboard dark brown hands scrub and slap cloth in a long porcelain sink. Outside, sweltering heat. Sticky thick air. White starched sheets billow in a summer wind on the back porch, two rows draped across a clothesline tied from the stair post to the green-latticed side.

Many days I live in my yard. I *try* to make sense of the people around me but nature draws me out of myself. I love the feel of earth: the squishy mud between my toes after a summer rain. To walk on spongy, feathery moss is like stepping on crushed velvet. I never wear shoes, but hold my sandals in my hand so that when Mama calls, "Erin Rose, keep your shoes on," I have them close. I love picking wild violets growing in soft green moss beside the garbage can Mama puts at the end of the drive. At times I have to search for them, some smashed by the garbage can or covered with a blown-away piece of trash. However, the violets grow back—up beside or down or under the garbage can or a little ways beyond. I pick them and pull the stems over my ear to wear them in my hair.

In the backyard, clover covers the ground. I separate tiny stems and braid them together for bracelets.

I wonder sometimes if there's a leprechaun hiding near. I squat and search for four-leaf clovers, as persistent as the bees buzzing on the scattered white blossoms. To spot a four-leaf is to find a pirate's treasure. When I do, I run inside, ecstatic, calling Mama. I put the lucky charm in one of my books, whichever one is my favorite at the time.

In my porch swing I hear the birds, feel the breeze under the trees, and see everything going on down the street. Here I listen to summer rain and watch mists rising. On summer mornings I sit in the swing and eat thick, juicy tomato sandwiches and drink ice-cold Coca-Cola for breakfast. On Wednesday nights, I sit on the front steps, where I hear sounds from the little Negro church across the field behind a neighbor's yard. Ironically the church sits in Blood Field or The Bottom, where the Saturday-night knife fights take place, usually cuttings or stabbings. When the air is very still, I feel drawn from a distance to the Gospel soul-singing and the clapping and the rhythms of the music so different from that in my own church. I feel a deep bond with the spirit and the passion of Negro music.

We are lucky to have so many black people around us and working for us. I know all of them, and they know me. I love being with them—laughing and singing and hugging. After summer rains Valley Road gets soggier as it stretches past the row of Negro shacks. On any given day women sit on tiny broken-down porches, balancing baskets between strong legs as they shell peas, while little tots crawl up and down the steps and old men fan themselves. On summer weekdays lively children, clean and shiny, come out of The Bottom on their way to school, knowing come fall they'll be in the fields picking cotton. An occasional wagon loaded with hay passes through. On other days wagons filled with watermelons, tomatoes, okra, or other local crops head for The Bottom, mules straining through the mud. One time I see a mule is dressed for the occasion, donning a Scotch-plaid cap, his ears sticking up through holes. Some wagons circle, stop, and display local produce like an old-fashioned fresh market.

Minnie Belle, a "colored girl," who's a middle-aged woman, works for us. She hangs up the rugs on a line she has tied from tree to tree and beats each rug with a broom. Each week she gives the pots and pans a special cleaning; she takes them outside, drops them beside my old sandbox, and scrubs them down with sand to remove old grease stains. I'm always right beside her, wanting to help. And she pays as much attention to me as she does her work. She calls me "Baby," just like Daddy does, and keeps me laughing with her stories and her singing and her tickling.

And can she cook! On Fridays Minnie Belle fries fish, and I mean all the fish—the head and the tail—draining the pieces on a torn brown bag. Then after serving lunch to Mama and me, she sits on the back porch steps and gnaws around fish eyes with gusto. I slip out to sit beside her and ask, "Why don't you sit at the kitchen table?" She reaches over and jiggles my cheek tenderly: "Baby, I like to feel the outside!" She lets me taste the crispy fried fish tails that taste like burnt potato chips.

I love Minnie Belle. And I feel she loves me, too. When I'm sick with a cold, she searches for peach bark—finds a tree, cuts out a piece of bark, brings it to our house, and drops it in boiling water to make tea. After the bark steeps for a while, she sweetens it with honey. Then Minnie Belle serves me her special cup of tea.

On summer days I go with Minnie Belle to town for Mama's errands. Minnie Belle is tall and broad shouldered with long legs and wide, flat, shoeless feet. With sandals in hand, I like to walk barefoot, too, despite stubbed toes from buckled sidewalks cracked upward from the roots of mighty oaks that line the streets. To keep up with Minnie Belle, I hopscotch down Church Street over cracks to touch shadow-spots and run across squares that scorch my bare feet. We turn north at Valley Road onto a dirt road where either hot dust flies up my legs or sticky mud sucks between my toes. Once I heard Mama tell Daddy that Minnie Belle grabbed a knife and stabbed her husband one Saturday night in Blood Field. She didn't kill him, just cut his shoulder for making her mad.

In summers we always keep plenty of ice in our refrigerator in the kitchen and also on the back porch in an old icebox that opens at the top to drop in large blocks of ice. From Bennett's Ice and Coal Company, Uncle Willie delivers the ice. When I hear the wagon wheels squeaking down our drive, I wave and run beside the old wagon loaded down with huge ice blocks and call to Uncle Willie, "I bet I can beat you to the steps!"

He takes off his straw hat and waves it high, "Naw, ye kent, Missy!" He pops the whip. "Git up der, Mule!"

I take off and then wait at the steps and giggle as I watch Uncle Willie drive the mule wagon, calling "Whoa-a" and stopping at our porch, his white hair wet now and glistening in the sun. "Ah see ye der, Missy. Ye beat me agin!" Grunting, he lifts ice with long tongs to drop into the icebox. On the way out, he stops at the curve, as he always does, and chisels some ice chips into the cup I hold. I grin. I have enough for two ice cones I'll pour grape juice on. "Thank you, Uncle Willie."

Once a week a black man with one arm cuts the grass with a sling blade. He swings that blade so smooth and low to the grass that the yard looks manicured by scissors. No one considers him "crippled"; his one powerfully strong arm makes up for his lost one. Though he is also middle-aged, Mama calls him her "yard boy." The police named him Trust after he worked for years as a trustee at the county jail. As a teenager Trust got into a fight with a man who stabbed him repeatedly in his arm—Trust nearly killed him in retaliation. Trust lost his arm and his freedom. After getting out of prison, he won the respect and the "trust" of the town. His yard work makes him extra money.

On one of those exceedingly steamy summer days, Trust stops a minute to take off his straw hat, bends it, and wipes the sweat from his brow.

I walk up to him. "Would you like a glass of water?"

He bows his head at me. "Thank ye, Missy, don't mind if I do."

I lead Trust around to the back porch and call Mama for a glass of iced water. The kitchen screen door snaps open as Mama walks out holding the glass and ... hesitates. Quickly I reach for the glass and say, "Thank you, Mama."

I hurry to give the iced water to Trust, who waits by the back steps. He smiles broadly, "Thank ye, Missy. Bless ye." He drains the glass of water in one long gulp, places the glass on the edge of the porch, puts on his straw hat, nods, and tips his hat to me.

Mama frowns down at me, her lips pressed together. "Come in the house, Erin Rose." She walks to the edge of the porch, picks up the glass, and knocks it hard against the porch banister. The glass cracks into three big pieces that fall onto the porch floor. Mama bends over, picks up the pieces, and drops them into a garbage can.

"Mama, why did you break the glass?"

"Erin Rose, we don't drink in a glass used by a colored!"

"You can wash the glass."

Mama shrugs her shoulders and sighs as if I had stretched her last nerve. She speaks quietly, slowly, determinedly, "Our colored help drink from a jelly glass just for them. And there's always the spigot outside. *When will you ever learn?* Now come in the house. I don't want you around a colored man!"

Chapter 5

The sea stills to a warm rocking motion. I know Daddy is near. I lay my head back and stretch my arms out, legs rising with the gently rocking sea, Daddy's hand under my back. I watch clouds float across the sky and feel as if I, too, am lying on one, bobbing my arms, and then drifting. When I no longer feel the touch of his hand, I clench my fists, the sea ripples against my cheeks, legs give way, and I fight to stay buoyant. His hand suddenly touches me again. "Baby, if you fear the water, you'll never float or swim."

I know love—that pure kind between Daddy and me. Without any restraints or judgments or expectations, that giving of yourself and accepting of the other. Our unconditional love lasts for twelve years, and I'm devastated when it's gone. My childhood ends when Daddy dies, and I spend the rest of my life craving that kind of love again.

Through the years, though, when I feel alone and lost, there is that gray place where I go and know Daddy's presence. It feels like a warm embrace. I just close my eyes and peer inward into the shadows of ghosts and time, and here I find that lost part of myself ...

From North, South, East, or West all roads point to Oak Glen, North Carolina. If you're driving on Church Street, you'll find yourself in a long feathery tunnel of tall water oaks, their branches arching over the street with tree tips touching tree tips. In the expanse of vivid green stands our old Victorian home—a better term might be eclectic Southern Gothic because I've never seen another like it.

Built by Daddy's parents in the late 1890s, our house was the second one on Church Street and also one of the first in Oak Glen to have an indoor toilet. A large wrap-around porch spreads across the front and sides, one porch corner curving parallel to the bay window like a crescent moon. Supported by white Corinthian columns, the roof slants and three large windows in front and back give light to the second floor. The roof then rises in an octagonal shape with space for a third floor. On each front corner a turret juts up with small stained-glass windows. From the street it looks like a haunted house on Halloween night, but it is my house of magic.

I wait here for Daddy when the sun sits above the last treetop in our yard. When I see the little blue Ford turn into the driveway, I run as fast as I can, jump up on the running board, and ride around the curve into our backyard, hugging Daddy's arm through the open window. My dog Snowball, a white furry Spitz, runs after us, barking and tail wagging. The car stops. I jump down. And here Daddy and I stroll through my Garden of Eden, crunching autumn leaves and acorns and eating tasty pecans that Daddy cracks and hands first to me and then my dog.

In season we pick small green apples off our trees to take inside to make applesauce; or we venture behind the woodshed to find plums which we eat on the spot; or I pull Daddy into the grape arbor where the vines curl up and across in thick tangles forming a living ceiling of juicy black-purple grapes. First, I show Daddy my secret code—which vine to pull—that makes the arbor open and lets us through into my imaginary tunnel.

On the back porch steps we sit and watch the sun drop, splashing golden between treetops. Daddy and I watch how the sun paints scattered acorns with a thin coat of gold. We sit till shadows creep across the bottom step.

Twilight and Mama's call bring us in, Daddy to kiss Mama and then to cook supper. Mama hates cooking, so we wait for Daddy to do his magic. First, he strikes a match to light the kerosene stove, which Mama despises to do. (She hates the wood stove, too.) Usually, Mama goes to the living-room to hear big band music on the radio—Tommy Dorsey, Benny Goodman, Harry James—or to listen to the new episode of *Sherlock Holmes*.

I stay with Daddy in the kitchen to help. I watch him begin his specialty: stew beef, potatoes with lots of pepper, and puffy biscuits. After putting a pot of water over the flame, he drops in the chunks of meat and then peels the potatoes and carrots and lets me drop them into the bubbling water. He rolls out dough on the porcelain table with a Coca-Cola bottle while I sprinkle flour on top. After that, I push the top of an empty pickle jar through the dough to cut out biscuits.

While the food cooks, Daddy reads the *Charlotte Observer,* and I run outside to pick tiger lilies that grow near the house. From the kitchen windows enough light slants on the ground for me to find them, then cut and arrange them in another pickle jar that I set on the table in the alcove off the kitchen. Supper ready, I run to get Mama. With Daddy sitting at the table, hot food steaming, Mama humming a dance tune, I am in a warm cave.

I remember one night when Daddy is painting the kitchen. He stands on the kitchen table to reach the high ceiling with his brush while I, his appointed helper, sit in my grass skirt on the floor stirring paint—Daddy bought one for me at Carolina Beach. I also wear homemade leis around my head, neck, and feet. Since I want to be a dancer, I'm wiggling my hips to the Hawaiian music. I'm listening to records, stirring paint, and jumping up every other minute to hula with leis, paint stick dripping.

Finally, Daddy puts down his brush and announces, "That's not the way to do it." It's one of those hot, muggy summer nights, and Daddy has his shirt off and is painting in his shorts. He drapes a towel around his boxers, pulls them low over his hips, and says very seriously, "This is the way you hula." And he starts dancing on the tabletop until we laugh so hard neither of us can stop.

Sometimes on cloudless nights, Daddy and I just sit on the back porch steps and look up at the sky. In the clear space over the driveway, Daddy points to the night sky and the galaxies of stars forming: the Big Dipper, the Little Dipper, the Milky Way, the Bear. He picks me up so I can see clearer. We look for unusually bright stars; he lifts my arm and with his hand over mine guides my finger to trace the patterns. I can feel Daddy's arms holding me and hear him saying. "See the Big Dipper, Baby? It's tilting, about to spill out some stars. Look, there's the Milky Way. Its stardust has spread a milky rainbow." I wonder how far this Milky Way goes and whether we can slide down it together and then follow the North Star home. You can never get lost if you know the North Star; it will always be low over the hedge in our front yard. And the Man in the Moon guards our home; Daddy and I, on a cloudless night, have seen his face.

Lightning rods rise like tall spears from the octagonal roof. Daddy tells me how they attract lightning during a thunderstorm so it hits them instead of our house. These thunderstorms fascinate me: winds whipping, trees bending, nature flashing her power. I like the sound of crashing thunder after the sky splits and the sound of rain falling in torrents like Niagara Falls. I sit in the swing on the porch, unafraid, and feel the rush of cool air and smell the ripe pears from the nearby tree. And I know I'm safe.

After heavy rains in the spring Daddy and I look for arrowheads in the backyard. Except for the time when American Indians roamed here, only our family has lived on this land. As Daddy says, some of this land is still virgin soil. Time and weather have pushed arrowheads near the surface; sometimes the land yields up several of them in the same spot. Daddy points out the stone tip stabbing the soil, its pointed head glints in the sun. He bends over, pulls out the arrowhead, and wipes the mud on his pant leg. "No telling how long this one has been here," he says. Soon I can discover them, too. I start a collection in a tin box.

At the end of the center hall, there is a tall black safe where Daddy keeps his money. Still, a decade and a half after the big bank shutdown in '29 when his family lost nearly everything, Daddy doesn't trust the bank. The black safe guards his valuables: insurance policies, the deed to the house, some old letters, war bonds, his stamp collection, foreign coins and cash, and the big family Bible with dates of births, marriages, deaths, and dried roses as markers for special verses.

I place my tin box of arrowheads beside Daddy's valuables. Whenever he opens the safe, twirling the combination back and forth (which I memorize but never whirl correctly), I open my box and take out the pieces of flint and count them while Daddy counts his money. Rubbing my finger across rough surfaces and touching the sharp ends, I see that none of the arrowheads are the same, each shaped with distinct strokes, each a different shade of gray or the color of sand, a few slightly pink. Daddy says the Indian carries *who he is* with him—his roots and his pride of ancestry—and that the color of the stone is the color of the earth from which he comes.

"Arrowheads are as different as people," Daddy says. "All from the same source in nature. Just from a different place, with a different look."

I sit on the floor with my arrowheads for the longest time and think about Daddy's words. I imagine young Indian warriors chipping away with stone striking stone, flakes dropping like the last flicker of a sparkler on the Fourth of July, and then more chipping, stone against stone, bone against stone, their hands artfully shaping flint into notches and sharp edges. The past unfolds. I imagine scenes as if I'd been there.

In early morning before dawn I hear the *woo-woo-woo* of the mourning dove and see shadows still silvered by the moon. I see Indians hunting deer in the forest with arrows and bows made from yew, right here in our backyard where we now collect arrowheads. A young bronze Tuscarora with egret plumes in his dark hair slips silently in his moccasins through tall grasses in our yard and pauses, pulling bowstring taut, and waits, eyes intent on tangled underbrush for the tip of an antler to stir. Then at the right movement, quicker than light, the arrow swishes through the air, the deer leaps free, twigs snapping, the wings of roosting birds flapping. And I pick up the arrowhead that must have missed its prey. Were these arrowheads crafted here? Did Indians live here in our yard? Then where was their burial ground? Where our house sits? Do I sleep over old bones of warriors?

I imagine ritual burials with long posts rising up near our porch, supporting the animal skins stretched tight for grave-beds so the dead can face the sky, souls waiting to return to the Great Spirit. Were they shot down by the white man? Bodies left, bones bleaching, they sink into the ground as rain settles dust, making the world one big tomb. Do the ghosts of the unburied hover here? I ask Daddy so many questions, and he answers them in ways I can understand.

Now, I sense Daddy's answers and stories have given root to my imagination and use of metaphor. As a child, I had no words to give meaning to what I perceived. I knew the land brings up arrowheads like the sea surrenders shells. The land holds all the dead, many in unmarked graves, with their tokens; the earth knows their secrets. And that makes the past live with us.

"Erin Rose," Daddy says, "remember your roots. Remember your land. They make a big part of who you are. And remember your name. No one can take your name away from you. Only you can soil your name, and *only you can lose who you are.* Then it's hard to find what you've lost."

"Daddy, how can I lose myself? Do you mean if I go somewhere and then can't find my way back?"

"Well, something like that. Don't worry about it, Sweetheart. Just remember: ask questions about everything. Look and look to find answers. And when you find the answer, trust yourself. Be true to your thoughts, your conscience."

I'm sure all the answers to my many questions can be found in Daddy's books. Daddy's large bookcase he bought when he was a student at North Carolina State University sits in our living room. On the shelves are sets of *Harvard Classics, Stoddard Lectures, Complete Works of Shakespeare,* an anthology of *O. Henry* short stories, Mark Twain's *Autobiography, Aesop's Fables,* Edith Hamilton's *Mythology,* and a Bible. I sit on the floor turning pages trying to read, getting tearful. "Daddy, I can't read some of these words!" He puts down the newspaper and looks at me and smiles. "Don't fret. One of these days, Baby, you'll be reading them all."

I wish I could recall all the things Daddy told me. Most of the content I remember vaguely. *Aesop's Fables* I shall never forget—the antics of the animals and our laughing at them I cherish. The tale about the little creeping tortoise and the spunky hare is my favorite, probably because Daddy encourages me never to give up—just plod on. Whenever Daddy travels to Charlotte, he buys me lots of books, beautifully illustrated. I sit on the floor somewhere in a corner with the books stacked up around me and devour them for hours at a time. This practice becomes a large part of my life. Often I identify with the characters and connect to them as people.

When I'm old enough to study history, I look out at our land and wonder even more how much it has witnessed death, cruelty, war. Daddy's not here to answer, but voiceless trees could. The oaks are so old. Maybe they watched the Indian boy dragged through soil and felt the hemp tighten on its bark and the weight of a body hanging. The oaks must have seen slaves beaten and the blood dripping into the earth. The oaks must have stood in silence and witnessed General William T. Sherman's troops march through the land, felt fire from scorched fields, smelled musket powder, and known the scent of blood of Rebels and Yanks alike, blending together, staining deep in the soil. The oaks remember ancient stories that lie everywhere, deep and hidden.

Our house on Church Street sits about four blocks south of the train track, each block with its own traffic light. Especially with the windows open on summer nights, I awake as regular as clockwork and listen to the train, the whistle wafting on the breezes across vacant lots, the rumbles droning down the track and willing me back to sleep.

If you grow up in a small town, you know the sound of a train. You tell time by its arrival, men checking pocket watches to see if the 10:00 or the 4:00 is on time. And some part of you still hears that train call, low and mournful in the night, and knows it, too, has a story to tell.

Chapter 6

As long as I remember, my "job" was to pick up pecans that fall on the ground from our four huge pecan trees. About six years old, I drag a big brown burlap bag about as tall as I am around our backyard and drop in a few pecans with my dog wrapping herself around my legs and nosing the bag. One of our trees near the property line is so tall about a sack of pecans fall into Mrs. Macaulay's yard next door.

When I'm circling the tree and stooping over to retrieve the nuts, someone pushes up the kitchen window, leans out, and shouts to me in a very gruff voice. "You stop that right now. Get out of my yard!"

The Voice scares me nearly to death, even though it belongs to our kinky red-headed neighbor with a bulldog overbite. I jump back, stumble on the sack, and fall down with pecans spilling every which way. I wonder what Mrs. Macaulay's yelling about.

"Did you hear me, little girl? The nuts that fall on the ground on my side, in my yard, are mine. You get away from there! You and that dog of yours! Get!" She waves a flabby white arm back and forth as if she's coming after me.

Frantic, I grab my bag, pull it to the other side of the tree, drop it, and run wildly to the porch as fast as I can. Mama is furious and leaves to give Mrs. Macaulay "a piece of her mind." They never speak again to each other, but at no loss. I don't think they ever spoke before.

Later, when Mama tells Daddy in the living room, he explains, "She's just a lonely, cranky old lady who likes nuts. And we have plenty of those around here." He pauses, chuckles to himself, and says, "I mean ... we have plenty of pecans here to share."

"You said it right, Jake, the first time. *Nuts.* We have 'em all around. Shall I name a few?"

"Leah, don't."

Mama is already holding up her hand, starting to count on her fingers: "Number One next door, Cranky Macaulay ... Number Two across the street, Witchy Millicent ..."

"Oh, Leah!"

I interrupt Mama. "Do you mean Miss Millie? She hides paper bags under her coat."

Daddy changes his conversational voice to serious: "Now, Erin Rose, that's Mrs. Millicent across the street. She's really a nice old lady. People talk about her because she always wears that old black coat that hangs on her like a cape, so big they say she could hide something under it ... why did you say 'paper bags'?"

"I peeped in the window of her front door, Daddy. And she has little brown bags lined up and down the hall."

Daddy turns to Mama. "Leah, did you know this?" Then he turns to me. "Why did you do this, Baby? When?"

Mama yells, "Oh my God! You've crossed the street! Erin Rose, I've told you never to cross the street. You could've been struck by a car!"

"And, Baby, that's not nice to peep in someone's house."

Mama adds, "You could've gotten caught!" And Mama turns to Daddy. "Jacob, what do you think Miss Millie would have done?"

"My God, Leah. The woman's not a witch! She just looks like one."

I think of her long white bushy hair. That big black coat. The little dirty front door windows. Those brown bags lined up and white sheets covering something. And Miss Millie humped over, digging. *Wonder what she's burying?*

I'm beginning to get teary-eyed, and Daddy picks me up, goes to the davenport, and sets me in his lap. "Everything's all right, Baby. We just worry about you because we love you, and peeping in someone's house is like going in without permission. We want you to grow up doing the right things." He leans over and kisses me on my wet cheek. "Do you understand?"

"Yes, sir." I sniff. We hug.

"Daddy, I see Miss Millie a lot from my window when I wake up early." (My bedroom is on the front side of the house.) "The first thing I do is pull up the shade and look straight across the street to see what Miss Millie's doing. And she's usually dragging bushes down the sidewalk, while everyone's in bed, and hiding them in her backyard."

I'm holding Mama's full attention now as well as Daddy's.

"Tell us what you see, Erin Rose," Mama says.

I speak slower, trying to paint the exact scene popping into my head. "It's real early and the air is gray so it's hard to see across the street. Then I see a black shape come out of the fog. It's covered from top to bottom in black. It wears a black cover on its head and a long black cape that almost touches the ground. It looks like a crooked old man, all bent over. One arm drags something long and heavy and covered up."

Daddy interrupts. "Is this something from one of your books, Erin?" He hesitates. "Or are you making it up?"

"No, Daddy! I don't make up stories about real people. Just the ones in my head."

"Jake, let her finish. She knows everything that goes on around here! And I want to hear it."

"I know it's Miss Millie because she drags that *thing* into the backyard, and she comes back around, walking straight with a shovel. Her hat's gone and her white hair hangs down her back. Then she hunches over and digs holes in the yard and goes back after some bushes. After she drops something in the hole, she puts a bush and dirt in and hits the ground with her shovel like she's pounding on top of a grave." I turn to Daddy. "Does Miss Millie get bushes from the graveyard like everybody says? Why, Daddy?"

Mama raises her eyebrows, tilts her head at Daddy, and shrieks with laughter. "I told you, Jake ... I told you so! I know she steals shrubs from her neighbors! Mary, right next door to Millie, has been missing plants forever!" Mama's so tickled and excited over my discovery, she spills her coffee.

Daddy just shakes his head and tries to be firm. "Leah!" He turns to me. "Baby, I'm concerned about your sleep. If you wake up so early, don't pull up the shade. Just stay in bed and perhaps you'll go back to sleep."

"Oh, no, Daddy. I'll be wondering what she's up to. And I've got to see! Oh ... one time a roll of toilet paper fell out of her coat."

Mama is watching Daddy and holding her fingers over her mouth, sniggering. And Daddy's trying to keep his teacher-preacher voice without laughing—I can just tell. "Or maybe, you could sleep better in another room for a while. Want to try?"

"No, sir, it wouldn't do any good. 'Cause once I start waking up early, I keep doing it." I shrug.

I don't tell Daddy about the dreams that wake me up, and even though I forget about them afterwards, the feelings they create remain. And the sounds of the house I hear while in bed: the scrape of a tree limb, the crackle of the fireplace, the whistling of wind between window and sill, cracks that sound like the sharp splitting of kindling, creaks that echo like rusted door hinges, and the greatest sound of all—the hum of silence. *The breathing of the house.*

Later I'll hear *all* the stories about Miss Millie. People say they see a black figure leaving the cemetery, dragging something along the road right at the moment night slips into dawn. The shadow of a witch hiding a large shopping bag under a cape. During the day townsfolk witness Miss Millie on Main Street visiting stores where she picks up on impulse whatever she sees and wants. The clerks write down what she takes and report the theft to the store owners, who in turn send a bill to her family members, who are well-off, according to the town's standards. Her family pays and her deeds are hidden in the closet to protect their name and to avoid the embarrassment of having a kleptomaniac in the family.

On Sunday mornings Miss Millie goes to the First Baptist Church. She washes and curls the usually dirty, wild white hair, pulling it back and taming it under a stylish hat. Now she is dressed in a fashionably tailored suit with a fox stole wrapped around her shoulders, its tail and fake eyes hanging over a bit. She makes a very imposing figure— rather tall but solid and sturdy like an opera star. Every Sunday, even in summer, she sits alone in her furs in the same pew in the same spot next to the aisle while her family sits on the other side of the church.

I like to sit behind Miss Millie and stare at the glass eyes of the little dead fox hanging down her shoulder. The little fox and I stare at each other while the preacher declares in a loud voice and then a louder voice that we are going to fall into the pit of Hell fire because of our deeds. Poor fox. He's already dead. But he hasn't been burned.

In church I feel as trapped as that poor little fox must have felt. To avoid my fear that the floor will split open and drop me into fire, I look at the stained-glass window on the wall near me. The sun shines through the glass upon Jesus walking down a small dirt road and holding a little lamb in his arms. His face is calm and pleasant with an *inside* smile. He seems likeable and full of love for the lamb. The stained glass makes the colors bright and the outside world beautiful. I wonder why this painting is even in the church. The feeling the preacher instills and the feeling in the painting are incongruous, a word I'll learn later.

On early summer nights Daddy and I take long walks all over town with my hand in his, with me looking up at him thinking how tall he is (though he's only medium height). Black hair, soft brown eyes, dressed in khaki, Daddy is all earth tones. Sometimes we walk down South Main, stopping by an empty lot that serves as a baseball field, and watch boys play ball. (Daddy played baseball in high school; my Uncle Henry says he was good enough to become a pro.) Often we walk as far as the north side until we reach the train track and there wait for the faithful passenger train, the Boll Weevil, to clatter down the tracks and stop at the old depot to pick up Oak Glen's mail.

There, as always, waiting patiently, is Old Amos, black as night and dressed in an even blacker train conductor's uniform; in rain or shine, winter or summer, he wears that heavy coat with shiny brass buttons and a conductor's black hat, proud as a general. Old Amos reaches into his pockets that bulge like an old mail bag, ready to hand a stack of letters to the train conductor. Everyone knows Old Amos has walked all day up and down Main Street so people with last-minute mail can hand their letters to him to put on the train. They know that he keeps vigil over each piece. Knowing he can't read, a few tease him by asking for their mail back. When he can't find their names, Amos—fearful—stutters, curses, and shouts nonsense while the "gentlemen" stand back and chuckle.

46

Amos, like a caged stray, yelps out in fear during mocking sprees. He wants just to be left alone to save everyone from traffic. He steps in the middle of the street and raises his hand when the stoplight turns red; then mumbling under his breath, "C'mon," he waves his hand for cars to go with the green. People laugh. No accidents. He walks proud. Though unacknowledged, Old Amos has gained the town's trust.

Old Amos is what folks call the "town character"; he just showed up one day, a young black man, homeless and slow-witted, who loves trains. The town lets him sleep in the depot; workers on the trains give him clothes; he does errands for businesses, the sheriff, a lawyer or two, or the judge; he eats what he can find or is given. He came to town as a young silent loner and remains a loner, now old and silent, unless he's mumbling wordless nonsense to himself.

Near the depot Daddy and I listen to the train rumbling and *clink-clanking* toward town, the horn piercing the night with a mournful sound; we watch the train slowing, the great wheels screeching and rising steam swishing like a mighty dragon's breath. Then all is still. People outside the depot mill around, waiting for the unloading and loading.

Suddenly, with one hand full of mail, Old Amos hands it to the conductor, turns, and with his free hand tips his hat at Daddy. He calls out, "Howdy, Mista Jacob, suh, and lil' Missus." He tips his hat again at me.

Daddy nods his head and replies, "How're you, Amos? Hope you're doing well."

Old Amos shakes his head. "Yeah, suh. Thank ye." And he grins an almost toothless grin while he nods his head.

"It's nice sunny weather we're having," Daddy remarks.

"Yeah, suh, Mista Jacob. A fine day the Lord hath made." He keeps tipping his hat and bowing his head, tipping his hat and bowing his head, in a happy rhythm as he backs away.

Daddy calls, "Amos," and walks towards him. "Have you had supper yet?"

"No suh ... but I et me sump'n today, suh."

Daddy pulls a bill from his pocket and hands it to him. "Why don't you go by the Greek café—you know, the one down the street across from the hotel?"

"Yeah, suh. I know th' place. Men in front sit'n smoke their cee'gars."

"That's right. Well, go around to the back and knock on the door. Tell them that Jacob O'Donovan sent you for the supper special and hand them that bill. There's a bench out back where you can sit and eat. And you keep the change they give you back."

"Oh, thank ye, suh ... thank ye, suh."

"The change should be enough to buy you breakfast in the morning. Just do the same thing. Tell them Jacob wants a breakfast plate."

"Lord bless ya, Mista Jacob. Bless ya, bless ya," he repeats over and over as he shakes his head back and forth, going out into the coming darkness.

As we turn toward home, I look up to Daddy and he smiles at me. I think how much taller Daddy appears. To me he's a giant among pygmies just like in *Gulliver's Travels*, the book we read together.

Chapter 7

In the backyard Daddy has built me a large playhouse resembling a small log cabin, stocked full of dolls and doll furniture: a bunk bed, a clothes chest, a rocking chair, a complete kitchen, and even a sink with running water, as well as a child-sized table and two chairs where I can sit and look out the window. Some days I pack a peanut butter and jelly sandwich to eat there. A child's wicker rocker where I rock my dolls sits at the playhouse door. This is where Ruby Jean finds me.

When Ruby Jean moves to Oak Glen and appears in my backyard that same summer morning, I am elated. We become instant friends when she smiles and calls out, "I love your playhouse! Can I play?" This becomes our home base.

I am seven, and she is eight. She's pretty with big brown eyes, full lips, and dark brown hair that hangs long and silky with a wave at the end. Her skin tans evenly, about the shade of Mama's coffee with cream, and boys will never call, "Hey, Freckle-Face!" like they do to me.

Every day we play: Dolls in my playhouse, Dress-up in my bedroom, or Music in our living room when Ruby Jean sings and I play the piano. Or we just roam around to find something to do in our neighborhood.

Sometimes Lucy Mae, the black "help" of Ruby Jean's mother, plays with us. She is around 16 years old and skinny and sounds just likes Scarlett's personal slave Prissy with her high-pitched soprano squeals.

Some afternoons when Ruby Jean's mother goes shopping, we set up the Victrola and call Lucy Mae to come dance with us.

"I's workin' now," she whines in a high soprano.

Ruby Jean insists, "Aw, c'mon, Lucy Mae, show us the camel walk. We won't tell on ya if ya don't work." She assures Lucy Mae her mother will spend a long time shopping.

She shakes her head and then grins. "I do declare, ya girls, what am I gonna do wid ya?"

Light on her feet, Lucy Mae prefers dancing any day to cleaning house. We push back the davenport, wind up the Victrola, and drop on a record. Giggling, Lucy Mae soon snaps her fingers, buckles her knees, sucks in her lips, and starts a bowlegged walk with her neck pumping in and out like a chicken to a drum beat. Ruby Jean and I fall in behind her, imitating Lucy Mae's every move and gesture, and we camel walk back and forth in rhythm across the living room, losing all sense of time except to rewind the Victrola.

Then suddenly Ruby Jean spots her mother through the front window and yells, "There's Mama!" Lucy Mae grabs the broom, Ruby Jean stops the music, and we scramble with the Victrola back to Ruby Jean's room just as the front door opens.

"Laws me, dere's a lot of sand under dese chairs!" Lucy Mae claims in her whiney voice as she pulls the broom back and forth from under the davenport. "I's has to move der furniture! I's got on to duh girls, yes, Ma'am, for tracking in, Miz Beacham."

Every Wednesday Ruby Jean and I head to the courthouse. On Court Day the traffic is heavy. Everyone from miles around in the county travels to be a part of the fanfare like a summer picnic without food. A stately colonial courthouse faces Main Street; in a place of honor, the statue of a Confederate soldier stands out front on the grassy manicured lawn. The back driveway circles behind the jail and beside a row of public toilets, each marked either MEN, WOMEN, or COLORED.

Along the side of the courthouse, a chinaberry tree spreads its shade across the entire area, easing some of the hot mugginess of summer. Men gather in small groups in the grass to gossip, chuckle, talk politics, smoke cigars, and listen to the county patriarch—old and crippled Judge McDowell in his white suit and Panama hat, who leans back to sit on his spine in the captain's chair under the tree. Along the wall of the Cotton Land Hotel next door, men sit in ladder-back chairs, talking and waiting for the court bell to sound.

Curious, Ruby Jean and I slip between the groups listening to this or that (we don't know what). We watch smoke rings circle up; we smell the mixed scents of tobacco, Old Spice, cloves, and sweat; we hear "I'll be god-damn if that scalawag wins this case!" and then the bell clangs.

Dressed in Sunday best, everyone follows the crowd into the courtroom. We watch the bent-over judge lean on his two canes and wobble like an afflicted old crab from side to side down the aisle of the first floor. All the black people trudge upstairs to the balcony. All the white people follow the judge, who looks determined, like a general leading his troops to battle.

Occasionally, I go with Ruby Jean to the McKenzie Funeral Home across the dirt road from her house. Because she has no piano, Mr. McKenzie, the owner, allows her to practice on the piano in the funeral parlor, a large room with a private outside entrance.

When I go with her, I always get anxious. After all, it *is* a funeral home. I'm afraid of what's around me—that primal fear of death, that invading presence of the unknown, that disturbing atmosphere of pain and loss.

Nothing seems to bother Ruby Jean. She tells me all about the place. "There's a lab upstairs with a dead body. Blood is draining from a tube stuck in his side. And in the chapel parlor there's a casket with the top open. But you can look right at the dead man. Wanna go see him?"

"Maybe we should start practicing the piano," I say quietly.

"Oh, don't be such a scaredy-cat, Erin Rose!"

I sit on the piano bench and listen to Ruby Jean play her monotonous rising and falling scales on keys like a robot. I wonder when some door will pop open and reveal a dead body. Ruby Jean plays for eternity. Scales up and down, up and down, then repeating the exercise an octave past middle C, now upper in the treble, crescendoing just like my fear. Suddenly I stand up and rush toward the door. "I have to go!"

Ruby Jean lives on Valley Road, a narrow dirt road less than a half-block away from my house. Her small house faces the McKenzie Funeral Home; the back of the funeral home faces a sizable empty lot next to my backyard. We always cut through the vacant lot, going back and forth, to and from, our houses. One day when we're crossing, Ruby Jean says, "Oh, Erin Rose, I wanna show ya something! Stay close behind." She turns in the direction of the funeral home's garage.

"Oh, I don't wanna go there! The hearse is parked inside. It's creepy!"

"No, it's not." She reaches out and catches my arm. "It won't take but a minute."

I let her pull me inside the garage, which is dim, its rolled-up metal door halfway open. We sneak in around the hearse parked next to the wall where a narrow vertical cabinet hangs. We're in between the cabinet and the long black car. I feel uneasy and start to leave, but Ruby Jean suddenly pushes me back and whispers, "Look who's here!" She yanks open the cabinet and runs as fast as she can out of the garage, stopping just long enough to slam the door down.

And there I stare into the sunken eye sockets of a hanging corpse. I stand a foot away, mesmerized by the skinless mouth with its long yellow teeth grinning. The body is dark leather stretched on bone, like a piece of meat left too long over an open fire. A heavy wood club stands by his fingertips, and two balled-up babies lie at his feet. His vacant eyes keep staring into mine.

Suddenly I can hardly catch my breath. I feel hot, sick, closed in, walled up by the hanging dead man before me and the parked hearse behind me in the semi-darkness. The rest is black; I don't remember how I escaped. Did I start screaming? Did I pass out? Did the funeral director find me? Did Ruby Jean return?

After the initial shock, I have no recollection of the rest of the day.

This incident has no bearing on my friendship with Ruby Jean. I push the scene into a back blank space of my mind, and I go on as if it never happened. This "delay" or "suspension" of consciousness would become a safety-valve throughout my life—like Scarlett's "I'll think about it tomorrow"—when I'm faced with loss, fear, and betrayal.

From that day I take the long way to Ruby Jean's house, avoiding the dirt path that curves around the funeral home from my yard. Instead, I walk down the sidewalk on Church Street, turn left at the corner of Valley Road, and stay on the opposite side from the funeral home. I never look in that direction.

On her porch Ruby Jean waits for me and waves. "Let's stay on my porch and watch the cars come see Spaghetti. Someone stopped from New York this morning. They asked me if that dead man is still hanging up on the wall!"

"Why would they drive this far to see a corpse? That's yuck!"

"They didn't, silly. They're on their way to Myrtle Beach and heard about it. Every summer it's like this. 'Specially on weekends."

"How in the world do other people know about him? And find him?" I ask her, amazed.

"Beats me. But look at the license plates. They tell you the state they're from. We can keep count of the states. Make a list."

"Ruby Jean, why do you call that thing Spaghetti?"

"That's the name everybody calls him. Father says he's Italian. Guess no one knows how to say his real name."

"That's crazy—*spaghetti's* food. They could call him Antonio—that's not hard to say. Or call him Tony."

"No. It's too late. He's been around forever. No one would know who we were talking about."

I'm full of questions. "Whose babies are at his feet? Why are they there?"

Ruby Jean shrugs. "I don't know. Why's it matter? There're twins. Always been there. Probably born like that—and somebody dumped them. Rolled-up in little balls and gettin' black like Spaghetti, and he's as black as a nigger now."

Later, when I go home, I tell Mama about the dead man, but she already knows about him.

"He's been in that cabinet a long time," says Mama. "I saw him once when I was a little bit older than you are right now after we moved here from Georgia—that was in the early '20s. I went upstairs in the McKenzie Funeral Home, which was a furniture store, too, when it was on Main Street. Spaghetti wasn't in a case or anything then. Just hanging on the wall. Tied up with rope under his underarms and hung on a hook. I'll never forget that! I didn't know a dead man was hanging upstairs until I walked past and saw him. Nearly scared me to death!"

"That's not right," I say, "to keep a dead man hanging up!"

"No, but that's the way things are sometimes. You may not like what people do, but there's nothing you can do about it."

"Mama, does everyone look like that after they're buried?" I feel so sorry for the dead man and terrified of what happens to people after death. "But, Mama, I thought we all go to Heaven and become Angels—if we don't fall into Hell. That's what they say in church."

I can tell I upset Mama. She backs away from me, shakes her head all around, and lifts her eyebrows. She sighs and picks up a pack of Camels. "Erin Rose, don't worry about it. Don't even think about it. There's nothing you can do about it anyway. Honey, just worry about what you *can* do. And ... uh ... uh ... just ask your daddy."

"Well, who was the dead man, Mama? And how was he killed?"

"Oh, he was just some white trash who worked in a carnival. They say he got into a drunken fight one Friday night, and someone hit him on the head with a carnival tent stake. No one knew much about him, except he was Italian. You know how people are in this town. They can't remember or pronounce any word that's not Scotch or English. Someone called him by the only Italian word they knew or could pronounce—Spaghetti."

Mama pauses. "If someone's last name isn't traced back to a Highland Scot, he's either rubbish or the enemy." She reaches for her cigarette burning in the china ashtray and takes a long draw. She shakes her head. "It's a wonder they didn't toss him in the garbage. Instead, McKenzie hung him on the wall upstairs for people to see. Opposite those tall windows. And you'll never guess! People said when the lights were on in that room at night and the train rumbled through, the passengers on the Boll Weevil could see the hanging body through the windows."

"Mama, why didn't they bury him?"

"There's a law that a body can't be buried unless someone claims it—at least, that's what everybody says. But I think the real reason was money. There was no one to pay for his embalming."

"He had no family?"

"Yes. His father came to claim the body, but he had only a little bit of money to pay for burial. Told McKenzie he'd be back if he could get the money, but if not, then McKenzie could do whatever he wanted to with the remains. Now every time the funeral home moves to a new place, McKenzie drags Spaghetti along."

By the '60s news about Cancetto Farmica has spread up and down the coast; adverse publicity stirs up discontent, especially among Italian-Americans. A total of six decades has passed since his death before Farmica is buried at the Hillside Cemetery on September 30, 1972, when the humanizing effect of the Civil Rights Movement reaches the rural South. Anonymous donations from local citizens pay for a solid bronze coffin and porcelain vault. Farmica's grave is covered with six feet of cement to keep curiosity seekers from digging him up.

Chapter 8

During rainy days I traipse up the squeaky stairs to the unused rooms to roam around, to seek the unusual, to incite fantasy. I wander through dust-mites and spider webs, listen to the staccato of raindrops on the roof or the brushing of branches. I love this meandering through dark, musty rooms and rummaging in old trunks.

I pry open an old brass lock and lift the heavy top of one old trunk, sturdy like a captain's seaworthy chest. Ladies' old-fashioned dresses pop up and tumble over the trunk's edges: velvet, silk, cashmere, linen, batiste—a few with brocade and some with crocheted collars and cuffs. I explore more. I find pieces of yellowed lace, dainty crocheted doilies, a baby's quilt, and old stamps from all over the world.

Excited, I run downstairs and call Ruby Jean to walk over to play dress-up. We become Southern Belles and float down the stairs, taking turns being Scarlett O'Hara wearing a white picture hat and holding a fan we make from notebook paper. We smile, hold a hand out for a kiss, giggle behind a fluttering fan, and curtsy. Soon we tire of being beauties and seek more adventure by rummaging in the trunk.

At the bottom we discover faded photographs of people I've never known—probably O'Donovans. We try to match people together in different ways and spend hours making up stories about them; sometimes we act out our imaginary scenes. If there's a photo of someone I feel close to, I keep it in a cigar box tucked in the back corner of the old trunk. It seems, especially on rainy days, these people are still around me in this forgotten room. A few framed portraits on the wall follow me with their eyes.

One of these portraits is my granddaddy, Daddy's father, whom I named Jayjo when I was two. Daddy says he used to be a proud gentleman planter in the late 1880s to the mid-1930s who drove around looking at his land, checking his crops, and overseeing his workers good-naturedly. He started when he was young and handsome with thick black hair, broad shoulders, and a fit physique.

In the portrait he looks straight at me: the beginning of a smile—that crooked shape of his lips—and I feel he's about to laugh, happiness rooted in his eyes. This room was Jayjo's room for a long time before Daddy moved him downstairs. Now, he's a bent-over old man, balding but sporting a thick white moustache that catches and holds food—pieces of scrambled eggs, bits of bacon, and mush. He keeps his teeth in his pocket. All day, it seems, Jayjo sits on the front porch in a green ladder-back rocker, rocking and chewing his gums, or he reaches into his baggy pants pocket and pulls out a dirty pocket knife, a spoon, and an apple that he meticulously peels and then scrapes with the spoon. Then he rocks and he gums the spooned apple with juice that runs down his chin. He's happy still—just rocking, watching people pass by, seeing at sunset flames touch leaves to spread a bright red hue inward and over *his* apple trees like a huge burning bush. His eyes twinkle then as if he knows something the rest of us don't know.

On my way to the side of the porch where the swing waits, I skip in front of Jayjo who calls, "Baby, come sit with me."

I hate him to catch my hand; his skin is sticky, soft, and mushy. His pants stay unzipped and he smells like pee. I usually run from him, but sometimes I stay for a second or two; then Mama scolds me, "Erin Rose, don't get around that smelly old man!" Daddy, though, plays checkers with him sometimes after he gets home. They use an old crate turned on its side, just right for the checkerboard. When Daddy lets him win, Jayjo laughs deep in his belly.

Upstairs in the same room next to Jayjo's picture hangs the portrait of his wife, Daddy's mother, Emma, my grandmother. Not a pretty woman at all, but a "plain Jane" with an obvious prim and proper bearing; she tilts her face up to give a somewhat snobbish impression. A tight, high-neck black dress intensifies a chilliness, her eyes cold enough to pierce right through me, and I wonder if she can read my thoughts. If so, I know she wouldn't have liked me—she'd never approve of my free thinking and I look too much like Mama, everyone says.

Emma dies at an early age before Mama and Daddy marry, so what I know is mostly from Mama's and Daddy's stories. Daddy tells me that his mother, Emma Grace McEachern, became an orphan at the age of ten when both her parents died. Emma moves from Marian, South Carolina, to Oak Glen, North Carolina, to live with her older sister Vivian and her husband, Alan John, who become her legal guardians.

At a young age Emma's skill at needlework is remarkable. In her *spare* time she crochets doilies, dresser scarves, fashionable collars and cuffs, and baby clothes; she sells them by walking through the neighborhood door to door. She saves every penny she makes. When I imagine that little girl—about my age orphaned, totally dependent, living in an unfamiliar town in someone else's home (though it's her sister's)—my heart goes out to her. What must she have felt? Even though welcomed and cared for, Emma must have suffered a loss of identity: she, an outsider, growing up in the John home of *nine* children. My impression of Emma from the harsh image of the old black-and-white portrait and Mama's description of her softens greatly. I soon learn that Emma displays quite a bit of independence and spunk. In contrast to a 1890s "lady," she's liberated way before her time.

Soon young Emma becomes caretaker of Sister Vivian's home: Emma does the housework and tends to her nieces and nephews. Later Emma starts working in the millinery shop that Vivian has recently opened on Main Street. Instead of paying her sister for working at the shop, Vivian deposits Emma's earnings in a special account.

In 1891 Emma meets a widower, Franklin O'Donovan, a "gentleman farmer" who owns around 400 acres of farmland in Chesterfield, South Carolina, and in Anson and Union Counties where he grows cotton, corn, and sugar cane. His own mill grinds sugar cane and processes the juice to make molasses, a staple food for his tenants and a commodity for country stores.

Almost immediately, Franklin begins corresponding with Emma, whose sister Vivian keeps pretty tight reins on her even though she's 27. Most of their courting is done secretly by letterwriting, which continues for a year. Much to the surprise of her family, Emma elopes to Chesterfield to marry "Mr. O'Donovan" as she always calls him.

In the ancient trunk I find a stack of old letters, dated 1892, written in fancy script that cover seven consecutive months. The letters are still tied with faded yellow satin ribbon and a bow, the way only a young woman would do. I am pleased beyond measure to hold in my hands Emma's love letters, written by her and to her. The letters are very proper and grammatically correct, and she addresses Franklin as "Dear Mr. O'Donovan"; he replies and addresses her as "My dear Miss Emma," and they both sign their full names. Emma talks about going to the theater in Oak Glen, to concerts, and to Wednesday-night prayer meetings. She describes taking care of her sister's sons and helping Vivian choose hats for her millinery shop.

A handsome and dashing figure in old photographs, Franklin confides about long hours working on his farm; the long, lonely nights; and "how much I would enjoy a young lady's company." From his writing he sounds easy-going, affectionate, and quick to express his feelings.

Emma soon becomes more personable. She is undoubtedly hesitant to tell her sister about him. She writes, "It's not that they would not approve of you but rather that they don't know you." Emma explains that her sister has been keeping her money plus some family allowances in an account for her. She fears she will lose the money if she elopes, but she does not want her family to break them up. Franklin assures her that all he has will be hers.

I am thrilled to witness history unfolding: a woman falling in love. Grandmother Emma becomes alive for me while I read. No longer straight-laced and logical, Emma metamorphoses into an impetuous, passionate woman in love, courting Franklin unbeknown to her family by secret meetings, love letters, and an elopement she eagerly anticipates and carefully executes.

She tells him when to meet her train in Chesterfield, instructing him "not to bother with much fuss over a wedding—keep it simple but nice," and explaining "I'll be wearing a white cashmere dress." And then in her letter there's an added note: "Mr. O'Donovan, you better have a preacher with you."

In 1892, three months after they marry, Emma buys property with her own money and opens on Main Street her own dry-goods store—the forerunner of the department store. She names her business the Emma G. O'Donovan Store. Daddy says his mother is featured in *The Raleigh News* along with her sister Vivian John as the first women in North Carolina to own property and to manage businesses. Emma's store becomes quite popular with women, because not only does she sell bolts of fine material, but she also designs, sews, and fits made-to-order dresses. Later she orders and sells ready-made dresses; this innovation brings even more customers. From all over this part of the state people in buggies and wagons come to Oak Glen to trade, often out of curiosity to see a business owned and operated by a woman. Emma's store remains very successful for several decades.

For a few years Emma and Franklin live upstairs over her store until she gives birth to her second child. Quite the matriarch, Emma rears four children, rules her family with a stern hand, runs the household, manages her store, and holds the money with an iron fist. She plans to build a home on Church Street, which then is a dirt road on the outskirts of town where only one other house stands—the District Judge's—and near where the town has planted small water oaks. She adds to the blueprints two turrets, stained glass, and space for a third floor; Southern Colonial changes to Victorian. In time other homes appear and generate a fine neighborhood that someday witnesses the town growing up and around it.

Franklin (my Jayjo) remains the "gentleman planter," piddling with his farmlands in Chesterfield and in Anson County. Their daughter Eloise later moves to Winston Salem and marries an executive at R. J. Reynolds; the oldest son Richard sells insurance and gambles a lot, his parents often picking up the tab; the youngest son Henry plays football and organizes—along with a couple of his "buddies"—the first football team in Oak Glen. In the family portrait display he wears the first football uniform. He attends every game and then talks about each for the rest of his life, socializing on Main Street, often leaning back against a building in a ladder-back chair along with other men, mostly storeowners and professionals. And he continues to live in the home place on Church Street.

The second son Jacob (Daddy) has no chance to graduate and get an architectural degree. During his senior year Daddy chooses family over career and leaves State College to return home to help the family financially. America has entered the Great War. Richard joins the army, soon goes to fight the Germans, and leaves his family holding his empty bag. Being a big-time gambler, Richard has acquired big-time losses. He has signed notes on family property to back up bets and has acquired the consequent losses. Daddy must help pay off his brother's gambling debts to save the family property, including their home. In time the O'Donovan's financial situation stabilizes, and for a while Daddy opens his own business, a battery shop, the only one in town.

Daddy likes to use his hands, whether building something he designs or working on cars. In the second decade of the 1900s, cars become more prevalent in the small-town South, so owning a battery shop becomes profitable. If a battery goes dead in those early cars, it has to be rebuilt, which Daddy does by pouring acid into vertical compartments. Since he literally can take a car apart and put it back again, automobile owners frequent the battery shop.

Often Daddy puts his drafting table on the back porch and sketches blueprints of buildings and houses. Now sometimes he draws cartoon and fairy tale characters and popular figures on wood, paints them, and cuts them out for my bedroom. On my wall I see Mickey and Minnie Mouse, Goofy and Donald Duck, Little Red Riding Hood, and Pinocchio. Above my bed are the little Dutch boy and girl. Charlie McCarthy, the ventriloquist's doll, sits on my mantle.

Chapter 9

I grow up under the shadow of the Great Depression. Though that *ugly* word appears in the late '20s, the Depression affects everyone for decades. For some people its effects are worse than the effects of war. When the stock market crashes and the banks all close in 1929, the U.S. economy hits bottom, and the O'Donovan family finances are nearly wiped out. That is true for most people through the '30s, and the Depression brings with it suicide for some, starvation for others, and terrible hardship for most. But then there are the others: the money lenders, usually bankers, who gain fortunes.

In 1930 during the Depression years Mama and Daddy marry. At that time Daddy works as the head mechanic at Holland Ford on South Main. Mama is ashamed of Daddy's being a blue-collar worker who leaves for work each morning dressed in khaki work pants and shirt. Of course, he is lucky to have a job. After I'm born in the mid-30s, Daddy continues to work with cars, and Mama still feels he's not ambitious enough. She and Uncle Henry keep reminding me (as I grow to understand them) of how brilliant Daddy was in college. They say a professor at North Carolina State College used Daddy's blueprints as models in his drafting class. Daddy's dream was to become an architect. Disenchanted, Mama says, "Look at Jacob. You'd think he'd feel letdown ... but he doesn't seem to mind." They forget why Daddy dropped out of college to keep an open house for his family.

What if it's 1929 and all of your money—your earnings, your savings—is in your bank account? When the bank closes, the money is gone. In the meantime owners of businesses have to make their payroll and to pay creditors for merchandise; farmers have to pay their workers to cultivate soil to plant seeds, bulbs, and gather in the crops; men stand in long lines hoping for jobs from moneyless employers; doors are shut with signs that say OUT OF BUSINESS; families need cash to buy food; grocers are broke. Fields lie bare save for smothering weeds, wilting plants, and rotting fruit under a Southern sun. And on ... and on ...What can you do? Go to someone with cash for a loan.

The townsfolk go to Stafford McCraw, the president of Liberty Bank, after it shuts down. He has cash on hand, lends families large sums of money, lists their properties as collateral, and demands all loans be paid in full by the end of 90 days.

I grow up hearing tales of the sufferers. For 90 days the O'Donovan family keeps the Emma G. O'Donovan Store in business and the farms running, but they can pay back only two-thirds of the money by the due date; they ask for an extension of 30 days to pay the remaining one-third. Mr. McCraw, an old family friend, refuses; he wants the land, and he gets it—everything but the home place. Such goes story after story. Soon the name McCraw is venom to every resident of the county. However, the McCraw family become multi-millionaires almost overnight, and by the mid-1930s McCraw owns the town.

In the 1940s when I'm young, Daddy sings a song to me—one that's popular then: "I'm a Million-Dollar Baby from the Five-and-Ten-Cent Store." He'd laugh and say, "That's really true. I was born in Rose's Five-and-Dime Store." He gets such a kick from telling me this and seeing my puzzled look, but it turns out he means he was born upstairs in the O'Donovan store that was lost during the

Depression years and by the '40s became Rose's Five and Dime.

As the Depression hits, Emma dies of a stroke. The money and the land probably would have gone with the closing of the banks even if Emma had lived, but without Emma to manage, all the rest of the O'Donovan assets vanish. The family can salvage nothing. Daddy saves the home place by assuming a mortgage he pays for the rest of his life, and then Mama must pay it off. Mama says *that* is her luck: to marry a man of reasonable wealth before the bottom drops out the next day.

The O'Donovan home is my springtime Garden of Eden, but it has always been Mama's Winter of Discontent. It is not her home but Daddy's Home Place. Since her wedding day Mama has lived here with her father-in-law and brother-in-law Henry and whatever O'Donovan needs a temporary place to stay, including the ones in coffins. Most people say "You can't go home again," but Daddy thinks you can.

Daddy's brother Henry lives upstairs in his bedroom since Henry's time is his own to manage, and he supposedly takes care of their papa while Daddy works. Uncle Henry owns a little second-hand store off Main on a side street that dips down into The Bottom, where he sells to the black folks in town everything from men's shoes and boots to women's clothing. Actually, his store resembles a small dark hole in a wall that smells of moldy earth and stale fish from the next-door fish market. Sometimes Mama has me take a message to Uncle Henry, and I nearly choke walking down that alley. I dodge old sticky Coca-Cola spills on the sidewalk along with tobacco spit and hold my breath as long as I can to escape the scents of sweet pickle, rank fish, and sour feet. However, Uncle Henry slips out each day at dawn and stays away all day and most of the night, sometimes working. Because he has no car Mama and I wonder what he does during those late evening hours when the stores are closed and no one is downtown. Daddy doesn't know either.

I hate Uncle Henry's appearance: skin pasty-white, body paunchy, body odor musty like his store. His pants hang under his belly and his cuffs hang over his feet in very wide shoes. He always wears a wide-brimmed fedora with the front curved down like Humphrey Bogart's. However, my vision does a double-take sometimes: I see an attractive young man, blonde with a muscular physique, dressed in Oak Glen's first football uniform—the photo from Henry's high school senior year.

When Uncle Henry sees me, he calls, "Hey, Baby," pats me on the back, and shakes my hand with his soft, fleshy one. Every midnight as regular as clockwork, he slips like a ghost into our house. We hear the whiny squ-e-e-e-ak of the heavy door open and shut, then the heavy thuds falling up the stairs to the bedroom where he has slept his entire life.

Spring to Mama means spring cleaning. Mama scrubs every inch of the house downstairs with Bon-Ami and Lysol. Of course, she has domestic help to do the cleaning. I clean the French windows and the wall and floor molding. She's proud of having the old house shining. Out of curiosity—and determination—Mama goes upstairs to check the condition of Uncle Henry's bedroom.

Mama is in his room. I hear a door slamming and Mama huffing down the stairs screaming louder than the Rebel Yell.

In Uncle Henry's room Mama finds rows of Mason jars and Mason jars and more Mason jars without lids—jars of *pee* lined up neatly against the walls. Amid the rows are stacks and stacks of yellowed newspapers piled nearly halfway up the walls. Mama is mortified. She is *not* going to touch that damn hog pen. But it *will* be cleaned.

When Daddy arrives home, Mama is waiting in the driveway. She starts fussing before he's out of the car. I hear Daddy saying, "Just when am I going to see him? After midnight? Or before dawn?"

"Well, Jacob, just stay up all night. Or go upstairs right now and clean it up. After all, he *is* your brother. And I want his *pee* out of my house before noon tomorrow!"

I awake early in the morning to see what's going to happen. I can hardly wait! I love excitement—as long as I'm not caught. Then, I hear a loud commotion upstairs—a deep voice, furniture being knocked around, heavy feet plodding, a stomp on the stairs! Yeah, Daddy's *got* him ... before he slipped away! Usually my curiosity gets me up and going to investigate—I usually hide and watch. But Uncle Henry is so paunchy and clumsy that I suspect he's spilling a lot of pee on the stairs. The fumes of old sour pee—awful! This time my imagination must fill in the details while my head is buried under the cover. We need to decontaminate!

How long will it take Uncle Henry to bring down a year's collection of daily newspapers? He reads all of them: *The Charlotte Observer, The Charlotte News, The Raleigh Observer, The Raleigh News, The Oak Glen Exchange, The Wilmington News, The Fayetteville Observer, The Washington Post, The New York Times*—I count on my fingers until I run out of fingers and names. Oh, I forget— *Life Magazine, The National Geographic, The New Yorker*, and others.

After midnight I hear the same stomping on the stairs and down the hall to the bathroom. Uncle Henry! He's no longer living in the chamber-pot past.

Some days Mama has "all she can stand." She calls Agatha, and we walk to the bus station on the corner of Main and Church to wait for the Trailways Bus to Hamlet. Daddy has to drive there after work to get us, but he doesn't seem to mind the extra trip for Mama to be with her sister. Mama and Aunt Agatha have fun together, and I get to play with my cousins.

On other days, when Mama wants the car, Daddy rides the Greyhound Bus back and forth to work. When Mama has the car, we head straight to Hamlet. I watch Mama sit at her dresser, rouge her cheeks, paint her lips with her little finger, and arch her brows carefully like Joan Crawford while she hums to Glenn Miller on the radio.

Hamlet, 16 miles away, is "wet." On the edge of town Mama stops at The Hub, a popular drive-in tavern with beer and hamburgers and fries that has a dance floor with music playing continuously from loudspeakers hanging in the shade trees. We stay in the car, and Mama sees someone she knows. He leans against the car, his arm stretched out on the open window, and they talk and Mama laughs. Then he comes around to the passenger side, and Mama tells me to get in the back; he slides in and hands her a beer. For the longest time I sit slumped in the corner of the back seat of the little Ford coupe and drink Coca-Cola, dropping peanuts into the bottle, one after another, until they bubble up out the top. Mama and the man laugh and laugh at nothing and drink more beer with the music blaring. These afternoons I hate Mama. She doesn't flirt with Daddy.

Jayjo has a stroke and lies paralyzed. Daddy has already moved him to a downstairs bedroom, and Mama's nurturing nature suddenly takes over. She nurses him day and night. She props his head on a pillow and feeds him, or sometimes she holds his head to spoon down soup. Every day she bathes him and changes his pajamas and sheets; she talks to him sweetly and always stays near. I hear her mutter, "Oh, God, help me make up for being so mean to that old man. I've been so indifferent." I know how Mama feels: we could see only the physical remains of him—his outer weakness that keeps him from taking care of himself. We miss the inside. At nights she sits and holds his hand until, one night, he finally dies in his sleep.

In the small-town South, ritual rules. Food starts arriving as soon as the coroner announces a death. If there's grief, it apparently disappears with apple pies. And so it is with Jayjo's death. "Well, he lived a good, long life," everyone says, and now "he'll be sent to his Maker" in grand style. His funeral is a celebration of life—no time to mourn. A couple of days before his funeral the undertaker returns Jayjo to our home, embalmed, washed, and dressed in his best cleaned suit with a new shirt and tie. The men "lay him out" in the dining room, which is now filled with flowers and burning candles.

They open the coffin. Jayjo lies stiff and ready for his wake in the old Irish and Scottish tradition: open-casket viewing with plenty of food and drink but no alcohol in this home-place, the unspoken edict of his dead Scottish and staunch Baptist wife. Relatives, neighbors, friends, acquaintances, and curious visitors soon arrive to view the corpse, to talk about how *good* he looks, to pray, to reminisce, to eat, to drink, to joke, and to share recipes. A few volunteers sit up with him through the night, never leaving his body; the men with legs crossed on knees smoke cigars and share old repeated stories, still chuckling over the same lines. Smoke from tobacco and candle flames curl together, making an undulating circle around the body, as in days of old, keeping evil spirits from the dead.

On the day of the funeral most people, especially family and participants, wear black. The women also wear hats and small white gloves. The police and funeral-home director put signs Death in Family and Slow Funeral in various places: in our yard, in the street near the curb in front of our house, at the church, and at various intersections where the funeral procession passes. The flower girls, designated women friends of the family or women of the church, take the wreaths, flowers, and potted plants from the house to the church and then later to the grave site. Black-dressed pallbearers close the coffin, put a flower spray on the casket, and carry the coffin to the hearse. Family cars line up behind the hearse, and the cortege stops in front of the church, where pallbearers lead the procession into the house of worship. A pallbearer reopens the coffin for the service conducted by the minister and chosen speakers. Daddy recites the eulogy.

When Jayjo's coffin is finally sealed, the ritual is repeated with pallbearers returning the coffin to the hearse, the flower girls packing flowers in cars, and the police leading the hearse to the family cemetery plot where the monument stands. All the cars drive with their lights on as part of the funeral cortege. Other traffic stops along the route.

At the graveside the family sits under the canopy where flower girls place a few flowers and pallbearers put the coffin to rest. The minister leads another service and says a final prayer, and a reception line forms for people to give their last condolences. Their duty done, the family returns to the home place to eat again and entertain guests.

And Jayjo is left lying beside Emma in the cemetery.

Chapter 10

One Sunday morning I run to the porch to get the *Charlotte Observer* for Daddy. I see big red letters across the front page, and I know at once something *big* has happened. Daddy reads the red headlines aloud to Mama: "America Under Attack; Pearl Harbor Bombed." Seeing fear flush in my face, he assures me that we're safe. "Our troops will get the bad guys. Fort Bragg's right around the corner!"

As if to prove his point, Daddy drives us to Hamlet to the train depot. Often on Sunday afternoons, Daddy, Mama, and I drive to the train depot to watch the trains come in. Hamlet is the main junction of the southern part of the state where trains meet—a major artery for going up and down the Eastern Seaboard. I hold my breath in awe when a large engine screeches to a halt with billows of steam hissing out from under and around the great wheels. What tremendous power for me to see and hear. The train is real. Close enough to touch when the steam dissipates.

On this drive to Hamlet, we stop at the depot to watch all the commotion. "You see, Erin Rose," Daddy says in a low voice, "our troops will keep us safe." Troops upon troops fill the depot and the trains: soldiers and sailors on furlough or weekend passes with young wives or sweethearts waiting eagerly on the depot platform; or soldiers and sailors under orders for combat, anxious to fight yet afraid, waiting until the last minute for the deep tones of that ALL ABOARD ... instantaneously, they sling duffel bags up on the steps and jump on, hanging onto the side rail, out of windows, waving at loved ones running along with the train, hearing again ALL ABOARD for ... Camden, South Carolina; Columbia, South Carolina; Denmark, South Carolina ....

To ride a train is to be part of something much greater than yourself—the same feeling I have at times when I look out at our land. I think back to times Daddy would put Mama and me on the train to ride to Raleigh to visit Aunt Isabelle, Mama's sister, who works in the lingerie department of Ivey's Department Store. Mama shops all day, we visit Aunt Isabelle, and we return home the next day.

Soon after the ALL ABOARD, the black porter, commonly called the "News Butch," dressed in the same black suit as the conductor, comes bumping from side to side with racks of sandwiches and drinks and snacks and newspapers, his voice booming out like a tobacco auctioneer: "Ham and Cheese, Coca Cola, Roasted Peanuts, Cracker Jacks, Hershey Bars ..."

On the pretext of having to use the bathroom, I walk down the aisle, too, swaying back and forth with the clanking rhythm of the train, sensing I'm moving fast within a vortex of even greater speed. The power heightens the vividness of views from wide windows: flashing bits of sky, trees, countryside, telephone poles; country homes snap past with each clack of the track like a kaleidoscope.

Now, in 1942 I am seven years old. The entire town is bustling with ideas about how everyone can contribute to the war effort. Everywhere there are posters of Uncle Sam, a looming figure, dressed in a red-white-and-blue suit with top hat, his forefinger pointing straight at you: "Uncle Sam Needs You." The home-front battle cry is "Grow your own food and help win the war!"

Daddy and I plant a Victory Garden. We buy vegetable seeds that come in white envelopes with red and blue stripes at the top and a picture of the vegetable beneath a star-studded flag. In moist earth we sprinkle seeds, cover them, and place each envelope upside down on a stick to name the vegetable row: radish, pepper, butter bean, green bean, corn, cucumber, tomato. I wait and wait for a tiny seed to push through the soil into a sprout. I slip out early in the morning to see if Daddy and I can really make life.

Hearing about the war is like listening to the radio or watching a picture show. It doesn't seem real. At home, life goes on as usual, though the preacher on Sundays prays for our troops. And I wonder, how does God fit into all this? If He's so powerful and the Head of All Things, then why doesn't He stop the fuss?

I sometimes think of Daddy as God ... *not really, but they're a lot alike.* Daddy knows everything. He fixes everything. He's my confidant. If I decide to confess something "bad" I've done, I confess it to him; he listens and asks me what I think I should do, and we come to a fairly easy solution—a whole lot easier than the church's fire-pit way. Daddy and I never talk about church or my Sunday school lesson or why Jesus loves us, but he takes me with him to Sunday school every week. Many facts about religion puzzle me so, yet I never ask Daddy Bible questions, because he answers my questions before I even ask.

Mama tells me never to question anything in the Bible—that's what *her* father told *her.* "That's sinful, Erin Rose. Just do what you're told." From her tone I fear the thoughts in my head will cause my body one day to fall into the fire-pit. Sometimes in church after the preacher has finished, I look carefully down at the floor to see if it's opened to Hell's fire before I stand to leave, regretting my thoughts have been so free willed.

My home and the church are simply separate. Daddy and Mama and I never say grace before a meal, yet Daddy from time to time reminds us how thankful we should be and Mama has me say a prayer every night at bedtime before she tucks me in and kisses me. Since Mama doesn't go to church with us and Daddy never brings up the subject of church at home, I never connect the two. However, Daddy's stories sound a lot like Jesus' parables—just a different way of talking that makes a whole lot more sense than the church does.

Sometimes I have bad dreams. I awake in darkness and hate to slide from my warm bed to slip down the long black hall by the creaking stairway to reach the only bathroom in the house. On some stormy nights I hear raindrops like fingers tapping and loose tree limbs rasping on the slate roof, a floorboard groaning, winds howling. These sounds and shadows make me feel creepy; I hold my breath and run as fast as I can to my parents' room and jump in the bed to cuddle close to Daddy.

Usually I find comfort in the shadows of this house I love—the creaks and cracks and hisses are its breath and heartbeat. But what makes me so afraid at other times? Threatened by the presence of something ... something I sense as tangible and all-consuming as a fog drifting in and around me. Could it be my future?

On the east side of our house, two doors away, the John Hospital looms up on the corner of Church St. as a daily reminder of human suffering. Built by Daddy's first cousin Dr. Timothy John this tall brick edifice casts gloom over the neighborhood. Across my backyard, eastward, I can see the ambulance pull into the hospital drive and stop at the back door, the stretchers sliding in and out, sometimes covered with a sheet, sometimes not. I wonder who the people are. What are their stories?

On hot summer nights I lie in bed with my windows wide open to let in breezes through the screens. In the '40s, even in the South, there is no air conditioning, just the relief of high ceilings and large iron fans. At times the breeze gently sways the thin Priscilla curtains that spatter the bright moonbeam on the floor. When the night is very still and all the lights are out, I hear sounds reverberating ever so faintly from the hospital: a clatter of dishes, a sudden scream, a human drone sustaining a tone like a wearisome bagpipe, the staccato burst of *gong … gong … gong …* I don't like being this close to Death's Edge, the moment either of passing on or awaking, not understanding who or what makes the decision and why.

Across the street on the north side, beside the little Episcopal Church, a wide stretch of land dips down into The Bottom, the site of those deadly fights. I think of the dried-up corpse still hanging in the funeral garage on the west side and the family dead periodically laid out in our house. I imagine spirits, sometimes unfriendly ones, hovering around in the darkness. On Saturdays when I go to the picture show before the feature films, the morning newsreel replays scenes of skeletal bodies stacked up like pieces of firewood. There are scenes of skeletal men with protruding ribs leaning against wire fences, eyes sunken, staring … waiting. I try not to look at the faces, but I'm spellbound by this horror that spills into my sleep at night.

Awake I believe I'm in a land that's safe and free from such inhumanities, but my dream self doesn't know the difference. *Nazi troops always come at night, marching, marching, marching in unison the high goose step down my street and pausing at our walkway. The troops march up our steps, pound on the door, and kick it open. Jackboots stomp into my room, and I, a child, wild-eyed, the blanket clutched around my chin, stare in horror through the space between bedpost and bed. Black jackboots shine in a slant of moonlight beside my bed.* I awake, too terrified to scream. I feel safer when Daddy's near, but dreams disregard time and place.

Our Victory Garden is already growing and I'm proud of our war effort. Certain foods are now scarce and rationed, and our school is also selling stamps for U.S. Bonds and collecting metal and tinfoil.

My mama's war effort is smoking cigarettes. She smokes so much I think I'll have enough tinfoil to build the wing of a fighter plane. I am delighted. I run around picking up the pack of Camels and ask her, "Don't you want another cigarette, Mama?" I wait anxiously for her to finish a pack so I can remove the inside foil and roll it up into a tiny ball. I also help the war effort by chewing packs of gum all day long to add the wrappers to Mama's tinfoil. Then day by day I watch the ball grow until it's large enough to take to school for the drive. I'm excited because I'll probably win the second-grade contest.

Central School is collecting scrap metal. On the far side of our backyard an old barn still sits, used as a carriage house when Daddy was a child. Now it's an eyesore full of junk. Mama helps me pull out my grandfather's old plow and his other long-discarded farm equipment. Then she pays someone to haul all the junk to school to help us win the war and me win the second-grade scrap contest. Mama's patriotic effort arises, I'm sure, from my never-leaving-her-alone pestering.

At the kitchen table I sit with Mama to separate sugar, meat, coffee, and gas ration stamps and to figure out when to use them. The Rationing Board at the courthouse decides the number of stamps to allot to each family according to need. The gasoline clerk, for example, gives more gas stamps to doctors, for they make more house calls than they get office visits. Many women who never worked before now work as clerks to distribute the ration books to each family. As the war escalates, more food and household products are rationed, and without enough stamps no one can buy these. And some items are altogether unavailable, such as nylon stockings, hairpins, chocolate, rubber for tires, car parts, or toothpaste in a metal tube unless you turn in an old used one. We brush our teeth with baking soda.

The fire horn blasts through the night: a repeated *bong-bong-bong*. Fear once again takes my breath and holds it; my heart beats hard, as loud as the alarm signal itself. Quickly, people respond to the air-raid drill, assuming it's just a practice "blackout." I wonder if it's real. We do have Fort Bragg nearby, a major target, and German submarines are sinking boats off our Atlantic Coast—making us all "sitting ducks," in one of the most dangerous spots on the map. Everyone turns out the lights, pulls down window shades, puts out fires—even the tiniest spark. Some people drape blankets over the shades to block out a candle flickering or coals left glowing in the grate. In each neighborhood, air raid wardens patrol the streets, checking for any light and ringing the bell of any house where the smallest hint of light seeps out.

Once during a blackout someone bangs on our door. I nearly jump out of my skin. In heavy darkness, with me hiding behind Daddy, he opens the front door, and there stands a man in a black hard hat that looks like a helmet. For a moment my heart rapidly beats to the rhythm of goose steps of thousands of soldiers in their Heil Hitler march.

"Hello," Daddy says. "Something wrong?"

Instead of German words come English, thinning the night and my heart beat.

"You have a bit of light showing, sir," the warden warns.

I take a deep breath, look down at his tennis shoes, and exhale.

"From under the front shade, sir."

Daddy replies, "Sorry about that, Donny. You're Donald Smith's son, aren't you?"

The young man nods. "Yes, sir."

Daddy remarks, "You're doing a fine job here. Got some good eyes. It's probably the fire. I'll get right to it." Daddy finds a small piece of coal, still smoking, a spark inside. With the poker he crushes it to ashes.

These temporary intrusions of total darkness and silence create somber times and that infinitesimal moment of paralyzing fear for a waiting child, afraid of hearing the thunder of planes or the stomping of jackboots.

Memory is what you remember and what you forget, the unconscious holding on to everything, not discerning between images from film or print or real life. Nor does it distinguish between past and present. It is all the same.

Downtown Oak Glen suddenly is a lively place, full of American troops in local bars. On Saturday afternoons Ruby Jean and I stroll along the street taking in all the sights. At the corner of Main and Church, a few doors from the Glen Theater, soldiers crowd the sidewalk, leaning against the buildings and smoking, waiting to get into the crowded bar. Other soldiers stumble out, blocking the whole sidewalk, and Ruby Jean and I walk around them, stepping off the curb into the street on our way to Carolina Drug to get a cherry-Coke after the picture show.

The drunk guys don't frighten us because a lot of them on the street are hometown boys on furlough "raising Cain." Anyway, we've just viewed the picture show of either handsome soldiers or sailors dying for their country heroically. Why shouldn't they drink a beer? Or two?

Sometimes we see a sailor or two with a cigarette dangling from their lips and beers in their hands leaning against a building or a car. I love looking at sailors in neat white uniforms because they make me think of Uncle Bobby, who is in the Navy. And they remind me of the sea that I love: white tops of waves splashing and gray ships rolling on the tide. Then loud, lively music thrusts through the window of the bar along with a crash of a chair and the sight of someone thrown through the door. Ruby Jean and I hurry through the crowd trying to look nonchalant, but we're excited by the sounds, sights, and smells. There's a kind of thrill in being close to danger, especially when you're safe at home, merely talking about it.

In 1941 Oak Glen becomes the site of the first glider base in the United States. Daddy says our county's favorable weather conditions played an important part in the Army's decision. He explains all the strategy to me. The glider is a new concept for the U.S. military, but the Germans have used it since 1940. The army recognizes the effectiveness of these silent gliders loaded with troops and supplies, including heavy weapons and jeeps that land behind enemy lines. In essence, the glider is a plane with no engine or artillery, towed by a regular plane that releases the glider near a spot considered safe. When the glider is released, the pilot steers it safely to land within enemy territory. The Glider Training Base trains pilots as well as selected soldiers from all over the country.

The new glider pilots help fill the streets downtown, already full of soldiers from Camp Maguire needing a bit of recreation. The army holds monthly dances at the base in an airplane hangar and invites the community to attend. These dances host well-known bands, including Tommy Dorsey, Benny Goodman, and singer Vaughn Monroe. At moments of selfish indulgence, I hope the war continues until I'm old enough to attend an army dance and jitterbug in an airplane hangar to live music. Then a thought pops into my head: *that is a long time away and too many soldiers will die.* Already, on the street, we pass soldiers and hear comments: "I got my orders." ... "Gonna be shippin' out soon."... "See ya, Buddy, on my way to Berlin."

A member from nearly every family in Oak Glen has joined a branch of the service and gone off to war. In those houses a vacant bedroom awaits, and a Blue Star Service Banner or a Service Flag in the front window honors each serviceman in the family. At the glider base, housing has become a problem. Since the Army Corp of Engineers has built the base as a temporary habitation, they have provided housing for only single men; married soldiers must find a place to live in town. Many of the larger Oak Glen houses have spare rooms, so families eager to befriend soldiers and their wives welcome them into their homes. The soldiers, in turn, welcome the home atmosphere and that special Southern hospitality. Many make close bonds, and a few soldiers return here to live after the war.

We rent a downstairs bedroom to a tall good-looking captain and his young, friendly dark-blond wife and newborn baby. Sometimes the captain and Daddy sit on the back porch and talk of baseball and war; inside, on the davenport, Mama holds the baby in her lap and listens to the young wife talk of home in Oregon. They stay for nine months or so, until he receives his orders to ship out, and she has to drive alone with her baby across country to Oregon.

The day is steaming hot. Daddy checks over her car again and again, loading her luggage and baby stuff; Mama holds the baby; the girl opens her pocketbook and dumps out piles of cash. This must be her first experience of moving and traveling alone and managing money. She opens the glove compartment in her car and shoves in loose bills and more bills—all the money she has, hundred-dollar bills just hanging out of the compartment. Daddy is concerned whether she knows the way, Mama at last hands her the baby-girl, I am in shock at seeing so much money thrown around, and finally we say our good-byes.

She's off. I feel very sad. I am aware, suddenly, of the aloneness of separation. The unexpressed grief about what may happen. The sudden danger for the unprotected glider pilot as well as the young wife with baby left to battle for herself. Daddy has pointed out to me that the enemy can't hear the silent glider, but they certainly can hear the aircraft pulling it. The effects of war. My great fear of death.

Chapter 11

In the summer of 1942, I am seven, and I fall passionately in love with my Uncle Bobby, 17. On the day he comes, I am sprawled on the living room floor writing him a letter on Mama's stationery, stopping only to ask Mama how to spell a word. In the second grade that year I learn cursive writing and practice it all the time by writing letters to my sweetheart. I know I'm his sweetheart because he ends his letters with SWAK (Sealed With A Kiss); even across the envelope on the back, he prints another SWAK. I am so excited, I can hardly write, thinking about seeing him soon. At the open windows a mild breeze waves the curtain sheers back and forth. I sit and wait. From the distance I hear a faint whistling on the wind that sounds stronger as it gets nearer, closer to home. Then I know.

Tall, blond, blue-eyed, and incredibly good-looking in his white sailor uniform, he marches up our front walkway to the beat of his whistling, "Anchors aweigh, my boys, anchors aweigh ...," and I yell to Mama, "Bobby's here!" I rush down the steps to meet him, his arms held out to catch me.

"Hey, Sweetheart, you've grown up!" Bobby picks me up and swirls me around and then kisses me on the cheek. I hug him tight around the neck and feel as though I can never let him go. He puts me down, plops his sailor hat on my head, and we walk the rest of the way into the house, his arm hugging my shoulder and my arm reaching up around his waist. I chatter all the way inside the house: "You're early!

We were going to meet you at the bus station. Aunt Agatha's coming and we're gonna cook a big supper. She's made your favorite banana cake—don't tell her I said so." I lean my head back to see his face and the blond hair now curling from the growing-out crew-cut, a few strands falling on his forehead. His skin is a tropical, golden tan. He takes my breath away. School will start soon, and I cannot wait for the girls there to see him.

Bobby is Mama's younger brother, who has lived in Raleigh for the past five years with Isabelle, their older sister, after their parents had died. During the summers Bobby comes to Oak Glen for long visits with us, sometimes alternating visits with Mama's other sister Agatha in Hamlet. During his junior year when the U.S. entered WW II, he waited eagerly to join the fighting. After high school graduation Bobby quickly joined the Navy before the draft could get him. After his basic training, the Navy sent Bobby to the Gulf Coast at Pensacola, Florida.

As long as I can remember, I've been crazy about Bobby, who has been like the brother I've never had. Now that I am seven, I know how it feels to be in love. I already know about love. I love my Daddy every day in a quiet, still way. I love the trees in my yard and the purple-red sunset when cold is settling in for winter. However, with Bobby, I feel passion, the loud something that makes me run and shout and dance on top of the table to fast music. Bobby is an unexpected parade that you've only heard about but want to join before it goes away. And now he's here.

We walk up the steps holding hands. Bobby drops his duffel bag in the hall as Mama hurries through the French doors, her eyes lighting up. "Bobby, we didn't expect you until tonight." They hug and kiss. "Did you take an earlier bus?"

"No. I got a ride. Would you believe—a guy from Camp Maguire?" Bobby falls into the nearest chair and reaches up to his shirt pocket to pull out a pack of Lucky Strikes. That's what I'm going to smoke someday. He keeps talking. "I was in this bar and some soldier sits down next to me and we start talking. Come to find out he's leaving in a couple of days to get back to Camp Maguire." He blows a smoke ring out into the living room. "So I bum a ride. Beats riding the bus any day. He let me out at the corner."

Daddy comes home early to help Mama cook that special fried-chicken supper with all the Southern trimmings for Bobby's homecoming. Aunt Agatha arrives earlier than expected with the banana cake and her husband Ben and my two cousins. The evening is festive with reminiscing and laughing and very little talk of war. After kisses and good-byes, Aunt Agatha's family leaves. And we have Bobby to ourselves.

In the living room Bobby pushes back a few chairs and calls me. "Come on, Erin Baby, I've got a new dance step to show you. You'll be the only one in your class who'll know how to do it!"

Bobby drops a '78 on the Victrola and starts singing along with the record: "Don't sit under the apple tree / with anyone else but me." He guides me into the jitterbug, pulling me between his legs and flipping me over his head to the beat of the music. We dance until we're really together with the music and its beats. Then Bobby pulls Mama up to dance a slow tune until she is laughing at their dipping. Laughing, too, Daddy teases Mama that she's going to split her dress.

The next day we play cards all morning. First, five-card rummy, then gin rummy, and finally poker. Using small matchsticks for money, we play blackjack with deuces wild until we both get tired. Bobby pushes all the matchsticks to the center of the kitchen table and says, "Let's play for the pot." I win. Bobby claps and says he's so proud he's made me into a gambler "who can hold her own with the entire Army or even the Navy for that matter." He leans over and kisses me on the cheek. "Sweetheart, just keep your cool."

We share secrets, too. After supper before dark, Bobby borrows Daddy's car to buy some cigarettes and take me for a ride. It's been a while since he's been in Oak Glen, and he wants to see some "old familiar places." When he gets to the Maguire Road, he flies down the highway to the South Carolina line and crosses over to drive to a place that sells beer. I promise I won't tell on him—about the beer or the speeding. Maguire is not far and the road passes a lot of bars. I feel all grown-up and elated. I love the way Bobby drives the little Ford coupe faster than Daddy does, with windows down, music blaring, and wind rushing through my hair.

Bobby continues to visit us each time he's granted leave. My friends finally see him in his sailor uniform and just stare at him and giggle. On his last leave, in 1944, Bobby brings home for a few days a girl named Pearl from Newport, where he is stationed.

At first, I don't like her a bit, because she's with Bobby, but she smiles at me and gives me a Chinese doll with a little black Chinese house with gold trim made like a stage that you can take apart and put back together. Pearl's only gift is for me because she says I'm Bobby's favorite. She has a tattoo of a bird high up on her thigh, and Mama spots it when Pearl puts on her bathing suit and comes out on the back porch to sit in the sun with us. Mama has a fit. Of course, Pearl doesn't know that Mama has a fit, but I do. Mama raises her eyebrows the way she always does when she's displeased and turns her head and clears her throat really loud. Then she quickly goes back inside the house instead of sitting with us on the steps. She doesn't talk to Pearl for the rest of the day.

After Pearl leaves for Newport, I am delighted. Her return gives me Bobby all to myself. Mama, though, worries him to death. She follows him around everywhere, fussing about the "questionable" girls he is forever "getting involved" with and when he is going to "settle down" with some "nice" girl. Bobby just shrugs and grins, which really irks Mama. When he sees me behind the open door listening, he winks at me and says to Mama, "Hey, Sis, don't you know I'm waiting for Erin Rose?"

After supper while I'm helping Mama with the dishes, Daddy and Bobby sit on the back porch and talk about the war. The back door is open, and we can hear snatches of their conversation through the screen door. I know Mama is eavesdropping as well as me. She frowns, looks up, and pauses with a dish. It seems that the war is accelerating more and more every day, and most of the servicemen are biding their time, waiting to get their orders for overseas. Mama's hands are still in the soapy water and her eyes fill with tears. Bobby is saying he thinks he'll be shipped out anytime now. I drop the dish towel and walk out of the kitchen.

On the front porch I sit on the steps alone. I don't want to see anyone. I ache inside. Shipped out ... Does that mean shipped out to the fighting and bombing like what's in the picture shows? *I see airplanes painted with a circle like the sun on the tips of wings and men with squinting eyes who dive down to crash on the deck of an American ship, and the sea rushing in so fast it knocks the sailors down and washes them away. The ship tips over backwards, the stern sinking into the sea first, the bow sticking straight up in the air, and finally it slides down quickly under the foam where giant waves roll over it. Some of the sailors are pulled into lifeboats after being burned. And I see John Wayne losing his leg when he gets on the hospital ship.* Suddenly, I don't want to watch any more war movies.

The night is dark. No stars out at all. Even the moon is gone. I feel as empty as the sky. Only a black sky and a black porch. There's no light here. But I don't want to go inside the house because I'll have to see Bobby and that hurts too much. I sit and stare at nothing until I hear the front door open.

"Sweetheart, are you out here?" Bobby asks.

"Yes."

"You mad with me or something?"

"You're going overseas."

"Probably. Looks like it."

"Are you going where the fighting is?"

"I suppose. Don't know exactly where yet. Somewhere in the South Pacific if I'm sent."

"What if you don't come back?"

"Hey, what kinda talk is that? Sure, I'm coming back. Why, I'm taking you on your first date, remember?"

"I remember."

"And when you turn 16, I'm taking you to your first big dance. How can you forget that?"

I sniff. "I haven't forgotten."

"Why, I've got so many places to take you, Sweetheart, I gotta come back."

I swallow hard over the hurt in my throat. I don't want to cry in front of Bobby so I sniff three times real fast, but that doesn't help because when he puts his arm around me that makes me really cry. He holds me close until my sobs become sporadic sniffles again. Then he pulls off his sailor tie and insists on wiping my nose with it because he doesn't have a handkerchief. After wiping my nose, he tosses the tie up in the air and says to it, "Well, here's looking at you, kid" in his best Bogart voice with a cigarette hanging between his lips. And I cannot help but giggle as we watch the tie land on top of an azalea bush.

"Come on, Sweetheart, we need to dance."

In good spirits now, we rush inside, drop a record on the Victrola, and jitterbug the night and reality away. Even

90

Mama joins us and starts dancing the Charleston. Time passes fast. Bobby looks through the stack of records and chooses another one. He smiles at me. "Erin, Baby, let's dance a slow one."

The music starts and we dance: "I'll be seeing you in all the old familiar places..."

This is our last dance.

Bobby never makes it to a heroic battle scene that I often imagined and feared. He stays stateside, trained and ready, apprehensively eager, on hold. But the war passes him by, much to the relief of Mama, my aunts, and me. Our prayers are answered, temporarily. The atomic bomb drops on Hiroshima in August 1945, and newspapers fill pages with the mushroomed destruction that soon ends the war. Bobby completes his four-year tour of duty in the war's early aftermath. In September 1945 Bobby turns 21 and gets an honorable discharge. He drops by to see us for a very short visit, but he is not the man who left. I note his fingers now have turned cigarette-stained yellow and fingernails bitten to the quick. He appears restless, his hands shaky. I look into his eyes and they don't focus on me; there is something lost there. Is he disappointed he never got to fight? After all, he waited four years to be "somebody" in battle. Does he miss belonging to a team? For four years he slept, ate, worked out, and shared the hopes of his buddies. What will he do now? He leaves soon for Baltimore to visit his brother, Thomas, and, perhaps to get a job.

Like thousands of other veterans after a war, either temporarily dislocated or permanently, Bobby finds himself trained to fight with no war to fight in, jobless, a part of another "lost generation" isolated from the mainstream, no longer bound to the nation's needs yet unprepared for civilian life.

I am 11 years old in January 1946. It is dreadfully cold, and the chill goes deep into my bones so I feel I will never be warm again. When they bring Bobby home, the coffin remains sealed shut so no one can see his badly burned body from the Baltimore fire. They put his coffin under the window of my bedroom. Since my bedroom faces the front porch, it is the one closest to the main door and the most convenient for people to reach. Anyway, they just have to move out my bed.

As fate has it, four months after his discharge, Bobby is dead at 21.

People come in all day and part of the night. They cry. Someone falls over the coffin, sobbing. People take turns sitting with him. And Mama is inconsolable. Her excessive sobbing is so loud and long Daddy puts her to bed and calls Dr. Harry, who lives across the street, to come over and give her something. You would think she loves Bobby the most.

I stand in the back of the room and silently stare. I don't remember being told anything about Bobby's death until the coffin arrives at our house. When I finally discover that it contains Bobby's body, I can't believe it. The news is beyond shock or grief or anything I've ever felt. The ache is like having a knife stuck in my chest. I can only stare at that *thing* in my room. Then, when no one is around, I walk up close to the coffin and just stand there, losing track of time. I reach over and run my hand along the wood grain on top and gently stroke the sides of the coffin.

When they first bring him in, I want to die, too. I can't face knowing he's gone. Then I start thinking *he's not there*. I keep standing, rocking back and forth on my toes to the rhythm of *he's not there, he's not there, he's not there* ... As long as I can't see his body, I can believe he's not there. I can believe whatever I want to. I can believe he will be back someday. He said he'd be back to take me on my first real date. He promised. The spring I'm 16 he'll take me to my first dance. He promised.

Chapter 12

In the New Year 1947, after Bobby's death, winter settles in for a long season: cold winds not letting go, limbs scraping the roof, boards creaking in the house, fire crackling in the fireplace. A dull grayness invades the rooms from outside and from within. Daddy leaves early in the mornings to drive to Bennettsville and returns in the late afternoons in the growing dark of the short winter days. He brings the only bit of light into our home.

When school is out, I hate to go home. My only bright moment in mid-afternoon is spotting Snowball on the front steps waiting for me. And that undeniable second she spots me and streaks up the walk with her "happy" face, mouth open and lips split up in her special dog-smile, her fluffy tail wagging. I drop my books and we cuddle, neck to neck, a perfect fit. I hug her longer, hanging on, postponing the time to enter the house and see Mama crying and smoking and staring at the ashes of dimming coals, burned too low to give out heat.

"Mama, I'm home."

Surprisingly, Mama is up and about and acts eager to see me. Of course, she expects me to start my homework and then practice piano while she goes through my papers to keep tabs on my grades. Then she walks from one window to another and stands gazing out, smoking. Mama seems to have no friends in Oak Glen, and she never has anything to do if she's not cleaning. She flips on the radio to the music station WLBG and hums along with the songs she knows. "C'mon, Erin Rose, dance with me!"

The radio plays a tune fit for the Charleston. Mama showed me the steps when I was a little girl; I'd wiggle my knees together while my arms hung low, waving across my knees at the same time, trying to keep up with Mama. At 11 now, I hope I can follow her better. For a rare moment we laugh and lose ourselves in the music. I remember what Aunt Agatha says about Mama's laugh—it is genuine and spontaneous. I haven't noticed it for a long while—not since Bobby's death.

Everyone deals with loss in different and separate ways. Mama and I stay poles apart within our own narrow cold-winter space: Mama indulges in crying and senseless questioning of fate, God, and her brother Thomas, who left the apartment before the fire, and falls into deep anxiety over the slowness of firemen, the lack of warning devices, and the reasons why Bobby was so overcome with smoke. She paces the floor and turns to chain-smoking as some type of substitute for answers. I seek a private spot where I can be alone to sit and cry or to sit and think when I can't cry. Sometimes I can go into a nothingness like a coma. Or I write in my journal.

In a silent world you are forced to be still. To think, to remember, to release that which is repressed. Of course, you can read, sleep, drown in fantasy, or escape reality however you like. No one knows what's going on inside your head. However, when my world stops for a while and I'm in cold silence, I like to snuggle up in a blanket on the davenport in front of the fire and stare at a particular shape made by the burning coals. Or if our yard is covered with snow and the air is too cold, I cuddle in the wingback chair and stare out the bay window, focusing on a snow-sculpture. And I *meditate*. (This *word* I do not know at eleven, yet that is what I do.) Often I get ideas, and suddenly I understand something that I didn't know before. It's strange: I'll know the answer before I think of the question. I just look at nature. *Cold winds lash at trees. Naked limbs lifeless. Spring brings buds.*

And life *does* go on—like the seasons.

The freezing winter *does* turn into a chilly early spring: ice breaks, snow melts, patches of snow appear around blue crocuses. Before I know it, rain comes and warm winds; the narcissi bloom with bright yellow jonquils, trumpeting spring and the renewal of life—right *here* in our yard.

Coming home from school, I spot it—even before my dog. There it is—the "bush burning," not burning red, but the forsythia burning bright yellow at both corners of the front yard. The flowering bushes opened after I left this morning. Now the mid-afternoon sun over the western hedge keeps them on fire. And nearby in clumps, standing at attention, are yellow jonquils pointing their trumpets to the sun.

Pushing open the heavy wood door, I call out, "Mama, have you seen the flowers? And a robin landed in the grass! Spring's come!"

Everywhere I can smell a special freshness in the air and hear myriad *cheep-cheep-tweet-chirrups* in the tops of trees. On the birdfeeder lands a pair of cardinals and a robin hops to peck a sunflower seed. And I think, "Life is good! No more signs of death."

Carolina summer arrives with playing baseball in the park, swimming in the river, and fishing in the creeks. And with it comes the overbearing heat and humidity. However, the gardens ripen with watermelons, squash, juicy tomatoes, and mouth-watering white corn-on-the-cob. In the backyard Daddy fries fish in a large black iron skillet on the brick fireplace grill and dips hushpuppies in the big black iron pot. We have wiener-roast parties; Daddy straightens out old coat-hangers to pierce the length of each hot dog, and we hold them above the fire. When the fire simmers down, we roast marshmallows the same way. On the back porch Daddy churns homemade ice cream packed in dry ice. Though Daddy's red-velvet roses grow abundantly against the white of our house, he plants more roses near the windows on the west side with me supervising. And the oaks stand strong with feathery green tops cascading down the street.

All is well. I, too, am stronger than I was seven months earlier when Bobby died. I can swallow his death now, digest it, and let it become a part of me. Like osmosis, grief seeps into my pores and becomes a faint underlying shadow.

Soon lengthening shadows bring early night. The air is cool enough to wear sweaters to football games. Early autumn grasses turn yellow, and leaves spatter the woods with red, gold, and orange. We rake leaves, Snowball jumps on the piles and scatters them everywhere, and we rake them back. We pick up pecans. Life goes on.

Then winter winds once again lash at trees, whip through my hair, sting my skin, wail by my windowsills. Ice forms on naked limbs, darkness covers the earth, and life shrinks again into a narrow space.

Momentarily, the Christmas magic that my parents create several weeks early lessens the cold winter. In the bay window Daddy sets a large cedar tree and encircles it with strings of colored lights. The tree spreads the sweet freshness of cedar throughout the rooms. After supper we decorate the tree with multicolored balls, so thin they reflect the tree lights. Mama places candles on all the windowsills and lamp tables. She arranges nandina from the yard in tall cut-glass vases, the red berries trailing down. She decorates the mantle with garlands of greenery: magnolia leaves, holly, and more nandina with its bright red berries. From nearby woods Daddy has cut down mistletoe and brought home bundles, the tiny white berries clustered like little bunches of minuscule grapes. Daddy hangs the mistletoe from the white molding over open French doors leading into the dining room. In fact, I remember fresh mistletoe hanging over every door and Daddy saying you have to be kissed if you stand under it. Our entire house glows in anticipation of Christmas Day. And I glow in excitement for the morning when that wonderful being will bestow upon me everything I wish for. Santa Claus I don't mention anymore, but Mama does, so I go along with it, and he never lets me down.

Two weeks before Christmas Mama is busy with errands: shopping, wrapping gifts, giving the house a December "spring cleaning," and assigning me to pick up pecans on the ground to place in several small baskets with nutcrackers. Aunt Agatha arrives from Hamlet, and she and Mama drive to Holly Hill Cemetery outside Wagram to clean the family lot that has their parents' and Bobby's graves, a trip they undertake every major holiday and birthday, taking the appropriate flowers and décor to fit the occasion. This cemetery has no caretaking services, so the two of them have a lot to do: raking fallen leaves and branches, weeding, picking up the trash, smoothing over the graves to keep a nice mound, and sometimes adding dirt to a grave that has caved in a bit from too much rain. I can hear Aunt Agatha exclaim, "Mother would turn over in her grave if she could see this hole on top of her!" I can see her and Mama when they're finished, going to each footstone, leaning together, heads down, reading the stonecutting aloud. I see them going to Bobby's grave last, short sobs choking out the reading. Mama always returns home tired and nostalgic, but this time she is extremely sad and tight-lipped.

About a week before Christmas Eve, Mama rides the bus to Hamlet to visit Aunt Agatha. School is not yet out for the holidays, so Mama makes plans for me to go home with a friend and stay until Daddy picks me up on his way home from work. Past the time he was to get me, the phone rings at my friend's house. Her mother tells me that Daddy isn't feeling well, and that sometime after supper she'll drive me home. When I get there, Mama is not there, and Daddy is lying on the bed. For Daddy not to be up-and-about is most unusual.

"Daddy, what's the matter?"

"I need to rest ... a bit, Baby ... you all right?"

"I'm fine, Daddy. Are you sick?"

He hesitates as if he's trying to catch his breath. "I have a pain in my chest ... Think I strained a muscle ... You know that big ... pickle jar? I was trying to open the lid and I strained ... too hard. That's all ... I'm okay. Need to rest."

"When's Mama coming home?"

"She'll be home soon ... I called her."

From that moment on, my mind is hazy. I try to remember the rest of that night, but I cannot piece it together. It's a bad dream: I'm in a room of dense gray that becomes fog wrapping around me, and I keep turning around but I can't find a way through; above the fog, shadows shift back and forth, and I'm under water, trying hard to surface.

Tiny drops of memory split the gray, and I'm sitting up in my bed, watching the open door of Mama and Daddy's room. From the hall, figures go in and out of their room—a man, a woman in white, and Mama. I'm so confused about time. Is it night? Is it the next morning? Days run together. No one talks to me. My head strains to know what's happening. I feel invisible.

Suddenly, I am in the living room. It must be Christmas morning because dolls and books and games and packages cover the floor and a stocking hangs full of fruit from the mantle. But what happened to Christmas Eve? I don't remember it. Did I drink the eggnog that Daddy makes? Did he read me the Christmas Story from the Bible? And then recite "The Night before Christmas," with me filling in words when he pauses, as he always does, while we sit by the fire?

Then a memory drop splashes: it is four days later—December 29th. Mama says, "Daddy is sitting up in bed. He's had a heart attack, Erin Rose, and needs lots of rest, but he is so much better now. I can dismiss his nurse today, and you can visit him."

Daddy leans back on pillows and his eyes sparkle when he smiles at me rushing in, holding my two new dolls. I am the only one with him in the bedroom. He exclaims, "There's my Baby, so grown up!" We hug, and I prop up on the pillow beside him on the bed.

"Oh, I've missed you so much, Daddy. You haven't even seen my two new Christmas dolls."

We talk about how pretty each doll is. One is a blue-eyed, curly-headed blonde Southern Belle, dressed in an old-fashioned pink hoop-skirt. The other doll is a brown-eyed brunette with bangs, wearing a white fur-trimmed red velvet jacket with matching short circular skirt trimmed in white fur around the bottom, a red tam with a fur ball on top, and ice skates. I remember the dolls because Daddy tells me what he likes about each one. However, I can't make up my mind which one is prettier. I want to know which doll Daddy likes better, so I can choose that one as my favorite. He insists he likes them equally, for each is beautiful in her own way.

"What? Two different dolls that are the same?"

He asks me, "Baby, why do you have to choose? Accept each one as she's made to be. You can love each the same."

Stubbornly, I insist, "But, Daddy, I want to know which is *best!*"

Daddy shakes his head, smiles at me, and starts to tell me something, but suddenly his words are unintelligible. Why can't I understand him? Suddenly, I think he's playing a game with me—speaking Pig Latin!

"Daddy, don't do that!" I lean over, prop myself on his chest, and stare at his face. Still, he emits guttural sounds. I draw closer to decipher this foreign babble. I watch his lips and then look up at his brown eyes that touch me with love while he struggles to tell me something that I struggle to hear. His eyes hold my eyes; I try to keep his. But suddenly they start rolling back and down, back and down, like a doll's eyes roll under her lids when she's held upside down. Finally, the brown is gone.

Silence strikes.

I sit and stare as close as I can get, mesmerized by Daddy's muteness and the whites of his eyes.

Suddenly, the visiting nurse jerks me from the bed and pushes me away. "Get out of the room and *stay put!*"

I sit in the living room with Aunt Agatha and my cousin Noelle, who asks me why I'm so puffed-up and mad.

"I hate that nurse. I want her to go home."

Daddy's bedroom door opens. We hear the nurse praying.

Later I'm in a room with adults coming in and milling around. I remember only one person—Aunt Agatha's husband Ben—coming up to me and putting his arm around my shoulder; he leans down and whispers, "I am so sorry, Erin Rose."

Afterwards, they all become forms drifting in another gray room. And again life ignores me. I'm invisible.

Days later something draws me down the hall to the open room at the end, silent as a tomb. Others have gone for an early supper, and I slip in alone, amid shaded roses and dust-flakes floating in streaks of sun. At sunset, that time in between fading day and nearing night, I stand beside Daddy's coffin beneath three tall windows dressed in sheers, hanging like a shroud. Slowly, heavily, my eyes sink low to face a face I love. There, in his coffin, he lies like a man-sized doll on quilted silk.

For a long time I stand there, looking down at the chalk-sculptured face. He looks a lot like Daddy, I keep thinking. Instinctively, I reach to take that familiar hand so warm and strong and responsive, and gasp at the cold marble I touch. Quickly, I jerk my hand back, feeling the nerves in my fingers and palm frozen to stone, the sensation overwhelming. I shiver. How can this be? My breathing is shallow: I wipe my hands together again and again, trying to sling off the stone that sticks like grief.

Then quick as a spark, a thought brightens my mind: that's not Daddy in the coffin! But he's here. I feel Daddy's warmth all around me, especially around my shoulders like a hug. When Bobby's body lay in his coffin 11 months ago, it was my imagination that convinced me Bobby was alive. But this time is different. This time I feel Daddy's presence in the room. I look at the gauzy Priscillas hanging from the windows behind the coffin forming a veil ... separating me from a place where Daddy watches me. From deep inside, I know a moment of Truth: Daddy is alive on the other side of a veil somewhere, as sure as if I could see him, touching me, giving me breath to live.

When Mama discovers me in the darkening room, she rushes in and scolds, "Child, whatever are you doing here?" She turns me around and hurries me out as if the body were contagious. Others wandering into the room look surprised and disapprovingly at me, a lone child at Death's door for, after all, I am only a child and know nothing.

At his funeral I remember walking down the middle aisle of First Baptist Church, following the coffin carried by pallbearers to the front. I never shed a tear because I carry my moment of Truth. Then with time it fades. And I lose the veil.

Emptiness aches like a hunger pang, and I cry for what cannot be. I remember sitting by the bedroom fireplace, looking at the fire and eating a banana sandwich Mama has made. Relatives gone, this is the first time Mama and I are alone at suppertime, and it is also the first time I recall feeling close to her, sitting huddled up near the fire and eating a sandwich in silence. Daddy, if he were here, would be cooking us a big meal; but Mama's sandwich is okay, really, and the two of us almost touch in the near darkness together by the fire's warmth, both feeling the terrible void left by Daddy's death. Mama insists that I sleep with her—she cannot bear being alone.

On many winter afternoons we have the same agenda. We tease about having our 4:00 tea. On especially cold late afternoons, when the wind is strong and howls through the treetops, chilly drafts whistle under the wood door from the porch to Mama's room. Even so, a thin shaft of winter sun lingers in the room as the fire glows softly in the grate. Mama brings in an old coal bucket stacked to the brim with small pieces of coal to perk up the fire. We pull up two chairs by the hearth beside the dresser bench.

When the fire catches brightly in the grate, Mama brings in a tray with hot tea with lemon, cream and sugar, and tea cakes. She puts the tray on the bench and serves tea, and I help myself to the china plate of tea cakes—you know, the thin crusted ones with mildly sweet powdered sugar and the taste of yeast. Mama doesn't like to cook, but in winter she loves to bake these. Sometimes she adds little sandwiches; I can't help but think of Daddy's pot roast and stew beef with puffy biscuits. Snowball slips in and lies down between us. Mama and I sit by the fire and drink tea and munch thin pastry and watch long tongues of fire lap around the pieces of coal, its gray ashes spreading in a pile, a spark sometimes popping out onto the hearth, and listen to the moaning of the trees around the porch posts. And Mama smokes and flips her cigarette butts into the fire. The day draws to a close, that time of day just before the need for lights and only firelight flickers, the cigarette's glow brightens when she inhales, and the incredibly sad longing that never leaves her eyes. The fire's warmth in a dim room, the yeasty pastry, the no-need for words bring a fullness that nothing else but Daddy could replace.

On these afternoons Mama and I become sisters; I am her companion, her confidante at 12. At times it seems as though I am the older one; she turns to me for advice. We have no income except Daddy's insurance money and a check coming to me until I turn 18. Mama is already worrying about how many years the insurance income will last, for she has a child to raise and put through college; she has absolutely no work experience and not even a high school diploma. In the '20s and before, high school had no 12th grade; students graduated at the end of the 11th, but Mama dropped out of school in the 10th grade, because she was bored, not because she wasn't smart; her reading and writing were better than most. As her adult confidante, I listen to all her worries. I become her sounding board, but for the life of me, I cannot give her advice. At my age I lack this kind of wisdom.

When I have a cold or simply don't feel "up to par," I'm suddenly a little child again. Mama heats a jar of Vicks and rubs it on my chest, warms a towel or soft flannel, and places it on top, creating a warm softness as I lie in bed until I sit up and breathe in the fumes from the jar. She keeps feeling my brow, adjusting the cover around my shoulders, and hovering over me with full attention. She brings me hot cocoa or hot tea and waits anxiously by my bed for me to respond to her nursing. Since our doctor lives diagonally across the street from us, Mama watches for him to return home in the afternoon. When he parks his car, Mama, panicking, rushes down our walkway and by the time he reaches his wide porch, she waves and motions for him. Dr. Harry responds, checks me over, and advises, as always, "Give her some Castor Oil ... or Milk of Magnesia will do."

The winter of 1947 is bitter cold. Mama worries about heating the old drafty house because a load of coal costs so much. Soon there is only one fire going and that's in Mama's bedroom. I have no choice but to sleep in her bed. Standing in my pajamas in front of the fire, I turn around to get warm before running as fast as I can to jump in the bed under the quilts.

Near the end of winter, all the fireplaces stand empty. Though fireplaces have always been the only source of heat in each room, the chimneys stopped up by soot no longer work. Mama wants everything clean and orderly, but now if Mama tries to build a fire, the air is blocked and down falls the soot to smother the flame; out floats backed-up smoke, choking whoever's at the hearth and coating walls with a shadow-smudge. The dingy curtains hang limp. Then Mama decides to close each fireplace by covering it with a fitted piece of metal, and install an oil heater in the dining room, the central room on one side of the house. This will be "our" bedroom. She'll arrange the dining room furniture in the back of the wide hall, and we will live in a small area on one side only.

"What about my bedroom? It's still where it's always been."

"No, Erin Rose. I don't want you way up in front of the house by yourself. Besides, the room's freezing without a fire. And you can sleep with me."

"But, Mama, I want my own room."

"Hush, now. I'm thinking about renting the rooms across the hall. We don't need them, and we certainly can use the money, especially now with the cost of fuel."

Renting a room to a couple during the war is one thing: he was an Air Force Captain training to go to war, and lots of people were renting to be patriotic. However, this renting to strangers for money is just embarrassing. None of my friends have strangers living in their homes. And I want my privacy back. I've slept with Mama for two months, and I can't write in my diary or journal anymore, because she watches me. And I do yearn for that small open fire.

I am now sadly dependent on Mama. Yet strangely the house seems to be alive. It has its own presence, standing in for Daddy. The long mahogany-paneled hall is like a huge wainscoted shield watching over us. In the center of one wall is a large chifforobe almost as tall as the ceiling. Inside hang Daddy's clothes: his khaki shirts and pants, his brown wool tweed coat, his fedora, his dark summer suit. From time to time I find myself standing before it. I open the door, rub my hand against the soft stubble of wool tweed, lay my head upon the sleeve, close my eyes, and breathe in his musk. The sense of Daddy's presence is palpable; it is like warm air curling around my shoulders. The air is so thick that if I should fall into it, it would hold me up.

Chapter 13

Times merge like a rapid current, and I am caught swirling, floundering in its vortex, trying to grab something tangible to pull me to stability. I don't know *when* things happen. It doesn't matter. It does matter, though, *that* things happen.

The renters come. And for about three years of my life, I suffer humiliation over the types of people who pull up daily at different times in our back driveway to enter their quarters. It's usually a couple and a child or two; the father, more than likely, works in the mill. I know I'm a snob but what can I say? I was raised that way—by Mama. Ironically, she needs their money. Really, I feel sorry for the renters. But I can't help it that I hate the smell of cooked cabbage, the scent lingering down the hall. Or the smell of a man's sweaty, dirty overalls when I pass him on the porch. Or the loud, gruff sound of their speech—the strange accents, the butchered verbs.

In the late '40s class division is still very pronounced in Oak Glen. In East Oak Glen the cotton mill reigns. Rows and rows of small houses, nearly touching side-by-side, each with an outhouse, form a village of mill workers with their own school and church. Unfortunately, the families suffer the cycle of scant wages, little schooling—older children leave school to work in the mill—and prejudice from those on "our side" of town. I ask Mama why she rents to just these poor white folks from the other side of town—the mill people. Aren't there other people from our side who need rooms to rent?

Mama answers resignedly. "Erin Rose, have you noticed how much this house has run down in the last two years? Do you realize that we haven't had a decent tub of hot water since your Daddy died? Not since I've had to give up all my 'help'? Who else would live here with cold water and rooms with just little heaters? The mill-hill is used to shacks and outhouses. We're only a step up from them."

I think of our old-fashioned kitchen (built in the 1890s) with the small wood stove and the small hot-water tank attached to the stove by a long, narrow pipe through which hot air goes to heat the water. After wood burns for hours, the tub water in the bathroom will be hot. If needed, large pails of water were heated on the old kerosene stove for baths. Daddy always kept wood in the stove and a box of kindling and newspaper nearby so that he could quickly start a fire early in the morning. Our "help" kept the wood fire burning, as well as the small coal fires, one per room during the day except for summer.

Mama tries at first but soon gives up. Something always goes wrong: new wood won't burn but smokes and wood must be split to fit into the stove. Anyway, it's too much work for just the two of us. Instead, she warms water in a large pot on the kerosene cook stove, enough to cover my waist in the tub. She carries that big pot all the way across the hall to the bathroom until that becomes just too much. I either bathe in cold water or heat it myself.

Now I am embarrassed by our kitchen. My friends have white built-in kitchen counters with electric stoves; we have an enamel-top table beside a large sink, a big pie-safe, an enamel-top, and a side table with a drawer for silverware. The kerosene cook stove smells bad. Before, I remember the kitchen scents of our cook Minnie Belle's fried chicken, field-peas with fat-back, and bread-pudding with cinnamon.

Her laughter, too, and her teasing and her humming of Gospel tunes and the light she brought to the house. Mama never learned to cook, so she opens cans and warms Denny's Stew and English peas or pork 'n beans and a ham sandwich.

Now that Daddy's been gone for several years, the insurance money has dwindled partly because Mama saves a monthly portion of the money for my college fund. So, sometimes, before the monthly check arrives, Mama has no money for groceries. That's when she gets angry about Uncle Henry's permanent stay upstairs.

"It's not fair!" she says to me. "Henry lives here for nothing: rent-free, utilities-free, tax-free, and I have to worry about the mortgage payment for this old family home that got your Daddy in debt. It's just not fair that Henry gives nothing."

She fumes and fusses and then turns to me. "Erin Rose, run down to Henry's store, see if he's there, and tell him to buy some groceries. If he's not there, then you'll find him somewhere on the street talking, probably on some back street, sitting on a bench with the old men and gossiping. Talking, talking, and laughing. That's all he has to think about. Sitting in a ladder-back chair, leaning against a storefront like he owns it."

I am humiliated by the chance that someone I know will see me walking down the sloping back street leading to The Bottom. Uncle Henry's used clothing store is tucked away, a dark cave in the slope of a building near The Bottom. From my house I hold my sandals, walk barefoot, and take my time, stretching it, leisurely. My mind retreats into fantasy, creating for me another reality within my surroundings.

To be less conspicuous, I avoid Main Street and turn on Valley Road, the narrow dirt road which passes the black folks' shacks and then dips down into the hollow. I stop to put on my sandals, pause a bit, and really *see*, as if for the first time, the shacks so close they almost touch the street's edge.

As usual, women sit on the steps of their porches and shell field peas and speckled-purple butterbeans, grown in their small gardens, while their tots crawl up and down the steps. Older children are playing "hide and seek," squealing and laughing, chasing each other in the dirt and dust. On one porch an old gray-headed man rocks, fanning himself with a cardboard fan like the ones handed out at church on Sundays—he watches the children play and chuckles along with them. The women, across the porches, gossip, often calling out an expletive like "Laud have mercy!" that initiates a roar of laughter up and down the shacks.

I feel drawn to them—their camaraderie, their happy nature. Each shack looks cozy, and I wish I could sit on the steps, too. I think of my house filled with every toy, game, and book available, but I have no one to share them. Ruby Jean is interested in boys now, and there's no one to talk to or play with at home. I remember sitting on the back-steps with Minnie Belle, who told me stories about the "root woman" peeling off the bark of peach trees to make healing tea. I think of Jessie showing me how to bake a chocolate cake while I "help" her. I miss them so much—their hugging, their teasing, their laughing.

I'm still on the edge of the road, in front of one of the shacks, pretending to buckle my sandals. One woman catches my eye, and I smile. " 'Morning, Missey. You gwine get too hot out thar. Betta' git in the shade for a spell."

"Thank you. But I have to get to the store for Mama."

"Betta' bes careful. Dis is Sat'dey. Go-to-market day. And a whole lot of crazies, good-for-nothin's, already up to devil-doings down dis road."

Suddenly, the old clanking watermelon wagon turns onto Valley Road and heads in my direction. I jump over the shallow ditch into a yard for fear of being sideswiped. The overloaded wagon jerks along, leaning sideways, rolling by, and the bent-over driver is aware only of reaching The Bottom. The hitched mule, snorting and straining in the heat, still sports the now-tattered straw-hat of Scottish plaid around his ears. Little kids giggle at the mule, and the old gray-headed man on the porch tips his hat to me. He mumbles, "Yah live in the big house, up Church Street, don't yah?"

"Yes sir, I do."

"Ah knowed yer grandpappy. Uh nice feller." He shakes his head. "Yah'sm. He was over thar at de jail." He points a shaky finger across the road at the small red brick jail.

Mama's father spent a lifetime in law enforcement. A memory flashes of me in a photograph as a little girl running up our walkway toward an elderly man with a thick and wide white mustache. He has stopped and is reaching in his coat pocket. A shiny gold star shines. That's my mama's father, who's digging out a piece of candy for me, as he always does. I wait for him when it's his time to come home and make a bee line for him and the candy. I am two or three years old. For a long time he's been Chief of Police; when he retires, already a widower, he comes to live with us. Needing to occupy his time, he becomes the jailer.

"Yah'sm. Yer grandpappy wuz uh good mon. Uh po-licemon—look after us."

"Thank you for telling me that," I say, "but I'd better be going. Mama'll wonder about me. 'Bye."

The woman with the bucket of peas calls, "'Bye, Baby. The Laud bless yah."

I start walking away, my eyes filling up, my heart aching. So much happened before I was born. Apparently, my grandpa Captain Kavanagh made amends for his earlier life.

All the way to The Bottom I pray. Not for protection

against a crazy-drunk with a knife or from a Saturday-come-to-town-gypsy kidnapper. I pray that none of my friends or classmates see me here, especially if I have to go into Uncle Henry's store. Even worse would be for someone to see him hand me a little brown bag of groceries. That would be far worse than being with Mama at the rummage sales she sometimes has on Saturdays, right across the street from here *in* The Bottom. In the large empty lot she parks her little Ford, along with a dozen or so other women, and drapes old clothes on the car, over the top, across the hood and trunk, and against open windows. Inside on the back seat she stacks worn-out pants and sweaters and hats. She sells mostly to black folks and Lumbee Indians and a few gypsies who camp out in tents on the north side.

Shadows fall across the entrance to Uncle Henry's store. Inside, mustiness invades my senses, and I can't see until my eyes get used to the dark.

"Hey, Baby," Uncle Henry calls and reaches past a customer to shake my hand, his palm soft and sweaty. "What can I do for you?"

I speak as low as I can. "Mama needs some things from the grocery."

He nods and waits for the last of the customers to leave and then locks the door. "Erin Baby, you wait outside, and I'll be right back."

I keep my back turned, trying to hide in the shadows, and wait long miserable minutes. Uncle Henry promptly returns from Main Street with a small sack of cans from Pender's Grocery. Of course, I take the little bag, another humiliation equal to the first, thank him, and hurry home.

That night at dinnertime Mama and I are sitting at the kitchen table, and, unexpectedly, Uncle Henry comes in. Jovial as usual, he speaks and sits down to eat. Once he starts eating, he never stops until he's finished everything in sight. Mama and I glance at each other and then stare at our plates to avoid watching Uncle Henry, who is slopping down food, dropping bits and pieces on his shirt, and talking with his mouth open.

"Yes sir!" he repeats for the thousandth time, "your daddy fell over heels in love with your mama the first time he saw her. Said she was such a pretty little thing ... I asked her for a date, before she met your daddy, but she turned me down. I was probably a little clumsy on the dance floor." He chuckles so many "he-he-he's" that his belly bounces.

I glance up at Mama. She looks like she's going to heave up the canned stew.

Completely stuffed, Henry (I'm not calling him "uncle" anymore) slides his chair back, stands by the table, and pats me on the back. "I promised your daddy I'd take care of you."

After he leaves, Mama and I just sit and stare at each other. Blue eyes merge with hazel. We hear the heavy front door shut finally. Very sternly, Mama says, "Do you see why I said, NO for a date!"

We burst out laughing. Then suddenly Mama says, "How about a game of cards? I'll clean the table, you get the cards and some toothpick-chips. We'll play 500 rummy."

Despite the "ugly" things in our life, we do have nature blooming as ever in our yard. The grass may not be as manicured as before, but it's still green with little scattered white flowers of clover. The purple grapes bulge from tendril-like vines that cling to the old wood shed and coal bin. Violets grow wild in the shade of the apple tree, and tiger lilies peep through tall weeds. To me, it's still my Garden of Eden.

Mama is proud of the many rose bushes growing around the house, many planted in the 1890s and still blooming a deep velvet red, despite years of neglect. When

Daddy was alive, he always took care of the roses, pruning, fertilizing, planting more. Mama especially likes the rose bush beneath our current bedroom bay window, the original dining room, on the south side where the room curves out from the rest of the house. There is a tall old shrub with unusually large red roses that have bloomed profusely through every summer since it was planted. One day Mama calls me to the window, alarmed. "Look at that!"

I stand beside Mama at the window and see a dead bush. It looks shriveled: no blooms or new growth. Only a few blackened buds appear, as if they have been burned. Yet the other rose bushes are blooming profusely.

Mama hastens outside but finds no clue. Then she looks beneath her window and sees a splash of stain on the house near the black buds. She looks up and discovers more stain, a thin yellow streak running down the wall of the house. Her eyes trace the stain up to Henry's window. She knows at once.

Darting upstairs in a huff, Mama finds again, under Henry's window, Mason jars—this time pee-stained and empty, beside a stack of new *Washington Posts*. When she returns, I feel my heart actually ache to see her face so dejected and eyes so empty. What can she do? Spend the rest of her life with pee falling from the sky? Mama just sits on the bed and cries. I recall Edgar Allan Poe's "The Fall of the House of Usher": the crack in the foundation of the Usher House is like the yellow streak running from top to bottom in ours.

Sensing how much life is defeating Mama, I try not to complain—especially about the renters. However, the presence of one oily-haired teenage boy is grossing me out. I can feel him staring at me. I am becoming paranoid.

As many older homes, our house has only one bathroom that we have to share with the renters. When I do, I feel like someone is staring at my body. Similar to a bathroom in a boarding house, the room is large and located at the end of the hall; an old bathtub sits on four lion paws by the wall opposite the door. To have to bathe in the same tub with what I think of as "alien intruders" is bad enough, but then one day when I leave the bathroom, I forget to turn the light off. The hall is dark and, when I turn around, I see a shining speck of light through the wood door. Is that a hole in the door? A peep-hole?

I walk back to the door. Sure enough, I can bend over, put my eye there, and see inside the lighted room. I am mortified. That creepy, pimply teenaged son of the renters must have been watching me bathe or, worse, peeping at me on the toilet, his eye on the hole while he stalks me on his knees by the door. And God knows whatever else he is doing.

I feel so desecrated. I want to die right then and there. This is my home. My life support.

My life has fallen to this.

Mama speaks to the family but, of course, they deny that their son would do such a thing. And no one has a clue how the hole suddenly appeared in the door. Mama hangs a thick towel on the inside of the door over the hole, and no one mentions it again. I keep my dignity by glaring at him in *utter* disgust and wanting *to kill him* whenever we pass in the hall. They soon leave.

When I'm 14, I decide to create my own bedroom. I am craving a place to write—besides sitting on exposed beams upstairs under the roof. Between the dining room (Mama's bedroom now) and the kitchen is the former "butler's closet," originally a small room used for a pantry, linen storage, and whatever else a butler needed it for. Though it's tiny, there's enough room to make a cozy bedroom.

Stubbornly, against Mama's wishes, I pick up furniture pieces from storage upstairs and drag and bump them down the steps to the "butler's" room. Seeing my determination, Mama acquiesces, knowing I'll just make a pallet otherwise. Now, my bedroom is finished. I love my décor—blue and white with slashes of bright pink. My single bed is pushed up against the wall. A dresser with a white ruffled skirt. Glass lamps sit on small round mirrors. Colorful perfume bottles with golden atomizers rest on a gold tray. Magazine pictures are tacked on the wall of Cornel Wilde in Robin Hood pants, Jeff Chandler as an Indian Chief, and Clark Gable staring right at you as Rhett Butler. Stacks of books and a basket full of movie magazines sit on the floor. I stay in my room as much as I can after school.

It is my space for privacy—I can sit on the bed to read or to write in my journal. I'll hide the journal in the nightstand or, perhaps, in a safer place. I am dying to write; that is, if I can keep my writing secret. So far, I've had no success.

In the fifth grade I wrote daily whatever I wanted to in a little white leather diary with a lock and key and then pulled the leather strap over to fasten the lock. Only my key could open the book, and I left the key tucked away inside my music box where the ballerina danced to *Swan Lake.* Mama found the key.

Another year I had a large black diary, and in it I began a story about a famous girl reporter, who flew around the world having exciting adventures. She was very sophisticated and she said "damn" a lot. I had seen *Gone with the Wind* and heard Clark Gable say the first curse word in film-making history when Rhett turned at the door and stated, "Frankly, Scarlett, I don't give a damn." I also started my paragraphs with "Frankly ..." I kept this new book carefully hidden in the bottom of my nightstand. Mama found the black book.

When I returned home from school that day, I could tell by Mama's look that she was on a rampage. She held up the black book. "What are you thinking, Erin, to write such curse words? Is this the way you waste your time? Is this the way you feel? I can't believe you have such thoughts. What in the world will people say if someone reads this? You should know better!"

Now I don't trust thinking aloud on paper. I have no privacy where I can put anything that won't be scrutinized. Only my thoughts are my own, and these I guard, locked up inside me, yearning to fly free. For a while I stop writing anything but schoolwork, and my imagination starts fading.

So much for my bedroom plans. There is no use in arguing about where I am going to sleep. Mama nags and nags and begs me to sleep with her. True, my little room is freezing in the winter, but I like being swallowed-up by quilts when the wind stirs like whirling groans and tree limbs scrape across the roof. Even in summer Mama makes me sleep beside her. When nights are hot and humid and the windows are open to still air, the large iron fan churns sharp breezes across the bed. And train sounds pierce the air and echo down the tracks above the rattling and clattering. I lie and listen to the cacophony of night. With time, an all-pervading darkness settles within the house, and, if alone, Mama cannot sleep. She calls the house her tomb. She wants me closer. Sometimes, I feel she is trying to draw me back into her womb.

I try to forget one summer morning. It is very early, that time of day before life begins to stir save a bird chirping, a soft breeze wafting through the open window, the shade being pulled up after lights out to catch the coolness of night after one of those hot days. I am sleeping with Mama. She lies on her side asleep, facing the open window, and so am I, asleep on her other side, turned toward the window. For some reason I suddenly open my eyes.

And there he stands.

On the porch in front of our room, Daddy's brother Henry stands close to the window, perfectly still, breathing on the screen, staring down at Mama. I am conscious of our thin nightgowns, the sheet, kicked off during the hot night, draping our feet. I shut my eyes quickly and lie very still and hold my breath. After a while, I open my eyes in a little slit ... and Henry is gone.

Our lives have fallen to this.

Chapter 14

In high school I whiz through diagramming sentences and accept that words must be placed in the correct spot of the sentence with no exception, like a jigsaw puzzle. The smart student must write exactly like the answer key. Forget the content; it's already known and proven. I earn A+s and 100s in English and Mama is thrilled. I earn A's in history and biology and chemistry, and Mama is pleased. But why didn't I try harder for the *plus*? Then I stumble through advanced algebra and come up with an A-. Mama has a fit. She's ready to high-tail it to school to see my math teacher, whose fault it is. We have a screaming match over that, so she decides I need to practice solving more formulas. I can do that on Saturdays after practicing my piano lesson. "Erin Rose, you should at least *try* to bring home all A+s!"

Luckily, I have nearly a photographic memory, temporarily that is. I can memorize whatever I see, such as part of a text page, long enough for a test. Just like playing the piano; for a recital I close my eyes and see the keyboard and music notes and feel the sound and rhythm.

Daddy bought me a piano when I was ten to see if I'd like playing it. It was an old used player-piano which played tunes when I turned on a switch. Like a yellowed roll of sheepskin with hundreds of little holes, the roller caused compressed air to blow on a hole to press down chosen keys. For hours Daddy and I played the old player-piano, listening to the tinny sound of songs from old Westerns and watching the "ghost" play all the notes. We had fun trying to sing through our noses along with the tunes. I loved playing. I started piano lessons and practiced on the old upright, assuring Mama I wouldn't punch the automatic roller. By the time Daddy died, he heard me perform in two piano recitals, the last one "pretty" good.

After six years of lessons, I can play just about whatever I want to. When I'm alone and play for myself, I feel transformed to another realm—far away from here: I am the sound, the rhythm. And I am determined to play Rachmaninoff's *Concerto #5*, which I practice on my own, even though my piano teacher wants me first to perfect Bach. And I love playing show tunes, but when Mama hears me, she'll call, "Erin Rose, shouldn't you work on your scales? And the technique exercises? I'll turn on the metronome—it's already set." Oh, how I hate that little pendulum that clicks at a predetermined tempo like a whip empty of feeling lashing your brain cut-cut-cut-click-click-click. Mak-ing-mu-sic-math. Mak-ing-writ-ing-di-a-grams.

On Sundays the pattern continues. I wear my gold five-year-perfect-attendance pin to the gender-separated Sunday school and sit and try to listen to what I've heard before: click-click-click-click ... with-out-think-ing-with-out-speak-ing ... and—God-forbid—without-questioning. Time creeps in church. As I did as a child I try to sit behind Miss Millie and the little fox around her neck and across from Jesus and the little sheep in stained glass ... and hope I don't step into the pit of Hell.

Then bless my new 11th grade English teacher, Miss Meadows, who's young and greets us with a sweet smile. We begin poetry and my imagination with words and images reappears—I feel really alive again, as I did playing piano alone. When Miss Meadows asks questions, however, I don't volunteer because I fear I'll give the wrong answer, and I don't want the class to laugh at me if I expose my interpretation that's so very much unlike theirs.

"Erin Rose," she says, "I enjoyed reading your homework discussion. Your interpretation was excellent. What about these lines by Emily Dickinson? 'This is my letter to the World.' I'll read the poem to the class; and, Erin Rose, you tell us what the poem reveals about the poet herself."

Oh, my God, why is she calling on me?

> This is my letter to the World
> That never wrote to Me—
> The simple News that Nature told—
> With simple Majesty
>
> Her message is committed
> To Hands I cannot see—
> For love of her—Sweet countrymen—
> Judge tenderly—of Me

I hesitate for a moment and then reply: "Emily Dickinson is shy and feels quite alone. She hesitates to communicate personally with others by sharing her poetry, which is her letter, because she assumes they won't like it or accept her thoughts. She thinks nature gives these thoughts to her to write that come from an unseen power like God. She seems apologetic that the words don't come from her originally.

"Thank you, Erin Rose. That's splendid!"

I cannot help but wonder if Miss Meadows has an ulterior motive. Can she possibly guess that I'm hoarding hundreds of images inside my head? Shattered parts spilling out from time to time in my night-dreams and daydreams?

The child inside me remembers in her own voice; especially, when awaking at night, I sometimes hear the child's voice speaking, and I quickly slip out of bed to catch the voice on little snatches of paper. I have to write fast in the dark to capture the words that fade like an invasive sprite who doesn't want to be caught by the mere form of letters. I think of a butterfly that lights near me, and the minute I move my hand closer, it flies away, lost. At times I hear my current voice speaking images in lines of poetry. If I keep still and don't try to remember or write, the phrases keep coming. Left alone the stories persist and develop themselves while I'm doing something else.

It's strange how putting words into print diminishes the beauty of the image, or the depth of the thought, or the intensity of the feeling. Like a painter trying to capture a scene from nature: even the best painting is a weak facsimile. That invasive sprite within teases me relentlessly to create—almost caught, it often flits away.

And then I meet Luke McLeod.

The harvest moon hangs suspended in the eastern sky, low behind trees. Its golden glow slants, caught between tree branches. It is autumn. In a few days I will be 16. I feel that life is waiting for me in some mysterious way as if my inner and outer worlds will finally converge.

Always an avid reader, I live as much within the worlds created in books as I do in my surroundings. The mysteries and passions of Gothic romances I find far more suitable for my nature than my humdrum, inhibited life in this small Southern Bible-belt town. These feelings and thoughts, though, remain safely hidden, and as I am looked upon as the proper young Southern lady who wears white gloves and hat to Sunday school, whose name is called out in church every year to receive another medal to hang on her five-year pin for perfect attendance, and whose name appears on the A honor roll every six weeks at the high school.

Leaving later than usual from the public library where I work part time after school, I stroll home, enjoying that in-between-time before darkness settles. Blue sky graying out, I walk straight into the moon.

I don't know when it happens. It's just there. A feeling in the air. A sudden sense of presence all around me like some unknown but familiar entity walking there beside me. I think of Jane Eyre, over the miles, sensing Rochester's call so strong that she can even hear his voice beckoning her. I think of Heathcliff in *Wuthering Heights* and his feeling of Katherine's spirit near his windowsill luring him across the moor, their unrequited love overpowering him, though Fate holds them together but forever apart. And a tremendous yearning comes over me for someone special in my life, but someone near whom I can touch and see. I think of Bobby— and his promise. But I want someone more than an uncle.

I could say I willed a presence. But no, it is more than that. I feel his eyes on my back.

After my birthday, I go Saturday afternoon with Megan to the local drugstore hangout. Teenagers stuff themselves into booths in the back and drink Cherry Cokes and listen to rock-and-roll music and a few popular crooners on the jukebox: Nat King Cole has replaced Frank Sinatra. Several couples are dancing. Others mill around and watch. And the rest of the usual crowd stand near the jukebox, talking, laughing, and waiting to punch another selection.

Megan and I lean against the soda fountain, sipping our Cokes, my back to the crowd. The music changes, and the baritone of Nat King Cole drifts across the room, rising over the hum of voices: "Unforgettable, that's what you are ..." I don't know when I first become aware of his presence. I don't know where he is. I don't know who he is. But I know he's watching me. My back feels his eyes staring. It's a while before I turn around. I know that when I do, I will look him straight in the eye. And I do. His eyes fixate on mine and hold them.

There he is. He wears light green pants that blouse like a paratrooper's, pegged at the ankle. A long gold chain loops from his belt to below his knee. A white windbreaker with the sleeves cut out reveals a bronze tan. His strawberry-blonde hair has just enough red to make the blonde shine. He has Elvis sideburns and a few waves falling out of place on his forehead, the sides swept back into a ducktail.

He stands by the jukebox and stares at me over the sea of faces. The look holds until the song stops and another starts. I can't divert my eyes. It's very strange for me to lock eyes with anyone for any length of time. No one has ever had this effect on me. I feel a bond that I've never experienced before. The music stops, the crowd shifts, he's gone.

I turn to Megan, who knows everyone and all the latest gossip. "Who was that blonde boy by the jukebox? He's suddenly disappeared."

"Which one?"

"The one in a white cutoff jacket with the bronze tan."

"Oh, that was Luke McLeod. He's been dating Sarah Beth lately … along with others. Beware! You don't wanna get tangled up with him. He's *bad* news."

"Why?"

"Because he goes from girl to girl … loves 'em and leaves 'em. And, so I've heard," she adds conspiratorially, "he always gets what he wants." And she tells me all she knows about him.

The afternoon crowd starts to leave, and our conversation stops. Soon I leave to go home. As I walk down Main Street, the music continues, wafting along on the wind the soulful crooning "Unforgettable …" and, I, too, continue feeling the heat on my back and the heat rising inside me, torched by a pair of eyes that I will discover are as green as the sea.

As I walk up the steps of home, the phone starts ringing inside. I know who's calling before I reach it. My heart thumps and thumps. "Hey, this is Luke McLeod. I just saw you in the drugstore with Megan. You doing anything tonight?"

"No. Not really." I can hardly catch my breath.

"How about a movie then? There's a good one in Hamlet. I've already seen it, so I know it's good. But I'll watch it again."

"I ... I don't know," I mumble. "I'll have to see ..." My God, what am I going to do? I really want to go, but I don't think I should. I won't know how to act around him. What will I talk about? Megan said he's been with so many girls. What about Mama? She'd have a fit if she'd heard what I've heard. And she won't let me go out of town.

"I'll pick you up at 6:45 then. We need to leave early to make the movie." Luke quickly says before I can answer.

During these days everyone is having a "nervous breakdown"—my mother has one every day, and I've never understood what it is. But now I think I'm having one! I feel jittery suddenly like I do before a piano recital when my insides vibrate so much I nearly retch before I go on stage. Before recitals I've discovered the current trend—a Coke with ammonia—will do the trick. But I don't have time to run to Carolina Drug. What am I going to wear? Do I have time to wash my hair? And, sweet Jesus, the Inquisition. Mama will recreate the longest and darkest one of all.

"And who did you say he is?"

"His name is Luke McLeod."

"Is his family the Hunter McLeods?"

"I don't know. I don't think so."

"Then where does he live?"

The Inquisition is so familiar. Next will be: what does his father do? Well, what did his grandfather do?

"Mama, I don't know his genealogy!" I shout. "You ask him, because he's gonna be here in a few minutes and I haven't finished dressing!"

"Don't you get short with me, Erin Rose. This is not like you."

"Please, Mama, leave me alone. He's nice, Mama." That word "nice" translated means he looks mighty nice to me.

"Erin Rose, I want to know who you're dating. You must have some idea about where he lives."

"Somewhere in the Sandhills. I don't know exactly."

I do know what *not* to say. In town he can't live on the wrong side of the tracks. And he sure can't live near the mill shacks or anywhere else in East Oak Glen for that matter. Living in the country depends on the amount of family land and Mama's approval of the last name.

Quickly I add, "He goes to Wallace High School."

Mama likes Wallace, because her family once lived there.

"And Alice Faye Stewart has dated him," I declare.

Mama regards her family as respectable.

"Well, I suppose he's all right then."

Bingo! I thought *that* bit of gossip would do it.

When I open the front door, Luke immediately starts talking. "Look what I gotta wear! Mother pressed the wrong shirt and put all the rest in the wash, and this one doesn't go with my pants. Will you look at this—a green shirt with *blue* pants!"

I feel such a strong pull toward him, it's like a huge magnet has been sewn inside his skin so deep that I may, if not careful, become stuck here forever. And I couldn't care less what he wears. "Your pants are navy. I like green with navy." I am looking in his eyes more than at his pants—I've already done that. "They look good."

Luke walks in and extends his hand to Mama, introduces himself, and smiles. Still holding Mama's hand, Luke shakes his head back and forth and comments, "There's no mistake who your daughter is, Ma'am. The resemblance is striking, more like sisters."

I breathe a sigh of relief. Luke obviously makes Mama feel young again, and at the same time he says his proper "Ma'am." Her questions are gone.

After a bit of adult small-talk Luke informs Mama of his plans to drive to Hamlet to the theater and asks her when he should have me home.

She hesitates but says, "I usually don't allow Erin Rose to go out of town. And I like to have her in about 10:00."

"Yes, Ma'am." Luke pauses. "You know, that's a really good movie in Hamlet. Have you heard about it, Ma'am?" He starts explaining the entire plot, adding, "I've already seen it, but I think Erin Rose will really like it." He waits a second or two and then adds, "I understand about going out of town though. My mother always worries about me, too. We can take in a movie here."

Mama wavers, "Well, I suppose I can make an exception tonight. The Hamlet movie does sound like a good drama. There's probably just another western here on a Saturday night. And since you're going out of town, you can have her back by 10:30."

"Yes, Ma'am. That's great!" Luke starts to go, pauses, and turns around to face Mama again. He shakes his head and frowns. "I don't know. Maybe we shouldn't go. I don't know if we can get back by then. You know, that'll take a little longer to drive. And with Erin Rose, I'd hate to have to drive over the speed limit."

I smother a laugh and hold my head down to look away. Megan told me briefly, above the clamor of the drugstore crowd, that Luke drives to Maguire to drink beer and to pick up girls hanging around the beer joint. And often on his way back home he and a buddy drag race, two abreast, down Lumber Road all the way into the Sandhills, outracing the cops who sometimes watch for him.

Mama nods understandingly. She smiles at him. "Be home by 11:00, then."

I can't believe it. Not only am I going out of town at *her* suggestion, but she's added an hour to my curfew.

Luke looks at me across the room and smiles as if he's acknowledging that we together are clever conspirators. He makes me one with him. A surge of warmth starts from my toes and spreads to the top of my head.

As Luke starts the car, he asks, "Is it true what I've heard about your Mama? That she went out looking for Rick and you when you weren't home on time?"

A flash of Mama's little black Ford coupe coming down South Main at the time my date and I were pulling out from the Milk Bar embarrasses me again. I pretended not to see her, but the couple in the backseat exclaimed at once, "There's your mother, Erin!" To Luke I tell the story again. "And we were on our way home. I guess everyone in town knows that story by now."

"Damn." Luke looks over at me. "I'm getting *you* home on time."

In the theater we sit on the side near the front. We slide low in the seat and eat popcorn from the same box and laugh during the movie at the same moment and glance at each other at the same time over the popcorn box. I am aware of his arm touching mine, holding the box low, and I feel again drawn into him. I sense I've known him for a very long time.

Later, after Luke drives through the second stoplight on Church Street, we see light. The lights from my house brighten the whole block. She's done it again. Not only are the front door lights on, but the ceiling lights at the corners of the wrap-around porch glare like prison floodlights, beaming over the yard. It is ten minutes before 11:00.

In front of my house the lighted pathway stretches quite a distance from the sidewalk to the porch steps, especially if you're being watched by Mama and the whole neighborhood. At the door Luke leans over and gently brushes his lips on the corner of my mouth. I stand still, anticipating more, but he just whispers "goodnight" and steps away.

The next day Megan calls after church. "Erin, you didn't tell me you had a date with Luke!"

"I didn't have time. He called me right after we left the drugstore, and I had to get ready in a hurry."

"I can't believe you went out with him. You know what they all say about him being so wild. And the way he is with girls."

"No, I don't know. I just know how Luke was with me last night." And I add defensively, "And he's very nice. I had a really good time. We went to Hamlet to the movies, stopped by The Hub to get a drink, and came home."

"Well, don't get fooled by the first date. Some guys have seen him in action snowing girls. I understand they all *do it* with him and he doesn't even have to try. Did I tell you that at Wallace High Luke hauled a keg of beer onto campus in his dad's pickup truck, set it up in the school parking lot, and sold beer between classes? He was expelled from school. That is, until his dad talked—I've heard—very convincingly to the principal—what Mr. McLeod said I don't know—but Luke was allowed back into school. And then his friends voted him class president ... Erin, are you going to see him again?"

I still feel the brush of his lips on mine. "Yes. If he asks me."

The following week everyone mentions to me some wild rumor about Luke. These rumors reported by the guys just don't fit the Luke of Saturday night. He is not the only one to frequent the town of Maguire after hours. A lot of guys after taking dates home meet at the hangout corner of Main at Will's Esso Station to exaggerate their adventures and make plans. You can see them parked on any given night, sitting on the fenders of the family car or pickup or fancied-up jalopy—talking, laughing, occasionally yelling out at another buddy passing by. Here the race challenges and the dares are made about crossing the state line into South Carolina, about ten miles away, into the "wet" town of Maguire. Our county has been "dry"—that is, without alcohol—since WWII. Outside Maguire these guys congregate at Hank's Grill to buy beer or, if they're so inclined, go to the honky-tonk across the street to pick up girls and whisper about episodes the next day at school.

I wonder if these tales are true or exaggerated so terribly that what truth there is becomes a lie, each speaker trying to shock. In the 1950s such episodes seem to be the measure of manhood. Like generations of men before, fathers smile knowingly, inwardly pleased, flattered about their sons' promiscuity with "loose" girls, beaming "Oh, he's a chip off the old block" and "He's just sowing his oats like his old man." He'll settle down with a "proper" girl someday. And collectively they uphold "her" virginity like a holy cross to preserve, protect, and finally take as a challenge. I keep thinking of looking in Luke's eyes. The Luke inside his eyes is not the one outside. I want the one *inside* his eyes to materialize.

Ruby Jean, a year older than I, got married at 16 a year ago and dropped out of school, and we haven't talked in years. There are times I really miss her since she lived so close that we'd visit each other on and off all day.

Megan, though, lives nearly across town on the southwest side. She's been my best friend since first grade. We walk two or three times a week to visit, we talk on the phone off and on all day and night, and we have all our classes together. She is my best friend. In our junior year both she and I have to do a lot of guesswork about boys and sex. We are somewhat obsessed over these topics, and it seems that's all we talk about. In the art of kissing we consider ourselves experts. Between the two of us, we know how every boy in town kisses. If we've missed someone, Megan asks around until she finds out from another girl. Of course, we've been to a lot of parties where we played "spin the bottle" or "post office." In algebra class, when we are bored out of our minds, we entertain ourselves by rating the guys who are called to the blackboard or just passing by. We use our own signals, usually a facial expression to indicate our evaluation. Oh, we're very subtle: from placing a hand over our face with wrinkled nose, to holding lips tight and shaking our heads, to lifting shoulders and looking quizzical, to lifting up eyebrows with a suggestive smile and turning head to the side, then to the reverse whistle—sucking in breath and falling back in the chair with a slide. Our algebra teacher is a short little woman with a bent-over back always facing away from the class while she writes formulas on the blackboard. We're safe.

Luke continues to treat me as someone very special. Our dates are pretty much the same: going to the movies; stopping by the Canteen, the community hang-out, to dance; parking at the pecan orchard, the "kissing spot," where sometimes couples park in a circle, turn on their lights, turn on the radio music, and dance. I'm still awed by

Luke and that feeling makes me very shy. He does all the talking. I never know what to talk about, since my life is so humdrum: studying for classes, practicing the piano, working afternoons in the library typing cards for the catalogue drawers. What can be any duller?

Then there's Mama. I can't give her the advice she asks for. I feel guilt when I leave her—always alone. And I carry inside me a sadness I try to hide. And I know Luke dates other girls—why not? We're not going "steady." I've been in line with Megan at the movies and seen Luke walk in with another girl and wanted to vanish on the spot. I can't help but wonder why he even dates me. But he always calls. And I feel alive with him.

I wonder how it feels to pitch rules and decorum to the wind and live just in the moment. Luke's vitality in grasping what he wants intrigues me. I wonder how he acts when he's with other girls. I want to see him in action. Be one of those "after-hour" girls in Maguire. But the consequences scare me to death.

Then there are times that his disregarding rules bothers me. For example, his spiking the only punch bowl at a school dance with vodka. The girls who don't drink alcohol have to go without a drink all evening or drink his concoction (sometimes not realizing it).

Then there is the matter of his carelessness—unintentional or simply indifferent to consequences? Just the same, his tossing rules to the wind almost cost me my part-time job in the county library. I work in the back office typing catalogue cards for new books. This task includes typing the classification number and all the bibliographical information on cards that help locate books in the stacks. The job suits me. I am accurate, fast, and interested in browsing through the new books coming into the library when I'm done typing. I have my own desk and schedule my own hours and spend time reading. And I earn my own money that I spend on clothes.

One afternoon Miss Woodworth, the librarian, and her assistant left to attend a meeting, where Miss Woodworth is to speak at the Thursday Afternoon Book Club. That leaves a girl at the front circulation desk and me in the back office. The two of us, therefore, are responsible for the Oak Glen Public Library.

Soon in walks Luke. He looks through the stacks and strolls in the back, calling, "Erin? Where are you?"

He finds me at my desk before I can reply.

"Whatcha doin'?" he asks.

"Hey, Luke. What are *you* doing here? I'm busy typing." Of course, I'm excited to see him, but at the same time anxiety consumes me. *No visitors allowed in the back.* I am in the Forever Indecision State whenever Luke appears.

Luke picks up some cards and makes a face. "You do this all afternoon?" He drops the cards down and plops himself into Miss Woodworth's swivel chair at her desk, plays with every object on her desk, leans back, crosses his legs, and says while he swirls a bit, "Hey, I like this!" And the first thing I know, he pulls out a cigar, lights it, and flips ashes into the paperclip tray.

Everything happens so fast. "You can't smoke here!" I jump out of my seat, start pulling up the windows beside the librarian's desk, and frantically fan the air, yelling, "Put out that cigar and get out of here with it! You're not supposed to be here. Only staff. She'll be back any minute now."

Everyone knows Miss Woodworth by sight and knows she is an old bat. Streaked with gray, her red frizzled hair stands out as if her hair were plugged into an outlet. She always stands at attention, even when walking, short and stout, poker-faced, unbending in her dark brown oxfords. "Hurry, Luke! It's time for Miss Woodworth to come back."

Luke shrugs indifferently. "Okay. Just came to say hello. See ya then." He ambles out the back door.

I leave the windows open for a little longer before closing them, wash the paperclip tray, straighten and dust her desk and chair, and start typing. In no time at all I hear the firm heels of her shoes. I keep my eyes glued to the typewriter. With wild hair and imposing voice, Miss Woodworth marches into the office. As always she says, "Good afternoon," and displays her painted smile and slight nod that puts you in your place.

And then she starts sniffing. She walks this way and that. She looks like a dog—a part terrier mutt. "Sniff-sniff ... sniff ... what is that I smell?"

I keep typing.

Before I can think of anything to say, she exclaims, "A-ha! What is *this* doing in here?" She holds a crushed-out cigar up in the air between her forefinger and thumb as if she's found a crushed snake on top of her file cabinet.

I am aghast. I can't believe that Luke put out the cigar there and left it.

She stares at me accusingly. And in the most Puritanical loftiness, she proposes, "And have *you* been entertaining young men in this office while I was away?"

The way she accuses me with her eyes makes me feel as condemned as Hester Prynne standing in the town square displaying her glowing Scarlet Letter for all to see. Miss Woodworth's reprimand hits deep because I have never gotten in trouble before, except with Mama.

And perhaps even deeper I am hurt by Luke's insensitivity.

For a while that little voice inside me nags and nags Megan's word "Beware!" But the word eventually gets lost somewhere in Luke's smile. And his incredible laugh. When he laughs, the laugh spreads all over his face, completely innocent in the moment's indulgence, just like a child's. And in that moment I see again in his eyes the Luke that I've started to love.

Dating Luke is exciting. It's like being on the edge of something. That edge I think I can never cross over, but I am attracted to that part of him that will ... and to that part of me that wants to be the wild gypsy free of decorum. To plunge into the forbidden, to embrace the unknown, and to fling open that closed door to light, exposing dark-stored secrets ... I want to see for myself all that lies there. The dark pulls at me. But I know it will be a long time before I open that door—if I ever do.

Spring is in the air. I can smell the lilacs at the edge of the driveway and feel the air cool and warm at the same time. It is that indefinite time of day again—no longer day, not yet night, a waiting time. When you don't mind the dull gray for you know the moon will rise.

I stoop down to pick some violets growing wild in the shade of the apple tree. I spotted them the other day scattered among weeds like purple clover. I break the tender stems off near the ground and soon have a dozen or so. I arrange the violets in an even bunch. They will look just right with my blue dress, and it feels so good to have cotton next to my skin again after a long winter of wool. The violets feel like velvet against my face. Even the air feels like velvet. And I have a date with Luke.

The thought of touching him makes me feel warm and cool at the same time like the spring air. Mostly warm when he touches *me*.

It is about time for him now. I walk inside the house and down the dark hallway and stop in front of the mirror. It has been in the same spot for three generations. The glass is not very large, but it reflects half of your body. Ornate mahogany with carved rosettes frames the mirror in a shape like a shield that is carefully polished with lemon oil. I think of the mirror as someone real—who just changes her face.

In my dreams the mirror pulls at Mama and me when we pass down the hall, and we cannot help but look in it; it wants us to keep it alive. Its face may be Mama's or it may be mine. *Or double-faced, or superimposed with one over the other or one becoming the other.* Sometimes I hurry past, afraid to see my own shadow. Otherwise, the mirror just hangs there, staring blank, hiding reflections gathered during the day, storing them deep. At night it watches every flicker of movement year after year, retaining tales like the old English scop, the keeper and shaper of ancient stories of warriors and queens.

"Mirror, mirror on the wall, who is the fairest one of all? Mirror, mirror on the wall, who is the fairest ..." I'm half awake, the other half sleeps, with a chant sing-songing over and over and over ...

When I was too little to reach the mirror, Daddy picked me up and held me in front of it and said, "Baby, look in the mirror and tell me what you see." I always smiled when Daddy held me. "See," he said, "when you smile, it smiles back." I giggled.

"Now what happens when you frown?"

Tonight I smile in the mirror. I pin the violets in my hair over an ear and examine my powder and lipstick, fluff up my hair, and adjust the neckline of my dress. Satisfied, I start to turn then look up at Mama's face in the mirror.

"Erin Rose, what are you doing?"

"I'm waiting for Luke, Mama. I told you I have a date. We're going to the picture show." I turn and walk onto the front porch and sit in the swing, waiting for him.

Soon Mama walks across the porch to where I'm propped up in the swing. "It's getting dark. Come on inside with me."

"I'm waiting for Luke."

"No." She speaks as if she's talking about the weather. "Not tonight."

"What do you mean?" I stop swinging. A tremor shivers through my torso.

"Erin Rose, I don't want you to go anywhere tonight." Mama shakes her head as she repeats, "No. Not tonight. Not tonight. No."

"But, Mama, you said I could go. And I reminded you this morning." The spring air turns heavy. I can't take a full breath. Night is approaching, unusually dark.

"I want you to stay here with me tonight."

"Mama, that's not fair. I stayed home last night and the night before that. I did my homework early. And I checked with you first."

"I get so lonesome, Erin Rose. My nerves just can't take it tonight. And the house is so dark. Like something is around each corner. I can't be alone in this tomb tonight." Mama pleads on the break of tears. "Come in now." She heads for the heavy wood door that creaks when she opens it.

I jump out of the swing and hurry across the porch. I push the heavy door and shut it with a loud thump. I follow her down the hall and into the kitchen.

"Mama, I can't just break a date."

"That's easy to do. Call him. Tell him you can see him another time." Mama starts picking up dishes from the draining board, satisfied they're dry, ready to put on the shelf. Task completed. Dismissed.

"I can't call him." My voice rises.

Mama sighs. "I get so lonely, Erin. My nerves just can't take it tonight."

"Luke's already left home by now and he'll be here any minute. And it's not *my* fault how *you* feel!"

Mama turns to me, lifting her eyebrows up then down, her nervous habit when she gets flustered. She enunciates each word equally, "I said you are *not* going anywhere tonight."

"Well, I want to go and I *am* going!" I shout back.

Before I can turn around, Mama yells back, "We'll see about that." She jerks open the drawer in the enamel-top table beside the sink. She reaches in and pulls out a butcher-knife—the kind that has a fat wooden handle and a blade like a meat cleaver. She stands glaring at me and pointing that long sharp knife at me. For a moment I stand mesmerized, staring at the knife point moving toward me. My heart beats so fast, the beats run together as one big thump enveloping my whole chest and my throat so much I can't swallow.

Mama screams as she moves. "Do you see this? I'm going to slice my throat like this!" She cuts the air across near her throat. "Do you hear me? If you leave this house, I'll slice my throat and you'll find me dead on this kitchen floor when you get back." Mama's voice is piercing, and her eyes glare at me, blank and cold.

"Do you hear me?" Again Mama screams and the doorbell rings at the same time, and I run from the kitchen down the long dark hall and reach the brass doorknob and stop. I pull open the door and there stands Luke.

"Hey," I whisper, take a deep breath, and pull the door shut.

"Hey. You ready?" He leans over and kisses me on the cheek and takes my hand.

"Uh huh," I murmur softly, barely audible.

"Sorry I'm late. I've been talking Mom into using her car. And she finally agreed. So we swapped. But she isn't too keen on driving my pickup to church. Man, on Wednesday nights, she's gonna get to church one way or another."

My insides are shaking. I want to cry or scream or run. I want to squeeze Luke's hand and run down the long walkway and race down the highway in his Mom's car going full speed with windows down and wind blowing my hair in every direction and keep going anywhere he wants to go and do anything he wants to do, even make love finally, rolling on the ground and keep rolling until morning and never come back. How can anyone understand how I feel?

Luke opens the car door for me and walks around to the driver's side. "You still want to try to make the movie? We'll miss the first ten minutes or so."

"Doesn't matter. Whatever you want to do." It does matter, I'm thinking. I feel I'll die if I have to sit inside for two hours. I want to be outside in fresh air, with no one but Luke. I want to say as much—to tell him everything. But I'm locked inside myself.

After the movie Luke brings me home, parks near the sidewalk, and asks, "Are we late?" He looks at his watch and shrugs. "Nope. We're on time." At once I'm aware of an invading darkness. Through the car window I see our house, its dark windows' vacant eyes, its angular roof and turrets looming like a haunted house.

Luke walks around to open the door on my side. I sit still, hesitate to get out. Barely can I move my legs. At the front door he kisses me good night. The porch is still dark and inside the house looks darker. I won't be embarrassed if the porch lights are suddenly switched on, even the blinding white of the ceiling lights showing me kissing Luke in front of mother, God, and country—not to speak of neighbors and cars passing up and down Church Street. Why doesn't Mama switch them on? Where is she? She always hears us coming up the steps. Dear God, I can't go in alone and find her.

I desperately want to ask Luke to stay awhile, at least to walk inside with me down the dark hall to the kitchen. I feel like begging him. But I can't form words to speak. Instead, I reach up around his neck, just as he's beginning to step back, stand on my toes, and start kissing him, passionately, long and hard, willing him to stay. After a while, he gently pulls my arms down from around his neck and clears his throat. He whispers huskily, "Erin, you'd better go in. I'll call you tomorrow." He gives me a peck on the cheek, calls softly, "'Night." Tears in my eyes, I watch him leave.

Inside, I stand in darkness. Mama's eyes haunt me. I can't kill the vision. The long hall stretches before me. I can't make it through this murkiness. I turn toward the French doors that open into the living room. I push them open. From the window a shard of moonlight slices the dark, sweeping enough light inside for deceptive shadows to play. My heart pounds. A pillow on the floor becomes a head.

Quickly I feel on the wall for the light switch, and the light from the chandelier floods the living room. I remember when it gleamed like new brass, or old brass when it was just polished; I'd imagine it caught sparks of sunlight through the window and held them long after the sun set over the hedge, and that was why the night was bright in the room.

Now it is dull, almost charcoal like dirty pewter, and I hardly ever turn it on anymore; I prefer the softer light from the lamp that doesn't show the cracks in the plaster so much. I remain staring at the wall with the crack before me, the wide water-ring stain on the ceiling and the dripping stain in the corner, the pink plaster there curling up like ribbon does when you slide the edge of scissors down it to make a bow. I'm choking, holding in my cries, prolonging my walk ahead.

I take three deep breaths—I've read somewhere that deep breathing helps to do something you don't want to do— and push open the other French doors into the dining room, Mama's bedroom. I hear no sounds. I walk across the room slowly without looking from side to side and swing open the door leading to the butler's pantry, my bedroom, then down the little hallway leading to the kitchen. I stop. I look at the kitchen doorway that's still open.

All of a sudden I have the impulse to turn around and run as I did earlier. But where will I run? I have no one to run to. I have only Mama. Oh God, *please* let her be all right. Don't let her be dead.

Quickly I walk in hugging the wall with my eyes staring at the dark ceiling. I am beside the table in the alcove, where Mama and I eat and where I put flowers when I was a little girl. I can still see Daddy dancing on the table and me, giggling in my hula skirt, slinging paint all over the floor.

I reach and pull the string for the naked light bulb dangling from the dingy ceiling over the table. No, I mustn't look at the floor yet. I hiccup cries for I don't know how long.

Deliberately, I glance at the floor and then stare.

No blood. No body. No knife.

The table drawer is closed. The knife is put up. The floor is clean. I let my breath blow out slowly. I feel a breeze from the open window. The yellow curtains stir slightly.

I hear the sound of a voice. Voices—low, laughing. A light snicker, a man's low chuckle, and Mama's "Oh, honey" floats in the spring air from the car parked in the back driveway.

Suddenly, I feel drained, empty in the pit of my stomach.

Chapter 15

Luke and I are still dating. You might say I'm going steady, and he's going ... wherever he wants. During my senior year in high school, Luke is at the University of North Carolina, so I see him only on the weekends he comes home. By the time I graduate, he's off to Myrtle Beach for the summer, working as a lifeguard. He comes home maybe ... twice. I go to the beach for a week with a house party of girls and see him for just one night. Ignoring me for the rest of the time, Luke hurts my feelings and makes me feel like a fool.

However, at the same time, that one night dancing with Luke on the beach at the pavilion under the full moon beside the rushing tide makes me fall in love with him all over again. Even in the dim light of the pavilion, I see his hair a golden auburn, his skin a tropical tan, and his eyes a potent green that captures mine in such a fixed way they consume me. It's more than physical desire. There's a depth within, a catalyst that gives rise to a budding hope; however, the inner Luke seems far away from the outer one.

How does the memory of that one night sustain me? And why?

Memory is a child without words to explain. The child sees the image, feels what that image conveys, perhaps identifies the smell, hears the sound, tastes the air, the grass, remembers. Everything we do creates memories. Living is remembering.

But who wants to live without understanding? Not only do I need *words*, but I need the *right* words to interpret what my inner child knows.

College gives me those words.

Even though money's been tight, Mama has for years saved money from each insurance check for a college fund for me. And now she has a job.

I choose the Woman's College of the University of North Carolina at Greensboro, commonly called WC, and later UNC-Greensboro when it became co-ed. The dark red brick buildings sit back, imposing, on green sprawling lawns with tall trees like many women's schools. This University was first established as a college for women because UNC-Chapel Hill accepted women only as juniors and seniors, and it boasts a tough academic curriculum.

In late August I'm anticipating leaving soon for WC. Unexpectedly, Luke sweeps in to tell me he has quit college and enlisted in the Army. At that time the Korean War is over, but U.S. troops are still guarding the border. I know he doesn't enlist out of patriotism. It's just another momentary adventure. He leaves for Fort Benning, Georgia, that very day. I feel conflicted about Luke's actions, yet I'm truly glad that I, too, am going away.

WC gives me my roommate's name so I write to Lou, short for Louella, my soon-to be roommate, several times that summer. I like the writing—I feel we've gotten to know each other.

I arrive at the university alone—no Oak Glen folks at all. Not a soul to speak to—not even Mama. And even on the first day, everyone else has someone. It seems that each girl has brought a friend to room with and knows others from home to pal around with. Always shy with strangers and miserable around established cliques, I walk behind an invisible barrier. I want so much to break through, walk up to a group, and cheerfully call out, "H-e-y, I'm Erin," and babble like a bubbly cheerleader, holding my audience rapt.

Lou is a dance major from Charlotte. I am excited to meet her but on campus I find she travels with a Charlotte clique. Her group accepts me in a friendly way—that is, they allow me to accompany them to the cafeteria and invite me to their rooms to smoke Winstons, to play bridge, and to knit. I don't smoke. I don't play bridge. I don't knit. They reminisce incessantly about Saunders Park High School and social gatherings in Charlotte as if it were The Promised Land.

Knitting socks, for some reason, is in vogue. In time I learn to knit. Lou teaches me the knit stitch; Marie, the purl; Jane how to find and fix dropped stitches. A whiz at knitting, Geraldine helps me follow the sock pattern. I start knitting Luke a pair of red socks. Before I learn how to turn the heel, the foot is long enough to reach his calf. Such a tedious job. But I finish it. Months later Luke opens his gift, pulls it out of the box, holds it up, and says, "What's this?" No more said.

When we go to Aycock Auditorium for required lectures, they take their knitting in special bags and sit together. I sit beside Lou listening to the pling of needles intermittently, one after another. One time someone drops a needle on the concrete floor, and it echoes as it rolls down the auditorium to the bottom of the stage; a few snickers create a domino effect around the large room.

In the dorm when the girls aren't playing bridge, they knit together while they gossip. I feel more and more like a pariah. I begin to think that the whole second floor of Paige Dormitory is occupied by Charlotte residents. I'm tired of hearing about Saunders Park's Country Club parents and their social gatherings, their trips abroad, their shopping sprees.

Weeks pass. I miss Mama so much. Every week or so, she calls me. I hear my name announced on the loudspeaker, and I run downstairs to the receptionist's desk to reach the only phone for two hundred girls. It's worth the hassle. I nearly cry when I hear her voice. It's the only time I feel my identity. And I realize how much we love each other.

As Mama talks, I visualize her in one of my old sweaters, cramped up in her bedroom with the oil heater, sitting on the edge of her bed near the night stand, staring out the tall window, and blowing smoke-circles at the dimming daylight. Soon she'll return to the kitchen to warm a can of Denny's Stew. Then the dark of night comes. Mama's alone. My throat chokes. I don't want her to know I'm sad living away from home and all that is familiar. She has sacrificed too much to get me here—wearing my discarded clothes, taking her worn shoes to the old repair man on Main Street, eating from a can each night, saving each penny she can spare. Thank God I was awarded the Stafford McCraw Scholarship at high school graduation.

When I can speak, I tell her about my classes, the meals in the cafeteria, my roommate Lou who's friendly and nice, the library so big I can easily get lost in it, and all the fun I'm having at the Saturday night dances when we're bused to Carolina, State, and Davidson Colleges. "I've never seen so many boys in one place, Mama, and I've never danced so much." I don't mention I'd danced all night and met a Carolina boy I've dated several times as well as a Davidson boy who took me to his fraternity house.

Mama sounds pleased. "That's nice, Erin Rose, that a group of you go dancing together. And that you go to Davidson. You can meet some nice young men there. You know what I've secretly hoped? That you'd marry a minister."

Neither of us mention Luke.

Oh, Lord, what she doesn't know about what's inside my head. I shake my head, teary-eyed. How I wish she were here and we could talk. Really talk. Tears spill over. But she can't be honest with me any more than I can be with her.

When I return to my empty room (Lou's with her friends), I'm glad for the silence and I reach for a book. I focus on biology—it's objective, factual. I'm exhausted from *feeling*. Later, when the group stops by to get me for dinner, I say I'll go after I finish reading a chapter.

After a few weeks I sit on the bed "squaw" style with the Charlotte girls and try to smoke a cigarette. Geraldine says, "No, Erin. Watch me. When you puff on your cigarette, you breathe in a deep breath, hold the smoke in your mouth just a second before you swallow it, and breathe out your nose at almost the same time."

There I sit propped on a pillow bringing a cigarette to my mouth (as Mama does), and the whole crew—Lou, Geraldine, Marie, and Jane—lean in to check my breathing, and suddenly I'm choking and coughing so much Lou's beating my back, ready to turn me over for a Heimlich maneuver. Jane is handing me a glass of water, while Geraldine is nearly shouting "Breathe, Erin! Take deep breaths!" Marie opens the window and walks around swishing away smoke.

When I finally can breathe, Geraldine assures me, "That's a good start, Erin. Next time you'll know exactly what to do ... and you'll be inhaling!"

There's no place more dismal than a dormitory on a cold, rainy day. If I'm not practicing piano or studying in the library, I spend time in Marie's room knitting and talking about guys. She's going steady with a hometown boy she dated through high school who's going to State, so they're together on most weekends. If not, we head for a movie, sometimes just the two of us. Marie, short with a head full of dark, natural curls cut close, looks like a pixie with upturned nose and rose-bud lips. And she's sweet like one, not at all pretentious. She's an easy-going, attentive listener, who will probably always be a loyal friend. A home economics major, she is into dressmaking, tailoring, and upholstering. She doesn't share my interest in literature, but we both like fashions and classical music; I keep a stack of fashion magazines, and she has a nice selection of 78 classical records that we play in her room while we look at magazines and talk about fashions. Marie teaches me how to crochet. Rather quiet in a group, Marie understands my feeling sometimes alone in a crowd.

I'm still registered as a music major, and I've been adapting to a schedule that I deplore. I practice piano three hours a day in a practice room in the Music Hall; if I can't fit these hours into the afternoon, then I have to return at night to complete them, weekends included. Also, I have to take theory as well which is like taking math. It seems with each semester I'll be increasing the number of music theory classes, music history, a heavy concentration of technique, and monthly recitals before the music faculty.

I recall how different my high school music days went: going to district contests, usually at Flora MacDonald College. I'm so nervous, knowing the judges are listening to each note and trying to catch one off beat and looking for a wrist too high or fingertips too flat or elbows too far out. My shaking hands fly through my piano solo faster than ever, fingers slippery from sweat. The Superior rating I always get feels wrong. The rating just means I play better than someone else. My real Superior happens only at home when I play, alone, what I want to: *my* interpretation of *Clair de Lune* and Chopin's *Nocturne in E* and Gershwin's *Rhapsody in Blue*. I'm my own judge. I play what I feel—not according to theory or mathematical precision.

The university practice room is like a big closet with only room enough to place an old upright piano and stool.

There I practice alone to the *tick-tick* of the metronome, the count exact. I think of practicing Bach's Two-Part Inventions, the first note of each measure sounding with each tick of the metronome that goes on and on, one hand playing against the other. But what am I playing here in this little room? Any Chopin? Or Rachmaninoff with full chords at triple *fortissimo*? No, a simple little piece I played in 5th grade—to perfect my technique. I am bored to death and disenchanted beyond reason.

What am I here for? In my 20s will I play on stage with hundreds of people listening? That's a joke! And no way will I teach piano and have to listen all day to children banging the keys. Mama will be disappointed if I quit; my piano teacher at home will have a fit.

It makes no sense to me. In a small town I may have been good as my piano teacher's "protégé," but here at a university in a city with hundreds of girls from everywhere, I am intimidated. I feel as though I'm nothing. Great God, I feel alienated enough without having to be in this hole alone for 21 hours a week. But I'm being loyal to the wishes of my piano teacher, Owen McCaskill, who presented me in a senior recital on stage in the high school auditorium: a concert in two parts, the interlude featuring a guest cornet player.

For that program I performed a Bach Two-Part Invention, Beethoven's "Adagio" from the Sonata *Pathetique*, Chopin's *Nocturne in E flat,* Franz Liszt's *Liebestraum,* Claude DeBussy's *Clair de Lune,* and a modern composition, *London Fantasia.* I know this was a highlight in Mama's life. She had always wanted to play the piano, but she was denied lessons because her sister had taken lessons, hated them, and quit. Her parents were determined not to waste their money again with Mama. Her disappointment remained; I see that faraway look in her eyes when she sits near, listening to every note I play. Mama, though, plays pretty well by ear the popular tunes that we hear on the radio, and I have the training for classical.

I love to play ... but on my terms. Playing music is like reading beautiful prose or poetry. It takes me to another world. I close my eyes and become the music—the way I close my eyes and become the dance. Mama says it's the Irish in us.

I meet Diana, a piano major who also doesn't want to be one. We strike up a conversation in the Music Hall, mostly complaining about our hours in the "hole" and discover we both live in Paige Dorm on the same floor. We walk there together and talk all the way. Diana is from a small town, too; she reads a lot and writes poetry and doesn't know for sure what she wants to major in. The time flies by as we stroll across campus and laugh about our imagination, how we use it all the time—while we're in class, reading, writing, and just daydreaming. Then we start walking to classes together and have more long talks on the way to the Music Hall across campus. Diana likes the lively bus trips and dances at Carolina, and I tell her about the fun I had dancing and the boy I've dated since then. We plan to go on the next bus out. I am delighted to have a friend whom I have so much in common with.

One day Diana tells me to come get her about 5:30 to go to dinner. She's going to take a nap. "You may have to knock on the door loud to wake me."

Her room is only a few doors down from mine across the hall. At 5:30 I knock on the door and call. She doesn't answer. I knock again louder and call, "Di-an-a, time for dinner," and as I call, I turn the knob to see if it's open and if she's awake. The door creaks open a couple of feet, and I'm almost in the room. Then I stop.

With her head turned toward the door there Diana is, propped up against the pillow in her narrow steel bed, naked from the waist up, with her naked roommate under the cover, leaning over her, breast to breast. I am stupefied. Diana calls something. I mumble something as I quickly shut the door.

I don't recall the rest of the day. I do remember my feelings and then my thoughts. I feel shock ... I don't believe what I just saw. I disassociate myself from the scene ... I wasn't there ... those were just figures on a screen. I feel stupid ... why did I open the door? What were they doing? I feel betrayed ... the person I thought was my friend is not that person at all. I feel more like an alien ... I don't even understand the world I'm living in; I truly feel an outsider.

It is the 1950s. I've heard the word "homosexual" before, but I don't understand it. It's a word that's hidden in the closet or swept under the rug, a word that's sometimes whispered. I know it means men attracted sexually to other men, but what does that mean? And what do they do? Are women homosexual? Is that what I saw? What I would have given to have Megan here with me. She would've figured it out. But she's married now and lives with her husband in a dormitory at East Carolina University. I miss her so much. And I've lost her, too, by her marriage. I feel like crying. Am I ever going to find a place to fit?

Diana and I never speak of That Scene. Just ignore it entirely. And I have never spoken of it with anyone else—until now. We remain close class friends. In time we both decide to become English majors. By second semester we register for the same English courses, including Creative Writing, Poetry, and Shakespeare, and often study together. Nevertheless, I keep taking piano for the rest of the year, even though I sense my piano professor has no interest whatsoever in a non-music major. When I play the "little piece" he's assigned, he looks distracted and disgusted. Just what my ego needs! When I finally say I'm quitting, he agrees that that's a wise step.

It's mid-November before I hear from Luke. At boot camp in Georgia, he gains a new interest: jumping from planes. He transfers to an Airborne Battalion, hoping to be stationed at Fort Bragg, near home, but he's sent to Fort Campbell, Kentucky. During one leave Luke picks me up in Greensboro, and we head home. He now sports a crew cut instead of sideburns and a ducktail; the paratrooper uniform enhances his sexuality. The khaki shirt tucked in his pants fits "to a T," intensifying his broad shoulders and chest. When he hugged me earlier, I could feel muscles toned as hard as brick. His pants are fitted but blouse out a bit around his calf where they fit in the high-top boots. He exudes intensity. While he drives, I can hardly keep my eyes off him.

When Luke looks at me and smiles, there's no one else who can match him. I'm crazy about him, crashing in love with him time and again. Yet, after he takes me home, I feel sad. Something terribly important is missing. And I don't know what it is. Not the sex I refuse to have with him, but something far more intangible. What is it? If I don't know, then how can we fill that gap? Unspoken words? I don't know how to begin—and Luke doesn't listen.

On his last night home, taking me to my house, Luke pulls up to the curb, cuts off the car, and just sits there for what seems like forever. I am silent. Finally, he slides over, puts his arm around my shoulder, and says, "Let's get married."

I am flabbergasted. I didn't expect this! The girls I know would throw their arms around his neck responding, "Yes. Yes. Yes!" and cover his face with kisses. I can't do that. I don't want to get married. Oh-my-God.

"Erin, you don't give a damn about me, do you?"

"Yes, I do."

"You don't love me. You've never said so."

"But I *do*," I mumble.

154

"You don't act like it."

Am I lying? I don't know. I know I'm *in love* with him. I guess I am—or is it hormones? When I open the front door and see Luke standing there, my heart starts beating wildly and I feel instant heat running through me. I may just melt on him. When he smiles, it spreads all over his face. He glows. And I feel a glow inside. I can't wait to kiss him! I think this moment is what *joy* looks like. I want to hold the joy, embrace it—never let it go. To feel joyful—is that *love*? But the feeling never goes to the next step. We don't talk about how we feel. I don't want to lose him. I need to know the difference between *being in love* and *loving*.

"Well." Luke breaks the silence. "I just asked you to marry me. Don't you have anything to say about it?"

"Luke, I'm not ready to get married."

He leans over me to open the door. "Get out then."

All I can say in a pleading voice is "Luke ..."

"Erin, just get out," he says in a steely tone. "I'm driving this car as fast as it can go. I might kill myself."

I step over the curb. He slams my door and screeches away.

Luke is such an enigma. He's so unpredictable. His impulsiveness keeps me in a state of shock. Needless to say, I stay confused. Perhaps it's that very same fascination—the surprise element—that holds my interest. Until Luke entered the scene, my life had become a routine of school, piano practice, part-time typing job, Sunday school at the Baptist Church, organist at the Episcopal Church, the ebb and tide of Mama's depression, her social restrictions. Then here pops Luke like a sudden sun burst through gray clouds. How could I not be addicted to his presence? I am drawn to freedom. I crave spontaneity. I envy high-spiritedness.

When I was chronically shy as a child, I remember holding onto Mama's leg and hiding behind her thigh when I was four—or was it three?—whenever a stranger stopped to speak to her. Then through the years when I'm in uncertain situations, I feel a terrible sensation that I'm locked up inside myself, unable to move or speak even though I want to. Of course, I've outgrown a lot of this, but often when I'm with Luke this feeling returns.

Though we've dated for two years Luke seems uninterested in me. When I talk, he doesn't listen, or he cuts me off by changing the topic. That makes me clam up and feel insignificant. Why does he date me? Undoubtedly he can take his choice from a list of girls he's already sampled in more ways than he has me. Could that be it? He wants to have sex with me but knows he has to marry me first?

Anyway, after his pursuits he has come back to me so far. Obviously, Luke doesn't mind my silences; he talks a lot himself, plans the dates, and dominates the situation. And I feel comfortable with him, except when he belittles me. Then I think: that's just my weird reactions to Luke's personality. Besides, it's easier to be with the familiar than to risk the unknown.

On December weekends I continue going to Carolina dances and a couple of Davidson fraternity parties. I have no problem attracting guys and thoroughly enjoy flirting with them (which I become quite good at). After all, this is my first time away from home and my first taste of freedom being *me,* not Luke's girl. But I have to admit: I flirt and think of Luke at the same time, because no one measures up to him. Or maybe I don't give anyone else a chance.

At the Davidson frat parties, though, the first hour rushes by with introductions, identity synopses, but then time slows while guys drink excessively, well on the way to drunkenness, and girls act ridiculously silly. I don't drink. (Have you ever been sober at a frat party?) However, the Carolina dances I love: dim lights, a DJ with the latest tunes, everyone on the dance floor. I fall into the music, close my eyes, and drift, swaying to the rhythm, the music lifting me out of myself, free.

At winter break I'm happy to see Mama and Megan, who now has a baby that her parents keep while she continues at East Carolina with her husband. Her marital status saddens me, for "home" used to mean a lot of time with Megan on the phone and in her company. I visit to see the baby (the first newborn I've seen up close) and feel a sharp reduction in our camaraderie.

Mama, too, surprises me with her friendship with Preston, the sheriff. At the courthouse they see each other often, so now he comes over a couple of nights a week to see her. Mama's bedroom is also the winter sitting room with the only heater; the fireplaces in the other rooms are still too much trouble to use. I'm glad Mama has a friend, and I find him entertaining. He sits by the heater in the upholstered chair with booted feet propped up on the ottoman smoking his cigar and narrating his stories in the most drawn-out Southern drawl imaginable. He's a good storyteller—if you have time.

Still at Fort Campbell, Luke comes home on leave for the holidays. We date as usual, never mentioning his marriage proposal. Then a few weeks before Christmas he invites me for Sunday dinner with his parents and family, whom I've never met.

Luke slows down by a cluster of trees in the middle of the Sandhills, turns from the highway into a winding dirt drive, and stops his new blue Chevy before a modest white house. I can see how in the spring colorful azaleas will cuddle close around the porch on both sides of the house. A trellis stands by the porch, waiting for the climbing red roses. On the edge of the porch pots wait to be planted maybe with white petunias. As their house appears, I sense it'll be cozy. Luke tells me this is their second home; the original was a large two-story house built on the opposite edge of their farm in a more secluded area. They still refer to it as their home place, even though the house burned to the ground during the middle of the night along with all their possessions when he was about seven years old. Luckily, his parents, older sister, younger brother, and he got out safely. They had to live with other family members until his dad finished building the new, much smaller house; the church and folks in the community gathered clothes and other needs for them. Luke still nurses that old embarrassment of taking handouts, especially second-hand clothes. (That explains Luke driving to Charlotte in high school to buy tailored pants made of expensive material of his choice.)

Inside his home everyone (except his father) greets me as a long-lost member of the family: his mother, sister, brother-in-law, brother, sister-in-law, and four little nephews. It seems each one is talking at once, laughing, joking, dodging little boys whining "I'm hungry, Grandma!" The long dining room table stretches nearly across the room, displaying a feast: fried chicken, rice and gravy, sliced roast beef smothered with carrots and potatoes, homemade bread-and-butter pickles, fresh butter beans, creamed corn, big hot biscuits, cornbread, and sweet iced tea. On the side table sit two apple pies and a three-layered chocolate cake. My mouth must have dropped in surprise; Luke leans close and says, "This is just the usual Sunday dinner when Mom invites the family over."

What a surprise! I am amazed and, of course, a bit overwhelmed at all the noise and food. I realize I'm at a real Southern country dinner. Most of the meal comes from their farm: the vegetables grown, picked, frozen, and cooked by Luke's mother, whom I instantly like and feel fond of by the time I leave. I refer to her as Mrs. McLeod, but she insists that I call her Marty.

She is strikingly pretty with thick black hair and blue eyes from her Irish father, she says, yet she's strong and sturdy with the hands and legs of a farmer's wife, large-boned and square-jawed of German descent on her mother's side. Fun-loving, she is full of stories you'd love to hear and of old wives' tales you respect although you think you know better. Marty goes to the Holly Hill Church every Sunday morning (after she prepares dinner, which waits) and prayer meeting every Wednesday night.

Luke's father is a rather short, graying red-headed Scot with a very brisk, matter-of-fact manner that will make an enemy quicker than a friend. I already surmised this from Luke's description of his father's beating him with his wide leather belt when Luke was a young boy, leaving red welts all over his butt and legs. When Luke introduces me to his father, Mr. McLeod just nods his head with a "howdy-do," turns, and sits down at the table. A signal—I notice—that must mean he's ready to eat, because everyone starts sitting down in their usual places at once. The family bow their heads in unison while Father McLeod mumbles grace.

After dinner, Marty puts her arm around me and says, "Come along, Erin, let me show you our place."

The December day is warm enough for a light jacket. Tall longleaf pines border the farm, evergreens scatter around the yard, and the winter garden indicates new growth will come: even rows carefully tilled, old soil overturned, the smell of fresh earth. A row of collards, the large grainy leaves, bright green and curly, is ready for picking. Marty shows me where she'll plant field peas and butter beans and carrots, where the potato eyes are buried. I remember from so long ago, it seems, the garden that Daddy and I planted. Before I realize it, I'm spilling to Marty the memory of our garden. I must have gotten teary-eyed, because Marty puts her arm around me again and says, "Isn't it nice to have such memories?"

I nod and smile.

"Erin, have you ever been in a tobacco barn?" Marty asks.

"No."

She points toward the old barn across the field, turns around, and calls Luke, who's sitting on the steps of the back porch. "Son, walk Erin over to see the barn."

He gets up, walks across the yard, and yells, "Mom, she doesn't wanna' see that dirty old place."

"Yes, she does. Come out here," Marty shouts back firmly.

Luke saunters up, just looks at me, raises his eyebrows, and then says, "Okay, let's go."

The door creaks open slowly. The old barn is weathered and empty but sturdy. Inside there is a distinct mustiness from the scents of smoke and hickory and something sweet, no doubt tobacco. The earthiness of fresh hay. Hanging ajar, the barn door lets in the afternoon sun setting over the western field, which shoots a bright ray through the barn, piercing a part of the darkness with light. From the rafters hang a few spider webs in the floating dust motes and scattered on the ground lie some leaves of tobacco turned golden brown, though withered, still emanating a scent I can nearly taste as sweet.

The tobacco barn is silent with the resonance of imaginable sounds. True, the door squeaks when the wind blows, the old planks of the walls creak, the tin roof *plinks* at a bird's touch. But there are those other sounds: the re-echoes of fire popping, leaves groaning while turning, peat burning, sweaty men cursing the heat, and wagon wheels rolling outside.

I stand in the McLeod barn, my head full of sensory blends, and wish I were an artist. I'd bring my brushes and palettes here and create an impressionistic painting—with a little reddish-blonde boy leaning against the barn door.

"Hey. Are you still here or gone somewhere? And what are you looking at?"

"Luke, I really love the barn."

"Well, that's a surprise to me. There's nothing here. Just dirt. And maybe a mouse or two hiding in a corner. Can't imagine *you* in a barn."

"I'm just thinking about how the tobacco looks hanging and—"

He cuts me off, "Hey. That's an idea—you and me in the barn. But we don't have any hay. Why in the hell did Dad take out the hay? He always stored it here."

"Why are you mad about hay—you mean a haystack?"

"Erin, hay is pulled from the stack, put in bales and tied, and stored in a barn. Or the hay is thrown on the ground of a barn and stretched out in a pile over in a corner … and I'm not mad … I'd just like to have some now."

I must have looked rather dumb … or at least blank.

Luke shakes his head back and forth. "Erin, have you not heard of a roll in the hay?"

"Sorta."

"Well, if we had any hay, we could roll in it."

"I don't want to get my dress dirty."

"Don't worry. We don't have any hay. I'd never push you on the ground." He comes closer and tilts up my chin, his hands sliding up my face.

Leaving the barn, Luke points at the stretch of longleaf pines on the edge of the field. "See that narrow opening between the trees? Looks like a path cut out." Luke moves closer to me and turns my head slightly. "Right there."

"Uh huh." I love the scent of his after-shave and the smell of his skin with his shirt cuff rolled up, his arm right under my nose. And the shape of his hand. That has my attention more than the trees.

"Erin? Hey, are you with me?"

"Yes. I'm listening."

"You wanna walk through the woods down that path and see the pond? Did you notice it from the highway?"

"Yes. Is that your dad's pond?"

"Yep. He's stocked it with fish ... and I used to go fishing there a lot. There's a small dock we can sit on one day if it's not too cold. The water is dark like the Lumber River. In the summer there's nothing any better than to sit on the dock and hang your feet in that cold, black water."

Returning to the house, across the field, we step over the dormant rows, Luke holding my hand. The late sun on my back, I feel a warmth all over—not from just the sun or Luke's hand, but from this particular place: the pungent smell of earth, the fresh scent of pines, the yeasty kitchen, the togetherness of family. Life seems so simple here. Hard work, yes. *But everything is what it is.* No complexities of the head that you get in academia: the constant analyzing of *how* and *why* things are what they are.

Poet William Wordsworth, my prime study this fall, writes about living the simple life, close to nature and your own intuition, seeing the spirit of God manifested in nature and all things as he states in the poem "Lines Written a Few Miles above Tintern Abbey":

> A sense sublime
> Of something far more deeply interfused,
> Whose dwelling is the light of setting suns,
> And the round ocean, and the living air,
> And the blue sky, and in the mind of man,
> A motion and a spirit, that impels
> All thinking things, all objects of all thought,
> And rolls through all things.

On the front porch, saying my good-byes, I feel someone's eyes on my back. I turn around and see Luke's father in the doorway staring at me. His eyes are green like Luke's. I smile at him and see the corners of his eyes crinkle.

"It was nice meeting you, Mr. McLeod."

He nods and says, "Come back."

Still with his eye contact, I nod my head and say, "I will."

In the car Luke comments, "Well, you've made it with Dad."

"What do you mean?"

"That's the first time I've known him to invite someone back."

Chapter 16

Christmas 1953 is right around the corner. I've almost completed first semester—I just have exams to take when I return to WC. Luke's leave is almost over; he's due back to Fort Campbell the day after Christmas. The Christmas Eve dance is over at the Canteen, and Luke drives me home and parks in front of my house, in the same spot where he proposed a month or so ago.

He reaches over to get something from the glove compartment. Luke turns and grins. "Got'ya something." He hands me a small wrapped box with white ribbon.

I hold the small box, and my heart pumps so heavily, I think I hear it. Oh, no. Please don't be what I think it is.

"Well, aren't you gonna open it?"

I look up at Luke. He still grins with his eyes wide open with anticipation. I know he's excited, like a little boy, proud of himself. I open the box and see the smaller container inside that I expected. I am overwhelmed by what's coming and what I'll have to say. Slowly, I pull up the top of the ring box and see a lovely diamond solitaire. "It's beautiful!"

What else can I say? I don't want to hurt his feelings. He has bought me an expensive diamond on his army pay. I don't want to lose him. But I don't want to marry him. Not now. The very thought stifles me ... scares me to death.

"Here, let's see if it fits." Luke gets the ring out, pulls off my birthstone, and slides the diamond on my ring finger.

It fits like my skin. He leans over and kisses me tenderly. I am choked up so I can't speak.

Luke starts talking, rushing through this plan and that, and I'm not even listening.

I blurt out, "Luke, wait a minute ... I can't—"

He cuts me off immediately, "I know. I know you're not ready. I know you want to finish college. And I don't know where I'll be sent. But that's okay. We don't have to get married now. We'll leave that up to you. Whenever you say."

I hold up my hand and stare at my ring. Then I turn and look at Luke. I open my mouth to speak.

Luke interrupts, "Erin, honey, everything will work out." He pulls me over and kisses me, this time, passionately ... I'm rendered voiceless again.

Days after the news "Erin's Got a Diamond!" wears off in the dorm, I bury myself in studies, especially for English classes. Luke drives from Kentucky about once a month, and we spend the weekends at home. The rest of the weekends I suffer from the loneliness of a dorm on Saturday nights when everyone is gone with a guy or with other girls looking for guys. I feel old beyond my years. No fun riding the bus into the city alone. And where can you go—alone?

One weekend, however, the freshman dorms give a party with dancing and invite a busload of Davidson boys. My entire dorm seems to be going—girls, primping all afternoon and talking of nothing else. Suddenly I think what harm can it do if I go? I'm not married. I'm not even dating, it seems. When I voice my plans to attend, everyone agrees. Unfortunately, there are so many WC girls, they far outnumber the guys, and I have to admit at a girls' school, the girls are ferociously aggressive, each ready to grab a guy as soon as he steps off the bus.

I wait until the hullabaloo dies down and the crowd settles in the gym—couples dancing, girls everywhere partying. I slip in, stand by the door, and listen to the music. I feel a touch on my arm and look up at a tall, quite good-looking guy, who motions toward the dance floor.

Temporarily, I'm transferred to heaven. We dance and talk for the remaining time. When we walk to the refreshment table together, I notice nearly every girl's eye watching; at least I feel they do. Tad and I saunter over to a secluded spot, and he says something to make me laugh. I think of how much I enjoy his presence; he is attentive to me and seems smart judging by the comments he makes about his classes. I would love to date him, even if he were not so handsome.

Later, when he walks me back to my dorm, Tad says, "I hear you're engaged."

I catch my breath. He knows. So that's why—the evil eye, the frowns of girls at the refreshment table, the mean gossip of the ones who are alone.

"Yes, I am. I'm sorry—I didn't think it mattered for tonight. I would've told you. How did you know?"

"Oh, someone whispered it to me immediately— when we first walked to the dance floor. That's all right. I enjoyed tonight." He pauses. "But I'm sorry you're not free. I would've asked to see you again."

I want to shout, "Yes, I would love to see you again. I'm free tomorrow!"

A couple of girls walk by, and one of them nudges the other. Says just loud enough for us to hear. "Look over there. There're not enough boys to go around, she's engaged, and she gets the best guy in the bunch."

Tad must have heard her words. And the stranger is right. He *is* the best in the bunch. I feel like throwing my ring into the bushes. I'm just 18. Why should my life be so restricted? I could take off my ring and tell Luke no to the engagement the next time he's home. But I can't do that. Not with my sense of loyalty, my word, my sense of honor. Besides I would *never* hurt him.

At the steps of Paige Dorm I turn and say, "Tad, it was so nice meeting you. Thanks for all the dances. I had a good time."

He takes my hand. "So did I, Erin. Thank you for the night. G'bye."

"G'bye, Tad."

I live a scholar's life. I read and study and write for my first creative writing class. Actually, I embrace this routine, going inward, contemplating the discoveries I make about philosophy and religion in my literature classes. I am amazed that a narrative is so much more than a story; that it reflects the philosophical views of the narrator—and often the beliefs of the author. Brought up in a fundamental Baptist Church, I coin myself a rebel. I don't fit in with any group that brainwashes with the idea "Accept—don't question." My head is flooded with questions about the virgin birth, resurrection of the body, "being saved," predestination, reincarnation, the supernatural views of Wordsworth, and the Transcendentalism of Emerson and Thoreau. Now I am where I should be—in a place where I can seek answers and, most importantly, in an atmosphere conducive to studying and learning, whether in a classroom, in the library stacks, in my dorm room alone on Saturday nights, or in Peabody Park propped against a tree with book in hand gazing at the sky between treetops.

When Easter break is nearing, I can hardly wait to get home. I've become so homesick all I want is Mama to hug me and kiss me on the cheek. I want us to sit at the kitchen table, talk, drink hot tea, and eat that delicious spice cake Mama buys at the A&P. Exhausted from studying, writing papers, and anticipating final exams, I want just to sit on the porch close to Mama and feel April's breezes. See the North Star as bright as ever hanging over the long hedge bordering our yard.

When I do go home at Easter break, all the talk in town is about the upcoming pageant to crown the first Miss Oak Glen, who will represent the town in the Miss North Carolina Pageant. The merchants are sponsoring girls 18 to early 20s, and an official has called me.

Mama is excited. "Call him right now and accept. He needs to know as soon as possible.

"I don't know, Mama. What will I have to do?"

"The local pageant will be conducted like the state one. You'll appear on stage performing your talent—of course, playing the piano. You appear in a bathing suit, and then, finally, an evening dress. You can wear the one you wore in your senior recital."

"Mama, you know how I get stage fright. And in a bathing suit, wearing high heels? I'll get so nervous, I'll break my neck! And everybody staring at my breasts? No way."

"Erin Rose, I know you'll win. You always cover up your feelings and look calm and poised. Don't even think about being nervous. You've got it made. And your breasts— stick 'em out. Be proud of what you've got. I wish I had them. I've been flat-chested all my life."

"I'll think about it, Mama."

"Oh, I forgot to mention. The local winner receives lots of gifts from the merchants. Really nice gifts. And when you go to the state pageant, if you place high enough, you'll get money, scholarships, endorsements—"

"Mama, stop it! Don't get ahead of yourself. There's no way I'll place in the state. And I'm not sure of the local. I can't do things like this. I can't help it if I'm shy in front of audiences. The winner has to be a drama queen. It's all an act—a big put-on."

"You stop it! You have the potential to do whatever you want. Quit putting yourself down. You'll stay shy if you keep telling yourself you are."

"Well, I've never seen *you* as outgoing. Unless you're high on beer." I walk out and slam the door.

In the porch swing I try not to cry, but my throat grows a knot. I sniff to breathe. Why do we fuss so much? I feel so terrible when I yell at her. I know I shout from frustration.

In June 1954 I win the Miss Oak Glen Pageant. I enter the Miss North Carolina Pageant in late summer. Everyone I know is excited for me and pours on the compliments. Luke's mom and sister along with Mama are my biggest fans, cheering in the front row.

Luke himself never mentions it.

Chapter 17

On my wedding day I awake crying. I cannot control the tears or the sobbing. I feel the life I know is ending, leaving a great gap in the center of my being. I'm not prepared for the unknown that's ahead. My insides are shaking, my stomach is nauseous. It's like someone is forcing me on stage to play the piano without my having practiced the music. I'm still in bed too sick-in-heart to get up. "No-o-o." I pound at the pillow. My sobs rush Mama to the bedroom.

"Erin Rose, what is the matter? What in this world?"

"I can't. I can't, Mama!"

"You can't what? You can't get up? Why? What's wrong?"

I sling off the cover and stamp on the cold floor with my bare feet. I nearly push the chair over and start screaming, "I don't want to get married! I don't feel like I know him. Not really. And Luke doesn't know me at all." I start sobbing again, so hard I can't talk. My head bent down, I lean on the chair for support.

"Erin Rose, don't be ridiculous! You've dated him for three years!"

I'm sniff-sobbing, heaving for breath. "That doesn't … mat … ter. We're the same as … strangers. Why does he … want to … marry *me*?"

"*Why*? Erin, honey, he loves you."

Mama thinks my life's so simple. She doesn't have a clue. "I don't understand what that means, Mama. And we have no interests in common."

"Is that all? Erin, you've got yourself worked up over nothing. Fiddledy-dum! Haven't you heard people say 'Opposites attract'? Anyway, when you're married a while, you'll know how to work him—to get what you want. As they say, 'just play your cards right.' Finesse!"

She pats me on my arm. "You're a clever girl. You'll work it out. Now, come on, Erin, go wash your face. I'll fix you some breakfast."

I snap. "No ... no ... no!" I fall into bed again and pull up the cover to my nose, determined to stay in bed for the rest of the morning and longer if I feel like it.

"Erin Rose, what am I going to do with you? It's already ten o'clock. People will start going to church shortly after three. And you have to take your bath, put on your makeup, and fix your hair! We have to take your wedding dress to church early so you can be with your bridesmaids to dress. Mr. Bullock will be waiting to take photographs. Have you packed everything?"

"Please, Mama, please!" I shout. "Leave me alone!" I bury my head under my pillow. Here I'm begging to be left alone, and I'm already more alone than anyone else on the face of this earth. I ache for someone to listen to me. And understand.

Obviously, Mama is stunned. She has no idea what to do. I hear her pacing around the room, and I smell her cigarette smoke. I hear her deep breaths and sighs—I know the signs. She'll soon be crying that she's having a nervous breakdown. And I'm truly sorry I'm causing her distress. But I can't help myself.

Suddenly, Mama sits down on the edge of the bed, picks up the telephone, and starts dialing.

Alarmed, I sit up. "What are you doing, Mama?"

172

"I'm calling Agatha. She'll know what to do. What to say to you."

"No, Mama, don't do that. Don't tell Aunt Agatha about me." I try to reach the phone, but Mama stands up and turns toward the window. "No-oo-oo, Mama!"

"Hello, Agatha? You'll never believe this! ... Oh, no, we're all right ... I guess we are. But Erin is hysterical. She's screaming she's not getting married and sobbing like her heart is broken ... Yes. What can we do? I don't know what else to say to her. I can't get her out of bed. She's determined not to listen to me, and I'm lost for what to do. Everything is set. Her bridesmaids from Charlotte will be arriving ... okay, okay. I'll try to calm down ... I know, Agatha. I need to calm down to help her calm down, but I'm so nervous I can't stop shaking. Oh, I wish Jake were here. He'd know what to do." Mama sniffs, her voice breaks, and she's crying.

Still holding the phone, Mama sits on the bed again and listens attentively to her sister's words and intermittently interjects: "Oh, you think so? No ... I haven't talked about that. Do you think that's it? ... Well, we went to Dr. Harry to fit her for a diaphragm."

Oh, my God! They're talking about *sex*! And I hadn't even thought of that myself. Jesus! Just let me disappear. Their conversation has decidedly stopped my tears.

Mama continues to listen, nod her head, and mumble. "Yes, you're right. She'll need that ... uh hum ... but I can't get to the store now. I'm not dressed. And someone will be here soon for her suitcase ... You can get to the drugstore? Thank you, Agatha. Okay, I'll see you then. 'Bye."

"What was that about, Mama? What is she going to the drugstore for?"

"Erin, honey, when you're married, you need a syringe."

"Why?" I'm yelling again.

"Well, to cleanse yourself, honey. To douche."

173

"You mean to use that pink rubber thing hanging in the bathroom with a long tube? That *thing* you take enemas with? No way."

"Erin Rose, you use the little black device on the tube to take enemas, but you insert the larger, longer device into your ... uh ... other place to douche. But nowadays you can buy a syringe, much smaller, like a rubber ball you squeeze to squirt water into yourself."

I'm almost howling by now. "What else have you suddenly forgotten to tell me?"

Mama leaves the room, decidedly calmer now that she has Agatha to deal with her unreasonable daughter. It'll be at least an hour or so for Agatha to finish dressing, go to the drugstore, and drive from Hamlet.

Through the window beside the bed I see winter gray, the sky mirroring my spirit. Will the grayness go away? Or will it slip into an unfamiliar darkness? Is this a premonition of mine? Or perhaps it's this month of December that darkens my soul. The month that Daddy died. Why was my wedding planned two weeks before the anniversary of his death? Thoughts of Daddy run deep in late December. Mama just mentioned needing Daddy. She has no idea how many times I've ached to reach out to hold his warm, strong hand.

I remember those hands now. *Daddy stands chest-high in the dark sea water, his arms under my back as I float at ease, head back and bobbing, body uplifting in a cradle of cool ripples, a spray of sunrays above. He lowers his arms little by little, and his hands rise to touch. I love the feeling of being one with the ocean and the sky and his hands, drifting with clouds, unaware of time. I don't know how long it is before I'm aware of the absence of physical touch. Then I feel a flash of terror: the tumultuous fear of sinking into the dark sea water. I start jerking, splashing, fighting the water, and shouting "Daddy! Daddy!"*

174

In the next instant, Daddy calls out, "I'm right here, Baby! I'll never let you sink."

Sure enough, he's only a step away—standing as he was before, the water lapping against his chest, his black hair glistening. If I'd only, calmly, reached out, I could have touched his hand. Now I'm in his arms against his chest with my arms tightly hugging his neck, holding on for dear life.

He eases my arms down and bobs in the water with me. "Erin Rose, if you fear the water, you'll never be able to swim. Do you know that you were floating by yourself? Now trust yourself. You know you can float, so you have no reason to be afraid of the water."

"But, Daddy, what if I get afraid sometime when you're not there?"

"Then pretend I'm there. You know how to play make believe. Close your eyes. Take a deep breath. Then make believe my arms are holding you."

I rise and go into the familiar darkness I love. The darkness of the long hall of our old house. I walk on the old wood planks that creak, and I breathe in deeply the musty smell of the air here that ripples through me. My eyes rest on the tall chifforobe against the right wall that once held Daddy's clothes. I pull open the door and smell the cedar inside. But the space is empty. I wish his clothes were still here. I could run my fingers down a sleeve to reach for his hand.

I return to the bedroom and proceed to prepare for my wedding. Christmas colors will brighten the white church walls: magnolia leaves, ferns, red poinsettias, and red berry-budding holly. Candles will burn in gold candlesticks on the window sills, gold candelabras will flood the pulpit with flickering light, and the tall stained-glass window will brighten with Jesus and his lamb. My bridesmaids will be in crimson velvet, high crimson silk pumps, and crème poinsettias attached to matching velvet muffs and moss green velvet hats with short veils of gold mesh and velvet leaves.

And I will play make-believe.

In the afternoon at 3:00 Luke stands down front beside his best man, his brother Paul.

I'm standing away from the entrances, waiting for my bridesmaids to complete their slow rhythmic walk. Uncle Ben waits in the corner of the church vestibule to walk me down the aisle. Mama thinks he's perfect for the role of father of the bride, since he's my favorite aunt's husband.

I have time to look at Uncle Ben and drop my eyes before he sees me. What hypocrisy! Giving me away! Ugh!

He'd prefer taking me to the basement for himself when no one else is around and seeing how much pawing he can get in. How I despise that man—ever since I was a child visiting Aunt Agatha and sitting in the swing on their front porch. It was summer and I wore a sleeveless blouse with a low-cut neckline. I was about nine or ten with developing breasts. Uncle Bennie plopped down beside me in the swing; the first thing I knew was his big callous hand sliding over me down the neck of my blouse to pinch a nipple. Quickly I gasped and moved away. He started laughing like a horse neighing. I never said anything to anyone, for I didn't know what to do. I just avoided him. Through the years he'd rub up against me anytime he could trap me alone.

Now I have to touch his arm and walk down that long aisle. Someone motions for me, and Uncle Ben starts to loop my arm through his.

The organist strikes the first chord.

"Daddy?"

"I'm right here, Baby! Only a step away. Make believe my arms are holding you."

I slip my arm through Daddy's arm, and our fingers interlace. In my free hand I hold Daddy's childhood gift, my white Bible, now covered in white satin with a white orchid.

The organ peals forth Wagner's "Bridal Chorus" from *Lohengrin*. I glance at Daddy. He smiles at me and nods his head; I smile back and nod in agreement. We proceed down the aisle: Daddy, so handsome in the black tuxedo, and I, in the long bouffant gown of Chantilly lace over bridal satin, a veil hiding my face.

I float toward Luke and I wonder: after the "I do's," when he lifts my veil, will Luke really see the woman I am?

In the cold, dark December night we drive toward Washington, DC, where Luke wants to spend our honeymoon. Then we'll head home a few days for Christmas before we leave for Fort Campbell, Kentucky, where he's stationed. The university is closed for the holidays, freeing me for several more weeks. As we near the Virginia line, snow starts falling lightly on the banks along the highway.

I start wondering if I have the right clothes. Thank goodness, I threw a winter coat, which I don't wear much, into the car at the last minute. Of course, I have on my going-away outfit: a charcoal suit, a red pillbox hat with red pumps, and white gloves. And the white orchid pinned to my suit. I sit on my side of the car's bench seat as if it were a church pew—legs crossed, gloved hands in my lap, a lump in my throat. I want to slide over close to Luke to snuggle with his arm around me. But I stay paralyzed.

Soon Luke pulls off the highway and parks in front of a lighted motel. He goes inside to get a room, and my heart jumps to my throat, flips over, and falls into my stomach. I can think only that I don't want to go inside. I don't want to be here. I don't know what to do with myself. I wait for Luke to return. The wind has picked up, keening through the treetops a sorrowful sound, banging the Welcome sign back and forth. From the motel window, light shines on flurrying snowflakes that splotch the pavement. Elsewhere is pitch black save for distant car beams.

Luke hurries back with a big black umbrella to help me from the car to the lobby and then goes back for the luggage. In the room he asks where I want my bag.

"That's all right. I'll take it." I pick up my luggage and half drag it into the bathroom and lock the door.

And there I stand. In the middle of the bathroom. With my hat on, still in my white gloves. I find a glass to fill with water for my orchid and set it on the back of the commode, for lack of another place. I look in the mirror. Oh, my God. I've got a lot to peel off. I don't want to, but I can't sleep in wool—that's too scratchy. Slowly I peel off my gloves, one finger at a time—and put them up where they won't get dirty. I pull out the hatpin and take off the red hat and look for someplace to put it. Then my red pumps and my hose and then my wool jacket and my wool skirt—there isn't anywhere to put them!

"Erin," Luke calls, "aren't you about finished?"

"Just a minute."

Damn, I've hardly gotten started. I strip to my underwear and brush my teeth. It takes a while for me to decide if I want to wash my face. But if I do, I won't have any makeup on in the morning. Now what am I going to wear? I open my bag and ... damn, damn ... why did Mama stick the box with that rubber thing right on top in the middle of my gowns? Oh, Jeeze—the diaphragm is right beside it. What if I'd opened my bag in front of Luke? How embarrassing! Now where am I going to put these things? If I throw them away, Luke'll see them in the trashcan. I'll have to hide these underneath all the clothes and stuff.

"Erin!"

"Okay."

I start pulling out gowns. I pick up the first one—the white one. I throw it down. Ugh. I'm *not* going to wear that because Mama told me that virgins must wear white. And it's as thin as curtain sheers. No way. What *can* I wear? I shake my head—I have about every color. But they're all so transparent. I hold a blue gown up to myself and turn my head back and forth as I study it in the mirror. The ruffled top is okay, but no, it clings between my legs. No way. You can see the print of my hair there. I throw it down and hold up a pink. My God. I don't want to look sweet. Do I have anything else? I rummage some more in my bag ... *Was that the door?* Oh, here's something. A coral gown—not too light, yet not too dark. And the material is not flimsy. I put it on and turn all around to see what the light does, and suddenly I think about the time. I wonder how long I've been in the bathroom. I quickly place all the clothes into my luggage so we'll have room to walk.

I slowly unlock the door—don't want him to think I've locked it. I take a deep breath and walk out of the bathroom.

The table lamp emits a warm glow across the bedroom, and the wind wanes to a soft whisper. Luke? Where is Luke? I glance around the room. The bed is empty. The two chairs are empty. The room is empty. I go to the window and peek out between the slats where his car was parked earlier. It's gone. All I see is darkness and moving shadows of speckled trees.

Time crawls by. I keep sitting in the chair. I keep looking out the window. I start pacing up and down the room. The morning slides into my mind because I am pacing like Mama had in my bedroom when I refused to get up. I can feel her anxiety about getting me out of bed as strongly as I do mine—wanting Luke back in the room. Would he just leave me here? A sudden pinch of alarm prickles my body, and I start doubting. Can I trust Luke? Where has he gone?

179

Finally, I turn on the bathroom light and leave the door cracked enough for a night light. I turn off the lamp and slide into bed. I lie in bed, unable to sleep, brooding over the unreality of the day and grieving that I could be the only woman in the world who spent her wedding night without the groom and—let's not forget—with just plain fear.

Emotionally exhausted, I'm about to doze off when I hear the click of the door. Luke walks in.

"Hi!" he calls when he sees me lying in bed.

I'm so relieved. I can't be angry with him. I sit up among the pillows. "Where have you been?"

"Oh, I just drove to an all-night grill up the road a bit. Had a hamburger and some beer."

He looks at me and grins. "You're not going to head for the bathroom now, are you?"

Luke just shakes his head and laughs, starts unbuttoning his shirt, drops his pants, goes into the bathroom for a minute, and then cuts off the light.

Then I feel him sliding in bed. He reaches for me.

We return to Oak Glen and stay with Luke's family during Christmas. His mother and sister have started preparing the food. The decorations, the greenery and the bright lights are up. Marty has invited Mama over for a Christmas Eve party and for Christmas dinner; I appreciate how they include Mama, who'd otherwise be alone at home.

These holidays are my introduction to what a big family is like: children, spouses, in-laws, aunts, uncles, cousins, and maybe a friend who's alone. The amount of food his mother cooks amazes me. She's made everyone's favorite dessert: chocolate cake, fresh coconut cake, fruit cake with brandy poured on top, banana pudding, pound cake so moist it melts in your mouth with your choice of topping. And, of course, there's the Southern Country

Christmas Dinner: turkey, fresh oyster dressing, cranberry sauce, standing-rib roast, rice and giblet gravy, candied yams, buttered biscuits, cornbread, and vegetables from the garden—purple butter beans, field peas cooked in fatback, and homemade watermelon pickle. And from the grape arbor, homemade scuppernong wine. Eggnog.

When I ask Luke if his mom cooks like this very often, he replies, "Not really. Maybe on Sundays—but then she'll make just two or three desserts instead of five."

I lean over and whisper to Luke, "I don't know how to cook at all."

Luke assures me that he knows I must be able to cook something. "After all, you're a girl!"

I admit, "Does boiling eggs count? Oh, I can mix up pimento cheese for sandwiches."

He shakes his head and suggests that I do breakfast and lunch, and he'll cook supper.

Mid-afternoon on Christmas Day, Luke and I leave for a long drive through the Appalachian Mountains on our way to Fort Campbell, Kentucky, home of the 101st Airborne. In 1954 there is no mountain bypass or interstate highway, just a narrow road against a mountain cliff, slick like marble that juts out suddenly so it seems the road beyond disappears at a right angle that leads to another right angle. Luke easily swerves the '53 Chevy up and around the edge of the road, where the slope drops down below us. Looking up, I see the narrow road ahead, straight above us, and below is the road, like a step, where we've been. A giant roller-coaster with a preordained track.

As we climb, the mountain air gets colder, and patches of snow dot the countryside. Along the road snow banks the cliffs and marks the road. Between the ridges in the distance, pale light momentarily brightens, then fades quickly and darkness drops like a curtain to end the day. Soon the car heads down the winding mountain road. A cold moon shines on the packed snow in the valley and on the white edges of the road. We ride in silence, but I'm warm in the car snuggled next to Luke, my head on his shoulder. I must have dozed off, for in what seems like minutes Luke is waking me, saying, "Erin, we're coming into Clarksville, Tennessee."

We pull into the Welcome Center, visit the bathrooms, get a drink, and look in the backseat at the food his mother packed in a picnic basket. In the wee hours of the morning we sit beside the road eating turkey sandwiches and fruit cake. Then we head to nearby Fort Campbell. And I'm introduced to another world: the Airborne quarters for married enlisted men. That night we sleep on a doubled cot and walk down the hall to the bathroom.

"Luke, what if I'm going to the bathroom and run into a paratrooper?"

Luke just stares at me and grins. "Well, honey, you probably will! That's who's here. It's okay." He kisses me on the cheek. "Say 'Excuse me.' But if he grabs you and tries to hold you hostage, just yell. I'll come get you."

We go into Clarksville most nights to eat dinner and then, just to have something to do, stop at a bar. A beer for Luke, wine for me with a shot of Seven-Up—Luke's idea for me to drink. I soon learn that if I'm near the base or Clarksville, I'll find myself shoulder to shoulder, face to face with paratroopers. I'm getting used to their catcalls and whistles and even a few "Hubba-Hubbas." However, what gets my attention is that Luke stands out from all the rest—his posture, his rhythmic walk, the fit of his uniform, his salute, the blend of his sandy hair with khaki, his laugh, and the charisma he has with strangers. I'm awed by him. My heart beats faster whenever I look at him, and there is a weightlessness in my step. I feel a freedom.

Now at dawn I still sleep but sense the sudden space left by Luke when he rises. My back feels the lack of warmth as I turn over flat, my arm stretching out, touching the emptiness of cooler sheets. I roll over to hug the other pillow and smell Luke's scent, which I inhale deeply till I fall back asleep.

Later the sun slides through the blind across my face, and I awake smiling. I am so glad to be right here where I am. I lie in bed, remembering the morning of my wedding. I must have been stark crazy not wanting to marry Luke. I love being with him and sleeping with him. His laugh spreads all over his face. There is an openness about him that pulls me in, especially when the light captures his eyes; yet there remains a mystery about him. I still sense an unknown part of him. It's strange: I feel as if I've known him all my life, yet I don't know him at all. But I will, I promise myself.

On New Year's Eve we go to a party on base. Loud music, colorful streamers, funny little hats, noisemakers. Plenty of ice and setups on the tables. Beer galore. Twisted brown bags on the floor. Everyone seems to know everyone else—or the liquor makes them think they do. The DJ does a fine job with the music, and I love dancing with Luke.

Sitting at a long table with a crowd is another matter. Suddenly I feel alienated. The girlfriends, wives, dates act outrageously silly and giggly—high as the sky or drunk. But I'm cold sober. At times like this, I retreat into that shy, unresponsive self I loathe. I'd like to get up and walk away, but I can't. It's that same paralysis that sets in, and I'm unable to move. Therein is my frustration. My body is not in my control. How does this happen to me? What is it? Does it have a name? My insides experience a deep-seated fear.

Finally, Luke leans over and whispers, "Wanna go? C'mon." He pulls my chair from the table, slides his hand down to take mine, and calls out our good-byes. When we step outside, cold air strikes my face—the freshness stirs my senses. For sure, the temperature has dropped below twenty degrees, yet I'm warm inside. Luke holds my hand as we stroll across the parking lot. Total darkness wraps around us like a cloak, but the clear sky has spit out tiny sparkling diamonds that fall into familiar patterns, the same constellations Daddy showed me: the Big Dipper, the Milky Way, Orion, the Bear. Spontaneously I find myself pointing them out, calling them by name. Luke's warm hand and the brilliant stars lift me to the top of the world, the light slicing the darkness.

Luke opens the car door for me and I slip across an icy seat. He gets in, turns on the heat and radio at the same time, and hugs me, rubbing me down all over to get my blood flowing. From the radio pours mellow music: Nat King Cole, Frank Sinatra, Perry Como. There's a pause. Then out peals "Auld Lang Syne." Luke lifts my face, slides his hands into my hair, looks into my eyes, and says, "I love you." He leans down and kisses me.

Chapter 18

January finds me back at the university—a married woman. Not that it matters, except to change my last name to McLeod, a Scottish one, instead of the Irish O'Donovan. However, when you think of it that way, it is quite a difference, and I don't like the idea of changing my own identity.

I will miss Luke—no question about that. Yet I look forward to my new classes and the focus in literature on someone else's behavior besides Luke's and mine. I relish the thought of studying instead of waiting for Luke to travel from Fort Campbell to Greensboro to see me.

Now that I'm a second-semester sophomore, A's in English and sterling recommendations have cleared my way for advanced classes. I've been granted a "sacred" seat in poet Randall Jarrell's Advanced Creative Writing class that meets once a week in a three-hour workshop for "the best of the best," mostly seniors. A much-admired poet and literary critic, Jarrell, however, is reputed to be a terror, and I am in awe of my situation—excited and too nervous for words.

I've been waiting for this chance since the first day I arrived at the university. As a freshman, I walked with my roommate toward the academic building to check on room numbers so we could find our way to class the next day. Passing the coffeehouse, we noticed a 100 or so girls milling around staring, and someone shouted, "Who is that?" No one knew. After all, we were all newly arrived. There he went, driving a bright red MG with the top down, speeding onto the campus drive, zooming past the library, and streaking around the curve that led to the faculty parking lot like a cat with its tail on fire. In a flash I saw his black mustache, a heavy but rather short beard, and a black derby. His facial hair labeled him a non-conformist in this clean-shaven '50s. Later, I discovered our Romantic Stranger's identity: the acclaimed poet Randall Jarrell.

Now I see Jarrell everywhere. He plays tennis on the court in front of Paige, our dorm, in his little short white pants. He strolls in the halls, a dashing figure in a tweed jacket with suede elbow patches, so smoothly professional. Jarrell never looks in anyone's direction, walks staring straight ahead as if the rest of the world is invisible, or he's too far above to see it below him. Then again, perhaps he's penetrating the veil of reality to contemplate that stuff from which dreams and poems are made. Aloofness makes him a man of mystery.

Inside, the narrow back stairs lead up to the classrooms in Aycock, the oldest building on campus. I always climb these steep, squeaky stairs very slowly, focusing on each step, darkened and sunken like big black dimples in the middle, and slip in the back of the room and sit in a corner seat nearest the door. Usually Diana—a sophomore, too—accompanies me; or she sits in the other corner seat, saving me a place; or she comes in shortly afterwards. We support each other, often sliding down behind the seniors. The tall windows reach nearly to the ceiling and let in shafts of afternoon light that fall across the room. There we wait as unobtrusively as we can in the shadows for our professor-performer.

Jarrell walks briskly into the room a few minutes late as if he is a performer going on stage for a one-man show. He always carries a book and a folder of papers that he drops on his desk. We all wait stiff with mixed emotions: eager anticipation for the stage-performer to "get the show on the road" and heavy dread that today he'll pull out our papers to read and strip bare. Until the show begins, no one breathes a sound. In the room the tension is taut enough to snap. Jarrell calls the roll but never looks up, so anyone can answer for an absent friend, and he won't know the difference or care. He never bothers to know anyone's name anyway. When he reaches for the book instead of papers, there are silent sighs across the room. We are delighted, no paper-stripping today, for we have three hours of cultural entertainment before us.

Jarrell reads poetry in a voice that makes us see images vividly; the implied meanings and emotions fall from the undulating cadences of his voice. Then he pauses and calls our attention to a phrase, a word. He has a way of holding his hands out and gesturing with his fingers, his forefinger and thumb almost together when he points out an image in a passage he has just read.

In T.S. Eliot's monologue "The Love Song of J. Alfred Prufrock," a gentleman goes to an afternoon tea to declare his love to a lady. Jarrell tells us Prufrock, the gentleman, presents himself as shy, self-conscious, and inhibited, yet he passionately wants to act on his desires. The beginning reference ("Let us go then, you and I") suggests the incongruous parts of his character: one part wanting to declare his love, the other unwilling. Rationalizing he has time, he procrastinates. Yet at the same time he recognizes the truth about himself: he is trapped by his past behavior— always thinking, questioning, never deciding or performing or expressing himself. He will never declare his love. At this climactic insight, in despair Prufrock responds by wishing he were subhuman: "I should have been a pair of ragged claws / scuttling across the floors of silent seas." Here Jarrell holds up his fingers, demonstrating this image, and says, "This crab will grab for whatever it wants, unlike the troubled Prufrock, who just frets over inhibitions, paralyzed, unable to act. See how Eliot's crab image is central to the theme?"

Like Prufrock, I, too, have deep feelings left unexpressed. I think of the beginning lines when he identifies with the image of a sunset spread across the horizon "like a patient etherized upon a table." I, too, watch my own inertia: the passivity that postpones, waits, then fails to speak, to act. How often I'm reluctant to answer a question in class, to state my opinion to others, to tell Mama "I'm sorry" for so many things, to whisper to Luke "I love you," and just to walk over to a stranger and speak. I understand Prufrock's feeling of futility when he admits, "I have measured out my life with coffee spoons" instead of engaging in meaningful relationships, because he quietly floats around social gatherings of meaningless chit-chat. At college I've "measured out my life" with books and writing instead of close connections.

I take the poem back to my room and reread it again. Often when the 11:00 night signal sounds "Lights Out" and room check is over, I slip into my closet with a flashlight to continue reading or completing homework, a figure of me made of pillows under the cover of my bed. Occasionally, my roommate does the same in her closet, both of us leaving our hideouts about the same time to snack before going to bed.

Jarrell has a tremendous influence on my life. He's the first person to open my mind to see facets I've never imagined on a printed page. He fine-tunes my understanding of all the literary tricks of the trade. He pulls all the parts of a poem together holistically: an image uncovers the theme. His voice, along with his theatrics, saves me from drowning in reading just words without thought.

After weeks of Eliot, Jarrell chooses Hemingway's short story "A Clean, Well-Lighted Place." I'd read the story but had no clue what it is about. Jarrell starts talking about

Hemingway and suddenly I get a flash of understanding: *Meaning comes from its integrated parts.* Now without prompting I see the whole story. I perceive how the light and dark imagery, along with understatement, gives the story unity and meaning. Outside it is dark and late. Inside a small, well-lighted café there is a bar with only one customer, an old deaf man who's quietly getting drunk and doesn't want to leave. There are two waiters: one old, one young. The young waiter, eager to go home, closes the shutters, wipes the table, and tells the old man to pay up: the café's closed.

The older, kinder waiter does not want to lock-up even though it's two in the morning. He says, "I am of those who like to stay late at the café.... With those who do not want to go to bed. With all those who need a light for the night."

The older waiter starts wondering what he fears because life to him is nothing, just as man and God are nothing, so he has nothing to fear. All he needs is *light.* Fearless, he goes home to an empty room. However, he cannot go to sleep because it is night, the room is dark, and he is afraid to sleep in the dark: "He would lie in the bed and finally, with daylight, he would go to sleep."

What is *unsaid* is what is most important—this I realize about Hemingway's writing. Is this true for all of us? Do we omit words we truly feel? And so each one of us remains an enigma? The old waiter's statements are contradictory: he thinks life is nothing, yet he craves *light.* He does fear darkness because it's like death. But after he declares life is nothing, he experiences an epiphany: "light was all it [life] needed and a certain cleanness and order." The title signifies what is there and at the same time what is missing. The café has light inside, but the old man and the old waiter, without hope or faith, lack light inside themselves.

I can feel the old man's alienation and imagine how it's magnified by his deafness. I understand how he escapes both loneliness and darkness daily by drinking brandy in a well-lighted room; the older waiter escapes by working late with others into the night; I escape by obsessively reading books, often into the early morning. I know darkness—the literal darkness of night in my yard when tall trees block the sky of moon and stars—and I fear the unknown. Still in my room at night when no moon angles through the window, I require a nightlight. And as a child in the blackness of a shut funeral home's garage, I saw death hanging on the wall: a corpse in a cabinet, a black hearse waiting. I know the old waiter's horror at the thought of facing death if he falls asleep in the dark; I've feared falling asleep and facing a recurring nightmare, forcing my eyes open till dawn. The fear is the same. The fear of not knowing. The terror of Hemingway's nothing and the great need of inner light.

Thanks to Jarrell I can understand myself by reading, how easily I detect writing techniques, and how I can relate meanings of one story to another story or to a poem or to my life. A particular statement remains with me. Jarrell said, "See how the words 'the bare light bulb hanging from the ceiling creates a yellowish tint around the room' can create a dispirited mood." And I see our kitchen at home: the hanging dim light bulb, naked without a shade and the once-white walls now a dingy, cream-looking yellow under low light.

In Peabody Park near campus, I write in the afternoons under a large maple tree where I can look out at the grass and trees and sky and ponder with no one else around. Or I can lean back on the bark and read, then pause, wonder, and start my own stream of thoughts. Soon an hour flows into hours, a thought into thoughts, whether I'm sitting on golden leaves in the sun or resting on a hard cold ground snuggled in a thick wool sweater. But writing for class is hard for me, especially when I am bound by my own need for perfection and also by Jarrell's high expectations. I turned in my short story over a month ago and feel more anxiety over it as time passes. Will Jarrell like my work? I want him to exclaim to me his rarely stated signature line: "That's a fine piece of work!" At least this solitary spot on late afternoons in the park helps me create a somber mood and natural voice.

It's time for another three-hour creative writing class. The kind that makes my heart pound faster than I can count. I'm running out of time; sooner more than later my paper will turn up. Today in the deep silence of the room, Jarrell pulls out my short story from his stack. I nearly stop breathing. I feel as though God himself sprawls on his throne, legs propped up, pipe hanging out of his pocket, and divine hands lifting up my soul in supplication, deep voice droning my title, "Gertie at the River." There he goes ... with his melodrama. It starts with the title—"Gertie" (with a sneer)? He nearly chokes on my two Shakespearean allusions to Caliban and Miranda that he finds so funny. Here I've waited and waited weeks and weeks for feedback and dreaded as badly as death his one-man show cutting my work to shreds before the class. "Now listen to this!" he says to the class again in his choking laugh. And I listen to the rest of my work read in the wrong melodramatic tone. Jarrell exaggerates parts with theatrical gestures and facial expressions that indicate he's making fun of me, and a few student "intellectuals" think they have to laugh with him. I am humiliated.

Glancing around the room, I see at least half or more of the girls not laughing. Suddenly I feel a strong bond of empathy, unspoken, as thick as the previous pre-class tension. Nevertheless, by the time Jarrell finishes my story,

I feel so low I hardly hear what he says. I am crushed. He has left inside of me nothing but silence. *My voice lost.*

It is weeks, perhaps months, before I can write again. I don't want to write anything flawed—and it *will* be in his eyes. If only he had shown me what is weak, I could have rewritten the story or composed something new. I swear to myself that never again will I let someone take my thoughts and my emotions, twist them into tight balls, and say, "This is terrible."

Jarrell never marks papers or makes suggestions or grades any work, so at the end of the semester we each go to his office for a single conference. He pulls out my folder, looks inside, obviously for the first time, then looks up surprised. "You've done only one writing!" I just nod and sit like a zombie. "Well," he says and hesitates a moment, "if that's all, I'll have to give you a B." I don't reply, just nod, and leave.

My illusions crushed, I seek my place of solace—in the shade of my tree in Peabody Park. Here I look at the grass and trees and sky and clouds drifting at leisure, molding, reshaping monsters and ghosts, sea crests and billowing sails. Yet inside my voice is silent.

"I thought I'd find you here," Diana says as she plops down beside me. "Did you see Jarrell?"

"Yes. I got a B. That's a relief. I feared I'd flunked. With only that one written disaster!"

"Erin, do you really understand what he said to you that day?"

"I've seen enough and heard more than I ever want to, Diana." I am not too far from crying. "My feelings are hurt. I've never been laughed at. And I've never made below an A in English."

"Erin, you wouldn't listen to me after that class. Jarrell said, 'This is some of the best writing I've seen! But it has some of the worst with it.' Just remember the first half of his statement! You're only a sophomore, Erin, and fifty percent is the *best* of any he's read. That's great!"

Tears run down my cheeks. Not for the paper or the semester grade, but because I have a friend who cares. Words tumble out through a parched throat. "Thanks, Diana. I'll try to remember that."

I take breaths of fresh air, and a bit of calmness seeps through my pores like a fine drizzle. Inside my voice is strong. No one else needs to hear it.

But I know me. I'll keep inside, probably forever, the second part of his statement that kept him from saying, "That's a fine piece of work!"

Chapter 19

Finally, spring semester ends. And soon I'll be taking my first plane trip to Fort Campbell, Kentucky, home of the 101st Airborne and Luke. There I'll stay for three months until September when the fall semester at the university starts again.

First, I take my things to Oak Glen, visit a few days with Mama, repack summer clothes in my biggest piece of luggage, stack novels of Jane Austen, the Brontës, Thomas Hardy, Henry James, Victor Hugo, and at the last minute squeeze in my new *Better Homes and Gardens Cookbook*, my roommate's wedding gift. I figure anyone can cook. Just read a recipe and follow instructions. Mama thinks I've lost my mind taking so many books with me that I can't even pick up my bag. I've assured her that there's bound to be some kind of airline employee to pick up my bag from the car to check it on the plane and that Luke will carry it later. But I do have to figure out about my dishes.

"What dishes?" Mama asks.

"The ones I'm taking, Mama, my fine china and crystal! What did you think? And, of course, my sterling!"

Mama really thinks I'm crazy now. She just can't understand why I need all my "good stuff" in a one-room apartment Luke has rented right behind a filling station on the highway near the base. He says there's nothing but fields around, and I'll be able to see the paratroopers jump early in the mornings. (Doesn't he know how late I sleep when there's no class?) Anyway, if I have to cook, what's wrong with putting a linen tablecloth and two candles in crystal holders on a small table in the kitchen along with Royal Doulton china and Old Master sterling at two place settings? Maybe I can find some wildflowers in the field, out where the paratroopers jump.

"Oh, Mama, I'll get some sturdy boxes at the A&P and tissue paper from Roses, and we can pack the dishes and let the airline take care of it. Luke's dad is driving me to the airport in Charlotte, and he'll pay for everything. No problem."

Well, I get my way. All my "goodies" are airborne with me, and I'm dressed to kill. In the '50s travelling women dress up in high heels, a hat, white gloves that touch the wrist, and, of course, a "churchy" dress—in my case, over a crinoline to make my skirt puff out. (When I sit, it goes up!) I hope the plane seats are large enough to accommodate "the puff"; I'd hate to make the stranger next to me miserable. My picture hat, though, *is* a little much, but it perfectly matches my outfit. Oh, my. If my seatmate is a soldier, he'll just have to sit at attention.

Do I need to say that our tiny apartment can barely hold my things? One narrow closet has almost enough space for one crinoline. However, in the corner a ladder-back chair leans in a foot of space where Luke keeps his pants. The double bed takes up all the room: it is the central and *most* significant piece of furniture. We spend all our time there unless we're bathing or eating. It serves as sofa and chair. My side is against the wall, so I have to crawl across the bed to slide into the sheets. The knotty-pine paneling makes the room so dark we have to leave the light on during the day.

I soon learn that *Army* time is not *my* time. Luke is up at 4:00, gets in about 5:00 in the afternoon—hot, exhausted, starving. He heads for the shower, eats, falls asleep, wakes up to polish his boots for 30 minutes, then gets ready for bed for the night, and is asleep by 9:00. (Of course, "quickie" sex slips in there somewhere.) And I return to my romantic hunchback of Notre Dame and Luke is snoring. Thank God for my cache of books.

Unseen strangers live in the four other units that are attached to our apartment; in front the lone filling station, where cars never stop, waits. I keep heavy drapes pulled across our front window, leaving the little window in the kitchen as our only source of natural light. Its thin white ruffles catch the radiance of the sunrise. And for a while I feel the brightness and savor the warmth of our place.

Every morning I wash fatigues, socks, and underwear in the small kitchen sink and hang them up to dry on a clothesline behind the building. Who do I know who has washed a fatigue? I had no idea how thick the material is. Bringing in a fatigue from the sun is like carrying a body into the kitchen to place on a tiny enamel table to iron. But no matter what time it is, I see planes spilling parachutes into the sky, dotting it with hanging stick figures. I think of hundreds of eagles with wings spread, sliding across the sky in slow motion. What a thrill that must be—suspended in space, bobbing in the wind, gliding. Free.

There's not much for me to do outside. Except for the small parking lot out front behind the filling station, I have nowhere to walk. In the back there's only the clothesline, fatigues hanging like ghosts over dried earth, weeds, dust. But there's the sun powering over all. I take a couple of towels out back to lie in the sun or sit back against the brick building, to read a book and occasionally look up to watch the plane drops. The field of dry grass spreads out as far as I can see. I love the sun! I love to feel the hot rays penetrate my body and sizzle down my arms and legs, heat spreading inch by inch until I blend with the sun. I'm used to hot and humid Carolina summers, but also to the large trees there that give shade like giant umbrellas. Here in Kentucky in the middle of a treeless field, I may as well be in a desert, except for the human fliers who drop and disappear like straw in the wind.

The day will soon fade. Slowly a dimness will creep into the silent bedroom. After I finish reading Henry James' *The Turn of the Screw*, I lay down the book and search the room with my eyes, expecting perhaps to see a ghost or some other lost spirit. My imagination is fierce. I check the front door to test the lock and bolt. I stare at the drawn curtain as I usually do and wonder what I might see if I opened it. Suddenly I have visions of a tall, thin man with shaggy black hair in a long black cape, peeping in some invisible hole at the edge of the window where the drape doesn't quite touch ... and then looking up at me with a ghoulish grin.

I pick up Victor Hugo's *The Hunchback of Notre Dame* and read again about the strong, brave, crippled Quasimodo trying to protect the beautiful gypsy girl Esmeralda. What would I do without my books as an Escape Map? With them I can fly far above the world to my own little airy dimension and stay until I want to drop back to earth.

Every day Luke drives our only car to the base, leaving me stranded. I do not communicate with the outside world. We have no radio, no record player. We do have an old black phone with a circular dial, and I call Mama every week and lie about having a wonderful time because I don't want to worry her. And I know my mama! If she thinks I'm not happy *all* the time, she'll call Luke and threaten him ... and maybe call the highest ranking general on post. She'd make it worse without intending to, like the time in high school she went out looking for my date when I was five minutes past curfew.

So I describe our weekends spent dressing up and going out to nice places to eat and dance, sometimes to live music. Taking long walks in the park holding hands. Going to the movies and walking down the street with soldiers along the way whistling at me. (Mama loves that.) The fun I have listening to Luke and his buddies exchange stories in a bar and flirting on the side when Luke's not looking. (Mama loves that, too.) I talk about the books I'm reading to prepare for English classes in the fall. On the phone I leave Mama happy.

Then I call Luke's mother, sometimes twice a week, to find out how to cook one of his favorite meals, like pot roast or country-fried steak. Marty likes explaining to me how to cook. I record her steps and actually try to follow them, because I know she'll quiz me about success (or failure) next time. And she loves to hear about my first meal when I threw out the frying pan with the steak Luke bought the night before, because I spot a speck of green on a T-bone, which I took for mold. Of course, the speck could have come from the green hand-printed label on the package. Or from my new steak knife that hasn't been washed. Or from that rusted old pan stored in the apartment with lord-knows-what burnt into the metal. Though a steak may not smell, I'm not going to take a chance on green.

That brings on Luke's first flare-up. Marty knows his temper, like his dad's. He strolls in, famished, as usual. And he sees the fine china plates, the real crystal goblets, the decanter of iced tea, the gleaming silverware—all on an Irish linen tablecloth with a lit blue candle to match the plates.

"Wow! Look at you!" Luke gives me a big hug and a kiss. "What ya got cookin'? I'm starved."

Then he notices no activity on the stove. His eyes fall on a plate of sandwiches, cut in triangles with edges trimmed. A closer look: peanut butter and jelly.

"Where's dinner?"

"Oh, I've made sandwiches and iced tea. I know how you like peanut butter and jelly. I've used that really good grape jam."

"Where's the steak?"

"Oh, I threw it away. Something was wrong with it."

"What?" Luke raises his voice at me for the very first time. It's close to a shout. "You threw out my steak? Nothing was wrong with that meat!"

I snap back. "It was green!"

"Green? What're you talking about?"

"Well, I'm going to sit down by candlelight and eat." I speak in that woe-is-me-how-dare-you-speak-to-me-in-that-way voice. I pick up the plate of sandwiches and put them on the table. I sit down and pout. Take a bite of sandwich. Silence. Then, "I've really worked hard trying to prepare dinner. I've even had to go into that dirty old filling station to get a match to light the candle. I'm not going in there anymore. Not my fault if the dern meat you got was green!"

By that time, Luke is laughing so hard I want to hit him.

"Am I *clean* enough, Your Majesty, to sit here and have a flute of tea?"

I look up. Correct him. "A goblet."

I remember then how Luke's mother laughed over the phone at my story, and I can imagine how his dad mumble-giggled in the background. Marty also loves to hear how I wash and iron Luke's shirts—she finds that so endearing. And she's so glad he goes to bed early to get a good night's sleep. These phone calls make me feel warm and less isolated. After tallying up events, I realize that life here is not so bad—as long as I have Luke.

And I do have time to read. My daily companions are the characters in my books. It's amazing how these printed pals sometimes voice my own thoughts. When I stop reading, my book pals leave and I'm left alone. My own voice becomes my best friend. I have one of those double names, typically Southern: *Erin Rose*. I think of myself as Erin, my authentic voice. But I detect Rose's presence. Rose is still me, but another part—stronger, less confused, and more mature. It's like talking to yourself, but not out loud. A child would explain Rose's presence as an imaginary playmate. We converse telepathically. Same thoughts, same feelings, yet at times one deviates slightly from the other. Erin is a dreamer; Rose, a realist.

Such as the night I dream of Luke's hand—broad across the palm, well-proportioned, handsome. The vision is as clear as a close-up photo, a hand suggesting warmth and strength. Awakening, I'm puzzled. Why did I dream of his hand? Then I think of how much I love to hold Luke's hand. Can hardly restrain myself from touching it. Moments later, dream forgotten, a voice bursts in my head. "That's Daddy's hand," Rose says. The big light bulb pops on: Luke's hand looks just like Daddy's. The warmth I reached out for after Daddy's death is there.

I seek Rose for understanding and guidance. When I can't sense her, I am lost, feeling like a hostage of Anxiety. When Rose returns, I am at peace; we speak with one voice, and I am whole.

One Saturday Luke's unit buddy Tony invites us over to his apartment where he and his wife live, three doors down. Luke says Tony has a collection of jazz records that he thinks I'll enjoy hearing. Tony and his wife are about our age, went to college, and have been married about a year.

Tony opens the door with a "Hi, there, Lucas," with a loud, welcoming voice and a slap on Luke's back.

"And who have we here?" He greets me with a big smile. Tony is definitely not Southern—maybe a New York accent.

"Hi. This is my wife, Erin. And, Erin, Tony."

"C'mon in." Tony leads us into an apartment identical to ours and calls, "Vic, come meet Luke and Erin."

From the kitchen area comes a very attractive woman, in all white, blouse and slacks, with a wide gold choker, her dark hair pulled back in a French knot.

"Well, hello," she chimes. She's carrying two wine glasses and offers me one while we're being introduced. "I'm so glad to meet you, Erin," Victoria exclaims. "Oh, to have someone to socialize with in this despicable place!"

Tony interrupts, "Vic, well, where are *our* drinks?"

"You know where the beer is, Tony." Victoria takes a sip of wine and turns to me. "Erin, couldn't you have just clobbered Luke to death when he had the audacity to bring you to this dump?"

"It is ... uh ..."

"Heaven forbid," Victoria continues, "that was the most brazen act Tony ever did and got away with it. But what could I do? I left my good clothes in New York. I wasn't about to bring them here. I've complained so much that Tony says if I don't shut up, he's going to take my picture here behind the service station and send it to all my sorority sisters!" An odd-sounding laugh erupts from her mouth, like a continuous loud stutter with a hiccup.

The guys, beers in hand, leave the kitchen table and stroll into the bedroom area, where Victoria and I are sitting in plain straight chairs. Luke sits in the third chair, and Tony plops on the bed.

After a few minutes Tony looks over at me. "Where did you get those shoes?" He stares up and down my legs, finally at my feet.

I've just given myself a pedicure and polished my toenails to match my slacks. I'm wearing nice, fashionable sandals, but nothing special for a man to comment on. Surprised at his question, I respond, "Oh, I bought these back home."

"Oh, those must be the shoes Luke bought you. When he picked you up, walking barefoot ... down a tobacco road." Tony laughs and dips his head sideways with eyebrows up as if he's revealed a carefully kept secret.

I feel a red flush, like a fireball rolling down a wire after thunder.

Tony continues, with an unpleasant smirk, "He taught you how to wear shoes, didn't he?"

I just stare, not moving a muscle. Everyone else starts laughing, Luke the most. He always goes with the crowd, doesn't he? Why doesn't he take up for me for just one time?

I glance at Tony, and my inner Rebel surfaces. "You damn Yankee. Drop dead," I feel but don't say. I know, though, he's heard me silently, loud and clear, and seen my cold, piercing glare and tightly closed lips.

"Oh, Erin." Victoria flips her hand at Tony as though she's brushed him away. "Ignore the fool. He *is* one when he's drinking." She turns to Tony. "Let's have some music!"

He brings out his expensive collectible jazz records and begins his endless "know-it-all" discourse about jazz musicians, until Victoria breaks in about the New York apartment they just bought.

"Do you have any idea of the outrageous price of wall-to-wall carpet? Well, Daddy bought it for us. Then we chose the designer furniture. You wouldn't believe how much we've gotten! And then we've had to store it. Just listen to this!" Victoria itemizes each piece.

The evening drags to an end.

As we leave, a heaviness pulls at me. Everywhere I go I feel lonely. Luke isn't bothered, but then he's a knight on a white horse who saved a small-town Southern gal.

Summer is ending. What will it be like to find myself alone again in a single bed? No longer sleeping in the curve of his body, my back against his chest, his arm over my waist, his leg thrown over mine. I've gotten so used to our love-making every night, every day—even his reaching for me in the middle of the night. I take in all his smell. Luke is always so clean; even his sweat blends in with the scent of soap, shaving lotion, and the faint intoxicating smell of musk that I breathe in deeply, the full scent arousing my whole body. When I awake in the morning, I roll over to smell his empty pillow and drift back to the sensations of the night and relive each move, each breath, each whisper. I arise from bed and carry the feel of the full length of him.

Somehow I'll have to focus on my classes, a full load of literature and advanced psychology. Luke anticipates being sent overseas in the fall to either Korea or Germany.

On weekends I can spend time with Mama in Oak Glen.

Chapter 20

On weekends when Luke remains at Fort Campbell, I return home. Mama and I have long talks on the front porch, rocking in the rocking chairs or gently swaying in the side-porch swing. Sometimes I can't make sense of Mama's thoughts but I try to understand. She worries about me all the time. Even when there's no reason, she creates one.

She told me that she had feared something mentally or emotionally was wrong with me, because I hadn't begun talking yet at two years old. She took me to the family doctor for an exam and diagnosis. "She's not stupid," Mama told the doctor. "I know she understands me. She just looks at me with those big blue eyes and smiles and does what I ask, but she doesn't talk. She hasn't even said 'Mama' yet."

The doctor looked at me, hiding behind Mama, hanging on to her dress, peeping out from behind, and looking straight into his eyes. He laughed and shook his head. "Leah, there's nothing wrong with your daughter. She may be a little shy. Don't worry about it. She'll talk when she wants to. She's a girl, isn't she? So when she starts talking, she isn't going to shut up." Soon after that visit, I started talking in paragraphs.

Memories echo, recreating such vivid scenes that I relive them. A déjà vu of forgotten pain: I always want Mama near, close enough to run to and touch, or run behind to hold on to. I am very young, and we are visiting Aunt Agatha in her home in Hamlet. It is early night but dark, and I am outside and see Mama get into a car with someone. In the darkness two bright red lights beam a spot on the sandy ground and move slightly, then accelerate down the narrow country road.

In desperation I cry out—no one hears me; I run—no one sees me; I rush into thicker darkness toward the dimming red lights on the curvy road—no one notices my bare feet bruised from gravel and sharper bits of stone.

The car is gone.

I am alone.

The feeling of abandonment and of being lost in the blackest night is nightmarish. Fright keeps me running after her until I reach the highway. I slip, fall down the embankment, and land in a hole, my leg jammed against a jagged drainage pipe.

The curtain closes. I have no recollection. Then I see lights in the kitchen. Aunt Agatha is holding me, propped on the kitchen counter with water running over my leg. She holds the skin tight, and blood runs down the drain. I am screaming. My leg is on fire. She pours a bottle of liquid over the long cut, and I scream louder. Someone else is with her, and they roll gauze over and over my leg—so tight. The curtain closes again and stays shut.

The next morning our family doctor checks my leg and bandages it even tighter. He says, "Your aunt was wise to pour hydrogen peroxide into the deep cut." There is nothing more he could do. The four-inch scar grew with me, very noticeable. Mama exclaims from time to time, "Erin Rose, you could have cut your leg off on that broken pipe! Don't ever run near the end of a ditch!" No, I never do. But I dream of running in darkness after red shining lights fading out. Yes, Mama, I know how it is to be in a black hole—hurting, longing, clutching.

As we sit there I think back to childhood at a time when I try to make sense of our neighbors' actions. That is near impossible in my neighborhood. Since I'm often outside, I usually see the milkman when he comes. I know his red pickup truck. He drives up to the back steps, and Mama walks out on the porch smiling. Her fun-loving look I don't see much. I run to the steps, just to watch what's going on. Holding a big jug of milk, he walks to the porch, and they talk for a long time. About what, I don't know. The jug is filled with special homemade buttermilk that he knows she likes. He is a red-faced, bulky man, somewhat tall, but not as nice-looking as Daddy. Speaking too low for me to catch his words, he makes Mama laugh. Then Mama acts silly. Hanging onto the porch column, she moves in a sort of swinging motion and giggles, lifting her brows into that Joan Crawford arch. A little voice inside my head is saying *Daddy wouldn't like this milkman hanging around.* Later, on every beach trip when Daddy drives by the dairy farm as we approach Springdale, Mama exclaims, "Oh, there's Fred's home!" I would recognize the red pickup parked next to a small, plain brick house.

I try to understand another day about Mama. I can hear the church chimes through open windows of that Sunday morning Daddy and I wait for her. I am so excited because she's never before gone with us to church. It's like waking up on Christmas morning and finding a gift that you've never expected. Daddy pulls out his pocket watch to check how much longer it'll be before he witnesses his monetary bribe: she'll go to church if he'll take her to Charlotte to buy a new outfit. Stepping on my toes, I try to see myself in the old mirror in my new clothes, wanting to look pretty like Mama. Like a magnet, the mirror pulls Mama up behind me, and I watch her adjust her new wide-brimmed hat that dips down slightly in front.

Dressed in white, Mama looks so beautiful. Her white linen suit has large fashionable shoulder pads and big black buttons, and it fits her so that her waist appears very small. Her coat has a round collar low enough to show the double strand of pearls. A narrow black ribbon wraps around the crown of her white hat. I love her hat. It's like Scarlett O'Hara's.

Mirror, mirror on the wall, who's the fairest ... suddenly, my singsong chant stops.

Mama jerks off the hat and flings it down the hall; it lands near the front door. She starts raging. "I hate that damn hat! I'm not going to wear it."

Daddy steps forward but, before he can say anything, Mama shouts, "I'm not going anywhere looking like this! That damn hat will rot before I put it on again. And look how tacky these shoulder pads bulge out on me!"

Daddy sighs. "Leah, you look fine."

It's like Daddy's thrown oil on the fire. His choice of words hits a nerve. From him she wants more than "fine." Mama turns around and nearly springs on him like a cat. He dodges her, grabs her hands, and holds them until she simmers down.

What makes me so afraid?

Now as we rock back and forth she speaks to me as an adult, telling me stories I've never heard about her, growing up in her early teens in southern Georgia. I've never thought much about her young years, but now, after maturing quite a bit and reflecting on my own life, I want to know all about her. When Mama was just the middle sister Leah, she admits she hated her sister Isabelle most of the time.

Four years older, Isabelle was always dressing up, trying on one dress after another that their mother had made her. Isabelle kept looking in the mirror, putting on airs, especially if she was expecting company. During these times Leah sneaked into Isabelle's room and watched her sister, noting how pretty she was with bright auburn hair and those tilted blue eyes. Isabelle got the red in her hair and her slanted eyes from their papa, but on Papa the slant became squinty.

While Isabelle ignored Leah's adoration, Leah eased her way to the dresser and one by one opened each bottle and, imitating Sister (her name for Isabelle), she put a small pat of cologne under each ear.

Isabelle, irritated when Leah opened her best toilet water, snapped at her. "Don't you spill that like you did the last time you were in here messing with my stuff. Just go away."

"I'm not bothering your stuff! I'm just looking."

"Well, get out of my way. I keep bumping into you while I'm doing my hair."

"You better be nice to me or I'll tell Mother who'll tell Papa about you slipping out of the house the other night to meet your boyfriend."

"Leah, that's a flat-out lie and you know it."

"It is *not*. I heard you creeping down the stairs after everyone else was asleep—so you thought. And I saw you from my window, in the moonlight, running up to Billy waiting for you by that big azalea bush in our yard."

"You pesty little spy!" Isabelle shouted.

"And I saw you kiss him."

There was a long moment of silence. Then Isabelle smiled sweetly, and her voice slipped up an octave. "Leah, do you want to keep my new toilet water?" She reached over and picked up the blue bottle. "Here, let me show you how to wear it." Isabelle gently put the applicator under her sister's ear. "See, just one drop here and one drop there. Oh, you smell so good." Isabelle held out the bottle. "It's all yours." Then she bent to kiss Leah on the check.

Leah paused. "I don't know if I want the toilet water. I was sorta looking forward to seeing Papa beat you. He never hits *you*!"

Isabelle cringed. "Please, Leah." She was about to cry. "I'll take up for you next time. I'll even *lie* for you so Papa won't beat you again. You've just got to learn how not to make him angry."

"Okay. Promise?"

"Cross my heart!" Isabelle swore with a flip of her head and a dramatic crisscross over her ample breasts. The *promise* Leah secretly preferred over toilet water and a sister's beating.

But she still hated Isabelle at times when she got a longing to play the piano and Papa wouldn't let her take lessons because Isabelle got bored with *her* piano lessons. Papa said he wasn't going to waste his money a second time for a girl's passing fancy. He sold the piano and Leah couldn't pick out her songs anymore. And then she hated Isabelle even more when her mother made Isabelle a fashionable dress of the prettiest material from the new bolt her papa brought home. She could still see Isabelle prissing around in her new outfit and handing *her* the latest hand-me-down.

Mama's stories are always interesting. Her vivid details make me see scene after scene like a stack of photographs, so clear I think I'm really there, feeling every emotion she experienced. Now I want to hug the young girl Leah.

"But, Mama," I ask, "Why did your papa *beat* you? Do you mean *spank* or *beat*? How did he do it?" This admission is way beyond my imagination.

Mama hesitates, and then breathes a deep sigh. She admits, "No spanking. He beat me. He'd say, 'Leah, go to your room!' I knew by the tone of his voice and the look in his eyes what was coming. He came to my room. Closed the door. He stood still and stared at me. I stared back."

Mama blinks her eyes several times, then looks down with fear. "My heart was beating so fast, I couldn't look at his face. Instead I watched him unbuckle his belt, and I heard the jerk when he tugged it from his pants." A tear rolls down Mama's face. "He reached out and pulled me toward the side of my bed. 'Bend over!' he ordered. And I bent my waist over the edge of the bed and left my feet on the floor. Papa reached up my dress and yanked my panties down. 'Hold up your dress,' he demanded. I tried not to cry out with the first lash, but if I didn't, Papa would just hit harder.

"By the time he was finished, I could only moan and cry softly, my bottom throbbing and burning. I lay still and listened to the buckle clink against the iron railing of my bed as he slipped his belt back on. Mother knew not to come 'mother' me, and my sisters—Isabelle and Agatha—were too terrified to even think about me. But later after everyone was asleep, Mother slipped into my room with some ointment and rubbed it over my red welts. By morning they were black-and-blue. Mother wrapped the torn skin with soft cloth."

I want to reach out to Mama, squeeze her hand, say something comforting. But the shuddering of her face from remembered fear and dejection and something else—a hint of a darkness sliding in—holds me back. *I've seen her eyes that way before, on me—piqued? Hostile?*

A sharp image flashes: *I'm running to Daddy and he's picking me up, swinging me around, and Mama's walking away, but she glances at me with those same dark eyes.*

I know not to get closer. Silence falls.

Then finally Mama speaks as if compelled to explain her papa. "My papa was a *good* man. I don't know why he always beat me. I probably did something bad like I always did, according to Mother. I was so stubborn; I just did whatever I wanted to, without ever thinking about the consequences or the feelings of others. Besides Isabelle and Agatha, who was the youngest, there was Thomas, who was the oldest. But whatever went wrong, the blame fell on *me.*

"Even when Isabelle and I skipped Sunday school which was her idea, I got caught and punished. I once thought I'd be Papa's favorite, because I was the only child that Papa named. Mother told me he named me *Leah* after a heroine in a French novel he liked."

Fall stretches down our street in a blurred tapestry of caramel browns, rusty reds, bright yellows, and muted greens. In our yard pecans nearly cover the ground. We hug our sweaters closer as a cool draft whisks around the corner of the porch. Mama draws deep on her cigarette, the tip glowing red. It feels so good here with Mama. The silences being comfortable, we don't force the talk. I describe what's new at the university, what the girls do when they're not knitting socks, red ones for Christmas, and how six of us went to the movies and sat together in one row in the middle of the theater in Greensboro. The movie was *Love Is a Many Splendored Thing* starring William Holden as a soldier who's killed in action. His girl is to meet him at a certain place and time; she's there, but no William. Instead, the title song gets louder and louder, and we see him walking up and fading out into the sky. Everyone's crying, literally *boo-hooing.* We have about two Kleenexes and pass them down the row for the sniffs and tears and sobs and snivels. And by then, we've started laughing so hard at ourselves that we're even closer to hysteria.

Mama is now the county's Veterans Service Officer with her office in the old courthouse on Main Street. If you want to find it, just go to the intersection of Main and Church and look northeast to a patch of old oaks and cottonwoods. There, snuggled under the oaks, stands our pillar of justice. Inside massive curving stairs, now sagging hardwood, lead up to the rotunda where the judge's chambers are, with private steps leading down into the courtroom. Upstairs, across the narrow hallway, near the judge's office is Mama's office, rather small but lively.

On court day there is a plethora of people and sounds and scents drifting down the hall: loud talk, creaking floor, burnt cigarettes, sweet sweat from aftershave, and cigar smoke. Over all, the smell of earth after rain. Mostly, the officials (men) of the court await their times, lolling around or in-and-out of Mama's office: defense lawyers, prosecutors, bailiffs, deputies, the sheriff—all talking at once. Mama enjoys the good-natured arguments, the joking, the latest news, and local gossip. She always finds men so much more astute than women. And she loves politics. Most of all, the men acknowledge her competence, show her the utmost respect, and treat her as a professional. The court bell clangs for court to start, dispersing the pre-court groups and bringing in crowds of whites, who settle in the first-floor courtroom, sitting on pews. Last admitted, the Negroes march up the narrow, steep steps located on each side of the vestibule that leads up to the balcony. Sometimes a Negro leans over the balcony rail to take in an important testimony.

Mama tells me about a man in his late 20s who stopped by her office one day this week to thank her for helping him get into school. Clark had recently been discharged from the Army after serving his time in Korea during the war and also for the past two years guarding the Korean border. Mama helped him with his GI Bill papers and college application requirements for a scholarship. Clark wanted her to know he was doing well in his classes and was grateful for her advice that persuaded him to go for a degree at State University. Mama's face glows with pleasure as she talks.

"You really *do* like your job, don't you?"

213

"Yes. I really do. It feels good helping these young men. And what would I do all day and night by myself? I'd be glad to work on Saturday and Sunday. Except for the weekends you come home."

That familiar ache eats away at me. I think of high school days at home and Mama depending on my company alone. Her threats of suicide and that utter sadness consuming me when I left for a date. Still, when it's time to go, I see Mama sinking within herself. I feel guilty for leaving her here with those empty night hours and lonely weekends. Nothing ever changes with Mama despite her new job.

In a nostalgic tone Mama starts reminiscing about my Uncle Bobby. "You know, Clark reminds me of Bobby: his blonde hair and that smile that's more of a grin. And him being a veteran of the Korean War just over with many other ex-service men trying to get their lives back. You know, I think of Bobby and *his* war, World War II, with the young men out of service without a clue about what to do. No one there to guide him—there was brother Thomas, of course, who shared his apartment, but that was all. Bobby was just lost. My little brother, dead at 21."

"Mama, don't go there. It's no one's fault about his accident."

"I don't know. If someone had only tried to set him on the right track, that would have made such a difference. But he wanted to strike out for the big city to seek his luck."

"Maybe there weren't as many opportunities after World War II. And there's never been anything substantial to do in Oak Glen without special training. Bobby could have asked for help, Mama."

"No. At 21 he was more interested in carousing and whoring around with girls who hung around Navy bases. He died because he was drunk, you know. Broke my heart. Passed out on the sofa. His lit cigarette started the cushions smoldering."

"I know, Mama. His sealed coffin was placed in my bedroom! You remember? And I loved him as much as you did and even more even though I was 11."

Mama pulls her sweater closer and hugs her arms. "It's getting chilly. Let's go in and forget sad memories for a while."

"Okay with me. And I'm getting hungry!"

We start toward the front door, and I stop. "Mama, do you remember Bobby used to say to me that I was his girl, and he was coming back to take me to my first dance when I turned 16?"

"Yes. I remember."

"And the month I turned 16 I met Luke, and he took me to my first Prom. That made me think of Bobby. You know Luke sort of reminded me of him. Bobby was so carefree and fun-loving, he made my heart flutter when he charged in with his duffle bag. And I loved him so much, even though he was my uncle. At 11 years old, *that* doesn't matter."

"We all loved Bobby. Everyone did. He was so full of life," Mama declares.

"*Luke'll* be lost for a while from me, but thank God—not forever! He expects to be sent overseas, maybe to Korea."

Darkness is coming now. As we leave the porch to go inside, I notice how dark our hall is. This old house is so dark and cold. I can understand why Mama doesn't bother to light and warm all the inside. A couple of rooms is all she seems to need. I remember when I was younger that I was terrified to cross the hall sometimes in the dark to go to the bathroom. I'd hold my breath and run. But most times the darkness comforted me, like right now. I feel a sense of warmth. A sense of ease—like floating on water in darkness, drifting along to the stars. I stop by the chifforobe and caress the wood and smile. Daddy's here. His presence is so strong.

Strange. I used to wonder if spirits lived here. I wouldn't want to live here though by myself like Mama. The house might not shield me from going over the edge to the land of illusions.

We eat ham sandwiches and potato chips. Then we have coffee and spice cake. I notice a couple of beers in the refrigerator—that's different. Mama's never kept alcohol here.

"Mama, do you remember when you and Daddy and I sat on the back steps and watched lightning bugs? And Daddy told me how to catch them?"

"And you wanted to drag out that large Mason jar you could hardly pick up!" Mama laughs. "You were so determined. You had to have your way."

"Daddy was afraid I'd drop the jar and break it. Because that jar was what he put his pickled pigs' feet in!"

"Ugh." Mama makes a face and laughs.

"But Daddy found a smaller pickle jar and some kind of cloth to put on top—"

Mama interjects, "Gauze. Yes. That was it! To cover the top to keep the bugs inside. And he helped you catch the lightning bugs. Then you brought the jar to me to put the rubber band on top around the gauze."

We both laugh together.

"Then Daddy says, 'Baby, look up at the sky!' I looked and saw dozens of stars across the sky. I got so excited! The stars were sparkling so, I thought they were moving! And I called out, 'Mama, Daddy, the stars look like lightning bugs!'"

Mama smiles and adds, "Then you ran towards us shouting, 'I've caught stars in my pickle jar!'"

Mama wipes one eye at a time. "I miss him so much, Erin Rose."

For a moment we are both silent, and then Mama tells me one of the most horrific stories of her childhood when she lived in Georgia.

It all begins when her Papa's deputies call him from that one particular Sunday dinner, and through the open window she hears the gathering men out front swear and cuss, threaten and mumble about a Peeping Tom. Her mother continues eating and her sisters and brothers stare at their plates, the idea of excusing themselves never occurring.

If only she had waited to shed her Sunday dress for a playsuit when dinner ended, her sisters might have detained her. If only she had known what was in store for her, she might not have ventured so quickly toward the big cottonwood tree that faces Main Street.

Not to miss something of this magnitude she jumps from the table, heads out at once across the backyard, down the dirt road, across the meadow, through Uncle John's trees at Four Corners, where stands the big cottonwood that holds her tree house, which Uncle John built for her. Quickly, she climbs up the ladder nailed to the tree and pulls up to the floor. She knows Papa and the men will pass by here, as do all the roads leading to town.

There, she props herself on her knees and hides between the branches. The white starched dress, pleats folding obediently down the front, is incongruous with the surroundings. Her bold eyes seem to mock: "I know a secret." The thought never occurs to Leah that this secret she'll carry to her grave.

Time passes slowly when you're a little girl in a starched dress, propped up on hard, splintered wood, head between planks. She waits. She stares. Her eyes go blank as if she is somewhere else, inside herself, sitting like a manikin, waiting. She is seven years old and loses herself in the cottonwood, looking through fresh young leaves of spring.

Leah sees a world of green and the rainbow colors of wild flowers in the meadow and, in the yard across the street, drops of purple-blue and yellow. Her cottonwood fans out, creating a circular world of space and shadow, of shafts of light and obscurity that grant her freedom to climb, to sit and to watch the world through slants and, then, if she's ready, emerge like a butterfly from its cocoon. And a butterfly she is, flitting around wherever she pleases, sampling this and that, until threatened, and then she slips back into her trusty old refuge.

A tomboy, playing with the neighborhood boys, Leah is forever getting into trouble, wandering around the town square, in and out of stores, pausing on the courthouse lawn before the imposing statue of the town's namesake, some Revolutionary general she's kin to. And then she misses her curfew, is late for supper, running home, knowing she'll get the belt from Papa—"lessons" to learn and remember as certain as the red welts on her backside.

The sun is no longer directly above. She can tell by the light streaks on the west side of the tree. She takes off her tight patent shoes still dusty from running, removes her stiff petticoat, and pulls up her dress above her knees. What she would give for her playsuit! Her cramped clothes are for church and Sunday dinner.

Leah leans back, stretches her legs, and wiggles her toes. How long will she have to wait? She knows the men went north and will have to return this way if they head toward the jail. Even the air is stuffy. Though it's spring, the past few weeks have been dry in southern Georgia; everyday people stop on the street to look up at the sky to predict rain. She can smell the dust of the red clay of the winding path that runs below the cottonwood branches.

At first, she hears twigs snap in the underbrush behind the tree house and then dried leaves and shuffled straw. Angry voices break the afternoon stillness. She shifts forward and peeps through the cottonwood. At last, she sees the men, each with a shotgun in his hand and a gun tucked in his pants. Two deputies pull the black man by rope tied to his hands in front and tied across his ankles just loose enough for him to drag his feet. From behind, Papa shoves him into the clearing. The captured one stumbles, nearly falls, and then receives the blunt end of a shotgun in the middle of his back. He is knocked face down in the dusty path under the tree house. "Git up, you nigger bastard, spying on our women."

From the hanging branch above, heavy foliage covers the tree house and shades Leah with protection from the much-too-bright Georgia sun and the heated men. At the sound of Papa's voice, she ducks down and lies flat on the tree house boards. Through a crack she sees Papa's imposing figure in his sheriff's black uniform, his silver belt buckle and badge glinting from slanted sunshine. He holds his shotgun and pokes at the young black man, cuffed, legs tied, inert where he fell, and rolls him over. "I said git up, nigger!"

The young man opens his eyes and looks straight up at the tree house floor. Leah sucks in a deep breath, and her dress moves with a life of its own. Its crispy swish sends her into a paralytic dread. It is only the man, though, who stares, who holds the gaze of her hazel eyes through the wide crack.

Terrified of discovery, she wills herself breathless and the man silent. Does he see me? Can the others? She stares into the fated man's eyes like those of a frightened woodland creature—shocked, alarmed, beyond outrage. And is there something more—hope? Papa pulls him up, pushes him with his gun, and half-drags the man down the road toward town; the excited men follow and stamp the earth, kicking red dust up like a dust devil.

She sits, cross-legged now, hands together, and chants: "Papa is a good man. Papa is a good man. Papa always knows what's best. Because Papa is a good man." She knows she should go home, and she's sure she'll be belt-spanked for jumping up from the dinner table ... so she might as well run to town first.

Leah clambers down the ladder and crosses the street. Parallel to Main Street an alley leads to the jail right across from the courthouse. She could run down the alley and arrive before Papa and the men. However, news of the capture has spread. Nearing the town square, she hears a lot of commotion. The street is filling up with men home from church or from their farms for dinner. Even some women and teenaged boys and a few older children are hanging around the street, and she easily slips through the gathering crowd. But soon, the crowd starts moving, like one huge beast, toward the jail and she is trapped in its momentum.

A couple of neighborhood boys, friends of her brother Thomas, spot her and yell, "Leah, what'cha doing here?"

"I wanna see what's going on!" One catches her hand and lifts her up. She knows Papa doesn't allow her near the jail, but she talks Rodney into letting her sit on his shoulders.

Behind the jail on the edge of a dirt drive, men are building a fire pit. A hole has been dug. She watches men place straw in the hole and then dried limbs across the hole as if they were building a campfire. They stuff smaller twigs and more straw in between. A deputy places one tall post straight up in the center.

Leah asks, "What're they gonna do?"

The beast moves forward, slowly, rhythmically, in unison, caught up in an emotional snare. With legs crossing around his neck, she leans over Rodney's head and scans the still-gathering crowd. She would not be able to run away now if she'd wanted to. She feels the excitement of the multitude. It's like the air before a storm—heavy, stifling, electrically charged. The young black man is led out with a rag stuffed in his mouth and tied at the back of his head.

The crowd shouts obscenities at him. A half-dozen white men hold him beside the post. Papa cuffs his hands behind, and a deputy ties his ankles and his waist to the stake. Several men pour kerosene on the straw and wood at his feet and then saturate his clothes and skin.

Rodney has edged up closer. By now Leah is so caught up in this event before her, she never gives a thought to how conspicuous she must be with legs and dress wrapped around Rodney's neck. At least she's high enough to see. She looks down at the man. And she hears a long, low, agonizing groan. Only then did she apprehend what is really happening.

A few yards from the fire pit, Papa pulls out his pouch of tobacco and taps the tobacco gently with his forefinger onto the paper he holds. Slowly, he meticulously rolls the cigarette. The crowd becomes silent, watchful. To Leah this silence is deafening. She can't watch this. She starts squirming to get down. Her stiff dress swings up and out, the starched fabric ruffling like paper or tender beginning to spark. At the sound the man jerks his head toward her. She looks into his eyes and sees such unfathomable fear that his silent cry she tucks inside herself so deep she won't have to hear it.

When Papa nods his head, a deputy empties a gallon of kerosene on top of the man's head. Papa takes a few puffs from his cigarette and tosses it at the man's feet.

Swoosh.

Once ignited, the flames rush up like a burning wind. Straw pops, limbs crack, sparks fly skyward. Smoke thickens, yellow tongues and red tongues flip out and curl up, snap into anger burning out of reason.

Rodney holds her in his arms and she buries her head against his neck; but then she becomes as mesmerized as the mob and watches flames rise higher and higher and listens to its continued drumroll. She feels the heat on her skin. She smells fumes that sting her nose. Hypnotized by the horror, she holds on to Rodney's neck to see what has happened. When Rodney lowers her to the ground, she's trapped by the close crowd. She pushes against legs to get away. She could hardly breathe from the smothering smell of burned flesh and kerosene. She thought she was in the circle of a flaming hell.

She glances down finally at her Sunday dress. Her white sleeve is smudged with soot. Papa will really be angry now.

In the dark of the kitchen, almost like a womb, we remain silent, both lost in memories, each a kaleidoscope, changing in pattern and perspective. You know, everything does change, but it remains the same.

Again we sleep together in Mama's bed. I lie awake and listen to sounds of the night. The house settles down too—the creaks, the squeaks, the scraping of limbs on roof. Then the faint whistle of the train in the distance coming down the track.

Chapter 21

The next time I'm in Mama's kitchen, Luke is with me. I'd gotten a ride earlier from Greensboro with a college friend going through my hometown; the ride saves Luke from having to drive the extra distance to get me. He picks up plates of barbeque, hush puppies, candied yams, and slaw along with some beer in Rockingham and heads to Mama's. That's one choice I can always predict—barbeque! The minute Luke passes the state line into North Carolina, he begins craving pit-cooked, minced barbeque—unique to North Carolina. It takes just a few minutes for the kitchen to sound like a party. Mama turns on music, and Luke talks steadily about what he's done for the last two weeks.

After a couple of beers, with the music playing, Mama jumps up and pulls Luke from the kitchen table, announcing, "I wanna dance!" She wraps one arm around his neck and pulls his arm around her waist and starts moving slow, back and forth to the rhythm of the slow tune. He dances with her but gently pushes her away a bit as she keeps getting closer. Mama keeps snuggling as close as she can get, and I keep looking. Slowly I feel a flow of heat rising up my neck and face. I know my face is flushed red. I am so embarrassed. I sit at the kitchen table, drinking a Coke, nibbling a bit of leftover spice cake to have something to do with my hands. The music changes to a fast tune. Mama changes to a jitterbug, and Luke hangs in with a slower shag; soon they're blending the two dance styles. When the music stops, Luke pulls out a chair and drops down, and Mama, swirling around for the last time, plops herself in his lap, throws her arm around him, and leans over, calling out "That was fun!" and kisses him on the cheek, for Luke quickly moves his head so she misses his mouth.

I am mortified. What is Luke thinking about my mother? I can't believe what I've seen. I know Mama is lonely. I know Mama loves to dance. And I know Mama is high as a kite. How many beers has she drunk? But what can I *say* now? She's my mother, for God's sake!

Luke is already standing and pushing her away. "Here, Leah, why don't you sit down?" He leads her to the table. He looks up at me. "Erin, why don't you get your things? It's about time to go, don't you think?"

We always spend the night at his family's home. I want to run out, away from embarrassment, away from the pity and disgust I feel. At the same time, I can't stand the thought of leaving Mama alone.

We say our good-byes. Walking to the car, I don't say a word, my throat lumpy, my insides dry. Luke puts his arm around me. "Hey, I'm so glad to see you." He bends over and gives me a long kiss.

At 20 life remains the same for me, just like it was when I turned 16 and started dating Luke, except for spending nights out and having sex, of course. Oh, I am still tremendously infatuated with Luke; he takes my breath away by simply walking into the room. I am in awe of him, especially when he smiles and looks straight into my eyes. Even if he doesn't say sweet things to me, it doesn't matter, because I can tell he feels the same electric buzz that I do. Besides sleeping with him (which gets better and better) at his parents' house when he's home from Fort Campbell, one—maybe two—weekends a month, I live in a university dorm or at home with Mama. It doesn't feel like we're married at all, just going steady. And at times Luke still seems like a stranger.

It's mid-afternoon in late autumn. Luke turns left from the highway into the Sandhills and winds down the dirt road through colored woods, crunching scattered leaves like gold and burnt orange confetti. We reach a sizeable clearance edged with tall longleaf pines and see his parents' home: the one-story house of painted-white wood with green shutters. Whatever season it happens to be, I love the view and sense a welcoming. Spring still brings bright red azaleas, tall white lilies, and purple irises around the house that are replaced by summer's sweetheart roses growing on trellises by the porch and rich red impatiens trailing up the walkway. Winter's view of bare trees against gray sky will welcome me later with smoke rising from the chimney and the hope of chicken dumplings and hot cornbread. Now a tremendously old oak tree and a few golden maples shade the house and the nearby tobacco barn. The McLeod home lies in a patch of green winter rye like an oasis in the middle of plowed fields of tobacco.

As Luke drives down the road, it curves near the barn, and Luke asks, "Can you smell that?" He points towards the barn. "We're at the end of October, and Dad's busy curing tobacco."

"Yes. It smells sweet ... and a little smoky. Sorta like hot spice tea ... or wet wilting roses. I like the smell, Luke. If you take a deep breath, the scent goes all in you."

"It smells like sweet hay." Luke pulls down the window and waves at his father, who's left the barn and walks across the field. Luke parks at the back of the house.

We wait for his dad. Mr. Luther McLeod is an enigma. Though short he holds himself straight, but his eyes watch the ground when he walks and I don't think he misses a trick along the way. Cocked over an eye, his straw fedora, the brim curved down, covers his once-red-now-gray thinning hair and receding hairline. He wears work pants and a long-sleeved dress shirt, even in the summer for his fair skin. He waits until he's right beside you to speak. Luke moves first and gives him a big hug, patting him on the back, as men do, and says with enthusiasm, "Hey, Dad!"

I move closer and call, "Hi!"

Mr. Luther reaches out to shake my hand, pumping it up and down, and remarks, "Howdy."

When we walk in, Luke calls his mom. You know the feeling when you go to a house. It sends out its own vibes. It talks to you, way before anyone else arrives on the scene. And you instantly recognize its essence: a simple charm. You catch the flavor of the home: the scent of vanilla, the touch of down in a handmade quilt, the taste of apple pie. You know the people inside before you meet them, and you already feel welcome. You can pour yourself a glass of iced tea, take off your shoes, stretch out on the sofa, and close your eyes to the world. Luke's home is that way.

In the den, open to the kitchen, the vibes are strong. Knotty pine, fashionable in the late '50s, covers the walls. Early American maple furniture blends with the worn hardwood floor, sheeny with lemony wax. A handmade quilt is tossed across the soft green sofa, dotted with pillows covered in green and embroidered with bold orange and canary-yellow flowers. Freshly starched ruffled curtains hang crisscrossed at the double window. A quick glance at the room seals my impression of family warmth, despite some of the stories Luke tells me about his father. I mention to Luke I think his dad is shy. Puzzled, he shakes his head and says, "Naw. He's mean as a snake."

Luke calls again, "Mom!"

The back door slams, and Marty hurries into the room. "Oh, Luke, honey. Erin! Bless your heart, child!" She gives each of us a big hug. "It's so wonderful to see you both!"

She leans down to turn on the driftwood lamp. With the sun falling into the trees and no artificial light yet, the pine walls now cast a gloom around the room. While she chatters about the family in the backyard and dinner warms, I get caught up in my impressions just looking at her. No pretension. His family's just plain, down-to-earth *good* people who care about you regardless of where you come from or where you're going. That's Mama McLeod, as most everyone calls her. She looks like a mom or a grandmama or your favorite aunt. She sees that you soak in a tub of hot water, eat your belly full, sleep in a clean, soft bed, and are blessed by a prayer if you need one, or even if you don't. You're safe for the night—her prayers keep away the nightmares. I liked her at once, the day after Luke gave me an engagement ring, and I feel the same way about her now. Though I still call her Mrs. McLeod.

I always associate Marty with food and flowers. Her roses grow large and bright, her azaleas spread rich and full, and inside, her African violets stretch out and bloom profusely on the kitchen windowsill. Even in the middle of the day, from the kitchen come the scents of coffee brewing and cornbread baking. In the center of the den hangs a picture of Jesus looking up with his hands steepled in prayer.

The backdoor slams again and then again. Everyone's coming in, eager faces smiling, obviously proud Luke's already made sergeant. They make a big to-do over me, complimenting my looks, my clothes, my "brainy" endeavors. His cute redheaded sister Jewell runs over to hug me. She's three years older than Luke but seems younger because she's so petite.

"Erin." She kisses me on the cheek. "Hey, are ya still making straight A's?" I made all A's my previous semester and Jewell was just as thrilled as she was when I won Miss Oak Glen and then went up to the Miss North Carolina

Pageant. Jewell's always been my head cheerleader and, to my chagrin, hasn't stopped talking about either accomplishment. But "cool" Luke has never mentioned either ...

"Hey, Luke, bet ya Erin's so smart, she'll set *you* straight!"

Luke just looks at his sister and raises his eyebrows. "*Yeah*," he responds in a monotone, "that'll be the day."

I really like Jewell. She's a friendly, loving, uninhibited cut-up. She teases and tells jokes and has been known to do outrageous things. Once last year Luke drove us to Fayetteville for dinner—that is, Jewell, Mama, his mom Marty, and me. It was a fancy restaurant with a bar and live music. Jewell was having the time of her life, squirming around in her chair, moving her arms up and down, and shaking her head to the beat of the music that she jumped up from her seat, climbed up on top of an empty table, and started dancing.

I knew Luke and his mom were humiliated; Marty clapped her hand over her chest and gasped as if she was having a heart attack; Luke jumped up like he'd been shot, stumbled over a chair trying to get to her. But Sister Jewell was too quick. She was already singing, gyrating in rhythm, and guys from the bar—mostly Fort Bragg soldiers—surrounding her, clapping, shouting "Go! Go! Go!" to the music. Mama's eyebrows went up and she turned to me with a shrug and a grin; I covered my nose and lips and swallowed my laughter. By then Luke had returned to the table and slumped down in his chair as far as he could slump with his hand holding his head down.

When the band stopped for their break, her admirers lifted her down from the table and started to disband. Luke strode over and firmly pulled her back to our table. He was obviously livid with rage and mumbled between his teeth, "Let's get out of here!" Of course, if we had been in Oak Glen with my friends around, I would have been embarrassed, too. But Luke didn't know anyone there, yet still he overplayed the rage. That was the last time we went out socially with his sister.

At 16, Jewell had quit high school, run off, and married her boyfriend. By the time she was 22, she had three children, had earned her GED, had passed a Civil Service exam, and had an excellent clerical job at Fort Bragg, commuting back and forth. There is no question about it— she is very bright and as charismatic as her brother Luke (when he wants to be).

I look at my watch. I know the story. *It's ten minutes before six.* Sure enough, Mama McLeod is taking food to the table. Jewell is taking biscuits from the oven and placing them in a napkin-covered basket. Cornbread is already on a platter. I ask if I can help; Marty hands me the pitcher to pour tea and place the glass by each plate, except the one at the head of the table. *It's five minutes to six.* Marty is hurrying to pour vegetables into large bowls. Quickly Luke sets the bowls on the table. Jewell has just finished carving the meat. *It's three minutes before six.* Chairs are out, plates and glasses set, all food is on the table steaming. Daughter-in-law Bonnie already has the five children, with washed faces and hands, sitting quietly at the covered card table, the one-year old there in his highchair. *It's two minutes before six.* Marty asks everyone (already waiting by their chairs) to sit down. Mr. Luther McLeod sits down at the head of the table, and Marty puts a steaming cup of coffee by his plate. She sits beside him. *It is six o'clock on the dot.* That's the time that Mr. McLeod has his dinner. All is well.

Marty says, "Father will say Grace."

All heads bow but I glance up at the picture on the wall in the dining room. Jesus and his disciples sit at *The Last Supper.*

Mr. McLeod mumbles low, "Bless-these-and-all-our-blessings-amen."

Luke has forewarned me that if dinner is not ready at 6:00, his dad will either knock the dishes off the table and throw the food in the garbage or simply slam the door and leave without eating, shouting, "You Goddamn woman!"

Mr. Luther is puzzling. Although he has a quiet manner, Luke says, "He can strike you quick as a snake." I can't imagine what it would be like as a young boy to be repetitively beaten as Luke was. Mr. McLeod would jerk off his belt and shout at Luke to drop his pants, and he'd beat Luke with his belt over and over again until he caused streaks and bruises, broken skin and welts. I could hardly shake Mr. McLeod's hand without seeing Luke as a young boy. My insides shudder as I remember Mama's description of her father's whippings. But I've never seen those actions. And I like Mr. McLeod. Sometimes when he shakes my hand, I look in his blue eyes or at times I see them across the table looking at me, and his eyes are soft and mellow. His eyes don't look evil.

Everyone talks at once: Luke's mother, Jewell and her husband Jack and their three sons, Luke's brother Paul and his wife Bonnie and their two boys, ages all one to six, Aunt Bertha and her husband Earl from New Hanover County near the beach, who just happen to be passing through town, and the next-door neighbor Annie with her new cocker spaniel pup Sparky, who is running circles in and out of little screaming boys' legs.

Luke and Paul eat like they've never eaten before. Even I eat two big pieces of cornbread loaded with butter. Marty bakes a cornbread "cake" in a large iron pan and breaks it up with her fingers into parts the sizes of pizza slices. As I eat, I hear snatches of conversations. Bonnie and Jewell are discussing babies and when best to potty train and how adorable each one is baby-talking and how old each was when he started walking. Marty and sister Bertha are reminiscing about their parents' farm, where Bertha and her family live. She and Earl have refurbished the old farmhouse and restored the old windmill so it's as good as new. They have so many pecan trees now, they've started a nut farm. "Can you believe that?" laughs Bertha. "Earl's even put up a sign that says *BERTHA'S NUT FARM.*" Marty and her sister laugh hysterically. "And that fool, he had cards printed. Givin' 'em out to ever-body. Goin' to houses and leavin' them callin' cards—you know, like them old timey ones saying '*We've come to call. We're at home at Bertha's Nut Farm. Come visit.*' Mercy me! He ain't got the brains that God give'em."

"Oh, Mart, I'm selling pecans in Ziplocs, pint or quart. And I'm making pecan pies to sell. And pecan rolls! You know, what Ma used to make—pecans and chocolate or caramel with brown sugar rolled into a bar and covered with powdered sugar? They really sell."

Aunt Bertha calls me, "Erin, child, come see me and visit the old place. You can come one of the weekends Luke's at the Army base. We'll have a good 'ol time. God love ya!" I thank her and promise that I will.

I know the men will talk all night, since the World Series has just finished. Luke's voice overpowers the others. "Man, talk about a good game, remember last year when Willie Mays caught that ball over his shoulder? Damn. That's never been done before. Everybody said it was gonna be the best catch in World Series history!"

Paul adds, "Yeah, and Mays turned and threw it back to the plate! God! Did that crowd holler. The Giants' fans went crazy!"

Mr. McLeod cuts in, "What about that Dusty Rhodes feller? He hit homers or a RBI every Goddamn time he went to bat."

Luke says, "Think about how much money was made on that series with the odds against the Giants. The Cleveland Indians were sure to win—Christ, the Indians had won more than any team in the American League history. Look at the Giants—they hadn't won a Series since the thirties. When was it, Dad?"

Mr. McLeod without hesitation responds, "1933. Last year was the first time the Giants won the series since '33."

Paul calls, "Hey, Luke, you can always remember when this famous catch happened in the World Series."

Luke looks at him, "Yeah?"

Paul answers, "By the year you got married—1954."

By the time baseball talk is exhausted, the dishes have been washed and the table's cleared—except for the beer bottles. The older children are running around in circles in another room; the neighbor Annie and her pup are gone; Bertha and Marty are in the living room looking at old photographs; Bonnie and Jewell have joined me in the den. They still children-talk. I sit in the corner and reach for a magazine, flip through the magazine rack: *The Fayetteville Observer*, *The Farmers' Almanac*, *The Readers' Digest*, *True Confessions*. On the lamp table is the Bible. I don't see any other books. I choose *The Readers' Digest* and turn back to the joke page. The jokes are all too silly to be funny. I put it back in the rack.

Suddenly I feel so alone. This is my husband's home, but I am an alien. I don't belong here. I don't fit in. Oh, I feel welcome like a visitor, or as Luke's guest. No. Not as his guest—he ignores me. He hasn't spoken to me since I arrived. Why? Here I sit. Everyone has someone to talk to, so I chastise myself for being *me*. I'm not used to everyone speaking at once. I'm not used to so much noise and heavy laughter and "Bless your hearts!" It leaves me numb, tongue-less, clueless as to what to do or say. As time passes, instead of warming up, I become aware of a coldness creeping up inside me, more than I've ever known to this extent. Before, if I ever felt a coldness, it was temporary because I could go home.

I wish I were home now. Mama and I could be sitting on the porch in our rocking chairs, just rocking and talking. If the air was too cold, we could wrap a blanket around us; or we could sit in her bedroom, I on the bed, propped up on pillows and she, in her rocking chair, watching TV and talking along with the scenes. But that's not really my home anymore, not now that I'm married to Luke. *Where is home?* I don't have one. I want a place I can go to cry.

Finally, I get up and wander around to find Luke. I don't see him anywhere. I ask Paul if he's seen Luke. He says no. I turn to leave the room. "You know, Erin, I heard a car door slam a while ago. I bet that was Luke. Gone to see someone, I guess ... he'll be back in a little while."

Chapter 22

From the pier I look out over the New York harbor and watch the huge ship glide towards the landing. Luke is finally arriving home after eight months deployed in Germany. Our time apart has seemed longer than others. My heart is a dense, throbbing fist in the middle of my chest. I am thrilled, excited, ecstatic to be with him again. I can hardly wait to feel his arms around me and his passionate kiss. But I dread not knowing the outcome of the days ahead. I'm suddenly shy about a number of things, especially sex, since it's been so long. And we haven't truly lived together as husband and wife, just slept together on some weekends and a few months at Fort Campbell. He is an alien from Jupiter as far as I'm concerned. As for communication, Luke has written me only a couple letters. Then I recall that letter from Munich, no name or return address, just a photograph of Luke inside a bar with a girl snuggled up in his lap.

At once it seems the mighty black hull of his ship looms up like a huge black whale, and I stare at the ship with as much awe as Captain Ahab gaped at his great white whale—in fear and in love. High up on deck thousands of soldiers lean against the roped edge, waving and yelling and whistling, some fluttering flags, some hanging halfway over the railing. I'm in a daze. I've left Luke's parents at the roped-off pier and walked down steps to a platform that leads to the landing.

Suddenly, I realize I'm the only person between the crowd on the pier and the landing where the soldiers will unload. *Are they actually whistling at me?* I look around and, sure enough, I'm the only woman in sight.

This morning I've washed my hair so that it curls wildly. I wear a close-fitting, sleeveless dress and three-inch pumps. Oh, my God, I never meant to parade out here. However, if I return to the pier, I'll be parading *again*. I am so embarrassed. I wasn't paying attention—just daydreaming about being someone I'm not. This scene is like an old movie set. You know, all those World War II movies in black and white. Scenes of these flash in my mind, and I'm caught up, amazed how time repeats itself. I feel for a moment I'm in a movie, reenacting the drama, the old plot. *The troop ship pulls into port with the sound of patriotic song. Hundreds of uniforms rush down the plank, but the wounded hero pauses on the landing, scanning the crowd for the girl he left behind. Feeling her absence, he looks down dejectedly at the turned-up pants of his missing leg and turns away. Then the sound bellows, "Johnnie, Johnnie, wait!" The delayed heroine runs into his arms, tearfully declaring, "You're here. You've come back to me! That's all that matters." Music swells as they embrace.*

Tears flood my eyes. I quickly blink them away, wipe my cheeks. I know his flaws, but I *love* him, irrationally, irresistibly. And I so much want Luke to love me the same. I grieve for what I suspect I don't have. Pretend for what I've never had.

Soldiers and more soldiers rush by, departing, eager to claim a loved one. I wait. It seems such a long time. Then I see Luke through the crowd. He pushes through the others, drops his duffel bag, and reaches out to pull me to him.

His parents and I have driven to New York the day before, spent the night in a motel, and arrived here at the port early this morning. In two hours he has to meet his battalion to go to a South Carolina base. We have just enough time to eat breakfast with him and tell him good-bye again.

His battalion flies to the base, and he manages to get to Oak Glen soon after we do. It's around 8:00 that night when Luke arrives at my home; he tells me to pack a few things to return with him to the base and plan to stay until he musters out. Probably a couple days left before he gets his discharge papers.

We drive to a motel near base. Long talks? Time for some in-depth discussions? You can forget that. No lingering foreplay. Just sex and more sex. He has never been one to express his feelings, nor I. But Luke has always been tender and loving when we make love. This time it's different. He is insatiable. Not because of long absence. He has left home on the edge of adolescence and returned a full-fledged man chock-full of experiences. I don't need a photo to know he's been busy with German whores: He shocks me with his new erotic tactics. And I'm amazed, maybe shocked, at my own excited responses.

Then as we lie on pillows to sleep, Luke sighs and says, "Erin, we have to do something about the sex."

"What are you talking about?"

"It's you. You just don't know how to do much. Oh, I don't know," he says miserably. "Just forget it." He turns away on his side and goes to sleep.

Forget it? His words stab me. Not only is my skin left raw, but my heart is laid open, carelessly exposed. And he thinks I'm to blame. I've been intimate only with him. That doesn't make sense. What does he want me to do? Pick up guys on the street and say I want it different and wild? How can he be so cruel on his first night home?

In the morning I awake in daylight shadows of an empty motel room. Luke has left early for the base and will be gone all day. What will *I* do today? No car. Not much money. Didn't think I'd need any. Just wait in this room?

His last words before sleep rise up like a great wave that crushes me. I am left limp, my spirit obliterated by his words. Like always when I'm put down, I slide into my imaginary cave, where I huddle in the darkness. I can't move until a ray of light invades the black. I need nurture. I can't live without nurture.

I walk to the window, pull back the drapes. The sunshine creates a golden day. I quickly dress, go out, look up, and breathe the sky.

When Luke was in Germany with the 101st Airborne from January until late August, I was at the university—taking extra hours and going to two sessions of summer school. Now at the start of September Luke has his discharge, and I have only one semester left to graduate, which means I will complete my degree in three-and-a-half years. I'll finish in January but graduate with my class in spring 1957.

In late August 1956, we apartment hunt in Greensboro. We need a furnished apartment on the bus line near the university. Soon I have to begin student teaching one senior class for the full semester in a high school close by while also taking a number of classes. I've gotten special permission to take on such a load.

For days we search for an apartment and find a lot of dumps with shabby thrown-together furniture, dirty mattresses, and old paint. Finally, we stop at a two-story white brick home on the corner of a nice residential street, very much like the old tourist homes in Oak Glen with the staircase in the entrance hall. The apartment is the entire upstairs. When we see the rooms, we sigh with pleasure; the mahogany period furniture gleams, the wall-to-wall carpet spreads over a large area, and the walls are painted a lovely blue. The bedroom is private with a door and adjoining bath, and the kitchen is small but cozy. And this location is perfect, near the university and a city bus stop. We agree at once to rent it.

On a Saturday morning I sit at the small kitchen table, slowly sip coffee, and look out the window. I am confused now ... I am not happy being married. It's like my entire life as I know it is gone. And I haven't gained much—maybe freedom from Mama's control—to replace what I've lost: companionship, laughter, *my* identity. And any bonding Luke and I may have had is gone. Luke was another person when he stepped off the ship in his uniform. He never talks to me, and he never, never listens. Since we've moved into the apartment, he's paid no attention to me. It's as if I'm not even here. For two months now, we haven't eaten a single meal together except for a couple of weekends at his parents' home in Oak Glen. Nor has Luke come home any night before midnight. Has he lost interest in me because I'm no longer an object to compete for? I'm no challenge? I'm a past trophy to gather dust on a shelf until another fits its place? Is that what he's doing every night, staying out late, testing girls for a replacement? Oh, he'll roll over in bed sometimes to have sex with me after I'm asleep. Now I have a new definition of the word "quick." If there were only someone I could talk to. Or better yet, if I knew what to say to Luke that he would listen to. I'm not going to argue with him. He always wins. And I've seen his red-hot temper if he thinks he's losing or someone else is ganging up on him.

I think of our marriage vows: *to have and to hold from this day forth ... for better or for worse.* I remember the solemn face of the minister as he asked each of us in turn if we would take the other as husband or wife, and I hear

Luke's deep "I will" as he pledged before God to love me. How can he turn away without giving us a chance?

After his discharge from the army, Luke planned to return to college. At first, he attended classes at a small college, but quit. Instead, he changed his part-time job at an industrial plant to full-time. Quickly he's moved up the ladder from office clerk to office manager to district salesman. I'm so busy with this schedule going to school and student teaching that I'm actually relieved at times that Luke is out. His excuses include going to bars with the guys and entertaining potential customers. Soon Luke becomes assistant plant manager.

In January 1957 I complete my Bachelor of Arts degree, earn membership into *Phi Beta Kappa*, and graduate *summa cum laude* with my class in the spring. Luke does not attend my graduation. Instead he drives Mama, his mother, and my aunt to the auditorium and then returns for us. He never even congratulates me. I go overboard in studying, analyzing, and putting my all into school. Generally, I succeed. But now I feel a complete failure. Perhaps I haven't put enough effort into our marriage. Yet I've tried everything I know to do. Maybe the fear of losing Luke is too great to risk a confrontation. And I stubbornly believe the Luke I fell in love with will return.

Chapter 23

Teaching positions aren't available in the middle of the school year, so I experience what women go through in the business world. Burlington Industries hires me straight out of college as an executive secretary in the home office. I'm excited about working in the world of the city—dressing up, walking into plush offices, eating lunch out, taking time to window-shop, and best of all, no homework. I'm placed in the secretarial pool, where I'm sent to a different office, sometimes every day, to take dictation, type, transcribe from a Dictaphone, make appointments, and do whatever else the executive needs done. Quickly I find out who's boss when I correct the public relations executive's grammar. He starts to sign the letter, pauses, stomps over to my desk, and shakes the paper in my face.

"What're you doing—changing *my words* here?" he rages.

I reply, "I just corrected your errors."

"That's *not* your job, Miss ... whatever your name is ... you send the letter *exactly* the way I put it!"

"Yes, Sir!" I retype the letter with his errors. So much for women's equality.

When I go to the mailroom, the guys there act stupid. I first hear catcalls and long moans and suggestive sighs, and I ignore them, walk on. Such is a typical day.

A few days later, Miss Pittman, the supervisor of the secretarial pool, calls me into her office. A tall, large-built woman in a matronly dress, she stands with her usual imposing manner.

"Mrs. McLeod, I have a matter that I need to speak to you about. It has recently been brought to my attention that you're causing quite a stir in the mailroom when you go there. And not only there. You're causing a distraction to the men in the offices. And we *can't* have that in the workplace, can we?" Turning, she lowers her chin, looks down her nose, and grants me a fake smile, her lips puckering like she's tasting a lemon. "Do you understand?"

"No, ma'am. I absolutely have not acted in any inappropriate manner. I don't understand one bit. What're you referring to?"

"Your appearance."

First, her words surprise me. Then I feel sharply insulted. I've always loved clothes, fashion, quality of fabric and design. I am dressed appropriately. I've got more class than that cow! Finally, I respond, "You'll have to be more specific."

Miss Pittman suggests, "Perhaps you can dress more conservatively. Wear a higher neckline and looser clothing. Do you wear a girdle?" Before I can answer, she reaches under my cardigan and slowly slides her hand from my waist across both hips and over my entire butt. This touching shocks me as much as an open livewire—so unexpected, so alarming. Quickly I step back.

"Well," she says, "I see you don't wear a girdle."

"No. I don't." Rage rises to the top of my head, and I know I'm flushing red.

"Then *buy* yourself one. And cover up your neck. Oh, and buy a larger top. Appear more businesslike."

"Miss Pittman, look at my outfit." I'm wearing a blouse with a peter-pan collar that touches the bottom of my neck. What's wrong with it? My cardigan hangs like a jacket, covering most of my blouse. My tailored skirt touches the calf of my leg.

The supervisor ignores my request. "That is all for now, Mrs. McLeod. You may go."

The only changes I make are to wear horn-rim glasses even though I don't need any, pull my hair back behind my ears, and try to smooth down my curls.

In the spring I accept my first offer for a teaching job. I am so ready to make a change I'm elated. The problem is that the school is located in Morrisville, a little town twenty miles away. Luke agrees to rent an apartment there, and he'll commute to Greensboro. However, I'm left with no car and, of course, no city bus. My only choice is to bum a daily ride with another teacher at the same country school: an old red brick junior high with self-contained grades. The day before school starts, the principal hands me my schedule: one seventh grade class. I have to teach it all: grammar, reading, history, science, math, art, and physical education. So much for *summa cum laude* and my academic dream.

Early in the semester I have to change lesson plans for a one-day project to be done by the seventh-grade boys. After sending letters home to their parents, the boys bring to class *Ajax, Bon Ami, Mr. Clean,* rags, and sponges to scrub the walls and entrance to the cloak room to eradicate completely their scribbled words—*fuck, piss, pussy, peter, shit, bitch, ass*—and their illustrations. Of course, the girls love me: no longer giggles from the boys standing there watching when the girls hang up their coats and see nasty words and pictures. None of my texts on teaching methods and theories or educational psychology ever came close to my current situation.

Isolation follows me wherever I go. When my colleague lets me out at my front door, I enter an empty apartment, which stays that way until perhaps midnight or maybe a day or two later when Luke finally comes home. His whereabouts remains unknown. Why have I thought we'd enjoy our apartment alone together better than rooms in someone else's home? Luke's commuting has definitely backfired. It's like throwing the rabbit in the briar-patch. I am trapped without a car and in a new apartment complex miles from town. When will I get realistic? I was so excited about teaching my own classes—even that hasn't worked. Me—teaching physical education and math? It's a hopeless situation. When I return to the apartment, I sit and listen to classical music for hours and pretend I'm not me. If I indulge in thinking about *being me*, I'll lose my sanity.

Second semester I'm pregnant. I know I am.

For the first time, I'm so excited about having a baby though I know absolutely nothing about one. I've never even held one! Luke shows no reaction except on the cold winter day he finally drives me to the doctor. I've chosen a reputable doctor whose office is in his home, a considerable way out in the country from Morrisville. Luke complains about having to leave work to take me, and his impatience flares after a mile.

"Where in the hell are you taking me?"

I reply, "I'm reading you the directions. We should be getting near the doctor's house."

The winding dirt road continues through a forest of elms and scrub oaks and brush. Finally, a yellow ranch house appears with a large fenced-in yard full of sheds, cages, and a barn with animals roaming around.

"Erin, for God's sakes, what kinda doctor did you get? A vet?"

"Just a doctor. Probably an old-fashioned family doctor."

"Do I have to go in with you?"

"Suit yourself." I know Luke doesn't want to mess up the bottoms of his suit pants with dirt or whatever is out there. And I'm so used to doing everything for myself anyway I no longer expect his consideration. But his cold indifference strikes deep. My voice cracks, "I'm just about to throw up from this bumpy road, and ... smells." I swallow, holding back tears. "So stop your complaining!" I hiccup.

Luke quiets down, surprised at my outburst.

He gets out of the car and holds my arm as we walk up the gravel path. At the door the doctor's wife or assistant in a white lab coat meets us and tells Luke to take a seat in the living room. Silently she leads me to the doctor.

What seems hours later, the old white-haired doctor in a crisp smock leads me out, shakes hands with Luke, and tells me to call him in five days. I nod my head and say, "Thank you."

As we leave the porch, Luke turns to me. "Well? What did he say?"

"Let's get in the car. I'm so tired." I must have looked exhausted, because Luke walks around the car to open the door for me.

He starts the car, turns around in the yard, and begins down the trail. He looks at me, puzzled. "Erin, come on now, tell me what the man said."

"I have to wait five days."

"I heard him say that. For what? What's wrong?"

"To see if the rabbit dies."

"Pardon me! What rabbit? What are you talking about?"

"I had to give him a specimen of urine, which he injected into a rabbit. We have to wait to see if the bunny dies."

"Jesus Christ! That man put *your pee in a rabbit*? Are you kiddin' me?"

245

"That's what he said." Looking at Luke's expression, I start laughing so hard I can't stop. And Luke shakes his head, starting to laugh, too.

Still chuckling, Luke exclaims, "This is *unbelievable.* Here we are in no man's land with an old doctor, waiting for a rabbit to keel over dead. Damn. You can really pick 'em, Erin," Luke jokes. He pauses. "Just a minute. What does this mean exactly?"

"If the rabbit lives, then I'm not pregnant. If I'm pregnant, the rabbit dies. I guess the poor little bunny can't tolerate a pregnant woman's urine."

"Well, I'll be damned. I've heard everything now. Hey, Sweetie, make sure you don't pee on me."

Life continues the same. I imagined Luke would be somewhat excited, because he seems to be crazy about little children. He's the one who responds to his sister's three kids: picks up each nephew one by one, swirls them around, plays cowboy—falling on the floor, shot by one of their pistols. Walking down the street, he never fails to stop at a stranger's stroller to "goo-goo" at the baby and compliment the mother with a big smile.

I'm glad my pregnancy doesn't show until the end of May; otherwise, I would have been forced to forfeit teaching during those months. No pregnant teachers can be "exposed" in public schools. Luke and I move back to Greensboro into a small house in an old neighborhood. However, he waits until my eighth month in the heat of August to move us.

In the '50s the sex of a baby is guesswork and wonder from old wives' tales. If you carry the child low, it's a boy; if it's close to your ribs, it's a girl. Getting closer to my due date, I make lists of names for both. I like the sound of Alexandria for a girl. I mention the name to Luke, and he perks up over the subject for once and says, "If it's a girl, what about Claire?" The fact that he shows interest puzzles me, since he's not one to care about such things and the name is not in his family.

My gut quickly replies, "I don't like that name at all."

The subject's dropped.

Later the same day he's talking to me and calls me Claire. A funny feeling spreads up my esophagus like a morning-sickness gag. But he hastily covers his slip-up. He shakes his head, "I have no idea why I just called you *that*. 'Cause we were just talking about the name, I guess."

Shortly before the baby is born, I find out why. I find the name and address of Claire Downing stuffed in Luke's pants pocket. Ordinarily I never check his pants, but he's thrown them over a chair for me to take to the cleaners. I recognize the university address and at once look her up in my yearbook. Sure enough, during my senior year she was a sophomore. That means she's *here now* and will be graduating soon.

Luke returns home from work surprisingly early, tosses his briefcase on the nearest chair, drops his keys on the coffee table, and plops down on the sofa. Twisting his tie knot loose, he stretches his neck and then his legs out. "God, what a miserably hot day! Thought I'd melt on the sidewalk."

The floor fan whirrs.

Without a word, I hold out the paper with name and address. Then I ask, "What is this?"

Without hesitation or the least bit of remorse, he replies, "Yes, I've been seeing her."

You can't possibly know how rejection and betrayal feel unless you've experienced them. My chest caves in. My heart thumps loudly in a vacuum. My insides vibrate. The baby kicks, stretches its foot across my belly. I want to run. I don't want to hear any more. But my gut already knows. Intuition wears you out, but facts kill you on the spot just as surely as a pistol shot into your heart. I am dead ... silent ...

dissociating hearing words meant for that other person standing in my place. I can't breathe. The air is too hot, stifling.

Luke is talking like the weatherman pleasantly announcing that tomorrow will be fair and mild: "Erin, I was planning to tell you. Just didn't find the time. As soon as the baby's born, I'm leaving." He pauses. "And ... I want a divorce." He turns to leave the room. "I'm going to take a shower. Got dinner reservations at seven."

I scream, "Is that all you have to say to me? You *son of a bitch! When* were you going to *tell* me? When I'm *going into labor?*"

He answers in a deliberate, rational manner: "Erin, *I'm in love with Claire.*"

Infidelity rears its ugly, warty head. *He loves someone else.* Our marriage is a lie.

My thoughts are whirling images caught up in a current. The late nights out—every night—the excuses about his job—entertaining customers, socializing to get more business contracts, going to out-of-town meetings—all convincing excuses. For, after all, he's the new plant manager. I can't face this now. The thought of losing Luke— I just want to run from it.

And I do. I grab his car keys and run out of the house, squeeze my extra bulk under the steering wheel and screech out of the driveway. I'm crying hysterically. I race his new Cadillac down the road, oblivious to speed or direction. I hope I wreck it. Don't know where I'm going. Don't care where I've been. Speed makes me free. Flying down the highway gives me a *high*—a wonderful *dizzying high.* Don't have my pocketbook. No license, no name. Nothing. I'm *no one*, anyway. Just *me. I am the invisible woman.* He doesn't see me. Doesn't hear me. God knows, he doesn't touch me. Scooting down exits, swinging up ramps. Where's the traffic? I've passed everyone. I start laughing. Laughing and laughing that chokes the loud cries, I can't get my breath. High-tailing it to the country and trees, then a heavy, quick, unexpected *thump-bump* off the highway into a dim grove.

I open my eyes.

A branch of leaves softly brushes the window where my head lies. *Shush-swish-shush-swish.* On the passenger side other limbs hang low and drape the car roof, a few tapping like gentle raindrops with a staccato rhythm. I open a window to let in air, much cooler now that a few breezes stir. Through the windshield I see trees lined up like silent sentinels ahead.

The evening darkens. I feel at ease here. I want to stay in these woods and watch them fill with rain. The fresh smell of cedar wafts on a breeze, and the new coolness dispels my body heat like a dip in a lake. Even the baby is calm now, rolled up in a little ball, floating pressed against my right hip bone. I move my cramped legs on the seat, stretch, take deep breaths of fresh smells, my head in sync with the rain tapping like rhythms of poetry. Lines of Robert Frost drift in my head:

> The woods are lovely, dark, and deep,
> But I have promises to keep.
> And miles to go, before I sleep.
> And miles to go, before I sleep.

The world of Nature—earthy and pure—pulls me to stay. Someday, maybe? *Now it's time to go.* I run my hand back and forth across my belly; the baby flutters like a butterfly. "Little baby, you and I must go home." I pat the skin under which the baby lies.

But how did I get here? I remember crying uncontrollably and hearing a *thump.* The next moment I'm opening my eyes. It's like lying on the surgical table one minute and then opening my eyes the next: there's a time gap.

I get out of the car to figure out what's behind me. First, a sharp turn. Then the path weaves around tall trees and a jungle of underbrush only partially cleared. How did I drive so meticulously without running into a tree? It's like someone else drove the car. And how long was I asleep? Or passed out? Now how can I turn the car around to leave?

I pull into our drive. The house is dark—not even a night light shines. The side door is unlocked. Luke is gone. But he'll be back in the morning—I have his Cadillac.

I don't know what to do. How am I going to manage with a baby by myself? The baby is due in September, a month away, and this date has knocked me out of a teaching job for fall. And divorce is practically unheard of; it's something only movie stars do. I don't know a soul in Oak Glen who's divorced; a divorced woman is completely ostracized. Every baby needs a father. And God help me, I still love Luke.

I'm so devastated I'll go crazy if I don't talk to someone. Mama is the only person I have to talk to about such things, but I hate for her to know how needy I am. When she answers the phone, I burst out crying, just hearing her voice. Mama is shocked, of course, when she hears me cry and when I tell her what happened but she tries her best to console me. "Erin, Luke doesn't mean what he says. I know he loves you. Anyway, if he's seeing someone else, it doesn't have a thing to do with you. Erin Rose, you're pregnant. Men sometimes run around on their wives then. Just stay put. He'll change his mind."

My only confidante, Mama, doesn't understand the seriousness of my situation. The only close companion left, then, is *myself*—my fictional friends in books don't come near these circumstances. I'm used to talking to myself, in my head, that is; desperation hasn't quite reached the stage that I say it all out loud. My wise, dependable inner voice, though, mopes, too.

A few days after the Big Love Announcement, Luke comes home in the middle of the morning with a great big smile and a "Hey-y-y!" He starts grinning like a little boy who has a secret he's can't wait to tell. "I've got something for you! Close your eyes. Don't open 'em until I say. Be right back!" He almost runs to the side porch.

Like an idiot, I stand with my eyes squinted closed.

Suddenly I hear a *plop-scratch-plop-scratch* and a loud *thump* from the small table knocked over with a crash of glass, a boom, and a rumble. My eyes open wide. The blue and white china lamp lies cracked and broken; the crystal bowl of hydrangea is shattered across the floor, the flowers in a heap. And I hear excited barks.

Luke yells, "Damn! Hold! Stay!" He points his head at the mess on the floor. "I'll get it up. How about this!" He tugs at the dog to leave the dirt and smashed glass and grins again. "Isn't he a beauty?"

I see a pony-sized creature with clumsy legs, a big head, a big mouth open and heavily panting, showing his sharp teeth. From the small, pointed triangular ears, I know he's a boxer or partly one. Huge and obviously untrained. I love little dogs. Big and fierce-looking ones scare me to death.

Luke is patting the dog, "Come on, calm down now, feller. He's never been taught to obey commands. No discipline at all. But you should see his mother—a real beauty, a show dog from a breed of champions." The dog gives a pull and nearly drags Luke across the room to track a smell from the kitchen. Then he growls and heads toward me. Luke gives more commands that the dog ignores.

Luke continues his story about the dog. "Some mutt broke into the kennel and impregnated the mother. She had a litter of pups they couldn't sell so they got rid of all except this one. Of course, he's a young dog now, still growing. My golf buddy Crawford—you remember him, don't you?—well, he told me I could have the dog."

I haven't moved. Open-eyed, I stare at the dog as I would at a monster in a horror film, eyes glued to what I don't want to see. The boxer is big and boisterous enough to knock me over. Luke can't even handle him.

"You know, Erin, when Crawford offered me the dog, I thought about you."

Yeah, I think. Quite appropriate. A horse belly and clumsy legs.

"He'll be a great dog for you, Erin. The backyard has a fence around it. I know the yard's small, but the dog will have enough room. He'll make a great watchdog. He just needs to be trained. You have plenty of time to teach him commands. What else do you have to do? Come on over here, Erin, and pet him."

"No, Luke. You know I'm afraid of big strange dogs. I don't want him here. Certainly not around the baby. I can't take care of them both. No."

"But you'll get to know him. It'll be fun teaching him tricks. You're a teacher. Pretend he's in your class!" Luke laughs at his own cleverness.

"Are you really serious? Do you think I can handle that dog with this body? Don't tell me you haven't noticed that I'm as big around as a barrel now. I can't even bend over to buckle my sandals! And when I go outside, I nearly have a heatstroke."

The dog is fighting to get away—growling, shaking his head to get loose from the leash. "Wait a minute. I'm going to put him outside, let him run around the backyard. You'll see." The screen door slams. Then I hear Luke rummaging for bowls for water and food. The argument is settled—for him.

"God a-mighty, it's steaming outside! Erin, honey, I've got to go. You'll see—the dog will work out. Let's call him *Champ!*"

"I am *not* keeping the dog, Luke. Take him away or ... I'll call the shelter to get him."

"Erin, you're so negative about everything. I could hardly wait to bring you the dog. And you don't like my gift! You're no fun anymore. I worry about you. You're here, right by yourself, all the time. I'll be leaving, and this dog will make a good companion for you!"

My new companion? Luke's leaving me. So he's replacing himself with a passionately panting dog? I grit my teeth when I suddenly have an insane impulse to laugh hysterically. He's proud of himself for getting me a dog. Does he think that's enough? Is life that simple for him?

So be it. I try. But the poor dog stays outside. Bowls of food and water sit on the small back porch in whatever shaded spot I find. The second the screen door squeaks, Champ comes running and jumps up on me. He's so tall his paws fall on my shoulders, and his large head—face to face with me—makes him taller; I brace myself against the porch post to keep from falling. Across the yard stretches the clothesline I trudge to every day to hang up clothes, sheets, and towels I wash by hand. And Champ jumps at the longer pieces, often tugging them away through the dirt or mud. But what can I do without a washer or drier? When the baby comes, I'll hang baby clothes there and Lord knows how many diapers he'll pull from the line.

Poor Champ! I can't get angry at him. He doesn't know better—it's not his fault. I can't discipline him. He does what a dog does without a companion. Sometimes I look out the kitchen window at him and get all teary-eyed. He has nothing and no one, a prisoner in a fenced yard, and

I want to run out and hug him, to lay my head on his dirty neck, and to whisper *what a sweet dog you are!* Give him a bath, a treat (though Luke hasn't bought any) and sit with him on the back step when trees shade us in early evening. I must do something for this dog.

Then the day comes when I first see his erection. He jumps on me, his face right in mine, we're nose to nose, his paws strongly set on my shoulders, and I'm trying to push him away and I look down ... and oh, damn! His very pink penis, as long as my arm, shoots out in the mightiest erection I could ever have imagined! I drop the clothes, the basket, and run, as if for my life to the back porch, grabbing a mop to push at him—still excited, now growling at me and the mop. Somehow I get the screen door opened. I slam the inside door and lock it against this horny monster.

Champ continues to show his penis and run after me every time I'm near. It's already September, and I'm on edge, anticipating the start of labor. Oh God, will I be here by this clothesline? I just can't stand it anymore—this dog struggle. I finally call Luke at his office (I'm asleep when he comes in, always after midnight, and he hasn't yet gone outside to pet the dog) to tell him about the dog episodes and beg him to find a good home for Champ. I receive nothing but peals of laughter.

"The dog thinks you're in heat, Erin! You better run faster!" Another spill of laughs. In the background I hear Luke chuckling to Becky, his secretary, "Hey, Becky, Erin thinks the dog's out to rape her!"

I slam down the phone.

Nothing changes.

I know nothing about childbirth. It is the fifth of September. All afternoon I think I have gas pains, but by dinnertime mild cramps set in. As night creeps in, so do the pains. I have only myself to talk to, but recently I monologue with God all day. I wish He or She would talk back. *If this is it, please let it stop until Luke comes in!* But cramps continue sporadically and harder. I don't know how to reach Luke. Should I call a neighbor? I've only met the one next door. I no longer have any friends in Greensboro.

For hours I sit propped up in bed, trying to stay very still; if I do, maybe the baby will slow down. At intervals the cramping really hurts. When it slows, I take deep breaths and hear Luke's voice *"As soon as the baby's born, I'm leaving."* What if he doesn't come home tonight? I watch the hands of the clock reach midnight. He knows my due date is anytime now. I know I can't trust Luke. I struggle off the bed, wobble to the closet, pick up the overnight bag I've already packed, and slowly take it to the front door. I drop my pocketbook on top and return to the bed, plopping down to rest. I'm too exhausted to move. A squeezing ache runs its course and then tapers off.

It seems God has ignored my plea. *"Come on, Erin Rose, think of a plan! Do something! Call someone— anyone!"* my inner voice commands. From the nightstand I rummage until I find the phone numbers of my doctor, the hospital, and the police. I pull back on my pillow for a minute or so—who to call first?

The side door shuts. Luke. It must be Luke. It's after 1:00.

He strolls into the bedroom and looks at me surprised. "What're you doing awake?"

"Oh, I'm so *relieved* you're here," I say and sigh. "I've had pains all night—labor pains. I've got to go to the hospital."

Luke is taking off his shirt, dropping his pants, shaking his head, and yawning. He sighs. "Ah, Erin, you're okay. You're imagining it. Just go to sleep." He turns off the light, gets into bed, rolls on his side, and immediately falls asleep.

"Thank you, God. *I'm not alone.* You *have* heard me!" I gulp down a cry. I feel so comforted by what seems like an answer to my prayer. And I'm comforted by the presence of Luke beside me, even though he's asleep. I have another human being with me now. That calms me somewhat.

It's strange, the pattern we keep: Luke orders and I acquiesce. Even now, sitting in the dark, I do as he says. I wait. I watch the hands of the clock tick around for another hour or so of increasing pain. I try not to yell out. Finally, a sudden agonizing contraction forces me up.

"Luke, I've gotta go!"

He doesn't respond.

I slide out of bed, put on a robe, switch on the hall light, reach for the telephone book, and start dialing the number for a taxi.

Luke calls out, "Erin, what're you doing?

I'm bent over double. "Calling a taxi ... for the hospital."

Quickly he's up.

Alexandria is born around eight in the morning on the sixth of September.

When I awake in recovery, the nurse holds up the baby close to my face and tells me I have a little girl. I am overwhelmed at her tiny beauty and the fact that she's actually come out of me! At that golden moment, a flood-like rush of love for her like I've never known spills from the deepest part of me. This love is real ... pure ... *ethereal* like you feel when you see brilliant sunlight playing on colored glass, shifting patterns of a rainbow. I want to cup her face and look into her eyes and touch her skin to seal our bond that nothing can undo, but I'm too weak to move.

The nurse takes the baby away and tells me, "Let's get you ready to move to your room!"

I'm floating in a pool of warm, warm water, drifting and drifting. My eyelids so heavy they can't unfold. Sleepy ... drifting underwater ... resting ... sinking ... *Luke's going ... won't be home ... gone* ... the sheet's moving, someone pulls it back—and gasps. Screams. Shouts for someone. I'm trying to open my eyes ... why the hollering? I open my eyes. Everyone's calling. Running around. The nurse remains by me, shouting for a doctor, over and over, her eyes big and alarmed. My eyes aren't focusing.

Quickly a group of green gowns circle my bed, everyone talking at once, someone giving commands. What's happening to me? Two gowns grab my bed and start running and pushing it down a hall, knocking it against the wall. Passing scenes blur. The bed is knocked back and forth into an elevator, the gowns are in such a hurry. I slip in and out of darkness. In the light I keep thinking: *I have my baby. I already have my baby. I've seen her.* I open my eyes again. On the wall in the operating room the clock shows 12:00. Someone straps a gas mask on my face. I know I'm in surgery.

When I awake, the clock on the wall reads 3:00. Am I still in this same room—an operating room? The mere thought stupefies me. Above the mask I see a clock and a white-gowned doctor in cap and mask with head down between my legs at the end of a table. What is he doing? His arms bent, hands together, fingers flying, instruments handed up and another down. He's mumbling and mumbling; mumbles echo *I can't find it!* Then louder huskiness: *I can't find it!*

Eclipsing light.

Darkness.

My eyes pop open.

I've got it! There it is! A clipped blood vessel! Got it! The shout reverberates with the opening of my eyes. The doctor shouts like a wild man. *Get the transfusion going! Where're the bags? Why aren't they up?*

Green Coats move in a frenzy: setting up metal poles, holding up containers of plasma, one doing it wrong and White Coat jerking it from him *You got the God-damn thing up wrong* and flipping it over to hang. I feel needle pricks very faintly in my arms and legs and feet and hands and hear words: *veins collapsing—can't find a vein to hold—try her feet—her hands.*

No one seems to know I'm awake. I can't even move a finger. I can't speak. I can only silently scream. Feel silent cries.

For some time, a long time now, I've been aware of a presence at my left. His low monologue is aimed at me. I can't turn my head to see. But he knows my name and keeps calling me: "Erin? *Erin! Keep your eyes open.*"

The Presence knows I'm awake though drowsy. He keeps talking to me, calling my name. I'm so sleepy. Can't keep my eyes open. I see tubes running in me now. I try to count them—there are too many. *I'm so cold.* My eyelids feel as though a magnet pulls them and me *down, down,* the pull stronger than mine. I see my body like a small upright stick sinking: small—a stick swaying down in an ocean. *E r i n—* slow, low, muffled call ... faraway—I can't reach the voice. My eyes flutter. "Erin!" Firm hands cup my face and tilt my head to the side. "Come on, Erin, wake up. Hold those eyes open. Erin!" He leans close to my face.

I look at the face of the Presence for the first time. Blue eyes. Sky blue. So lucid. Intense. He's dressed in green. He smiles. "Hi there, Erin. You're back. Stay with me now. Keep those pretty eyes open. Look at me."

His eyes pull me in. I try to keep staring. The more I focus, the more radiant his eyes. I'm so tired. And cold. I'm freezing. Oh, I want to sleep. Go away. Wanna s l e e p.

"No, you don't! Erin! Don't you fall asleep. Look here!" He touches my face again, holds my chin up, and captures my eyes again and holds them as if he's pouring bright white light into them.

My Mystery Man talks and talks, his eyes never leaving mine. I feel he sees through me, and he cares. He won't let me drop my lids. "You're going to be fine, Erin. You're getting blood in you now. Hang in there. Hey, look at me. You're getting eight tubes of blood at the same time. And soon you're going to see that little girl again. Do you have a name for her yet?"

I listen so hard. I love this man. He really cares. Who is he? *Stay with me. Don't go away. I'm afraid. Please God, make the blood go in fast. And, you, with the ethereal blue eyes, I never want you to go. I'll never forget you. But I can't stand this cold!* I know I'm shivering, like nerves shaking, vibrating. Someone's stacking hot blankets around me. I can turn my head enough to see Green Coats massaging my legs. I turn my head again to the left side. Where is he? Where is my blue-eyed doctor? His Presence? I feel myself falling in and out of sleep, my Presence allowing me to, though I can't see him ....

I stare at the clock on the wall. 5:00.

I'm being picked up and put on a gurney. Gently, I'm being rolled down the hall. I push open my eyelids and strain to stay awake. The gurney ripples on rollers and carries me along through a haze, walls floating by like buoys. Everywhere figures like shadows move languidly, drift away. Where am I now?

Suddenly, I hear Mama. "Oh, Erin Rose, darling." She looks so intense, her voice catches, and I know she's about to cry, bending over me and kissing my forehead. "Erin, honey," says Aunt Agatha, who's kissing my cheek, "We've been waiting so long, we've been worried to death!" And Mama exclaims, "Oh, the baby! She's beautiful!" Aunt

259

Agatha agrees, "She's the most adorable child!" The two talk nonstop. They've been at the hospital since this morning. They can't imagine why I was taken back into surgery.

"Thank God, you're all right!" Mama starts crying.

"Leah, she's gonna be just fine!" Aunt Agatha leans over to hug me. Both look very anxious.

I'm so weak I can't do any talking. But the love from the two of them makes me warm, even though under the blanket I feel a few shivers. I'm so glad to see them, I am teary-eyed. I want to smile, but my facial muscles don't budge.

I look up and see Luke at the door. He walks around the bed, stops midway, and, as if to get my attention, touches my arm between the IVs with blood. "Hey-y." No polite kiss. No smile. "I've seen the baby." He looks across the bed and speaks to Mama and Aunt Agatha sitting near. They talk, always using third person "she" when speaking about me.

And the nurse comes in, stumbling around with a heavy supper tray. Quickly she deposits the tray on the bed, turns the crank around to lift the head of the bed, and stacks pillows at my back. Luke shakes his head back and forth disapprovingly. "What are ya doin'?"

There I lean-sit half off the pillows, eyes sunk back, mouth partially open like a Raggedy Ann doll. The nurse replies, "Time for supper, dear." She straightens me up, puts the tray in my lap and a spoon in my hand. The spoon clinks on the floor.

Luke practically yells, "Stop it! She can't eat now."

To remedy matters, the nurse sticks a spoon of mashed potatoes in my mouth. She fake-smiles and shakes her finger up and down. "We must eat to get strong."

I immediately start choking, with potatoes spilling out. Luke to the rescue snaps at the nurse "to get her stuff and leave." He cranks the bed down. "And get her cleaned off and fixed right." He nods toward me. "She needs rest."

My eyes dwell on Luke, watching for any nuance to relieve my uneasiness. He looks so handsome tonight. I can tell he's showered and shaved and dressed up, as if there's a special occasion. He has a date, I guess. The scent of his aftershave, so potent, goes through me, surging, stirring up latent desires so much I crave him. Even in my malaise, I can't help myself from staring and thinking that under this hospital light Luke seems to glow: the blonde hair with a reddish undertone, the changeable color of his eyes now shining green, the suntanned skin with a pinch of copper, and his clothes the color of sand.

I want to scream: "Don't leave me! Don't leave us!"

And I hear him say, "Well, I'd better go." He tells Mama and Aunt Agatha to drive carefully on their way home. "And, Leah, you'll be here for a while when Erin leaves the hospital. Right? Oh, by the way, Erin, I took the dog back."

I lie immobile as before. Does Luke know the full story of today? Does he realize I was near death? Was he concerned at all today? Or is he disappointed that I'm here still, breathing, living? *Does he prefer me dead?* That thought crushes me like a rockslide. I feel panicky as though my breath's knocked out. *Oh God, please, please make Luke love me.* That's all I want to do—to pray all night: pray to Luke's psyche, to his soul, to his mother, to God again, to the ceiling, to the clouds, to the door. My feelings are too intense; I must calm myself inside.

I think of the baby and my love for her. Then as if the baby's opened a floodgate deep inside, an outpouring of love swells for Luke. I feel another golden moment. This love is also pure and profound and unconditional just like my love for Alexandria. It is unbreakable. The miracle of it is that I can give Love without receiving it.

Chapter 24

I feel as though I'm treading water in a deep current, the strong undertow a constant threat, and all I can do is stay afloat one day at a time. This morning is calmer though with Mama, my only lifeline here.

I lie on a soft quilt propped up on the sofa and watch Mama hurry back and forth from the baby's room to check on her to the kitchen to sterilize glass bottles in a big pot. Baby Alexandria is sound asleep.

Mama heads toward me with a large mug of coffee and hot buttered toast. "How're you feeling, Honey? Do you want me to add jelly or honey to your toast?" She sets the tray on the coffee table, puffs up my pillows, and pulls the light flannel blanket up, tucking it in on the sides. We're still in the heat of September, but with fans blowing I can feel a slight chill every now and then. Mama makes a good nurse. I think of the many times when I was little with a runny nose that she'd heat a large jar of Vicks on the heater in the bedroom, rub warm Vicks on my chest, and bring me a cup of hot tea with honey. Mama plays nurse again for me and her new first grandbaby.

My body is slow to recover from the trauma of Alex's birth. My lethargy lingers from blood loss after forceps nipped a vessel (or the doctor did) and the sharp sting of sutures between my legs. And the devastating hurt in my heart, a deluge of sinking expectations. Can I hold myself up to keep from drowning in grief and depression? I should be celebrating the baby's birth—not daily dreading Luke's intentions that pull at me with greater force. I must gain my strength back to deal with life.

This coming weekend Mama will return to Oak Glen where she still works as the Veteran's Service Officer for the county. I'm learning a lot about babies by watching her: how to burp a baby, change a cloth diaper, dump poop in the toilet, wash diapers by hand with Ivory Flakes, mix milk formula and pour it into sterile bottles, drop nipples into boiling water for a few seconds, place my hand on the back of her head when I'm holding her, hug and hug her, kiss and kiss her, and sing to her while I rock her back and forth. Babies love rhythm and music and plenty of loving. Well, I can do that.

Mama buys groceries and all the baby stuff I need. She cleans the house, washes the clothes, cooks the meals, and welcomes Luke wholeheartedly whenever he comes home. If I can keep my sadness at bay, I feel more like myself again with her. I relish her attention and care that make me feel not only loved, but also worth something as a person. We talk about everything—the scholarships she's gotten for Korean veterans and for children of World War II militia, the applications and letters she's sent to veterans' hospitals for those suffering from postwar trauma, and my plans about teaching again. We laugh about old movies we remember and the legendary gestures and antics of the stars we try to imitate. While Alex is napping a longer block of time, we play cards: a game of gin or 500 rummy.

Then when Mama returns to Oak Glen, Luke's heavy indifference pulls me under. I cry for hours during the day even when I'm doing the baby's tasks. Little Alex looks at me with big blue eyes and seems to understand the unbreakable bond between the two of us.

Our pattern of life continues, and Luke comes and goes as he pleases. My body is healing, but my emotional state is far too delicate to upset the applecart. He doesn't mention leaving and I don't ask; if I'm up and about around midnight when he comes home, he's always civil and at times pleasant, occasionally, even wanting sex.

Sure, there are moments when I feel exhausted by the stricter schedule ... like having two night feedings—at 2:00 am, at 6:00 am—the baby taking forever to finish her bottle and I, near collapse, craving sleep. The continuous diaper washing, bottle sterilizing, the nonstop baby crying in between.

Then at four weeks Alex screams continuously in pain; I am scared to death, not knowing what to do. So I hold her and rocked her all night into the next day in fear and dread of facing another screaming day. Finally, I call her pediatrician begging for a quick appointment and begging Luke to take us. Her viral infection seems to last forever. Too tired and too anxious to rest, I sit in silence during her naps and pray she'll get well soon and sleep the rest of the day. I feel so alone in the world, sometimes inadequate to take care of my own baby, and unable to escape for a little while.

Though one night I do. Three-month-old Alex, over her earache and cold, has become her sweet, easy self again. But I'm on the verge of losing my sanity looking at the same walls for weeks (months?) without the sound of an adult's voice except on TV. Christmas music plays all the time on the radio; up and down the street bright Christmas lights glow from roofs and trees; red print glares from the newspaper *Good Cheer*. Everything is edging me closer to a pit of hysteria. I have to escape, just for a little while. However, I fear leaving the baby with sitters.

Finally, I call my neighbor next door to see if her teenaged daughter can babysit on that winter Friday night. I call a taxi to drive me to the main theater downtown.

The theater is packed. I have to sit in a back row in the corner. The movie is good; I relax and escape for two hours. Then it ends. The lights come on. I stand up. Across the crowd on the opposite aisle, Luke stands up, turns, and politely waits for a girl to join him, his arm slipping around her waist as he leads her up the aisle. I drop in my seat. My heart pounds against my ribs, my chest feels crushed, and I can't breathe. Seeing them together, I feel like a stalker— Luke will think I'm spying and explode. I know exactly who she is: the pretty blonde whose picture was in my WC yearbook, two years ago. Yes, she's Claire, the one he loves now. I've been traumatized by him so often that this particular feeling is familiar. But it hurts just as much as ever.

Suddenly, a flush of panic overcomes me. I am humiliated that he may see me alone on a Friday night: no friend, no transportation, waiting for a taxi, for God's sake. Quickly I drop my head down, pray he can't see me. When I'm sure he's had time to get out of sight, I walk to the nearest corner where there's an all-night grill, one of those greasy spoons on a side street with a flashing neon sign. I don't care who's inside. I want a strong cup of coffee and time to sit. I don't want to go home. My anger and disgust and hurt make a mile-thick fortress around me that'll keep the two-bit greasy low-life men in there away from me. At last, I ask the waiter to call me a cab.

Soon Christmas will be here. We make plans to visit Luke's parents and my mama. The baby and I will spend two weeks and he'll stay a long weekend and then return for us.

The entire McLeod family drops by to visit, to eat Marty's famous Southern Christmas Dinner, and to see the new baby. They have a fit over Alex, three months old and the only girl after their five grandsons now. Everyone gives his or her version of who she looks like. After Luke leaves for Greensboro, I spend the rest of the time with Mama until New Year's when Luke returns for us. I can't help but wonder if he's been with Claire, since this time is her Christmas break from college. But Mama's delighted that she was right: Luke's still living with us even after declaring he'd leave for good at the baby's birth. She says, "I told you his affair with that girl would taper off and it would soon be a thing of the past."

But the first of January Luke packs up and leaves. He's been offered a new position as the manager of a larger corporation in Dayton, Ohio. This is a promotion with quite a salary boost. His last words are "Honey, I'll come for you and Alex as soon as I get settled. And I'll send a truck for the furniture and stuff." Half of me believes him; half of me doesn't. For months I wait but still he hasn't called—not even for a "hello." Obviously, Luke is paying the rent and utilities since I haven't received a bill or eviction notice, but my money is slowly diminishing. He hasn't sent us a dime to live on. I don't know his phone number, yet I know I'm sure I can get it—*but I'm afraid to call.* He may say he's decided to divorce me after all. At this point in my life, not knowing is so much better than knowing. After all, I'm only 23 and living a restricted life, and I'm as naïve as ever.

In mid-April, though, when I pick up empty Coca-Cola, RC Cola, NuGrape, and Cheerwine bottles in a field down the block and take them to the nearby little country store—baby on hip and bag of bottles in my arms—to redeem them for the deposit to buy milk, I know it is time to call Mama. I've avoided telling Mama or the McLeods about my situation.

Immediately, Mama drives to Greensboro with her car full of baby food and essentials and hands me money to buy airfare to Dayton. "Erin, what are you trying to be—a martyr? Why haven't you told me and Marty that you've heard nothing from Luke? *What he's doing is not acceptable!* His parents both would have given him hell! Who does he think he is? No money? And you've no food?

My God, Erin! What's wrong with you? You're just going to sit back and take it? As smart as you are, and you're letting a man *starve* you to death? And *grieve* you to death? No man is worth that!"

I sit at the kitchen table, my arm propped up with my hand holding my head. Mama is right. Why do I let Luke run all over me? I can't help it! My voice is gone. My self is gone. I'm a robot Luke has programmed and controls. Without my voice, I can't act. It's just Luke's voice telling me what to do. When I try, I can't do anything right. At least Luke doesn't think so. I no longer have any self-confidence because I have no self. I don't know who I am anymore. It's like I've gradually disappeared. If it were not for Alex, I'd never get up again from my bed.

"Erin Rose, I'm sorry if I was harsh but, Darling, I'm so worried about you." Mama leans over, puts her arm around me, and kisses me on the cheek. "Is there anything I can do?"

Tears roll down my face. My throat chokes up. It's so touching to have someone care. I've been alone too long. "Just ... being with me, Mama ... is ... enough." I let myself go and cry.

At last I mumble, "I don't want to beg, Mama, or threaten him. He has to come back by his own choice. I don't want him because of an obligation. And I don't want to betray him to others."

"That may be so, Erin. But you need to face Luke and find out specifically what he plans to do. It is wrong to keep you in limbo, waiting ... for how long? And it's not just you now. He has a child to take care of, too. This burden is not just yours. You have to fight for Alex's life—how she will be provided for. There are three people to be considered here, not just Luke. He's got to be told that—or he'll leave you hanging on a string for God knows how long until he wonders if he's lost control of you."

"Mama, I get so emotional I can't talk. And Luke won't let me; he won't listen or he'll turn everything around and get me so confused that he'll put the blame on me. Or he'll make me believe something I don't believe! I understand what you're saying, but that doesn't mean I can do it. I can't argue with him. It's like I've been brainwashed by a cult, and I can't get away. I love him, but I can't understand why I do when I hate him half the time."

"Are you afraid of him? Then, Erin Rose, you tell him if he doesn't shut up and listen, he'll be issued a warrant for arrest by the sheriff's deputy for lack of child support—oh, you might as well throw in wife abandonment—and he'll have to argue his case before a judge! Men like Luke have to be made to follow the law and decorum."

My heart beats so fast, my chest aches as though I'm about to have a panic attack. Afraid of him? Maybe I am. I hate his verbal abuse. I'll run from it rather than confront him.

"Erin, call the airport for reservations now for a flight to Dayton. I can stay with the baby as long as you need me, but we can't pussy foot around any longer, because I do have a job."

I sigh and drag myself to the phone.

"And, Erin, don't go tomorrow or the next day. We need to fix you up. My, you've neglected yourself! First things first—you'll need an appointment for your hair, a manicure, a pedicure, and a day to shop for something to wear. You're going to walk into that airport and up to that bastard like you own the world! Well, we'll need a few days to practice that. And, Erin, you must set your mind at ease so you can get some restful sleep and get rid of those dark circles under your eyes. Get the right makeup."

"Mama, I don't have money for any of that. And I don't want to spend yours."

"Don't worry. I have a little bit saved, and you can pay me back later. Oh, forget that. You don't need to pay me back. To see the *former* Erin Rose again is gracious plenty payback."

The plane circles the airport, lands, and taxies down the runway, coming to rest on the tarmac, the brakes screeching and hissing, the passenger cabin shuddering, the propellers grinding down. My body synchronizes with the sounds and vibrations of the plane, and I feel sick with anxiety. Will he be here? What if he isn't?

I step gingerly down the steep steps of the plane, one hand holding tight to the railing, the other clutching my one piece of luggage. My high heels and snug skirt slow the movement of the passenger line. The sky has dimmed, leaving me in a twilight zone. I follow the other passengers toward the Piedmont gate that opens and I hear names being called and see lovers rush to pick up loved ones in swirling hugs. Children laugh and dash from mothers toward men, calling, "Mommy, there's Daddy." An old couple remains by the fence, she sitting in a wheelchair and he pushing it an inch at a time, and then both start waving and calling "Here we are!" at the smiling middle-aged couple pushing through the crowd. College students with tennis rackets and hockey sticks and book-filled knapsacks, one with a pink teddy bear and another with a Panama hat—all are connecting with someone for Spring Break. I feel so envious—even of the old woman in the wheelchair. I wonder where Luke's girlfriend is now on her Spring Break. I must stop that! *Be confident, Erin. Hold your head up and smile*—even if there's nothing to smile at—*fake it, fake it!*

The crowd disperses. I stand and slowly look around. And there he is, leaning against the far wall. Waiting for the crowd to scatter, I suppose. When he sees me spot him, he holds up his hand and starts walking toward me. I don't move. I let him come to me. I'm relieved and I'm afraid. I fear the unknown, but I'm smiling straight at him, holding his eyes as he moves closer. I take in all of him: a new fashionable suit—light taupe that blends with his blondish hair—a Carolina blue shirt, a matching tie, and brown kidskin loafers. He always glows. He already has the beginning of a suntan. His smile almost covers his face. "Hi!" He reaches for my luggage and sets it down. Then he takes me in his arms and hugs me, kissing me on the cheek.

"How was your flight? At least it was on time. Did you have to change planes?"

I shake my head and say, "No." This is all I've said.

"Well, let's get out of this place, before another plane arrives."

I know I appear calm, yet I'm so nervous I feel as if I'm about to vomit ... as though more than butterflies are flying around inside ... more like shattered glass. I absolutely hate myself for not acting normal. No wonder he doesn't want me. If I could only be an actress ... and play whatever role fits the situation! Then for at least tonight, perhaps I could have him wrapped around my little finger! But I can't. I love him too much. If we could only talk, maybe I could explain myself. But he never gives me a chance. Soon he will orchestrate the whole night. *Come on, Erin. Don't think that way!* Please!—I say to myself, to the sky—Please! Not the same pattern again! Please! I don't know why I talk to the sky—there's probably nothing up there either.

Instead of showing me where he lives now, Luke checks us into a motel near the airport. On the way he asks about the baby and says how much he misses her. He wants to know everything about her, and he listens to every little detail. At least he knows how to get me talking. When I describe Alex and her little gestures, I forget all about myself. I find I'm talking freely and smiling and even

271

laughing. You'd think that we're a regular couple. He asks if I have pictures, and when I say I do, he wants to see them when we get to the restaurant.

He takes my luggage to the room and says he has to go by his office for a short while, and then we'll go out to eat. He'll pick me up about 7:30 or 8:00—this will give me time to rest.

I ask, "Should I change clothes?"

"Not unless you want to. You're fine as you are. Oh, I forgot to say, Erin ... you really look good. Lost that baby fat, huh? When I saw you walk in the airport, I thought *Wow*—you look fabulous!" He reaches over and kisses me properly. "See you in a little while."

He leaves and I wait. Confused, of course. But at least I'm not as nervous. I decide to take a luxury bath and change to another outfit, one not as conservative as this suit.

Around 8:00 a soft knock sounds on the door. You'd think I was going out on my first date instead of having dinner with my husband of four years. Luke has also changed clothes to a sports shirt with no tie, displaying a tanned neck with a bit of bronze hair showing in the V of his collar. He wears a light gray sports coat that turns his eyes silvery-blue. Why does he have to look so damn sexy? And his eyes—I've never seen hazel eyes change into so many hues over time. He leans over and kisses me gently on the lips and holds up a bottle of wine in one hand and two long-stemmed wine glasses in the other. I'm about to say, "Well, you went to your apartment after all."

But he interrupts with "See? I remembered ... you prefer wine glasses to drink your wine because you think it tastes better that way!" He's busy removing the cork and talking about wines he's discovered recently. He pours the wine and hands me the glass. "You'll like this." He holds up his glass for a toast, clicks my glass, and says, "Here's to us—

together! It's so good to see you, Erin. It's been way too long."

We drink.

"Do you like it?"

"Yes," I respond, "this wine *is* good."

He takes my glass, sets it down, and takes me in his arms, gently kissing my neck on the side and toward the back and then around the front under my chin and slowly down my neck to the open crevice of my breasts. His hands move to cup my breasts and then slide up my face and to my hair, holding my head so that my eyes are looking into his, and he says, "You'll always be my love." His lips close over mine. He holds me so tight that I'm conscious of every inch of him. When he lets me go, I'm too limp to stand.

"Are you hungry?" he asks. He laughs. "I mean do you want *dinner*?"

Is he laughing at me? I back off. "Of course, I want dinner. Don't you?"

"We'd better go now, or I don't think we'll make it." He runs his finger along my lips; I open my mouth and bite down.

"Ouch!"

"You asked for it! I'm hungry!"

"Okay. Let's go." He caresses my backside.

"I have to fix my makeup. Two minutes."

"Make it one."

In the morning I open my eyes and look lazily across the room. Luke, already dressed, plops his legs on the desk, leans back in the chair, and talks on the phone. Sounds like business stuff. I sit up and call, "Good Morning!"

He places his hand over the phone, says, "Hi, I let you sleep-in a bit. Better get dressed now, though. It's about time to check out and get breakfast."

"Okay." I walk to the desk, slide my arms around his neck, and bend over to kiss his cheek. "I'm going to take a quick shower."

I hurry. I put on makeup and fix my hair as quickly as I can. I know how Luke is. When he's ready for something, he's ready. "Oh, Luke, you forgot to see the photos." I pull the envelope from my pocketbook and hand him the pictures of Alex. "Here, look at these while I finish packing."

I throw my stuff together in no time. Luke's quiet this morning. He's flipping through the photos, not commenting. I saunter over to him. "Oh, Luke, look at this one!" I pull out the picture of a laughing Alex. She's partially sitting up in her crib with her head turned toward me, and her little face is crinkled up in a six-month-old-full-blown laugh, her mouth open with part of a tooth showing on her bottom gum. "This one reminds me of you when you laugh."

He shakes his head slightly, puts the photos in the envelope, and hands it back to me.

"Don't you want to keep one for your billfold?"

"You just hang on to them. Ready? Got everything?" He picks up my luggage and waits at the door. "We can eat breakfast downstairs."

At the table a silence falls. I take a sip of coffee. I eat a bit of toast. This morning I awoke feeling comfortable and close to Luke, especially after last night's full-blown gambit: the romantic candlelight-music-wine and amorous words with foreplay and passionate lovemaking until dawn. Yet today there's not a trace of last night's Luke—he hasn't even looked at me. Nor touched me. His voice is brisk, his manner cold and unapproachable. *Hey, I'm not a pickup. Or a one-night stand. I am your wife.*

Luke keeps staring at his watch. "Are you finished?"

I nod, he motions for the waitress, hands her a bill, and tells her to keep the change. He holds the car door open for me. I slide in. He slides under the steering wheel, and I quickly ask, before he can start the car, "Luke, what's wrong?"

"I'm driving you to the airport. I think it's better for you to leave today. Your flight's in an hour. We have just enough time to get you there."

"My ticket's for Monday."

"I changed it to Saturday."

"When did you change it?"

"Yesterday. When I was waiting for you."

"Yesterday? *Before* last night? Before I was even with you? And you still slept with me after knowing you were kicking me out this morning?"

"Damn it!" he replies harshly. "Do we have to talk about this again? I've already explained it to you months ago."

"But *last night* … last night you didn't mention that girl. Last night you said—"

Luke interrupts. "My God, Erin, you're like a child! How can you make me responsible for what I say and do when we're both high as a kite and fucking the hell out of each other?"

He might as well have socked me in the gut. Is that how he perceives us—fucking instead of making love?

"I want *out* of this marriage," he yells. "*I love someone else!* I'll get a lawyer and do all that legal stuff. My lawyer will get in touch with you."

I remain silent. I focus on steel as a tidal wave hits my gut—rushing, surging, washing out layer after layer of emotion. I hang onto my image of steel: I see my teeth, my lips, my body made of steel—hard, cold, unbending, uncrushable. *Dear God, please don't let me cry.* Make me into *steel*.

When we pull up to the Piedmont terminal of the airport, Luke reaches in his pocket, pulls out his wallet, and picks out some bills. He hands me the money. I do not take it. He drops three hundred dollars in my lap, gets out of the car, and puts my luggage on the sidewalk.

I look in my lap, and in one big flash, I see myself as *a first-class whore*. I open my door and get out, letting the money fall on the seat and the car-floor. I pick up my bag and walk like a woman made of steel through the airport door. And I hold my head high.

The flight to Greensboro where Mama will pick me up is long. The skies are overcast. I sit looking out the window, expecting the plane to fly above the ocean of clouds so I can stay afloat, staring at the emptiness of the sky, losing myself in its vastness. But the plane rumbles through muddy clouds that wrap around the propellers and mantle the wings like night. The unexpected elevator dip takes my breath, and I wonder if anyone—besides Mama—would even care if I fell through space with the plane. I doubt it.

Mama and Alex meet me at the airport. My image of steel dissolves in Alex's laugh and her word for "Hello!" Only seven months old, she cares, too. Mama just hugs me tight, and I feel her heart breaking for me.

Chapter 25

I am so glad to get back home to Oak Glen. It has been a difficult and emotional move to my old house. You may say, "There's no turning back. You can't go home again." That may be so for *you*; but, for me, our home place is exactly the same as it was. It smothers me with protection from reality; it gives me comfort. How I love the long, shadowed hall with the old, tall mahogany chifforobe that once kept Daddy's suits from wrinkling, and the black steel safe that still holds my arrowheads. The hardwood floor still talks with creaks and squeaks, and the tree limbs whisper on the roof. Every now and then when I'm very quiet, I can hear the soft remnants of *Claire de Lune* resounding off old surfaces of the walls. And the night train hails me, clacking and clacking and screeching when I sleep, and I dream of old stories resurrected from the past. I know I'll have to heat water in a big pot for Alex's and my baths, but the long porcelain sink with its flat drain remains in the kitchen, and cool summer breezes from the trees waft through the screens. I feel refreshed, the tons of recent muck already drained away.

Like the aged wizard in a fairy tale, our old house resurrects me, returns my innocence. I believe again in the impossible: all those things that just *are*, yet exist unseen. I curve my outstretched arms to caress the hall space and circle around and around, my hands moving back and forth slowly as if I'm underwater and feeling the current softly pushing against my skin. I am energized. *I am myself again.*

Oh, Alex, how I hope you'll love this house and *know* it as I do. Someday you can be a ballerina and dance across the beams under the roof, the light through stained glass holding you up. And books! You can read books and books and books in the porch swing or in the old slip-covered chair, propped on pillows under the gold-painted floor lamp. You can look far away from the rooftop and see your entire world framed by trees. And there's nothing to keep you from your green years.

With friends from my past gone, also married and moved away, I don't have to explain my situation to anyone. Alex has become my life. I really know the essence of love now. And with Mama close I can *like* myself, doing all the things I love without feeling inferior to the other woman whom my husband loves. I am so tired of figuring out an unimaginable future. Mama keeps telling me that I can do anything I want. She dotes on Alex. She does everything for her and I let her: changing diapers, feeding, rocking her when she comes home from her job. She cooks dinner, insists on washing the dishes, and straightens up our rooms. My physical and mental exhaustion is slipping away. Mama and I talk into the night about anything and everything. She becomes the sister I never had and still remains my best friend.

Mama is there when Alex pulls up on her crib slats and stands for the first time. She is there when Alex takes her first step at ten months in July. And when she starts taking more steps, Alex wobbles with her arms outstretched toward Mama and me interchangeably. Together we try to guess words from her gibberish. We take turns reading to her from a brightly illustrated child's book, *Old MacDonald's Farm*. In a few months when I read about the cow, she slaps the picture of it and says "Mo-oo, Mo-oo" right as the book sounds, and she giggles until the next page turns and "me-ow" makes her hiccup-laugh, so on we go. The three of us have created our own world.

Preston, Mama's sheriff friend, visits us regularly with Alex waiting, arms stretched out for him to pick her up, hold her high, and swirl her around as she giggles that child-sound that comes from deep within. He puts her in his lap in the rocking chair, the one that Daddy rocked me in, and we watch *Andy Griffith* or *Gunsmoke* or *Ed Sullivan,* depending on the night he visits. And he rocks her to sleep, Alex holding her bottle until it drops, her head cradled in his arms while Mama and Preston and I talk.

In these summer months I play the piano again. On some days I play all day, starting with classical: a Bach *Prelude,* a Beethoven *Sonata,* a Brahms *Waltz,* a Chopin *Nocturne*; then Mendelssohn's *On Wings of Song,* Gershwin's *Rhapsody in Blue.* At night when I play, Mama picks up Alex and sits and listens.

When I say it's her turn, she'll ask, "What do you wanna hear?"

I reply, "It's your call!" By now Alex is asleep so I put her to bed while Mama tunes up. I play strictly by reading music. She needs no music, just hums something, and away she goes—ragtime, jazz, Charleston, a slow melancholy tune—all by ear, whatever she hears in her head. On some nights we sit on the front steps and listen to the sounds from the old Negro church, its music wafting on early evening air across the vacant lot between the little Episcopal Church and Miss Millie's house across the street. There's nothing better than the joyous sounds of Gospel and heart-wrenching emotion from hymns mixed with the blues.

Never have I felt so close to Mama. Sitting on the wide porch in the old green rocking chairs, Mama and I watch the cars go by and a few people stroll toward town. I talk a lot and Mama listens. And Mama talks and I listen. She tells me how much she still misses Daddy, how much she took him for granted for so many years, and how she wishes she could do those years over. But she was interested in having a good time, even sneaking to her sister's hometown twenty miles away to *party,* leaving Aunt Agatha to take care of me. Mama talks about how much Daddy loved me and how jealous she was at times. I don't want to hear this, even though it seems eons ago; as a child I sensed exactly what she's confessing now—an admission I would rather wonder about than hear.

"You were your daddy's great love; I had to take a back seat. That hurt and angered me so much. But I understand that now. It's so childish to be jealous of your own daughter. And now I have Little Alex here—just like having you again. And I want her to be the apple of everyone's eye."

Her words create pictures of the many times we sat and waited for her to join us, yet she never did. I see her at White Lake, sitting in a straight chair under a shade tree, legs crossed, holding a cigarette, while Daddy and I swim, splash water at each other, laugh, and I ride his back. The baseball games she never went to. She, sitting on the back porch alone, watching us plant our vegetable garden nearby but Mama stays in the shadows. The time Daddy pulls up a stool in front of the enamel work table by the old kerosene stove for me to squish the dough into a fat ball, roll the dough-ball flat with a Coca Cola bottle, and cut out biscuits with the top of a little jelly jar. Mama walks in and out of the kitchen, a non-player in cooking, a non-sharer in our chattering. I remember her eyes—blank and cold enough to make me shudder but ... most of all ... the sudden darkening like an unexpected overcast day, smothering the light. Her eyes darken each time I jump in their bed, squeezing in the middle, snuggling up to Daddy, pushing Mama to her edge ... but I was a child. *Did she hate me then? Should I ask her now? Or should we just leave the past as it was? Is it really better not to know certain things? The unsaid words? The dark that was?*

Now that I'm back in Oak Glen, it's as if I'm playing house again during the day. I bathe and dress Alex in a frilly little dress and bonnet like a doll. Alex, with her big blue eyes, listens to everything I say—or she seems to. She looks precious in her little pink dress and her little white sandals and the big pink bow I scotch tape to her hair.

Today we're going for a walk. I tie Alex securely in the stroller, and we roll down the wide sidewalk in front of the house and along Church Street, waving at cars passing by and the drivers in turn waving back at us even if we don't know each other—that's the Southern way. The heat's simmered down, and the oaks tunneling the street create welcome shade. There's even a whisper of a breeze. Bits of sun slip through scattered leaves. What a beautiful photograph that would make—the contour of light and shadow.

Then there's a sudden jolt where a long oak root, like a big human foot, has buckled the pavement, bumping Alex back and forward. She puckers up her lips and lets out a cry. I quickly pick her up, put my hand at the back of her head, and rock her back and forth, sing-songing, *"There-now-darling-you're-okay-Mommie's-got-you."* But she keeps crying, refusing to get back into the stroller, so—with Alex hugging my neck, her face buried in my throat—I turn around, pushing the empty stroller down the street, retreating into our yard. I welcome the green edge of our safety zone.

Having my apple cart upset even a bit knocks me into melancholy. I think of Luke. And thinking about Luke is the worst thing I can do. It seems such a long time since I've looked at him steadily—studying his face, his features. He's not really handsome like "a pretty boy." His *vitality* entices me more. When something amusing happens, his eyes crinkle in the corners, his head falls back, and he roars with laughter, immensely enjoying that moment. I see that laugh now and I want to fall into it—to fall into him, to be him, to feel what he feels at that very moment. I can hear him singing along with the music in the car, completely unselfconsciously, without knowing the lyrics or the tune, stumbling over words and terribly off-key; but he sings with gusto, enjoying himself more than the musician. I miss him so much. Every inch of my body longs for him. I want to *smell* him. I want to *taste* him. I want to *feel* every inch of him inside me. But I'm greedy. His body is not enough. I crave his heart so much I can hardly bear it.

The summer arrives early, the heat peaks quickly, and the humidity makes me feel as if I'm swimming in an undertow. Everything is still and listless: no breeze, no dog barks, no birdsong, no cars. However, in nearly each room by a tall open window an old iron floor fan stirs up air, the high ceilings create space and, outside, big trees shade the roof and porch—all fashioning our oasis.

Alex and I often sit in the living room near the bay window and watch the world outside, pointing to and naming what we see; often we sit on a quilt on the floor playing with blocks, reading her books—pointing at animals, saying their names, and imitating their sounds. Alex can say readily *Da-da, Ma-ma, bye-bye*; as for the animals' names, we accept whatever she says. She crawls, sits up, pulls up on the sofa, and takes a few steps by slapping down on the cushions. We sing songs, or try to, and make motions with our hands. Sometimes she sits in my lap at the piano, and we sing the tune I play. While she naps with her fuzzy red pig who sings a lullaby, I read. And think.

Time creeps. And I'm content enough to let it. Like Alex, I'm growing up, too, just in a different way this time. I'm getting to know myself and what matters to me.

When the sun finally lights the trees in the western sky, I hold Alex up high on the porch so she can see the burning colors of sunset; she points at the color I name. If I spot a star—the North Star coming early over the front hedge—I keep pointing it out and naming it as Daddy used to do with me. Alex seems to understand whatever I say. By the time Mama gets home, the heat has subsided, and the three of us go for a walk with Alex in her stroller. Time creeps on.

I've become very lackadaisical about the future, yet I know it's time to get practical … to face the fact that I must venture into Reality. My respite in Eden eventually must end. Mama can't provide for us forever. *I need a job.* However, in Oak Glen, getting a teaching job is next to impossible unless a teacher in your field dies. And even a death won't guarantee me a position. There's only one white high school here in this little segregated town, and most of the teachers are the ones I had, still going strong.

Mama suggests that I try Raleigh. "Erin, you'd have your Aunt Isabelle living there and your daddy's sister Eloise. Both of them would love to see you and the baby. Having family close by means so much, especially if you live alone. And Raleigh is not so far from Oak Glen. You could come home on weekends."

"Yeah, I think so, too, Mama. I agree. Raleigh has a lot to offer. A university close by, I can work on my Master's someday … but it's already July."

"Call tomorrow. Get an appointment with the superintendent. Tell WC to send your college record to his office."

The following week I drive Mama's car to Raleigh and stay four days with Aunt Isabelle, Mama's older sister, in her cozy little white house not too far from the city. I leave Alex behind with Marty, her other grandmother—Mama McLeod, who is happy to have her as long as I wish. By the end of the week, I have a job. All I have to do is hand over my credentials, take a writing test (an original essay on the spot), talk to an English Department Coordinator, and have an interview with the Superintendent. Immediately, I am offered a high school English position, and I sign a contract with Raleigh City Schools. I also find an apartment shaded by trees in a nice residential section on Glenwood Avenue on the city bus line. Mama has given me money for a deposit on the apartment, and the manager will let me paint the walls blue. Now Alex is assured a sizable family with Mama and me and Luke's family and Aunt Agatha and Aunt Isabelle and their families and maybe my Aunt Eloise, Daddy's sister. We are not alone. The only thing left is to find a nursery. We have the month of August to get ready.

It's as if everything is opening up for me, pre-planned. I don't have to think much about it. No mental anguish over making a decision. I've acted on what feels right—what feels good. No anxiety over being accepted by Raleigh City Schools. I instinctively knew I'd be placed at the top of preferred applicants. It's like following a map dropped at my feet already highlighted by a bright yellow magic marker that even a child can follow. I feel energized and happy. Does God have a predestined plan for each of us to find? Look at all the good things that have suddenly come my way without any effort.

Even though since college I've been agnostic about doctrine, I know there's a God. Somehow we're tied to our fate, but we have freedom of choice. Can't prayer change some aspect of the plan? Only the Luke-heartache prayers have been totally ignored—the ones in which I beg God to make Luke love me and come home. Undoubtedly, these prayers are wrong: Luke's never going to change. He makes me unhappy, miserable, and confused about who I am—Luke is not good for me. Now, I am much more content ... happy ... definitely more sure of myself—as long as I don't see him.

One afternoon in late August, a week before I'm to move, Aunt Agatha drives from Hamlet to visit and see the baby before we leave. We're sitting in the living room, drinking iced tea, while Alex naps. We're reminiscing, laughing, re-bonding as we always do, and the phone rings.

Mama returns from the bedroom. "It's for you, Erin Rose."

I raise my eyebrows quizzically.

She slips in the room and whispers, "It's Luke."

Quickly, I shake my head and form my lips in a "no-o-o." I jump up and head for the tall window to look out, cross my arms in front of my chest, rock back and forth, and shake my head.

"Erin! Pick up the phone."

"No!"

Mama returns to the bedroom and comes back hurriedly. "Luke says you might as well come to the phone, because he won't stop calling."

My heart pumps much too fast, a lump settles in my throat, and my hands won't stop shaking. He must hear me pick up the phone because I nearly drop it.

"Hello, Erin? What's *this* I hear? You're moving to Raleigh?"

Thank God, I'm not standing in the room with him. I know that tone. He's in one of his composed rages.

"Erin, talk to me. Why are you moving to Raleigh? I just now heard about it. You didn't tell me."

I take a deep breath. "I got a job there, teaching."

"*Honey* ..."

285

This one word pours out syrupy thick. The old charm and spellbinding tone that I know too well. This time it doesn't soothe my nerves but kindles a violent anger inside which I manage to control.

"Erin, you can teach here in Dayton ... live with me ... I don't want you to go. I can't lose you, Erin. You know I love you."

I listen, but my renewed strength in myself makes me steel again. As he talks, I become stoical. I answer calmly and decisively, "No, Luke. I don't trust you."

"But you can, Erin. If you're thinking about Claire, then don't. *I don't love her*. She doesn't mean a thing to me. That situation was such a mistake. I've learned my lesson. I've only loved you. And I want you and the baby back with me." He sounds pitifully moved. *"Why did you leave?"*

"Why did *I* leave?" I almost laugh. He has such an amazing way of reversing facts that even I get mixed up. "You don't remember when I flew to see you in Dayton? And after using me all night, you sent me home on an early plane almost before breakfast! My, you have a short memory."

"Honey, I'm so sorry. I don't know what got into me to treat you that way."

"Well, I don't know what got into you, but what you've gotten into for months is that younger blonde who you probably have stashed away now."

"Erin, I told you. Claire is gone. I never want to see her again. I want only you. That's the way it's always been."

"Oh, you haven't seen a lawyer yet to start divorce proceedings? You were very decisive about that the last time I saw you ... and I haven't heard from you since."

"I didn't mean it. Honey, I don't want a divorce! I was wrong, so wrong. I can't live without you, Erin. Just give me another chance ... let me prove it to you." His voice cracks.

"No, Luke, I can't live any more with your set of morals."

At this statement, he acts surprised. "What?" Quickly he goes into a raving fury. I have to hold the phone away from my ear. I hear him call, "Erin? Erin, are you there?"

"Yes."

Luke blurts out, "Don't you talk about *me* and *my* morals! You oughta talk to your Mama about hers. You're living with *her*. Ask *her* about *her* morals! Ask her about *how she's fucked me!*"

I slam down the phone, insides shaking.

I don't know how long I stand staring at the square black phone. His words an execution. Killing my life as I know it. Killing future plans. Leaving me hanging in a bottomless abyss.

My Technicolor world shifts to black and white. The film snaps, cracks before me, making images distorted, darker, indefinable. I am blood-drained white, dead. I'm the ghost figure who slides into the room where Mama and Aunt Agatha sit still, staring at the cold, immobile rage on my face and my obvious silent resolve.

I turn my head to Mama. I keep my voice low and calm. "I can't believe what Luke just said—how he had the audacity to tell me what he did." I wait and then speak slow, deliberate, void of emotion. "Mama, he said that ... he's ... he's had sex with you."

Aunt Agatha gasps and throws her hand to her mouth.

Mama turns pale, silent. I stare at her sitting up straight in that old Victorian settee, white as chalk, unable to meet my eyes, with that look you get just before you vomit.

She needn't speak ... I know.

My imagined sister is gone. My best friend is a fake. My mother is dead.

Chapter 26

Sunlight on face. Smell of coffee. A happy slap of a child's hand on my arm and the call of "Mama." A bitter taste in my mouth. Nothing moves me from the sofa where I slept last night. My steel returns—my body doesn't move. I don't think I'll ever cry again: a cry comes from a feeling. And I feel nothing.

Mama walks into the living room and says she's staying home from work today so she can take care of Alex. She's sure I didn't get much sleep lying on the sofa. Why don't I get in the bed now? She's put on fresh sheets. I don't reply. She picks up Alex and closes the French doors to the living room on her way out.

Unbelievable. The size of this house and the number of bedrooms empty. And only one bed set up in her bedroom.

Then the phone starts ringing. Mama sticks her head in and I shout "No!"

Mama's right. I hardly slept a wink. I feel completely unhinged. All night I dozed off, and then my mind jumped erratically from one traumatic scene to another. I tossed in a surreal dream with static friction: voices shouting all together *she's fucked me—I love you—I don't trust you— Please give me a chance—I want to be myself—Come on and dance with me—I'm leaving when the baby's born—I want to live!—We don't need you—It's only you I love—I want Claire—Ask your mama.*

Still I lie on the sofa as my brain runs amok. At once Mama's eyes, her fierce stare, flash before me. Her look, cold and determined. And at that moment *I know*. And I know when.

It was Christmas Eve three years ago when Luke's mother invited a few friends and family to drop by. Luke and I were staying at the McLeods' house that Christmas. Everyone stayed until past midnight, eating and plenty drinking. Luke said he was going to drive Mama home.

"Wait," I said, "I'll get my coat. I'll go with you."

Mama turned around and glared at me. "We don't need you. Luke is driving me."

I remember the look she gave me, as if I were some contemptible bug on the floor. *Her arrogant eyes.* I remember those eyes now and the feeling that I could not shake off. I froze on the spot. And the first thing I knew they were gone. Her look—her *eyes*—I buried in my Pandora's box—deep, fathoms deep, along with all the other things I've chosen to forget.

I lay awake in the guest room. Luke stayed gone for several hours. I could not go to sleep until long after he returned. Awake, I lay listening to the car door shutting, the mattress creaking as he slid in beside me and his breathing easing into deep sleep, and I felt an unfathomable sinking so deep my conscious mind could not go there in the morning. My *insides* knew it then. *It was my mind that could not grasp it* on that early Christmas morning.

And then I remember when Luke was stationed at Fort Campbell and drove home on most weekends and said he'd stopped by to see Mama first before driving to Greensboro to get me at the university. I was delighted that he was being so thoughtful to visit her and they were becoming friends.

The phone rings and rings and rings. No one answers.

Then more past images flood my consciousness. Sometimes on weekends Mama and Luke drank beer in the kitchen, and Mama would laugh and sit in his lap. She would pull him up from the kitchen chair to dance with her to the music from her little red radio. A few times she started kissing him in front of me while Luke backed away and she teased him with her arms around his neck until finally he would gently push her away and say "We have to go."

I thought she was making a fool of herself drinking too much beer and irritating me, not making real moves on my husband. How could it be anything else? She is my *mother*, for God's sake! But why didn't I talk to her about it?

The phone rings and rings and rings. I wait until it stops to take it off the hook.

Finally, late afternoon I get up and dress, leave the house, and take a long walk. Where else is there to go? My world is still black and white. The black oak tunnel leads to just blacker space. The Baptist Church with white columns on black brick is the darkest of all. In time I find myself at Oakland High School, still out for summer, and sit on its dirty white steps. Around me stretches a vacant lot and emptiness, and I continue to sit, mind blank, immobile like a cold statue. Then high school memories fall like soot. Abruptly, I drop my head and laugh out loud.

Can you believe it? My senior class voted me Most Likely to Succeed! I can't stop laughing—it becomes funnier and funnier, and my body heaves from laughter while my face is drenched from tears.

Somehow I fall asleep. I wake up curled up on concrete with my head propped on my arm. It's a wonder I haven't rolled down the stony stairs. I am exhausted. I trudge back home for lack of any other place to go. Immediately, Mama's at the door being her usual self. "Erin

Rose, where have you been? I've been worried to death! And the phone has not stopped ringing!"

Twilight has fallen, diminishing the light and leaving an ashy residue across the yard. Darkness grows. An early full moon appears through motionless trees and slowly climbs higher.

I sit on the porch alone to think.

Oh, how I wish I could throw out all the memories I abhor and remember just the good, retreat to fantasy and illusion so I can believe what I want to, and quit analyzing. Let someone else tell me what to do and what to think. Luke would be good at that; he knows how to take over completely. But I can't believe him or trust him ever. And my mama—I can't bear to be around her. I look at her and all I see is Luke on top of her and her arms hanging around his neck. Will I ever trust her again? What are we going to do—Alex and I? We can live in Raleigh alone, but we'll have no family there because Mama is close to her sister, and I can't come between them. I can't return to Oak Glen, for that means Mama.

Then I become pragmatic for the first time in my life: I don't have a car, and I won't ask Mama for a loan. How will I take Alex to a nursery in the early morning and return to get her? How will I get to school? On the city bus—my God! It will be a month before I get my first paycheck. What will I do for money? If I cut off all ties, Alex won't have a grandmother or a father—that's not fair to her. Is it possible that a person can change? I don't even have money for a lawyer.

The confessions come back to me. The Scene fills my head so lucidly that I'm there again, and I hurt again, just as badly.

I hear Luke's voice on the phone accusing Mama of adultery with him: "Don't you talk about *me* and *my* morals! You oughta talk to your Mama about hers. You're living with *her*. Ask *her* about *her* morals! Ask her about *how she's fucked me!*" As if he had nothing to do with it, and then he harps on her immorality to keep the spotlight on her.

I desperately want Mama to lie. *Mama, please lie to me! Please tell me Luke's a liar. I can't live with the facts!*

Aunt Agatha leans over to Mama, breaks the silence. "Leah, tell her that's not so. That is preposterous! Tell her that's a flat-out lie. Tell her he's lying!"

Mama still does not speak, just sits staring into space. I stand before her: a captive—my face of stone, my eyes pleading, waiting ... *Mama, I have to live with illusions to replace what does not exist. Mama, please!*

"Leah," Aunt Agatha cries out. "You know you didn't."

Still waiting, I stare at her, praying for that lie of denial.

Mama sucks in her breath as if it's been knocked out. Tears spill from her eyes, run down her face. She starts crying, mumbling in between sobs. And then like Tennessee Williams' unpretentious Blanche DuBois, she says, "You just don't know how it is to be without a man."

Inconceivable. As if I don't know. And this is her excuse?

My chest punctured, I turn around, walk out on the porch, leaving Aunt Agatha sitting there, wringing her hands, bowing her head and shaking it, trying to make sense of it all. In time Mama comes to the door and calls me in, as she used to do when I was a child. "Erin Rose, it's getting dark. Come on in now." As if nothing has happened.

"Leave me alone."

If I can't trust my husband and can't trust my mother, who else is there? I ask myself one question: *Which betrayal can I live with better?*

Luke is amoral. Mama knows better.

I have no respect left for either.

Both have hurt me deeper than deep.

But Mama was *my best friend.*

After he pleads with me to come back, Luke calls me six times a day for four consecutive days. The fourth day I answer the phone and tell him to come for me and Alex.

I cancel my contract with Raleigh City Schools, cancel my apartment lease, pack up, and move to Ohio.

We never again mention his accusation and her silent confession.

Chapter 27

Fall comes early. I can tell by the dip in the weather, not from trees changing colors in the city apartment complex. We have a little patch of grass, no longer green, and acres of concrete. One nice thing, though, is the long, even sidewalk—no bulging oak roots—for me to push Alexandria in her stroller, or her to waddle behind the stroller, pushing her doll. Decked out in her new fall clothes, she wears a thick red sweater and matching toboggan that bobs along with her.

It seems that Luke has a limitless amount of money. I'm not used to that. He is more than generous about letting me buy whatever I want for the apartment, for Alex, and for myself. We buy a white four-piece sectional sofa, his choice of the latest style in the market, and a brass three-way pole lamp. He picks out two Danish Modern lamp tables and coffee table and a large stereo, on which he instructs me not to play classical music if he's anywhere around. I hate the stark lines of Danish furniture, but his enthusiasm overrides my taste. I soften the sharp style with two softly curved crystal lamps and add blue and violet pillows across the sofa; I camouflage the Danish tables with books and magazines.

When I say I want to refinish my grandmother's dining-room suite (the pieces I slipped into the moving van and stored in the basement), Luke has a fit, claiming that the pieces are junk he doesn't want to look at. But after I have it refinished anyway and he sees the restored eighteenth-century Queen Anne mahogany china cabinet, buffet, side table, and large dining table and finds out the price they're worth, he stops arguing. I know then Luke likes my décor. For the first time, I buy a washing machine and dryer that live in the basement, where I later set up a playroom for Alex to ride her tricycle and play with her own kitchen set when I do the laundry.

To prove he can keep his word, Luke comes in every night. Alexandria, who just turned a year old, gets so excited seeing her daddy open the door that she laughs and wobbles toward him with outstretched arms. He responds with his own brand of spirited baby-talk and spins her around and then plops on the floor with her arms still around his neck, hugging him and giggling. As he tickles her and calls out a greeting to me, they romp on the floor while I finish cooking supper. I pause in the kitchen and watch them, relishing the look that Luke gives me, my love for them both overflowing.

One afternoon while Alex and I are strolling down the sidewalk, a neighbor across the street walks over, introduces herself, and invites me to her house to join a morning coffee group, made up of friends in the neighborhood. She says to bring my little girl, for other children will be there. I thank her and accept.

Bright and early, Alex and I get ready for our first visit, pleased to meet my neighbors. After introductions and the settling of a few children in the playroom and the serving of coffee, our lovely hostess turns to me and asks, "Who's the blonde girl who lived with your husband this summer in the apartment two units down from you? We saw him going in and out and assumed she was his wife. And you can imagine how confused we were when *you* arrived. We thought you were *probably his sister*! When it must have been the other way around! Oh, my!" The lovely hostess chuckles.

The room falls silent. I stare at the circle of *Coffee Club Friends* and each one, with the exception of the hostess, drops her eyes to her coffee cup.

"Excuse me." I put down my untouched coffee. "I need to get my daughter." I walk where there's the sound of children and get Alex, put on her sweater and toboggan, and return to the low mumbling circle of women.

"Thank you for the coffee." I pick up my child and leave.

That night Luke says he doesn't know what that nosey bitch was talking about. "The *blonde's not here* now, is she? Or is she hiding in a closet?" He goes to the bedroom and slams the door.

A few days later a bank statement is forwarded to our address to Mrs. Claire McLeod, the previous address of the nearby apartment marked out. I'm not surprised. My inner self keeps up with all the little dirty secrets that my outer self pretends to be dumb about. But why in the name of God did he move us practically next door—even on the same side of the street?

The ladies' coffee club I never attend again, nor do I ever see a member in person. Luke owns up to his summer fling and assures me again and again that the affair is over. He sent her away because *he wants me ... and us.*

That winter Luke becomes a bowling enthusiast. He bowls on his company's team and, as in everything he does, he is extremely competitive, determined to lead with the most strikes. In college I learned to bowl in a required P.E. class and did pretty well and liked it, but I have not played since then.

And now we're bowling. On most Sundays Luke takes Alex and me to the bowling alley, and I look forward to going out with him, if for no reason but to do just that— get out of the apartment since he's gone a lot during the week. I enjoy bowling for fun, but Luke changes the game into a trial of skill. He is determined to improve my technique. I pause and get ready to throw the ball; he stops me, corrects my stance, my posture, my arm alignment, and points out the exact spot where I'm to execute the ball. Half of my mind is on where Alex is, sitting on the leather bench, eating cookies and sipping juice, or quite possibly wandering off. Luke gets impatient with my lack of skill and concentration and angry with my lack of ambition to practice diligently. I find so much instruction unnecessary, bordering on ridiculous. And bowling with Luke is too tedious.

He insists that I join a team in the women's league like the other wives do. So I acquiesce as usual. I join and he buys me a bowling ball with my initials engraved in gold on a real leather case. That winter I call the baby-sitting service once a week and bowl with the other wives. They don't mind—they like my handicap.

And I think of all those things I miss—all the activities I did during college days. When have I been to a concert? Or a ballet? Or a play? Or a movie? Luke hasn't taken me to a movie since the army days. And I love to play cards. In college I played bridge a lot; during the past summer Mama and I played rummy, blackjack, and canasta—and that was fun. But Luke and I, for a long time now, haven't sat down and talked or watched TV together. He always has to leave.

And books! How I miss college classes and discussing books! Oh, but I do have Alex. We read books all the time and talk about the pictures and the story. I'll crawl up on her new white canopy bed, and we'll prop on pillows, pink ruffles hanging like soft threads spinning us into our own cocoon, and read book after book. I do most of the talking, and Alex watches with her big blue eyes, her blonde ponytail flipping back and forth, while she points at the pictures and imitates my words and sounds. I'm sure she understands. She's my world now. And that's great! I have a loving, permanent companion.

Dayton has open bars, serving alcoholic drinks in most of the restaurants. However, as in most Southern states, North Carolina does not serve alcohol in restaurants, so I'm not used to this drinking in public. (North Carolina does have brown-bagging in the nicer restaurants, where customers can order a setup: a pitcher of ice, a choice of mixer—club soda, Coke, ginger ale—and make mixed drinks from their own alcohol kept in a brown bag under the table.)

Already I'm used to going to Suttmiller's and ordering a Brandy Alexander or a Vodka Collins or a Grasshopper or a Toasted Almond or any mixed-drink tasting like a milkshake or a minty lemonade. And, of course, wine readily replaces water. And Grand Marnier becomes a sorbet.

At first, we go out often when I move to Dayton—that is, maybe once a week, then twice a month. Usually it's just the two of us, and I feel like I'm 16 on a grownup date. I love this time with Luke, because he treats me like a princess with undivided attention. He always chooses a place where there's music—if not a live combo, then a piano bar. I'm awed by his sophisticated manner and impeccable dress, stylishly worn with casual abandon. His confidence handles any situation—speaking to the hostess, tipping the maître d' for the best table with candlelight, ordering the right wine.

What a good-looking man Luke is in a rugged sort of way. His square jaw and blond hair with the bit of red undertone makes me think of Robert Redford when he looks straight at the camera with that eye contact that holds you, making you feel those eyes are saying more than a voice can speak.

How can I not remember the Romantic Luke? We dance until the last call for music or drinks. Lights dim, candles flicker, the alto sax drones a slow, indulgent tune. On the dance floor Luke holds me close, breathes in my ear and kisses my neck, and we move to the pulse of the music as one dancer. His hand slides down my back and clasps below, pulling me tighter and I, press against his erection and sway back and forth with him to the music's last beat. Those times are getting scarce, but a rare moment you don't forget.

Mama calls me every week. We talk about Alexandria and the weather and that's it. Since that devastating confession I can't be the same with her. As for Luke, my anxiety has shot up one hundred per cent.

Mama knows we're coming home for Christmas, but we run late driving 11 hours from Ohio through the snowy West Virginia mountains that wind like a roller coaster on its side. So Luke becomes a NASCAR racer, speeding around those mountain tracks. A lot of time I sit staring out the back window at where we've been instead of looking at where we're going. At times I'll switch to the backseat to keep Alex entertained—reading, coloring, feeding her doll, turning on her music box, and singing with her.

It's been four months since we've moved from Oak Glen. When we cross the North Carolina state line, Luke has to stop a number of times to find the right place to get genuine North Carolina barbeque: minced pork barbequed in a deep pit, served with sweet coleslaw, candied yams, and lots of hushpuppies. Then we know we're near "home."

Luke pauses in front of Mama's house before turning into the drive. No Christmas lights. Mama knows we'll spend Christmas Eve and Christmas Day at the McLeods— and she's invited. I look at the darkness. No light at all, save for a small one toward the back. I feel the blank windows like eyes, forlorn, watching me. *I ache.* If only my arms were long enough to reach around the house and embrace it, hugging it and hugging it. I am so weary of being sorry. *It* can't help its dilapidated state. And I don't have the money to fix it: replace rotted wood, paint it white again, add bright green shutters and a new roof, pave the drive over mud-holes, replant an acre of red roses. And I can't redeem all that's gone. So it stands, for the town to see: a replica of so many old Southern homes. Yet there're those rare times— not many—that it makes me shudder. Then, ground fog rising up, I envision Edgar Allan Poe's House of Usher with a crack running from roof to ground.

Only *I* know that this house is much more than a house—*it's a presence of both past and present alive together* ... it stirs up forgotten and lost memories like an old ghost with a magic wand. It's when I'm alone that the magic occurs and I see Daddy as a little boy running up and down the hall playing chase with his brothers and one sister hiding in the many nooks. I see myself—a little blonde girl lining up her arrowheads and Daddy beside me—counting his money he puts into the family's big black safe. I see a make-believe ballerina dancing to music-box rhythms on cross beams in the skeleton of the roof. And brighter than life, stained glass pouring out golden light over darkness. The air full of people—faint echoes of soundless voices resound when the wind rustles leaves of sugar maples close by. The richness of colors and words sparkle in my head visualizing myself in the back of the hall, notebook in lap, writing, sunshine towering through the transom. The darkness of the house knows me, and I feel comfortable in it, even though at times I feel so grief-stricken at Mama's loss of light. Only a faint glow in Mama's two rooms. And the massive darkness spreading.

After we return to Dayton from the brief trip, I am saddened by the amalgam of memories. I *ache* for the Christmas splendor of the past. My old home deserves to *shine* still: its gleaming brass chandelier reflecting across the living room, the lit candles in each front and side window beckoning a bright welcome, the spruce greenery winding with Christmas bulbs down the stairway and across the French doors, the tall Christmas tree reaching out in the bay window and, finally, a green sprig of mistletoe with little shiny white berries hanging from each door-frame, *waiting*—as was the custom—for a man to kiss a girl walking under it. Always I loved the mistletoe—even though the berries were poisonous.

That first year in Ohio I become friends with a neighbor in the same apartment unit. These apartments are built as an upside-down L-shaped duplex with a nice landscaped court in the center of the two to make a unit. Alex and my friend's little boy Sam, the same age, play together often in our courtyard. Lois' husband, a medical intern, works long hours in one of the city hospitals, and since Luke's gone a lot on business, Lois and I keep each other company. She is a godsend! I have someone to talk to.

Lois and Joe are New York Jews. Before them, I knew only one Jewish family in Greensboro. In college I never studied Judaism, and Oak Glen never had Jewish residents when I lived there. (In the early '60s, maybe, a few Jewish families moved to Oak Glen and assimilated into the community with the Scots, Irish, English, and two long-settled families of Catholic Syrians. Then the lives of Negroes were totally segregated, and many American Indians were also segregated into their own schools and living areas. Even people with Italian names were considered foreigners.)

My curiosity starts when I look through Lois's wedding book, and—dumb me!—I ask her why each man wears a little flat hat on the back crown of his head. Lois chuckles and I begin my learning journey about Jewish practices and rituals and food. Lois cooks a lot and introduces me to both Jewish and Yankee dishes. Especially tasty are Cantonese ribs marinated in soy sauce, brown sugar, and freshly grated orange rind broiled until crusty, and then dipped into chutney. She cooks beef stroganoff served over homemade noodles or *matzo* balls. One day Lois brings over to our apartment a delicious snack called *Taigelach*. She has rolled dough into long strips, tied it into small knots, boiled it in honey, and then dipped it in coconut and nuts. She laughs when she says it's most often served for funerals. For me, it could easily become addictive. My favorite entrée, though, is lox and bagels that she and Joe eat fairly often at breakfast: an open bagel spread with homemade spicy-mustard sauce, onion slices, and finally layers of thinly cut lox. I've never eaten this tasty salmon dish before.

I too enjoy cooking the strictly Southern food Luke's mother taught me to fix. Joe likes the way I chop up pimentos and grate cheese, add mayonnaise and seasonings to make sandwiches or spread on celery. He'll even eat the pimento cheese in a bowl with a spoon.

I invite them to supper—when I know Luke will be home—and cook dishes unfamiliar to them: Southern fried chicken (my special way); fresh purple butter beans cooked with a small amount of fatback; fresh field peas with okra on top, also flavored with fatback; rice with giblet gravy; and fried cornbread. Luke contributes the Chardonnay.

Lois and Joe keep eating and raving over the food.

"This is *so* good. Erin, I want you to show Lois how you cook all of this. Especially those mushrooms!" Joe points to the beans.

"What mushrooms?" I laugh. "Those are purple butter beans."

Luke cuts in. "This is nothing. You oughta taste my mother's cooking!"

I snap back—which is unusual for me, but I've been cooking all day—"This food is exactly the same! Your mother taught me how to cook each dish! And even the vegetables are from your mother's garden. Don't you remember? The peas and beans she picked and froze and packed in a cooler and brought with her when she came to visit?"

Luke shrugs, then grins. "Well, it tastes pretty good ... but you'll never come close to Mama's cooking. No need trying."

Both Joe and Lois look up. There's a silent pause. Subject dropped.

Luke continues, "You oughta taste Mama's homemade minced barbecue. She cooks pork about all day, pours vinegar and spices on the meat, and pulls the meat from the bone and chops it up like hash. It's wonderful! You eat it with cornbread. Erin, you wouldn't even know how to start. We'll have to bring you guys some back the next time we go home ... you know, North Carolina is known for its minced barbecue."

Luke stands up to open another bottle of wine.

"Hey, Joe," I say. "I won't tell your Rabbi what you're eating."

He looks quizzically. "What do you mean?"

"Well ... even in the beans and in the peas ... you can find little pieces of *pig*. I knew Lois wouldn't mind, and I just wasn't going to tell you."

Everyone laughs as Luke pours more wine.

Joe insists, "Erin, I bet our Rabbi would eat this meal, even knowing all the contents."

Occasionally, Luke and I go clubbing with Joe and Lois to eat, drink, and dance. Tonight Lois looks lovely in her red dress with the full skirt. Tonight everything about Lois is dramatic. Her black hair, long and thick, is swept up into a French knot with a jeweled clip. Her face is artfully made up, and expensive jewels dangle from her ears—ordinarily she's in sloppy warm-ups with a shiny face and frizzled hair and doesn't give a hoot. I envy her confidence around her husband. She is rather tall, a bit larger than I, has a low alto voice and an explosive temper that I've witnessed with her son—and with Joe, too, if he forgets to do what she wishes. We always have a good time, since the four of us like each other and dance interchangeably. Outspoken, Lois and Luke joke and kid each other and drink, Lois guzzling her Scotch faster than Luke.

Joe could pass for a football player sooner than a doctor. Taller and larger built than Luke, Joe looks quite handsome in a dark suit with his black hair and inquiring eyes, black and serious, a spark of light when he smiles or laughs. A superb smooth slow-dancer, Joe whisks me across the floor as if we are one, he's so easy to follow. We stay on the dance floor a lot, even stopping for another glass of wine between songs and talk about any subject that comes to mind, including literature. He listens to me and seems very much interested, always adding a relevant comment that makes me think. And he keeps me up with current books. I imagine his bedside manner with his wife is as effective as it would be with his patients. More importantly, Joe's a considerate man. At the end of the year, he'll complete his internship and become a full-fledged doctor on the hospital staff.

Sometime past midnight we four prepare to leave. Luke walks with Lois to the front door where a man who knows Luke calls him and they stop to talk. Lois chats along with them. Joe and I continue to leave, walking to the parking lot. When we stand beside the car, Joe leans down and kisses me. I'm surprised. But we end up with a very *nice* kiss. I start thinking how easy it would be to have an affair— to beat Luke at his own game. For a moment I can see how my heart and my head could be at great odds. Yet a man like Joe could easily win a heart. However, my head thinks of Lois and I know I could never betray a friend. My husband? I'd love to get even with him. Then again, it was only a kiss. Joe's too nice a guy to go further that way. And I wouldn't want him to.

A bagel and lox. I see or hear that phrase and my brain flashes: I'm cast into watery shadows. I kick. I push. I can't budge the weight of what's above me, around me.

The weather's now hot in late spring and Joe, Lois, Luke, and I plan an outing. It's Joe's idea. Lois has made a delicious breakfast of lox and bagels for us and added some *Taigelach*—the rest of this sweet dough we pack to take. Joe has borrowed a friend's camper and arranged for a very capable off-duty nurse to stay in their apartment to take care of our Alex and their Sam.

Saturday morning we're off until late Sunday afternoon. Luke has hitched his boat to the trailer, and Lois and I have loaded the camper with food and swimsuits and beer and wine coolers. Joe's friend has offered his lake property where we can stay near the lake. It's an hour and a half away.

We park under shady trees beside the lake; there's a ramp where we can put in the boat and a stack of wood near a fire pit. The lake water is clear, slightly warm enough for swimming. The place is private, safe, lovely, and quiet. It's the perfect setting for summer activities: boating, swimming, hiking through the woods, building a roaring fire, or just sitting back in a lounge chair drinking beer or wine and watching the water lap softly, lazily.

Luke's not so keen about the camping stuff. He loves racing his new inboard motorboat with mahogany interior that he keeps as shiny as he did his paratrooper boots. He spends most weekends working on his boat and racing it in a nearby lake or attending hydroplane races in other parts of the state. On occasional Sundays he takes Alex in her bright orange lifejacket and me for a cruise down the river. Once in a blue moon we have a picnic: fried chicken, deviled eggs, pimento cheese sandwiches, brownies, and iced tea. We watch Alex play on the riverbank. However, Luke usually ends up going too fast with a child in the boat. I spend so much time pleading with him to slow down and fearing for my child, I'm too tense to enjoy boating any more.

Now on the camping adventure Luke promises me he won't go so fast. We all go for a moderate ride first around the lake, Lois and I *oh-ing* and *ah-ing* over some fabulous lake homes, the wind slapping lake water in our faces as we stretch out in the back of the boat. Gradually, Luke increases the speed and before we know it the boat literally races above the water, intermittently skimming and splashing, no holds barred, then swerves around—one side nearly vertical, the other almost even with water before splashing down abruptly when Luke decreases the speed. Lois and I scream our heads off, our shouts lost to the wind and the roar of the motor, our voices subsiding into nothing.

Luke slowly docks and grins at us. "Would you *sissy ladies* like to get out?"

I want to knock that grin to the bottom of the lake. Lois, speechless for once, just glares and knocks Luke's hand away, refusing help to get up onto the dock. Joe steps behind her and holds her butt while she climbs—which doesn't improve her mood a bit. And still in the boat, I put on my most arrogant look, ignore all the reaching hands and say, "Thank you, but I don't need any help."

I put a foot on the edge of the boat, reach for the rope around the post, and pull up my other foot; the boat slides from the dock, leaving me hanging on to the rope. Both men pull me up.

"Erin, you okay?" Joe asks with concern and a quick eye exam. Luke just shakes his head.

"I'm fine," I answer Joe and start walking down the plank where Lois is waiting, concerned.

"Hey," Luke calls. "Why don't you two fix us some lunch? I'm starving! While you're doing that, Joe and I'll race around some more."

Off they go, like two little boys running away from mama.

After lunch, Joe suggests they fish. In back of the camper Joe has stacked the fishing equipment needed, and they decide to cast off from shore near the curve of the lake.

I've always adored swimming, from early childhood with Daddy holding me up and telling me not to fear to my college years when I swam in an advanced swim class focusing on strokes.

"Let's try the water even if it's cold!"

Lois readily agrees with me. Quickly, we change into our swimsuits, jump into the water, play around near the shore, and I start swimming strokes. We lie in the sun for a while, talking and drinking wine-coolers, and then dive back into the lake.

The men, tired of waiting for a catch, decide to join us.

Soon they run down to our swimming spot, Lois just treading water and I swimming long back strokes.

Joe says, "Wow! Look at Erin!"

They jump in and Joe swims to Lois; Luke swims towards me, goes underwater, and surfaces almost on top of me, throwing me off balance.

I tread water and he laughs loudly, "Gotcha!"

Then quicker than a splash he laughs, reaches up and pushes my head down into the water and holds it there. I reach up but can't budge his hand. I pull on his arm. When I do, he presses my head down farther, so I kick and wiggle but can't get loose from him. The struggle becomes an underwater battle. My upper chest starts burning. I can't hold my breath much longer.

In the water world below shadows are moving, elongating, in slow motion. I see a few bubbles. Limp, I panic. I burn. My head's dizzy. I fear I'm about to drown. I am horrorstruck by this world of darkness. Then I feel a sudden release and a hand pulling me up and a shock of air—but not long enough for a deep breath.

Still laughing, Luke holds up my head while I cough and cough, gasping for air. He's acting as if I don't know how to swim and calls out loudly, "What're you doing? Not holding your breath when you go under?"

I'm still choking.

Suddenly, Joe's there. "Luke, hold her up!"

They're both treading water and holding me up and over, and then Joe's pressing on my back with the heel of his hand, back and forth, and I'm spitting out water and heaving.

Joe says, "Let's get her to shore," and puts his arms around me.

Luke quickly pulls me away, "I've got her!" and starts swimming with his lifeguard hold.

Later at the campfire the guys cook steaks, and Lois magically produces appetizing food. I feel lifeless, cut off from the others. I lean back in a chair and stare at the fire, watching flames curling up under wood, spitting cracks, eating bark and splinters. A bright red changes to orange-yellow, blue, dark streams of smoke, bold stripes rising, *a beast raging.* I can get lost in the fire, forms wavering like underwater silhouettes. And the wine coolers—I drink one after another—have a way of calming my nerves and drowning my anxiety. A few more drinks ... and I'll know it's my imagination that sometimes sees Luke as two persons. Yet I feel so sad ... just craving for someone to touch me gently, lovingly—the way Joe curves his arm around Lois and she lays her head on the side touching his neck.

Everyone's in bed. I lie on my side and look out the small window next to the bed. The full moon sits on tall trees like a spotlight and throws silver across the lake, creates a pool with a moon of water so close to shore that if I were at the water's edge I could swim to the moon and become silver. So tranquil and pure ... in its coldness and beauty I'd be warm. Yet in the coolness of a spring night, here in this bed I lie under a quilt near Luke's body heat, and I'm cold. That invisible spot deep inside the center of me never warms.

Soon I fall asleep and have a nightmare.

Chapter 28

After our camping trip, I carry still the beauty of the full moon shining on the lake and remember the intense desire for swimming to the moon's reflection, so smooth and clear like glass and unbroken in the darkness. Then I think of the ripples to come, scattering its face into a thousand distorted pieces.

Last night I suffer tormented sleep: I swirl and tumble and gasp for air, slinging off the covers and rolling onto Luke, but rapidly recoiling in a delirium of fear. Then, out of fire a dream-tiger flares up as lucid as moon on water, and my mass of fears abate. Instantly, I'm back in Oak Glen at my *real* home, facing the tiger, our eyes lock: *I see a green-eyed tiger that rests on my back porch. Bright neon green glowing in the dark. I can't see its body, but I know it's there. I see only green-eyed slits angled down like reversed luminescent diagonals. Then I see it's sitting, staring: front legs stretched out, eyes fixed on me. I stare back, unafraid. I, too, watching, waiting, aware of the immensity of its innate power. The night totally black, the tiger sits near the wall behind the back door of the long hall. I go to shut and bolt the heavy oak door, and it's still there, eyes glinting through darkness. I stand in the doorway intrigued by the mystery and the sheer danger and the ethereal awe of a now bodiless beast, but instead of jumping back and bolting the door, I leave it open and stare into tiger eyes.*

All at once, there is light. And I can see a beautiful green-yellow-blue striped full-grown tiger loping from room to room in the house. The rooms are empty. I'm ironing clothes for children, not my own, but for children in my care. I'm pressing the clothes, white, to be worn the next day. I pick up the smallest child, who seems to be different from the rest, sensing this child is the marked one for whom the tiger has come. But as I clasp the child and hurry through empty rooms to protect it, this child suddenly changes into a baby tiger. Still determined to save this baby, I fly to the end of the hall and climb up onto Daddy's chifforobe next to the oak door. I reach out and pull the top of the heavy door open to let the full-grown tiger out. The large tiger passes through and out. I shut the door quickly, relieved. Then at once there are tigers all around, dozens loping through the rooms wherever I look. They're searching for this child, this baby tiger. I cannot escape.

I awake. Those slanted eyes in the dark still remain fixed on me. I think of the campfire and the myriad colors of the flames. For days the phrase "the eye of the tiger" keeps popping up in my head. I feel as mesmerized by those slanted green eyes that seem to hold a message as I do by the fire images.

This same dream occurs again. Then, maybe once a month or once every couple of weeks. Sometimes it's changed to the single tiger sitting on the porch. What does this mean? Intuitively, I feel the dream is important. If I could talk to this tiger, would he respond to me?

I close my eyes and focus intensely on the eyes of the dream-tiger and imagine he's here to communicate with me. I fall easily into a trance and ask:

Why are you staring? What are you waiting for?

You, the Tiger responds.

I'm not afraid of you.

I am you.
My inert power?
Your innate fire! Burning, burning fears.

In the coming days, I live with the tiger's words: "I *am* you." I try to analyze what I should do. After all, the words came from somewhere. Mainly, I need to eliminate my fears. That will take time and a lot of planning because my greatest fear is that Luke will leave me for another woman. Why is that fear so great? It'll increase my feeling of inadequacy? And I'll lose completely my sense of self. Perhaps I can nurture the potential tiger traits within me. Like the early Native American Indians who kept their own animal totem within, I must fight for myself. The tiger has what it takes to release me.

In late August I start teaching English in West Carrollton, a small town about a forty-five minute drive from our Dayton apartment. With the help of Joe, I hire a reputable retired nurse to arrive early in the morning to babysit Alexandria. I miss Alex terribly during the day, but she likes the nurse; I, in turn, enjoy my classes and welcome teaching again—having my own money, receiving respect again, expressing my thoughts without being put-down and having a sense of freedom.

Then, in November, I discover I'm pregnant.

Once you experience infidelity, you are always on the lookout for that slightest little hint. You don't really dwell on it, but the thought has a way of creeping in, nagging at you if your husband is away a lot, especially on overnight trips. And when it does happen, you are almost relieved, for you no longer have that sharp anxiety of wondering when it's going to happen again. No more suspense, just a familiar hurt you know well. And this time I learn of infidelity from Luke himself.

On an early Friday night in February, Luke hurries in, takes a shower, dresses carefully—more than usual—and starts to head out. He pauses to say Claire's in town. She has flown to Dayton from Florida to see him. Oh, my God, after all this time—since he dated her in Greensboro when I was pregnant with Alex and lived with her for his first summer in Dayton—they're back together, taking turns flying to see each other. He's going to the airport now to meet her. He hesitates a moment and then explains to me, "Erin, I'm spending the weekend with Claire." *He's telling me this?* "I have to ... to see if I still love her. I can't make up my mind."

I feel I'm struck with a brick!

"You said this when I was pregnant with Alex! The same girl! And I'm pregnant again now, too!"

Then in shock, my voice dies. If it should resurrect, will I scream, hit him, slam the door in his face, or cry and laugh hysterically? Both the scene and his words are unbelievable, especially when he adds, "Erin, if I decide again I don't want Claire and I love you, I'll be back ... maybe ... before Sunday."

Softly, he pulls the door shut.

Have you ever felt you've fallen over the ledge of a dry well and you have to stay at the bottom of circular walls you can't climb, too deep to be heard even if you had a voice? You've been there before, but familiarity can't prevent claustrophobia, walls inching closer and closer with three days to wait. And at the same time my imagination goes wild, and I see myself starring in a melodramatic comedy—too ludicrous to be real.

Yet I ache from grief and rage. I want to hit, kick, rip out Luke's hair, knock him up against the wall, but he's gone and no one's here to beat on. I want to throw dishes against the wall and dash them to the floor, but I don't want them broken. Get a sharp knife and rip up his clothes—nothing he loves better—and hurl pieces into the street. In fact, in all

314

the places we have lived, Luke has never had anything personal with him—except his clothes. (His golf clubs stay in his car.) I want to pack some stuff, get Alex, call a cab to the airport, and purchase tickets for whatever plane has seats. Go so far away he'd never find us. But I don't have enough money to get there and stay. That old Ford he bought me to get to school is a piece of shit that wouldn't even slide on sleet, and the roads are packed with either fresh snow or freezing tire tracks. What do you do alone on a Friday night in Dayton during a snowstorm? Add to that your future will be settled in three days by someone else— you don't have a say. Escaping into a book no longer works. Why doesn't Luke ever leave any alcohol here? Tonight I could drink a whole bottle of bourbon.

"Mommy ... Mommy, I'm cold." In her pink fairy pajamas Alex ambles into the living-room, dragging the little red stuffed pig, her sleeping buddy she got on her first Christmas at three months.

"Well, when I checked on you, darling, you were as snug as a—"

"Bug in a rug." She giggles.

I pick up Alex and hug her tight. And an overwhelming love flushes through me.

Alex starts wriggling. "Mommy, I want some hot choc'ket. The wind is cold."

"You can't feel the wind in your room, Sweetie."

"I hear it, Mommy. I know it's cold."

"Let's go make your hot chocolate. Then we'll put another cover on your bed."

Later I tuck in another quilt, and Alexandria wants me to read her asleep. "Which book?"

"The fairy book like my pajamies, Mommy." She points at her pajama tops to Peter Pan and Wendy flying through the air, and I search her bookcase. "Is Daddy not coming home tonight to stay? I miss him."

"No, Honey ... here's your book."

"Peter Pan flies to Neverland. Is that where Daddy's flying?"

"Daddy isn't flying anywhere tonight, Alex. He's driving."

"Has Daddy been to Neverland?"

"No, Alex. Neverland is not a real place. It is a make-believe land in the book about Peter Pan. Why do you think Daddy would like it?"

"Daddy acts like a little boy when we play Candyland and do puzzles. He sits on the floor and giggles when he's winning. And he talks baby talk to me when he tickles me. He laughs and changes his voice a lot."

"Darling, why don't you ask him about Neverland when you see him? Do you want me to read now?"

Alex snuggles on her pillow with Red Pig, and I turn to the first page ... and then I shift my position to look at Alex. "Honey, when I sit on the floor with you and play dolls, do I seem like a little girl?"

"No. You're Mommy."

"But we play together and laugh. I change my voice when I read."

She shakes her head. "No. You always Mommy."

We stay in the world of Peter Pan until Alex falls asleep. I close the book, tuck her in snug, switch on her night light, and lean over and kiss her. I, too, get ready for bed.

The wind whooshes around corners; snowflakes tap on windows. And the night hours drag by. Already I've tried to read three different books, but I can't focus on any of them. The face of Luke keeps flashing in my vision. I hear his voice resounding around the bedroom. I drop the books on the floor, and I switch the light off. I close my eyes and try to get comfortable. Again and again I hear *"I have to see if I still love her ... if I decide I love you, I'll be back ... I can't make up my mind ... I have to spend the weekend with her."*

His voice doesn't stop, becomes a menacing chant reeling around and around the bed. I turn over to cover my head with quilts and meet his lingering scent on the sheets. I inhale deeply and sob until exhaustion finally lulls me to sleep.

The phone rings loud and long in the still and chilly Saturday morning. I reach for it and glance at the hour of the clock: 9:00. Luke? My heart already pumps hard, seemingly in my throat. I lift the receiver and hear Mama's voice, "Erin Rose?"

"Hello, Mama. How are you?" I prop up in bed, hoping not to awaken Alexandria, who was late last night going to sleep, along with me.

Mama wants to know how we're doing with so much cold weather. She misses us so terribly she can hardly stand it. The pipes froze last night, but she remembered to fill the bathtub with water. "We're so far apart; why don't you insist that Luke get a transfer back to North Carolina or get a new job? You're all I have—you and little Alexandria." She sniffs and starts crying softly. "I'm so alone, Erin Rose, I don't know what to do. I love you two so much."

"Mama, please don't cry. I can't do a thing about Luke. I love you, too … Mama, I have to get Alex up and make breakfast. I'll call you soon."

"But you never call me anymore … like you used to, Erin."

"I will. I promise."

"Please call me. I have no one to talk to."

"I will, Mama. Love you. 'Bye."

I pull the curtain back and see a world of snow. Indefinable. Still. During the night a gentle snow fell, covering our small world white and deeply cold. Looking out my bedroom window, I see how snowflakes tapped the glass, melted into myriad shapes, and froze like ice in a design on stained glass.

Two days remain before my final edict: to have or have not. The grand prize—Luke. I'm still filled with anger and now humiliation, like a child having to wait to see if she gets the candy bar. Yet by late afternoon on Sunday loneliness sets in, and with it grief overcomes rage. I don't want to go through the long months of pregnancy alone as I did before. If I didn't love him, I would never abide this disrespect, and I grieve for what I've already lost: my self-respect. My reasoning is gone. My emotions are a tangled mess. When I do recognize the truth, I dismiss it because of my insistent hope that everything will turn out okay. As a child, Daddy saw to it that my life was fine. Then with Daddy gone, I tried to pray to the church God, but that dwindled away, leaving only myself to depend on.

But whose voice is that in my recurring tiger dream?

When the doorbell rings late, I will myself to answer. Why doesn't he use his key? Then I can pretend to be asleep. I don't think I can even walk to the door. The snow lightens the darkness of night.

Luke stands attentively looking at me. "It's over, Erin. She's gone. I love you."

He pulls me into his arms and just holds me. In that moment that's enough. I am so relieved, I let out a sigh and start sobbing. And life goes on.

In early spring we have a Parent-Teacher Conference Day, and already I've completed my appointments, which went very well. On this bright day I'm elated to have some precious time to myself to stroll down the sidewalk in the more artsy part of town, window-shopping, choosing at will a bookshop, a craft store, and then an art gallery to browse around, entranced by the portraits.

I enter Art Designs and slowly peruse a half dozen or so paintings and turn and suddenly stop. My God! I've never been in this store before; I've never seen this painting before. But there he is—*green eyes staring yet reflective in repose ... waiting. Stripes now black and white and yellow and green under a cerulean shadow that wraps around him like an aura with bits of white floating above and below, like snowdrops and cloud puffs and slips of paper under tiger toes and at the bottom in front of him a slash of red.*

There he is—My Tiger.

A large rectangular acrylic on canvass of a full-grown tiger in the same position and with the same appearance as the one in my dream. The one whose voice is in my head, speaking telepathically. This is far too much for a coincidence. I must have him—even if it takes every penny I have or will have. I don't ask the price; just pull out my credit card; say, "Wrap it!" A nice young man carries my totem to my car.

When I come home, Alex is playing in her room, and I start straightening our bedroom and wondering where to place my new picture. I pick up Luke's coat to hang it up in the closet, and a letter drops out of his pocket. I see Claire's name on the envelope. I rip it open. She writes about how excited she is over the baby. When is he coming to see her so that they can make plans to get married? Oh, my God, not again. Has he been flying to see her instead of going on business trips? What else is in store for me?

Not knowing when he will be in tonight, I call Luke at his office and tell him to get home immediately and hang up. I'm waiting at the door with the letter in my hand.

Luke walks in, shuts the door, and sees the letter. "I've been planning to tell you we need to get a divorce as soon as we can. I've promised Claire I'd marry her so her baby will have a name."

His statement is so ludicrous, all I can think to say is "Are you out of your mind? Have you forgotten I'm pregnant, too?"

He shrugs. "Erin, you'll be fine."

"Fine? You haven't any clue ..." I swallow hard to keep my voice from cracking, but my throat hurts so much and my mouth is so dry no sound comes. I just stand there like an imbecile.

"Time's really getting by. I've got to see my lawyer soon to get him started on the divorce papers." Luke strolls in the bedroom, gets his bag, and drops some clothes in it, leaving drawers pulled out and closet open. "Oh, Erin, I'm flying to Coral Gables on the next flight."

My voice suddenly returns.

"You're a crazy son of a bitch! You're not packing me up and sending me out like excess baggage because you screwed your girlfriend and got her pregnant, too! And what about me? And our child who will be born in four months?"

"I told you ... you'll be okay."

"Okay? You bastard, you don't know what it's like for me! And marry her? *You are married, you idiot,* to me! I haven't seen any divorce or separation papers. And you might as well not plop any down because I will *not* sign any damn paper."

"Oh, Erin, be reasonable! I've told you how it is." Furious, he slams the door on his way out.

I'm furious too and want to yell but instead I answer him in my head. How it is? At which time? In Greensboro when I was pregnant with Alex and you said you loved Claire? And then when I was starting over in Raleigh you literally begged me to come back because you really loved me? Then a few months ago you couldn't make up you mind if you loved her again—you needed to screw her for three days and nights to be sure? But, alas, you come back to me because you love me. Now she's pregnant and you suddenly love her again ... you know something—you are a piece of shit! You are incapable of loving anyone but yourself ... I reach down and heave a heavy brass candlestick holder against the door, which now has a deep dented scar.

Luke leaves for a couple of weeks and then returns. I ignore him as if I don't even see him.

In a few more weeks another letter drops carelessly on the dresser. He's still living with us as usual, and I continue ignoring him as if he's not there. Of course, I read the letter. Again, Claire is busy buying baby clothes and fixing up a nursery. When should she expect him?

Soon afterward, Luke informs me he's flying to Coral Gables again to see her. I then ask him what his plans are. "You certainly can't marry her without being a bigamist. Did you know that?"

He looks at me and sighs. "I am well aware of that, Erin. I'm going to give her money for an abortion."

I quickly add up time and wonder: this late? Then I'm aghast. "Luke, that's illegal."

"Not in Cuba."

In 1961 abortions were illegal in the United States and would be for another decade. Most people were shocked by the mere idea. The word itself, abortion, was synonymous with quack butchering, murder, life on the streets. However, under Castro's rule, Americans with money were welcomed in Cuba, where abortions were legal.

His mind made up, I'm curious about how he can pay for such a plan. Despite what an emotional turmoil this has been to me, I cannot help but feel ambivalent. Obviously, Claire thought Luke was single. Now she finds him not only married, but he's convinced her simply to delete a baby she was so excited to have. To abort a baby I could never do. And in a foreign country—alone?

The eternal wheel keeps rolling on and on, flattening out my life that's measured, not by coffee spoons, but by my husband's lies. And plagued by hundreds of indecisions, unable to act. Luke's old habits remain: staying out late and for days and ignoring me. Sometimes on Saturdays he takes Alex to his office to catch up on paperwork, and his secretary Becky is there to keep an eye on her while she draws pictures on the stationery and plays on the typewriter. Alex comes home chatting about how she and Daddy and Becky ate hamburgers at Becky's house where she played all afternoon with a deck of cards. The next day I drive his car to the grocery store and find on his back seat a brown bag with stained lacey panties.

By May I wear loose clothing—no maternity dresses allowed for teachers. I wait to resign.

Chapter 29

In the heat of August our son Brennan is born and, for the first time ever, I receive two dozen long-stemmed red roses from Luke, who's bragging to everyone he has a boy. I'll be staying at home with the children, since it's too late to get another teaching job. Mama comes to stay with us a week to help out. Lois is still my good friend, as close as across the yard. Joe is my confidant—what would I do without him to empty my soul to? It is Joe I call when I start having labor pains in my back. It is Joe who makes sure Luke gets me to the hospital while Lois takes Alex to their apartment. And, bless him, Joe hands me, upon my return, a large jar of birth control pills from the hospital pharmacy before they become available to the general public, at first, at an astronomical cost.

A couple of months later Luke comes home excited about the showplace house he's leased and already arranged for movers to come the day after tomorrow. He wants to take me right then to see it. He's like a young boy on Christmas Eve. "I can't wait for you to see it!" I'm not the least bit enthusiastic about moving with a new baby away from my friends Lois and Joe and to a place across the city I've not even seen. Also, I don't have the time or energy to supervise the moving. But away I go with Luke, carrying Alex and baby Brennan, to see this wonderful house.

"What if I don't like it?"

"You will. Besides, I've paid the lease. And the apartment contract's void now. Someone else is already planning to move in."

"And you haven't told me? How long have you known—"

Luke interrupts impatiently, "I've taken care of everything. Just relax. Enjoy."

If Alex is around, she always listens to every word we say. Now she quickly interjects, "Mama, we bringing Tiger to hang?"

I give her a big smile. "Yes, Darling. Tiger will go everywhere with us. He'll stay right above my bed!"

Luke looks at Alex in the rearview mirror. "You know, your mama's waiting for that thing to jump down on me. To scare me to death!" And he makes a wild rendition of a tiger attack, roaring while Alex giggle-laughs along with him.

Luke fills me in on the tremendous yard we'll have with a pond larger than the size of most backyards where wild ducks, tame enough to take bits of bread from your hand, live and wobble around. Wildflowers grow everywhere, around the pond and across the backyard. It's a custom-built house that's been a showplace for over a decade. Built for a retired couple with no children, the house was designed for gardening and socializing. I can see it from the highway, alone in a field so big we could keep horses.

"Are you going to ride a horse now?" I ask. "Have a place to put him? Feed him, brush him, comb him? Make sure he gets enough exercise?"

"Erin, I don't ride horses." He looks over at me and grins. "Used to ride mules though on Dad's farm. You can get a horse to ride if you want one."

"Oh, I think I'll pass on that."

"Mama, Mama ... I wanna a horse ... a baby horse, Daddy?" Alex's so excited her little legs are dancing back and forth. "Daddy, will ya get me a horse?"

"We'll see."

"Luke," I whisper, "don't promise her something you're not going to do."

"How do you know?" He turns off the highway.

I study the neighborhood of small houses built close together, probably in the '30s and '40s, some in great need of repair and others well kept. Obviously commercial growth is eating up the land all around, industrial buildings and high-rise apartments and service stations and grocery stores edging in closer. In a couple of years it will be at our door. The bustling highway runs parallel to the Miami River, where local motorboats dock along the shore and where pickup trucks and motorcycles park.

"Tell me again about the ducks, Luke. Do the wild-but-tame ducks that follow you around bite?"

"No ... oh, I don't think so."

"And how many are there?"

"Erin, do you really think I counted them? Hey, I did count a dozen. And a whole lot more were out at the pond."

"Well, where were the dozen you counted?"

"Why do you ask so many questions?"

"Because you've chosen this place for us to live in and you didn't ask my opinion."

"Is that what this is about? You wanted to make the deal yourself?"

"Of course not. If you've already paid for a year's lease and it's not suitable for us, can you cancel it? You've just signed it, right?"

"Erin, just shut up. I know what I'm doing. And you'll like it. There it is!" Luke turns off the road into a long drive that slopes down and then curves to the side of the house near the patio. "Look."

True. The property spreads nearly half a city block—with that much grass to mow. And though the one-story house stretches out like a ranch house, the walls are glass with inlaid wood. Luke's leased a glass house? That's why everyone stares at it. Obviously the ground was built up for the construction of the highway. Now the rain and melting snow probably drain into this yard. And up close the legendary scenic view changes. Luke points to a handful of ducks waddling excitedly down the dirt mound around the pond—quacking, quacking, quacking. "See—they're hurrying to the patio like a friendly old dog happy to see us."

The second we get out of the car Alex starts screaming because two ducks are quacking around her legs, and she can't get away. The others are inching closer to me. "Luke, get the door open!"

He does and quickly grabs a broom and starts shooing away the ducks like chickens. I tell Alex her daddy is a cowboy now, using a broom instead of a whip to get the herd going. She looks out the window in the first room, a sunroom, and turns to me. "He's not a cowboy, Mama."

I put my finger to my lips and whisper, "Shh ... he's playing make-believe."

She puts her finger to her lips, opens her eyes wide, shrugs her shoulders, and grins. Then she giggles. That's right—don't cry over ducks! We wait for Luke to show us the rest of our house.

"You'll love this big living room, Erin." The sun's going down behind the trees; shadows stretch across the backyard and into the rooms. Luke leads us into its dimness and quickly stops, holding out his arms on the sides. He turns around and picks up Alex. He looks down and says to me, "Watch your step, Honey. No carpet. Just nails sticking up."

He stands still, eyes searching, but no light switches are on the walls. The low sockets are for lamps. "Damn!

What crappy work. They ripped out the carpet and left this mess. What were they thinking of? Don't worry. I'll get carpet installed in the morning."

I peep around Luke. "Is this one room? My God, it looks like a bowling alley!"

Suddenly a new albatross hangs around my neck. Not only do we have this humongous room where our living-room furniture will fill only a corner, but the master bedroom is also bowling-alley size. I'll have to convert one corner of it to a nursery since there's only one other little bedroom.

Thank goodness! Long heavy dark drapes hang in the two bowling-alley rooms but no other shade, shutter, or curtain hangs anywhere else. Alex's four-piece bedroom set will barely fit in the small bedroom at the front of the house, and the early morning sun will glare like a huge spotlight on the glass wall here. The same is true for the front breakfast room and kitchen with a bare glass wall. Similarly, on the back and west side I can sit in the large unadorned sunroom and look out blazing glass at a nearly empty pond from drought, and the unkempt surroundings of a hundred ducks at sunset.

Luke will not discuss any need for shades. There's no use in arguing with him, because he flatly refuses to spend any money on drapes for a rented house. I can sew some sheets together and nail them up in some of the rooms, drape them at the top by day, and loosen them to hang at night. What a show place this will be. I'll keep the hammer on the lamp table beside my bed in case a sheet falls in the dark. From the well-traveled highway at night, if the lights are on, half of the house is a bright fish bowl. The other choice is to keep the lights off in the smaller rooms and sit in the dark. Or I can sit in a large bowling-alley room under dim lamplight or go to bed.

Did you know ducks drop more eggs than poop? Giant white eggs lie all over the yard for you to stumble over because they're too big to step on and smash. Luke says don't worry; the eggs are just dead-heads—not fertilized, so no duckies inside.

"If you don't like them, pick 'em up, and drop them in the trash."

Every time he talks about the house, I could just *slap* him.

By late November we have settled into our showplace—as well as could be expected. Then late one night—Luke, of course, is not at home—I'm taking a shower. I pull back the shower curtain, step out onto the bath mat, and reach for a towel. As I'm drying myself, I suddenly feel strange, really creepy. I feel as if someone's staring at me—and this sensation gets stronger until it feels like an electric current. I wrap the towel around me and turn toward the window. Without thinking, I walk straight to the window like a magnet has pulled me, flip back the curtain, and look into a man's eyes, his face pressed against the window. I open my mouth but can't scream.

I flee into our bedroom and dial the police, holding the only weapon I have—the hammer. Though the police arrive promptly, while I wait I feel the kind of terror I only see and feel in a horror movie. The police find a porch swing propped up under the bathroom window and large footprints in the mud.

After they leave, everything stays the same. There spreads the big field. There sits a glass house like a fish tank. There stands a lone woman with a hammer in her hand. There lies a baby. There sleeps a child. The crescent moon, cold and sharp, shines bright white. Across the curving pavement, silhouettes of tall black buildings stand, wait ... for dawn.

In the sunny morning Luke drives by and points at the glass house to show another important customer his home.

Before long Brennan will be tottering around the pond, feeding the ducks fat chunks of bread. I dread that day. He's so active now at 11 months he tries to pull himself up but shows no fear of falling and crawls everywhere swiftly. I have to watch him all the time. In fact, I need to watch him almost as much in the house as I would outside.

One day Brennan and I are sitting on the sofa and hear a *tweet-tweet-tweet* like baby birds in the back of and between our sofa cushions. I pick up the cushions, see a family of baby field mice nesting, and scream. Meanwhile, Brennan reaches for a baby mouse. I yank him up and run from the room and slam the door. I scrub his hands and put him in his playpen, and he struggles to crawl out. I call Luke's office, but he's not there, so I tell his secretary to stop what she's doing and find a rodent control service that will send someone out. This is an emergency. The serviceman gets rid of the nest, pulls the sofa into the garage, and leaves rat bait around the house. Later Luke tells me that it is now my designated duty to get rid of rats.

When Brennan crawls behind the refrigerator and discovers a shallow box of rat poison, I find him sitting there eating piece by piece what looks just like Captain Crunch cereal. I grab him and Alex and try to race to the hospital at night during a rainstorm in my slow shit of a car that doesn't want to go uphill. Finally, at the hospital I run through the halls screaming for a doctor, holding Brennan and fearing for his life. Alex trails behind me crying.

They take him from me, and Alex and I sit in the waiting room. I rock back and forth, head bent down, praying and praying.

"Mama, is Brennan gonna die?" Alex sniffles.

"Don't say that, Alex, don't say that." I could barely control myself. There's no way to reach Luke.

There's silence except for the rain beating on the windows, the wind roaring against the Emergency sign. Then I hear footsteps, and I rush from the lounge and see a nurse walking down the hall, holding Brennan, who's licking a lollipop. I hurry to scoop him up in my arms, crying and swaying back and forth, and Brennan sticks the lollipop at my mouth, says, "Uh, uh." Laughing, I lick it and I reply, "Yes, darling, good, good, good." The doctor has pumped his stomach. Despite the trauma, as soon as the doctor gives him a sucker, he's happy. Then I remove the lollipop—my imagination sees him choking.

The next day Mama's doctor calls. "Erin Rose, this is Derrick Willis. Your mother's in the hospital for dehydration. I found her unconscious in her home and called an ambulance. If you don't come as soon as possible, I'm going to have to intervene and have the state commit her to Dorothea Dix Mental Hospital for alcohol treatment because she's a danger to herself."

Chapter 30

Tonight I'm exhausted. When I arrive from Dayton this afternoon, Mama's friend Sheriff Preston meets me at the Fayetteville Airport and brings me home. Then I drive Mama's car to the hospital, where she lies with tubes of glucose draining into her arm. Her face is pale and ashen.

Early this morning I have had to take a leap of faith to trust Luke with our children. He is sympathetic when I call, assuring me I should go because Mama needs me. I tell him I'll call the professional nurse we've hired before and make arrangements for her to stay. Luke sounds concerned about Mama, for he was always fond of her. He promises he'll take care of everything.

At the hospital I have a long talk with Derrick, Mama's doctor, whom I've known even before high school. I trust him with my life and Mama's. Derrick tells me how Sheriff Preston found Mama unconscious on the floor after she didn't appear for work. He called Derrick, who discovered her dehydrated and called an ambulance. Mama will stay another day in the local hospital, and the following day we'll head for Raleigh and Dix Hill.

Night sounds surround me.

I lie in Mama's bed, snuggled up into a ball against the extra pillow. I don't change her sheets because I want to smell her. Close my eyes, sniff in deeply her earthy, jasmine scent to permeate my body. To be a part of her again. To see and feel the way she lives. Can I ever get to know her? *Really* know her.

At midnight the train calls through the darkness—rattling, clattering, keening *can't kill time, can't kill time, can't kill time* ... I awake from muddled dreams, thinking I can't change the past that traps the present. So what can I do about things that can't be undone?

I glance around the room in partial darkness. In this old house the rooms are never completely dark with the light outside—the moon, the stars, the old street lamp—pouring through sheer Priscilla curtains over tall windows in some rooms; on glass doors, the high transoms; the bevel glass at the front door; and the stained glass upstairs. I can easily pull up the window shade a half-foot or more with lights off and thick shade trees blocking the view from the street. At night I feel safe here and comfortable, the brass locks and heavy bolts on the doors shielding me. Of course, as a very young child, the long hall—always dim or shadowy—triggered my terror of bumping into the Nazi soldier from the picture show. And my Uncle Henry still sleeps upstairs; I just heard him tramping in at midnight so at least Mama does have someone in the house at night. Her bedroom is warm and cozy, her bed covered by a heavy quilt, and my grandmother's white crocheted bedspread she made for her first grandchild—that's me.

So what with the furnishings—if you're lonely? After work, from 5:00 pm until 9:00 am, Mama's alone. That I can't help her with. Yet she does have a lover, who's married (of course he doesn't love his wife anymore), and they have a standing Wednesday night date and see each other many other times. But this setup obviously is not enough for her. My advice to Mama? That's a bit of irony. I don't even take my own advice. Besides her current alcohol addiction, *what was it,* before, that made her drink all the time when she wasn't at work? To kill the lonely nights before dark thoughts seeped in and around, asphyxiating her? What were her dark thoughts? Her regrets?

Dix Hill. What a vision comes to me. Since I was a child, just this name alone has conjured images of a laughing lunatic with rotten teeth, ready to bite, a hideous growl, and long, tangled hair sticking out like a porcupine's behind bars. Children would taunt each other with "You're so crazy, you oughta be in *Dix Hill.*"

Derrick has explained the situation. Dorothea Dix Hospital in Raleigh is the only place in North Carolina for alcohol treatment. Other hospitals can only "dry-out" patients temporarily. Mama needs longer-term treatment. Dorothea Dix accepts alcoholics and places them in with all the rest, the less seriously disturbed along with the insane. Derrick advises that Mama should commit herself; if she refuses, I need to convince her that I will not hesitate to do it myself. I do, and Mama acquiesces for a month's stay.

On the drive to Raleigh I try to detach my mind from *why* I'm going. I focus on the highway and traffic; when we come upon the countryside, I zoom in on nature, which usually has a calming effect on me. Across the fields dullness has given way to bright green and pastels because of the hard rains and drizzle lately. The woods are now speckled with pink and white dogwoods. Soon forsythia will burst yellow like a sun rising. Spring is a great season to hope that life will be better, especially after such a long, cold winter and emotional traumas. I feel like stopping by the woods today, letting Mama and me get lost together in the green, scampering around the trees, laughing. Maybe then we can find the words we need to talk. But we have other things to do and miles to go. I wonder if Robert Frost ever found time to stop.

At the next traffic light, I look over at Mama. She appears very docile, sitting quietly, staring blankly out the front window barely breathing as if something's taken hold of her. There's a twitch in her cheek every now and then. Her chin and jaw shake slightly like a mild case of palsy. Overall, she looks very thin; my first thought is she's been existing on her special diet of Vodka and Valium.

"Mama, are you getting hungry? I bought sandwiches and snacks in the hospital cafeteria in case we got hungry. Maybe there's a shady place nearby to stop."

"I'm not hungry," she mumbles. "I don't feel good."

"There's the Welcome Center sign." I quickly switch lanes, whip down the exit, pull into the parking lot, and stop in a patch of shade trees. "This will be a good place for a car picnic."

I get out of the car and walk around to open Mama's door. "Come on, get in the back seat, and we'll have a picnic. You can stretch out your legs."

From the cooler I set out several kinds of sandwiches, small cartons of pudding, and cheese. From a sack I pull out crackers, potato chips, a small spice cake, and a thermos of iced tea. "Look, Mama. You remember this?"

I hold up the spice cake. "Remember how you always had this cake on the end of the kitchen table in front of the pie safe? I'd come in from school and eat about half of it, and we'd eat the rest that night."

Mama looks up with a tiny hint of a smile, a tear falling down her cheek. "I miss those times."

"Me, too." I hand her a plastic cup of iced tea. "Here, let's drink to us ... with tea." And we tip the edges of our plastic cups. I can't hold back my tears anymore. We hug and drip tears and drink tea and eat our picnic. That is, I eat and Mama nibbles at a potato chip, showing no interest at all in the food.

With the windows all down and the doors wide open, a cool breeze stirs through the car, whisking away traffic hums and gathering tensions of the day.

"This is so nice, Mama, sitting here with you. I'm sorry I haven't come home much, but it's really hard to fly with children."

No response.

And I try again. "Alex still runs from the ducks, and Brennan crawls everywhere. He really gave us a scare a few days ago." I commence with a summary of our recent trip to the hospital because Brennan ate rat poison, and then I just stop. It's not at all like Mama to show no interest in her grandchildren.

How I wish that someone would ask, *"Erin Rose, how are you doing?"*

I pack up the uneaten food to store in the cooler, get Mama settled in the front seat, and pull out onto the busy highway that takes us closer to Dorothea Dix. It seems the longer we ride, the jumpier Mama becomes, and her hands shake excessively. I try to free her mind of the fear she must be feeling.

"Mama, you're going to be fine. Dorothea Dix is a hospital. They'll tend to you and watch over you like any other hospital. No need to be afraid."

"Erin Rose, I'm not crazy!"

"I know, Mama. And they'll know you're not, too. But this is the only hospital that will keep you for thirty days—enough time to really help you."

Now that she seems open to talk, I try again. "Mama, you've told me lots of times how lonely you are. Do you think that's why you drink so much? Maybe drinking takes you away for a little while from the loneliness?"

She doesn't answer, just ignores me, staring at space.

"Mama, you know you can talk to me. Please say something."

"All that time." She sounds so forlorn. "There's so much time after I get home from work, day after day. No change. I'll always be there in that old house—it's gonna fall in on top of me. I can't fix it up. And it's so dark and empty. It's my tomb."

"Then it's living in the house that you hate so much?"

"Oh, I've always hated that O'Donovan home. It gets so creepy I think it's full of ghosts. You know, your daddy's mother never did approve of me. And I never liked his family—they all thought they were better than me."

"Mama, they're all gone now. Most of them are dead. No need to hate the dead. Have you thought of moving?"

"Erin Rose, don't be so naïve! How can I do that? I'm still making the mortgage payment!"

"Do you mean that house isn't paid for after all these years?"

"It was paid for—by your daddy. But then he had to borrow money on the property when his family needed it, and he was still paying the mortgage when he died. And, of course, they never paid back a cent. I had to keep making the loan payments. And because the property is worth so much more now, taxes keep increasing, and I keep borrowing to pay them."

"Why haven't you told me this, Mama?"

"What could you have done?" Her voice is tremulous. "No need for you to worry, too. It's not your problem."

"It is my problem, Mama, if it concerns you. You've always been there for me. And I can help you when I start back teaching in the fall. It would do no good for me to ask Luke for anything. He controls his money and spends it for himself." All the winter weekends at a ski resort, the expensive equipment and clothes, sick children alone with me and always in need of something, and I with no money and barely enough gas.

"Don't even think of it." She spits out each word harshly. "I wouldn't ask that son-of-a-bitch for air! I don't wanna talk about this or think about it. Or Luke. There's nothing I can do. And *I'd drink anyway*. I hate my life." Mama starts shaking all over.

As soon as I can exit, I drive off the highway and stop on a country road. "Mama, you've got to calm down. I never meant to upset you. Try to breathe slowly."

I reach over the seat to get the thermos and pour her some tea. "Drink some tea, Mama. And take some deep breaths."

I roll down the windows so we can smell the freshness of spring. Thank God, she's calming down a little. "You're going to be fine," I assure her again. "Have you thought of selling the house? You could pay the mortgage, buy or build a small house, and be clear of debt. You'd still have money left over to live on after you retire." *Oh, how I hate to think of my only home gone.*

Mama shakes her head. "I can't do that. I wouldn't have enough money."

"Why not? That is prime property, Mama. The land's classified Business now. It should be worth quite a bit of money."

"Not with the conditions of the estate. Your daddy did not leave a will. So after the balance of the mortgage is paid, two-thirds of what's left goes to the estate, and then to you, the only child. As his widow, I'd get only one-third."

"Mama, that's no problem. I'll just sign over my share of the money to you."

"Erin Rose, do you mean you'd give me your share?"

"Of course, I will. Why wouldn't you think so?"

"I don't know, Erin Rose. I never asked you because I thought you'd want all the money, yourself. That you'd never give it to me!"

"Mama, is that the way you think of me? You consider me that selfish? And after all you've done for me my whole life? That really hurts my feelings. That's your money after all you've been through these years."

"Oh, Erin." Tears run down her face, and she can't stop sniffling and then crying.

"Tell me where to go, Mama. Do you have a lawyer? I need to get that paperwork done while I'm here in North Carolina."

On top of the bare hill a weathered building of dark-red brick stands stately like a giant sentinel, dominating the view of the countryside. No fresh spring grass sprouts nor flowers nor shrubs. Only three trees grow in patches of dirt, their gnarled limbs still in winter dress. From the building, rows of tall windows stare blankly at the crunchy gravel road that runs up the hill, curves, and stops in front.

Mama and I wait a few minutes outside. Most of the afternoon is gone, but a couple of hours remain before sunset. It's that waiting time. If we could dispense with what we're both dreading, this could be a pleasant time, standing on top of a steep hill and gazing around and off into the distance at Raleigh's skyscrapers. But the air here feels heavy. Maybe it's this dismal structure and the windows looking fixedly at us that create such a creepy atmosphere. I look up and see bars on the upper windows. I look at Mama and know she's terrified. Then swiftly, clouds shift and darken, hiding the sun and staining the sky a dull gray. The wind starts up.

Holding hands, we climb up the cracking stone steps to the porch and stop at the heavy front door. A gust of rain spatters us before we can get inside. Impulsively, I hug Mama and reassure her that in a month she'll be healthy and happy she came. I kiss her on the cheek as an attendant greets us.

After Mama signs in and the papers are completed, the attendant leads her away. Mama follows her down the corridor like a submissive child. Soon she returns dressed in a drab gray dress, shapeless like a prison uniform, no belt allowed. The attendant hands me the clothing Mama has worn: the green sweater, brown tweed skirt, brown pumps and leather pocketbook, khaki all-weather coat, and beige scarf. Her purse contains her valuables—I look in to find her diamond, the Bulova watch, gold earrings and choker, a lipstick and powder compact, and money in her billfold. She stands, her identity stripped. The head nurse will oversee a small amount of money for daily snacks and cigarettes. I'm reminded she's to have no visitors or any phone calls during her stay.

We say good-byes in the waiting room, and they walk to another heavy door, this time one with bars in the upper part. I follow behind. Mama pauses and looks at me with a pitiful expression while the attendant unlocks the door with her heavy ring of keys. Mama hesitates, recoils, and shrinks within herself, and then gazes back through the bars. I remain immobile before the locked door, staring at the dim light beyond the bars.

Strange what you think of at a time like this. *Her eyes.* The varied images of Mama's eyes have haunted me, no matter what scene is replaying in my memory. *Indifferent eyes. Jealous eyes. Angry eyes. Arrogant eyes. Desperate eyes.*

I pull off Church Street and enter our driveway and stop. The lights I left on earlier, one in each area of the house, shine. This site welcomes me home like love radiating from a grandmother eager to see her grandchild again. No way is this place a creepy tomb or demonic meeting house of witches and ghosts. I've heard rumors here and there all my life about our home because it's different—old, dark in places, a Gothic shape, full of sounds that people would recognize if they'd stop to think.

I look at the large high-angled roof where the turrets point up around the high flat part—that's the magic space, totally mine, I thought as a child. My world of imagination, books, music, dance, and spirit—come to think of it, *there was something* protecting me up there, keeping me from falling. I felt its presence in the air just as I felt that presence like an arm around my shoulder when I looked at Daddy in his coffin. The same sense of *something*. I wrote all about it in my journal. Somehow I believed everything was connected, but I couldn't figure out how. I didn't like the word *God*—that wasn't *my* word. God belonged to the church and the minister and the Sunday school teachers who talked about punishment and Hell and sin, ideas I just didn't understand. I wanted another name. So until I could think of one, I went along with *it*. Or the *presence* of it.

How I wish I had a special place like this now! I catch myself smiling at the little girl Erin and wishing I could meet her again to claim that inspiration and confidence she had in herself. I go to bed thinking of the sounds I'll hear: the front door squeaking, heavy footsteps stomping on uncarpeted stairs, the box cars of the train clicking and clanging, something scraping on the roof. I set the alarm for midnight to greet Uncle Henry and give him news of Mama. This brief encounter is pleasant, and he's concerned about her. As soon as I'm in bed again, I'm soon awakened by bright sun seeping through the shades.

It's cold getting up, especially when I'm barefoot. Quickly I make coffee in the old percolator—I forget how good it tastes and smells throughout the kitchen and how homey it sounds when the water *pop-pop-pops* in the glass top, steam rushing out the spout. I make cheese toast and drink coffee and then decide I can't leave this house without visiting my childhood world—my magic place.

The upstairs hall still displays long portraits of the O'Donovan ancestors in either stiff black suits and white shirts or stiff black dresses with a touch of white at the collar. They look stern and a bit suspicious as their eyes move with you. That never bothered me. I'd just sit against the wall with my knees bent up to support my white journal, and I'd make up stories about each one, whatever popped into my head, often naughty little things like Great Uncle Albert winking at a woman in the pew when he was taking up the collection at the First Baptist Church. I even imagined him grinning in his portrait. By the time I invented my stories, we were good friends—the kind who keep secrets.

And upstairs the secret panel still slides open. It takes me a while to slip through, and I refuse to think about sliding out. Why do I sometimes see the child Erin as someone else? The fact that I'm here crawling in a layer of dust and soot says I'm still that child inside, trusting my fantasies.

When I stand, I see a smaller, darker place than I remember. No light. No glow. Just a maze of dark brown wood: long rafters sloping into space, narrow planks running parallel across an abyss of nothingness. Spider webs hang from nearly every rafter, every web connecting to another like crisscrossing dream catchers. Where is the light? I look up but do not see any stained glass.

I want to go beyond the dusky webs to the bright magic place. Did the child Erin make up this story? But I remember! And I'm going to look for it. I'm still Erin Rose O'Donovan. I'll have to walk a plank to get over to ... somewhere.

Even though I can barely see my feet in the dark, I take two steps, and I'm suspended on only one narrow plank, wearing shoes with more heel than a child's. I can't turn around. I can't slide back. There's just dark air on each side of the plank. I am really afraid now. How did my childhood self do it? Dust motes float by—I'm about to sneeze. My balance is shaky. No one knows I'm here. Where would I fall? The young Erin knew the danger, but she ignored it. She trusted herself and the spirit presence. In a trancelike state, she imagined herself walking or dancing over safely. So she did. Now I remember that presence of something and focus on it. As I walk, the air seems to clear. The place is lighter. The morning sun has risen. I take my last step and find the dark plank in a bright beam of light. I look above and see a stained-glass window made of a dozen shades of green streaming a shower of gold.

On the plane back to Dayton I feel good, even though I just left Mama at Dix Hill. Maybe she'll have something to look forward to—a new house to plan, a chance to get rid of the old house that haunts her. Oh, I'll miss it so, but I feel better about letting it go. The magic and that stained light are with me now. When I return in thirty days, I'm sure Mama will look and be more like herself.

I go to the Glass House feeling confident and loving and peaceful. I kiss the children and say hello to Tiger. Looking at his quiet repose, I feel his surety. In the old house there were times I felt him lying on the back porch—watchful—and sometimes hovering bodiless in the dark—protective. Now I know that I can walk in darkness if I trust the light will enter it—even if it's a meteor swirling around in my imagination.

By the end of summer I suspect I'm pregnant.

It's been a couple of months since I stopped taking birth control pills. It's been a little over a year since Joe first started me on them. My gynecologist insists that I stop the pills temporarily because in the early '60s no one knows what the long-term effects will be. As a precaution, the doctor advises me to wait, perhaps a year, before I start back on them because by then medical research will have more information.

After my trip to Oak Glen I decide to take control of my life. I get a job teaching in a close-by high school that starts in a couple of weeks. Now I plan to make my own money so I can maneuver some kind of change. Emotionally I can't go on like this ... alone every night with darkness spreading outside the glass, pressing and pressing ... oh, I don't want to become my mother. Hours creep by. I can't sleep I'm so distraught. I'm so tired I can hardly move ... too tired to have another baby.

Impatient, edging on a panic attack, I sit in bed watching the bottom of the sheet hanging from the window, waiting for a peak of dim light to signal another dawn when I can call Joe. We haven't talked lately; they have a new baby and now live on another side of the city. However, he senses my long crying bout and depression in my voice and says he's on the way. I've got to know if I'm pregnant.

Joe knows why I'm so distraught. He's well aware of Luke's meandering in and out of extramarital affairs and leaving me isolated most of the time. He cautions me to get myself together and to take care of my own mental health. He says he's going to give me an injection that can start my period.

"But what if I'm pregnant?"

Joe assures me, "If you're pregnant, nothing will happen."

"Are you sure?"

"Erin, the injection makes you start your period if you're late."

After a few days when I don't start, I know I'm pregnant and I feel protective. I feel this baby is special. I love the baby at that moment with a strong bond. At once I'm horror-struck that the shot could have made me miscarry. Who knows? I could have lost the baby. Then it dawns on me that this child is meant to be.

Chapter 31

The day is November 22, 1963.

I'm being rolled out into the corridor on a gurney. Walls loom above and stretch ahead and a blur of people rush around me. The bed's moving, swaying, wheels squeaking, the sheet tight like a straightjacket. I can't move. My eyes fall shut, the bed stops, I'm opening my eyes again. The TV glares from the wall, black and white blurring of cars moving, voices speaking all at once, and a voice bends over me, a nurse saying "The President's been shot!" Who's been shot? I try to focus my eyes on the screen. Who was shot? And where am I? The blur becomes a black convertible and a figure slumped over a seat and a woman climbing onto the back—don't I know her?—and men talking from the screen and other voices talking around the screen and I can't move held down on the gurney. I fall asleep.

When I awake again, I'm in a hospital room, and I can see clearly the doctor who was my obstetrician when Kayleigh was born six months ago. The sheet's been loosened somewhat, and Dr. Dietrichson's asking me how I feel, the way doctors do, not really expecting a reply.

"You've been sleeping for quite a while. You were brought to your room around noon after some time in recovery, and you're doing fine." He reaches over and pulls up a chair beside the bed. "Erin, you've lost quite a bit of blood, but the surgery went well. You had a puncture in the upper wall of your vagina." He holds up his hand and indicates with his thumb and forefinger: "About two inches wide. Since the puncture was so deep, I used extra thick sutures. So I want you to be very careful. We don't want any kind of pressure, any strain whatsoever that would make those sutures pull loose until you've had a chance to heal."

He asks about the baby, how old is she now and do I have any help at home. Now how old are the other children? Are there many stairs at home? He quickly and firmly states, "Erin, you'll definitely need some help. You shouldn't pick up the baby for several weeks. That would put too much strain on you now, and you shouldn't walk up and down stairs. Do you have any questions?"

"No."

He reaches over and takes my hand. "Erin, you spend all your time taking care of your children. And now you've got to take care of yourself. That means arranging for someone to be there when you get home to tend to you and help with the children for several weeks. Do you want me to speak to your husband?"

"That would be nice, Dr. Dietrichson. But I don't think that would make any difference. I'll handle it. Thank you."

"I'm going to have you stay in the hospital about three days. We'll see how you do."

I'm lying there bewildered about how I'll manage to look after myself and three children—six months, two years, and five years—and four bedrooms upstairs when Luke walks in. It's late afternoon, and he can't stay long, has to get back to his office for some reason. He stands listening to me recite the doctor's words when Joe, our friend and now a staff doctor, walks in. After a few comments, Joe turns to Luke and says, "Hey, Luke, whatcha got there," indicating the front of his pants, "a piece of lead?"

Both men laugh.

From the hospital bed I see Luke's pleased expression at having received what he considers a decided compliment. I look at Joe—no ... not Joe, too. I ache, not from pain, but from the words and laugh of a friend.

Room empty of others, dinner dishes cleared, hospital sounds echo: heelsteps, food cartwheels, that metallic bell of someone in need. I lie staring at the elongated shadows that creep in from the window at dusk.

The TV keeps rehashing this incredibly long day. John F. Kennedy, U. S. President, assassinated. And I, as vulnerable as he, could have shared his fate. *If I had not arrived at the hospital in time.* So much blood. It was everywhere. All over the bed, the sheets, the carpet, the bathroom floor. The blood would not stop gushing. God, I don't ever want to bleed like that again. To feel my life pouring out of me in one rushing stream that I can't stop. Not a thing I can do. Just wait. Wait for some turn in events that decides my fate. *To get me to the hospital in time.*

I keep thinking of Kennedy's children, almost the same ages of mine. What are they doing now? What are mine doing this very minute? I think of mine standing at the top of the stairs this morning when I briefly open my eyes while I'm being lowered down the stairs on the stretcher headfirst. I see again after the blackout: five-year-old Alex standing in her red pajamas with a pitifully frightened expression, the look of someone wanting to cry but feeling terror that runs too deep for tears, and two-year-old Brennan, confused and still, huddling against her, clutching her hand as if his life depends on it. No sounds come from baby Kayleigh's room; someone—I'm sure it was Alex—has given her a bottle. And then there's Luke, holding open the front door, oblivious of the fact that he's still completely naked in view of the medics, ambulance drivers, neighbors driving to work, children walking to the nearby school.

A devastating day.

Flashes of my own disaster won't go away ...

Earlier this morning I stir at the first sound of our baby Kayleigh's whimpering for her six o'clock bottle. Still half-asleep, I attempt to get up and at the same time Luke turns over in bed and reaches for me, pulling me down and rolling on top of me. Trying to squirm out from under him, I say, "I've got to feed the baby."

"She can wait." He starts pulling up my gown.

"No, Luke, I have to get the bottle." Kayleigh is really crying now, the kind of cry that every mother knows will not abate without milk. And I can imagine without looking that forlorn look babies get that leads to loud sobbing and kicking and soon screaming.

"Let me up, Luke," I shout. "I've got to go to her."

"No." He pins my arms down and I can't budge.

I'm furious. "I've got to get her bottle!" I strain to sit upright, trying to shift my position.

"Goddammit, not now," he says.

I start kicking his legs, butting his head, but he grabs my arms, pulls both over my head and holds them with his arm, then pries my legs apart with his knee. "No! You're hurting me."

He jerks up my gown. "Dammit, get still!" He thrusts his engorged penis into me so fast and so hard the piercing pain feels like my guts have been stabbed wide open deep inside. I hear my own half-stifled scream along with Kayleigh's hysterical cry. Then comes the strangest feeling that something's collapsed like a balloon bursting, then I'm drowning inside myself.

"Let me up!" I scream. "Something awful's happened."

Luke withdraws and blood pours out, soaking the bed and my path to the bathroom, where I stumble onto the toilet and flood it with blood. I grab a large bath towel and press it between my legs, and it instantly fills with blood. I grab another large towel and then another until two towels are stuffed between my legs and still blood is soaking the terry cloth.

I scream, "I need a doctor. Call my doctor. Have him meet me at the hospital. I'm bleeding to death!"

I hear the mattress squeak and Luke fumbling with the phone and calling out, "What's the number?"

I'm still standing with soaked towels between my legs, hearing sounds of movement in the bedroom and the baby's cries, feeling blood running down my legs. Then everything goes black. I'm blind. I scream, "Call an ambulance!" just before I pass out.

I vaguely recall being picked up and put on a stretcher by two men, then carried down the stairs with the children standing there watching. The next thing I know a siren is screaming and houses are flashing outside the ambulance's window beside me.

When I wake up, I'm in a small room on a gurney being asked questions by a young man in green. I keep asking him, "Where's my doctor? I want my doctor."

"He'll be here soon. How did you cut yourself?"

"I don't know. We were having sex."

"What were you using? A bottle?"

"What?"

"A bottle. You've been punctured with something like a piece of glass."

"I have not," I snap. "I've told you what happened." I'm as angry at the young doctor as I'm frightened I'm bleeding out. I'm sure no one's doing anything.

"We've put packing inside you. Some kind of object went in deep and cut you."

"It was my husband." I feel like I'm being cross-examined in court on the witness stand, and no one believes me. I start crying. "Please get my doctor." I'm sobbing. "Please don't let me bleed anymore."

Dr. Dietrichson walks in shortly, calming me with just his presence and reassuring voice.

"Erin, we'll have you fixed up in no time. We're taking you into surgery now. And you'll be fine."

That was a day I'd like to forget. But I can't: on the anniversary of this day for years to come, the headlines, magazine covers, TV news, and TV talk shows blare *Where were you on the day Kennedy died?*

I'm in the hospital for three days. After the first day and the ten-minute visit, Luke stays away and doesn't come back until he returns to take me home. Each afternoon and night during visiting hours, I lie listening for his footsteps. There's that moment of anticipation when I think he's approaching, footsteps down the corridor coming near then passing by, stopping down the hall where another woman waits. Luke never comes. I get exhausted waiting, not hearing a word. There's no one to visit me.

I should have anticipated his no-show after the way he was when Kayleigh was born. He'd taken me to the hospital, walked with me to the elevator, pushed the button, and as the elevator door opened he said, "When it's born get the nurse to call my secretary. Let me know if it's a girl or a boy."

When Luke arrives to take me home, he never says a word about what's happened. It's as if the entire incident never occurred. He never even asks me how I feel; it's as if he's giving me a ride home from the shopping center. Luke has a way of talking things down, minimizing their importance until they no longer exist unless they're important to him. However, he does make it clear he's not paying any more baby sitters. Anyway, he says, "You're all right." He deposits me like a package in the downstairs den, pays and dismisses the sitter, speaks to the children briefly, and leaves. He has better things to do. We hardly see him for weeks.

The day I return home is John Kennedy's funeral day. The parade of cars and the shots and the slumped-over body and all the rest of it and Jackie's bloodstained dress flood the TV screen again and again. And then the funeral cortege and Caroline at attention and John-John saluting. *If I had died that day, where would my children have been today?* The question overwhelms me. They would have had no one: neither grandmother would have been suitable, their father far less so. I sit on the sofa, afraid to move, and sitting on each side of me Alex and Brennan stare at the children on TV and the reruns of the violence. When Alex asks the question "Why, Mama?" I can only shake my head with an "I don't know."

For years after, on anniversaries I click off the TV, flip over a magazine cover, or drop the newspaper into the trash. Lay it to rest, I tell myself. And I try to. However, scenes from my past emerge bright red, then turn dark like an indefinable shadow. Each time I have a Pap smear, the doctor sees a dark area. Once I explain, the doctor looks at me strangely as if I were crazy or a liar, so I avoid checkups for years. Twenty or more years later, my hometown doctor mentions being puzzled by a discoloration like a dark stain or scar tissue. I volunteer nothing. He scrapes the area to do additional lab tests, including a biopsy. The hospital clears me, but that dark stain is forever imprinted on my body and my psyche.

As soon as I come home, Alex brings down what I need from upstairs. Baby Kayleigh's already downstairs so we make a pallet there on the floor next to the sofa where I sleep for a week or so. Alex picks Kayleigh up, helps to feed her, change her diaper, bathe her in a turkey roaster on the floor by the sofa, and do the laundry. She puts Brennan in the tub with her and bathes him and puts on his pajamas and fresh clothes in the morning. During the day she keeps her eye on Brennan though he often sits close to me during the day with that anxious look a child can have when he fears you may leave him.

What would I have done without Alex? And she's only five and missing kindergarten to help me.

My neighbors visit, each anxious to find out what's happened. Mistakenly, I mention surgery, and their eyes widen as they look at each other as if they have telepathy. "Just a little problem," I quickly add.

I can't live indefinitely in the den, so finally I carefully climb the stairs. If Luke comes home, it's after midnight. As for me, my body is taking forever to heal. After six weeks Dr. Dietrichson discovers infection and the wound has to be cauterized, adding more recovery time. I feel I'll never be well. But at the same time, I'm terrified at the thought of having sex again. The words *making love* no longer fit.

Some things simply can't be dealt with in present time. This trauma is one. For years I've felt an overwhelming sense of inadequacy because of Luke's other women. You always know. The click of a phone when you answer, the unfamiliar scent of Fabergé or Chanel when you have none on, the early morning hours when he comes home long after the bars have closed and the usual time for "entertaining customers" is long past. Then the more careless hints: lipstick on a collar, motel receipt for Mr. and Mrs. in a coat pocket, and the slip-ups when he calls me someone else's name. I've quit trying to ask about it all. Luke has a way of explaining everything so I appear irrational.

Now I'm sure my injuries stem from some physical defect in me—I just know it. At the last checkup with Dr. Dietrichson, I ask him, "What's wrong with me?"

"What do you mean?"

"What made my skin collapse the way it did? Is the skin in my vagina weak after having three babies?" That makes sense to me.

His thoroughly quizzical expression slowly turns to understanding. Abruptly he shakes his head, his lips pressed in a tight line, and he articulates each word loudly. "No! There's nothing wrong with your body, Erin. You're perfectly normal." He pauses and then asks me, "Do you think that you were somehow to blame? Get that out of your mind! Your husband was extremely violent. It was his fault."

The doctor's words don't assure me; they will never take root in my mind. I blame myself for trying to pull away and making Luke angry. I've never heard of marital rape.

I avoid the part of my mind that holds scenes too painful to remember, where images you don't want to see again can hide. I dwell in that place where illusions lie, near the place of fantasy that in time you can think anything is only your imagination.

In Ohio snow comes early before Thanksgiving. With the children occupied in play or asleep, I stare out the window for what seems hours at the world outside. Endless snow covers the yard, the shrubs, the trees. I no longer can see where our yard ends and the neighbor's begins or where the street begins or where the ground of the distant houses ends and horizon and sky begin. The windowpane frames a world of white, vacant space with no defining path anywhere. Sometimes the winds from the north blow especially strong, and the snow piles up in drifts against the glass patio door five to six feet high so that I can't slide open the door or see beyond it.

At least we're in a new house I chose and own, thanks to Mama, who made it possible from her property sale of the old home place when I told her I was pregnant with

Kayleigh. But I did add Luke's name to the deed, so he'll have to help with the few payments left.

Inside the children make their own world of imagination and music, quick squabbles and laughter. I become immersed in it. I welcome the release and freedom and spontaneity in being a child again. The only part that remains alive is sparked by child play. Alex and I sit on the sofa for hours playing Barbies. She dresses Barbie, and I dress Skipper. We take turns having our girls go for a ride with Ken or Alan in the convertible. Brennan makes furniture with blocks and Tinker toys, and together he and Alex design a Barbie house, the rooms partitioned with large cardboard boxes propped up for days all over the living room for the Barbie family and friends. Brennan sets up his Hot Wheels track down the hall or lines up Matchbox cars by his service station.

Sometimes with the help of *Child Craft,* we make musical instruments out of paper-towel rolls, a comb and tissue, cloth, a pot or pan, long wooden spoons, a vegetable brush and grater, rubber bands, popsicle sticks, and cake pans. I play records from the set of Children's Classics albums, and the children march to "Peter and the Wolf," drowning out the French horn with their instruments to frighten the wolf away, knowing the French horn sound is the entrance of the wolf in this Russian folk tale set to the music of Prokofiev.

Alex bakes little cakes on her Easy-Bake oven and feeds them to Brennan after he pours chocolate syrup on them and himself. I pile stacks of books up on the floor, some to look at myself and some to read to them. Kayleigh is captivated by books at an early age, trying to read aloud with me as soon as she can talk, even sooner with gibberish to the rhythm of my voice reading. Weather permitting, Alex and Brennan play in the snow, but they're usually too cold to stay out long, so they return inside, snowsuits dripping on the linoleum before Brennan changes into another snowsuit to go back outside.

Christmas nearing, I'm relieved that I bought most of the children's toys or put them on layaway either in late October and early November as I usually do before stores sell out of popular items. Luke has taken the toys to the plant where he's manager to keep until Christmas Eve when he'll bring the Santa stuff to the house. He always gets the toys put together, sometimes by the plant engineer, and calls before he drives the company van home full of toys to unload after the children go to bed.

Luke always comes through for the children on Christmas and birthdays and Halloween, probably because he likes to play with the toys and parade around dressed as either Santa Claus or Superman. Of course, his charades don't last long, but he makes quite an impression while they last. Usually he arrives before dinner so he can get Alex and Brennan and even Kayleigh roused up with Christmas excitement.

He hasn't called since early morning, so I go ahead and feed them, give them baths, help them place cookies in a plate under the tree for Santa, put them to bed, and then face the waiting alone on Christmas Eve. That night the wind swirls snow in a white fury across the yard, eddying in a tall, twisted drift against the door. Hours crawl by. I call the plant, receive no answer. I try not to get panicky. I don't know who to call or how to rectify the impending disaster my mind keeps imagining. Midnight creeps by. I sit in the dark on the stairs and stare out the window by the front door, aware of a knot in the center of my chest about the size of my fist and a dull *thump-thump-thump* of my own heartbeat.

The wind has died hours ago; the night is ghostly still. I sit and wait and listen to the silence. The silence of the cold predawn hours. Over the snowdrift our tree lights, still on, reflect on the packed snow like slivers of broken stained glass. Broken like dreams. Yet tiny pieces of color dare to shine. I stare at the pieces, trying to will myself to get calm, but my heart is beating so fast, I feel I'll start screaming.

I must do something. In another hour Brennan will be up, waking his sisters, and barreling down the stairs to see what Santa's brought. But there's nothing. Only the same presents that they've felt, shaken, and smelled for weeks under the tree. There's nothing else. I sniff, shaking my head, holding my breath—I can't cry now.

Maybe I could find the night watchman to let me in the plant. But where has Luke stored everything? The closet in his office isn't big enough. The storage room will be locked. The night watchman doesn't know me, so he'd have to get clearance from somebody and it's after three in the morning. He's probably not there on Christmas Eve anyway. Like everybody else in the world he is home in bed. And the snow. God, I'd have to dig out of the driveway, and the snowplows are not yet out ... and I don't have snow tires. I'd have to leave the children at home alone, and how could I get to the other side of town and back before they awake? Then I remember I can't drive yet after my surgery. There's no way. I swallow a sob.

My mind totters on the verge of hysteria. I have to think of something. What can I say to Brennan? I can tell seven-month old Kayleigh that Santa will come after her Christmas afternoon nap and she won't know what Christmas is anyway. What am I thinking? She won't even understand me. Maybe Alex will believe Santa doesn't really slide down the chimney; he comes by the highway, and it's closed now because of the snow. I can't tell them there's no Santa Claus and give them toys a day late. It's a quarter to four, and Brennan will wake at five. If I cry, I won't be able to stop. I keep touching my face to wipe away tears.

I sit and watch the wall clock in the foyer, feeling each invisible movement of the minute hand. I hear the inaudible sound of each second passing.

I don't know when I become conscious of a new sound. Like the stepping on shattered glass over and over. Or the way nerves sound when stretched to their ultimate tautness and they snap one by one.

A door slams. Whistling drifts over the snow. It's four o'clock. Luke pushes open the front door whistling, "Santa Claus is Coming to Town."

Looking up, he stops at the foot of the stairs, and the whistling fades. "Hey-e-e-e, whatcha doing sitting there alone in the dark at this hour?"

My throat aches so from not crying, I can barely swallow and I'm too choked to speak. My words are too strained to hear. "Where ... have ... you ... been?"

"Now, Erin, don't be mad. It's Christmas!" His voice rings throughout the house as he pulls me to my feet and into his arms.

"Shhh-shhh. Don't wake up the children, Luke. Where're the toys? They have to be unwrapped and assembled and spread around the tree. They'll be up in another hour."

"Hey-e-e-e, Honey, you worry too much. I'll get everything done. Don't look so serious. You're no fun anymore."

By 5:00 Luke sits on the floor adjusting batteries for the Aurora Speedway and tries to get me to race him. "Come on, Erin, you take the blue car and I've got the red. Betcha money my car'll beat yours around the track."

He proceeds to play with every noisy toy he sets up. You'd think he's a little boy on Christmas morning, oblivious to the noise he's making.

Finally, Alex and Brennan run downstairs to play. And I bring Kayleigh down. Luke goes upstairs to take a nap.

I make breakfast, play with the children, and then complete cooking the Christmas dinner. I set the dining room table already decorated, and then I slowly start, still having to be careful, upstairs, to dress and I meet Luke on the stairs hurrying down. He's already showered and shaved and dressed up.

"I've been invited out to dinner, and I don't want to be late."

I pause on the step and the front door closes.

Sometime after New Year's Luke asks me if I want to go out for dinner and maybe dance, if I'm up to it. It's been a little over a month since I was in the hospital, and I would have chosen a trip to the zoo over looking out the window at snow. However, he mentions this at the spur of the moment early in the morning, and I start worrying about not having enough time to get ready. It'll be a painstaking task. He leaves me money to buy something to wear and remarks that I need a manicure—and "Please do something with your hair." Then he reminds me to get a sitter who'll stay late. He leaves calling, "Hey, I wanta see you glamorous for a change."

And I'm not really up to that. The very thought of an all-day preparation to try to be what he wants to see makes me anxious. I'll have to get a sitter just to go shopping and then drive in this snow and ice to get to the mall. It's too late to get a hair appointment, and it will take hours to get a manicure without an appointment. To Luke glamorous means sexy and stylish. I'll have to stand up and walk all day and go up and down steps. And tonight I'll still be up and about. That's too much pressure on my body which will take another month to heal completely.

Then, I remember all those "passing inspections" of Luke. I'll be tied up in knots, not knowing if I've created the right effect: Your skirt's too short. Is that lipstick the right shade? You've left your nails too long. Your makeup needs to be darker because you're so pale. What did you do to your hair? Is that all you got to wear? I used to think all the anxiety was worth the cost of a few hours of adult companionship. But Luke's so critical, and he's still never interested in what I have to say. He goes where he knows everyone and ends up talking business. Sometimes there's an acquaintance who asks me to dance, and for a while in the presence of a stranger I'll enjoy male attention that makes me feel desirable and at ease with myself. Invariably, the waitress will say, as if puzzled, "You're Luke's wife?"

Luke occasionally talks about a circle of high-class call girls in a nearby city. Some of these girls model at noon at an exclusive restaurant frequented by business executives or whoever has the money and interest. There the men eat lunch, sip martinis, and watch long-legged beauties parade across a platform in sheer panties and bra or flimsy gowns, and men order merchandise or whatever. Luke tells me how he has arranged a night for one of his customers with the right girl, since he knows them well enough to know which one will best provide what the guy wants. This will seal a business contract or award a new client with a special bonus. Luke laughs about how he can always predict the match. "A short paunchy middle-aged Jew always wants a tall slim blonde." The descriptions of these other women end with his criticism of me and his suggestion that I should be with other men occasionally to learn something new. He says it as if it's in jest, but I think he means it. And I feel he'd respect and admire me more if I'd take him up on his suggestion. He likes a good challenge—to win me back if I should stray. Whether he means it or not, the comparisons make me freeze.

That's it. I'm not going. Not for Luke to compare me to someone else. I'm nervous just thinking about going out with him; he'll be drinking, and I'm not supposed to drink while I'm taking strong antibiotics. And he'll expect to have sex even with my wound not healed. I look at my hands and they're shaking too much to stop. I wish there was someone to talk to or some way to escape or a place to cry without the children seeing me. I walk slowly upstairs and close the bedroom door. The first sob comes with gasping breaths and resounds deep within, low and loud, reverberating into long, empty sobs.

I'll wait, though, to tell him that I'm not going out. "Luke, I didn't get to go shopping today without finding a sitter. And I tried all day."

I no longer expect Luke to be here. His business trips have gotten longer, sometimes two weeks long, and I don't know where he is unless I call his secretary Becky who always knows. When he does come home, he's getting worse disrupting everything. He never participates, just criticizes and demands. He hates seeing toys all over the floor and fusses about having no food for him, just kid stuff. (In my head I point out: *I never know in advance when you'll be home. And I'm not your chef who can cook a gourmet meal in a moment's notice.*) Instead, I offer to drive to the grocery store. He plays with the children for five minutes, perhaps ten at most, gets them keyed up for his attention, and then he suddenly stops, cuts them off, and expects them to be instantly quiet, calm. The camaraderie is gone. Yet they are always anticipating, waiting, on hold for something else, wondering what did they do to make Daddy stop?

I wonder how I can allow myself to be so completely controlled. Perhaps if I had a stronger sense of self, I wouldn't succumb to his dominance. But I'm so caught up in his power over me, I don't understand its almost hypnotic intensity. When I'm with him, I'm in an upside-down world and doubt my own sanity. At the same time, my nearly snuffed-out voice within cries in protest.

This winter of '64 is horrendous. It snows continuously, sometimes blizzards. Temperatures drop with Arctic winds that pile up more heavy drifts. The children are sick with colds, and Kayleigh, going on ten months, has a bronchial allergy that causes her breathing to sound asthmatic and finally develops into pneumonia. She's admitted to the hospital and stays under an oxygen tent for over a week. In Kayleigh's hospital room I stand and look at her through a clear tent and watch her cry, not understanding why I can't take her from the tent and hold her except at mealtimes. Her hair falls in ringlets around her face from the constant mist spraying in, and her screaming colors her face as red as her hair. She refuses to eat for the nurses so I have to be there at mealtimes. Each morning I drive Alex to kindergarten, pick up the sitter for Brennan, and hurry to the hospital to feed Kayleigh.

A few days after Kayleigh's hospitalized, Alex wakes up sick in the middle of the night with a temperature of 104. I put her in a tub of tepid water and keep sponging her off until I can get her to the doctor the next morning. He diagnoses her with measles, the red, hard-core kind. We have to keep the blinds closed during the day, and I have to be with her constantly, sponging her face, giving her liquids until her fever breaks. After finding a sitter, I still go to the hospital to feed Kayleigh and then return quickly to be with Alex. Poor little Brennan doesn't know what's going on.

After Alex's fever finally breaks, it looks as though I can bring Kayleigh home from the hospital. Then Brennan awakes during the night sick with a fever. I continue the routine. I place Brennan in a tub filled with lukewarm water for his sponging and look for red measles rash. Instead, I discover his skin is full of little blisters—chickenpox. Although Kayleigh has recently received the new measles vaccine, her doctor advises that she not go home until her brother and sister are no longer contagious. The doctor was really nice; almost immediately the two diseases flip-flop. Alex catches Brennan's chicken pox and poor Brennan gets the measles. I contact the retired nurse we have often used, and she keeps Kayleigh in her home for several days.

The days and weeks run together with the ice and snow and the winds from the North. And Luke drifts in and out of our lives for fresh clothes and inquiries and reminders that there is nothing he can do for the children. "After all, you're giving them medicine, aren't you? And, God knows, I'm paying those doctors enough to tell you what to do. Call me if you need me." His stomach queasy at the thought of vomit, he's ready to leave, but not until he excites the children, arouses their needs, then slips away from their love into the slippery dark.

Something in me nearly dies, but my children save me from the darkness I feel. After the illnesses there's light in children's laughter and sheer joy in their fantasy. I watch and then join in their play, experiencing that wonderful freedom of being in a child's mind, escaping into childish imagination—the world of pretend, fairy tales, and music and games. No pressures. No trying to fit a role that's uncomfortable for me. Just absorbing the reciprocal love and need of my three. However, when we put up the paper dolls and dress-up clothes, Flintstone blocks, Play-dough and blocks, finger paint and Battleship, and the children fall asleep, I slip into despair, floundering around in that too familiar darkness, searching for my lost self.

At some point I forget the passage of time. I look out at the snow lit by the street light, packed tightly into layers of ice, and at the empty street stretching into darkness as far as I can see. It's then that the loneliness overtakes me, and there's nowhere to go. I pull the drapes and black out the darkness. In the dim room I sit and stare at shadows lengthening around me. Then sometimes late at night the doorbell rings unexpectedly, and I hurry down the stairs and pull open the door. There he stands, missing his keys, the full moon casting a soft light behind, leaving him in a silver glow, and a smile spreads across his face and his eyes take on a life of their own. Luke has a way of standing still in the doorway and looking at me, and I feel a part of me just sliding into him. I'm no longer me. His presence lights up the porch, the stoop, the room, wherever he is. And those times magnify, pushing away any other thoughts. Even in the darkest shadow that special part of him I love waxes sterling in a tiny slice of hope.

Chapter 32

Luke is friends with the owner of Skyline Supper Club and stops by there often for drinks. Soon he's infatuated with Rita Vann, a nightclub singer, who's attractive with long blonde hair, a sultry voice, and loads of talent. At the Skyline she becomes quite a hit, packing people into the club so now they need reservations. Her voice is all he talks about, raves about. "You'll have to hear her, Erin."

And he takes me just once. We're ushered down front at a choice ringside seat by the maître d' as if Luke himself is the celebrity. True, she's attractive, and she's talented. Maybe not enough for the accolades befitting a Hollywood star.

One night after the late evening news Luke rushes in and flips the channel. "Guess who's on Johnny Carson!" Sure enough, there's Rita Vann being introduced by Johnny himself, and she makes a striking appearance, her singing well received. She's a hit on both a local TV and a daily radio show. Luke's ecstatic whenever her name is mentioned.

We live two separate lives though we still live together. He finds his life glamorous and exciting; he finds mine insignificant and boring. And he advances in his company: he's put in charge of negotiating with area bosses of the teamsters' union and once breaks a picket line and a bullet barely grazes his shoulder. However, Luke pays off the union guy under the table and so avoids strikes in his plant. Everyone has a price, he tells me. He's so successful in getting and keeping accounts, he's soon made regional director.

The telephone rings late one afternoon while I'm cooking supper. I leave several pots simmering on the stove and reach for the phone, juggling Kayleigh, bottle, and phone while Brennan dives between my legs, Alex chasing him and yelling, "Mama, tell him to leave me alone." I nearly drop the phone while a woman's voice repeats, "Is this Luke McLeod's residence?"

"Yes it is."

"Is he there?"

"No he isn't."

"Who am I talking to? Is this his sister?"

"No, this is his wife. Who's calling?"

There's a pause. Then she says, "I'm sorry. I must have the wrong number. I'm calling Lucas McLeod."

"You have the right number. He's not home yet. Who's calling?"

"But the Lucas McLeod I'm looking for is not married."

"Well, this Lucas McLeod is very much married. At this moment his three children are hanging on my hip and running around between my legs."

"Oh, there must be a mistake. I'm looking for the Lucas McLeod who's the regional director of Ohio General Motors. I'm his fiancé."

"Then you must be the one who's mistaken since I'm his wife." I hang up the phone, my heart's thumping as though I've been on a long race. I know it's beginning again.

Around midnight Luke slams the front door and stamps into the den, yelling, "What in the world did you say to Rita Vann when she called here? Her agent tracked me down to tell me how she got so upset she missed her performance. He was mad as hell with me. What did you say?" His face is red, he's breathing hard, and his hands are gripped in fists. "Goddamnit, what have you done?"

My heart thumping wildly, I'm watching those fists. I speak calmly. "I told her I'm your wife, not your sister. But she says she's your fiancé."

"My God, you just misunderstood her. Now she's so upset her agent can't find her." He paces back and forth, holding his lips tight and banging on a table. Then he bellows out a tirade of epithets at me and rushes out of the room. Once again, he's turned the tables on me so it looks as if I'm to blame. He's so irrational there's no point in complaining.

However, it blows over quickly; the next day it's as though the rage and the call never happened, as though I'd imagined it all. I'm only 28, but I feel old. How can I break this pattern, say "Enough!" and start my life all over again?

A couple of months later—time dissolves its meaning when you have nothing to measure it by—I'm checking coat pockets again. It's become a ritual for me, a sick scavenger hunt. I find a receipt for lease property. I call the realtor, telling him my husband, Mr. McLeod, has lost the receipt and doesn't remember the apartment number. He tells me the apartment leased to Mr. and Mrs. Lucas McLeod is #209. I recognize the general vicinity of the address, which is on our side of town, near Wright Patterson Air Force Base.

I look up at the painting of Tiger and know what I'm going to do. It's late in the afternoon before I can find a sitter for the children. But nothing could stop me from driving to the address. It's easy to find, so I drive straight there and park outside the apartment building.

I find the door, knock, and a woman's voice asks, "Who is it?"

"Erin McLeod. Luke's wife."

After a pause she answers, "I have nothing to say to you. Just go away."

"I'm not going anywhere. I'm staying right here until you open this door. And if you don't open it soon, I'm going to start banging on it until you do."

Slowly the door opens, just far enough for her to peek out through the crack. She says again, "Please go. I don't have a thing to say to you."

I reach out and grab the edge of the door before she can shut it. I slam it open with one hand, march inside, and reach up for her long blonde hair with the other hand, jerking it as hard as I can.

Something comes over me. It's as if I'm two selves at once, my self and that other self I'm observing from a distance. I'm hitting her in the face, on her neck, on her shoulder and chest, wherever my fist falls as she's tries to pull away, screaming, but I hold her fast by her hair. It's the first and only time in my life that I enjoy both inflicting pain on another human being and watching it being inflicted, and I can't stop myself. I want to kill her. It's a segment of time that's immeasurable. It might have lasted a few seconds; it might have lasted a few minutes. It's like being caught in a centrifugal force: you can't stop the momentum because it's more powerful than you.

Suddenly, I become aware of a man's arm pinning my right arm down and holding me tight against him while his other hand pries my fingers loose from Rita's entangled hair. Screaming, she runs into the kitchen and when his grip loosens, I swing around to face Luke and hit him in the face with my pocketbook. He ducks, holding his arm over his head, and stands there while I beat him with it.

Eventually I stop. Rita is peeking out around a doorframe, so I yank off my engagement ring and wedding ring and throw them across the room. I shout, "You have my husband so take these damn rings." I stomp into the living room, pick up a heavy wood coffee table filled with glass knickknacks, and throw it across the room. Then I knock over the lamps.

Throughout it all Luke says nothing. He doesn't move. He stands like a soldier in combat shock. Rita runs out the door at her first chance.

Now that I've finished throwing everything moveable, I glare at him in a cold rage and stomp out. I get into my car, start the motor, pull it in reverse, slam down the accelerator, and take off like a drag racer across the gravel in the parking lot. I keep flooring the gas, going as fast as I can, ready to hit anyone in my way. I can't stop. I watch the speedometer surge up, as if I'm still two selves. I'm observing myself, watching myself in awe. At 5:00 the area around Wright Patterson is jammed with traffic. I keep speeding; I keep weaving through six lanes. Traffic in all lanes is stopped for a light. The self who is driving sees the stopped cars but doesn't want to stop while my observer self shouts in my head, "Stop!" But I can't. I'm still caught up in the chaos of the last hour.

So I ram into the car stopped in front of me.

The jolt brings me back from wherever I've been. The man whose car I've hit walks towards me; a policeman appears at my window. The policeman does the talking, and I'm unaware of what I answer. No one is hurt. Both cars are banged up; the front of mine is by far the worse. We exchange insurance information. For some strange reason I'm not cited. The policeman asks, "Are you sure you're okay, ma'am? Your car is all right to drive home. But do you feel like driving?" He looks concerned. "You can go, but drive more slowly. Be careful, ma'am."

The insurance company pays for most of the damages, and Luke pays the deductible without saying one word.

Snow drifts are piled high, nearly over my head, against the glass patio doors. Luke is gone somewhere; I suspect he's with whomever his current woman is. I decide to go home to North Carolina for Christmas without Luke. Santa comes early for the children so that the three of them—ages two, four, and seven—can fly to Oak Glen with their favorite gifts: Alex's Barbies and their clothes in a little case, Kayleigh's playhouse and doll, and Brennan's case of matchbox cars and Hot-Wheels racetrack.

This is my first trip here in two years since Mama's month stay at Dix Hill. Now she lives in her new house—a one-story brick built after the home place sold. Her house is rather small, but it does have three bedrooms even though we five feel a bit cramped. Minnie Bell, who cleans for her, has cooked our Christmas dinner, leaving nothing for Mama to do but drink. This surprises me because her doctor and Preston have reported her sober for two years. So, why now? I had great hopes for her, but now ...

After Christmas dinner she eventually falls asleep on the sofa, too drunk for me to get her up and into bed, and the children play on the floor and in the chairs around her. They spend a week that way, playing Barbie, coloring in books, racing cars around the room, eating leftovers until I grocery shop and cook, and then watching their grandmother pass out in their midst. I pray that she'll wake up and be alert during the day so we can engage in adult conversation, but I fear she's lost again within herself.

At breakfast I suggest things we can do together, and I beg her not to drink any more vodka, at least for a day. But she denies she's drinking. If I pour vodka down the drain, she'd just find another bottle hidden somewhere. I'll not argue with her in front of the children.

"Let me get dressed, Erin. And we can take the children for a ride and get a milkshake. And we can stop by Roses—I remember how you used to run up and down the aisles, just looking … and end up at the candy counter where you'd shovel up pieces of chocolate into your little brown bag."

"Chocolate-covered nuts. I still can eat those all day."

"Well, let's get out of this house! It won't take me long to take my bath." Mama calls, "Alex … Brennan … Kayleigh, we're gonna take a ride! Soon as I dress."

The children respond with "yea-a-a-a-h-h" and start picking up their coats.

A worrisome time later, I check on Mama. She sits at her dresser, trying to put on makeup. One eyebrow crooked, the other one half-touched, one cheek a clown circle. She looks up at me. "I'm ready."

She starts to stand and stumbles, catches herself, and leans against the dresser. "Erin Rose, I … I don't feel … very … well."

A new vodka bottle, half-filled, lies between the trashcan and wall. What else can I say? What can I do? I'm ready to go back to the snow. But we have a couple of days left before Mama has to return to work and we leave for the airport. Asheville writer Thomas Wolf's words run through my head: "You can't go home again."

After the holidays end, we fly out and land in a snowbound city. The flight is late because of the blizzard conditions, and Luke doesn't meet us as planned. Instead, he's sent one of his employees to drive us to our snow-covered neighborhood. We find he's had no one to shovel the driveway or the walkway or the steps or stoop by the front door. The driver carries our luggage to the front door, so we have to trudge through the snow, two children trying to walk in the boot tracks of the driver's steps and Kayleigh holding on to my neck as I hold both her and the small bags. It's at least midnight, and the snow on the ground has long since turned to packed ice. A north wind blows, causing the kind of cold that chills you to the very marrow of your bones. Kayleigh keeps whining, "Mommy, me cold."

The driver politely piles the luggage in the snow on the front stoop and leaves before I can reach it or turn the doorknob. Holding Kayleigh in my arms, I unlock the door and push it open, and we—Alex, Brennan, and I—step into ice water that nearly touches my calves in my high-heeled boots. Alex squeals. Brennan charges through the water as I yell, "Get back! Don't touch the light switch!" But he's already flipped on the switch and shouts, "Mama, the ceiling's on the floor ... I'm freezing!"

I step in far enough to see the exposed water pipes between the upstairs floor and the downstairs ceiling, now in broken pieces.

Ice water covers both children's boots. Still holding Kayleigh on the stoop, I empty Alex's and Brennan's boots while they cry about wet-socked feet freezing and the only place to run is back into snow. No car awaits. Kayleigh whines with each blustering of Arctic wind, "Mommy, me cold!"

Like an old silent movie with a woman and child shivering in the cold, I knock on a neighbor's door to get the children warm and dry. My mind can't think any further.

Georgia Lee welcomes us, hurrying the children in by the fireplace with its shimmering ashes to take off wet boots and socks and then returning with stacks of towels and quilts and blankets while she calls for her husband. Miguel's already downstairs and bringing in more wood and stoking the ashes. With a fire and snug covers, they're soon warm. Miguel comes in with our luggage and then he checks our house: the pipes have frozen and burst. Everything—sofa, piano, bookcases, china cabinet, buffet, dining table and chairs—all the furniture I love sits in ice water.

A major in the Air Force and an engineer, Miguel quickly institutes an action plan. He puts his arm around me and says, "Erin, you and the children are welcome to stay with us as long as you need. We *will* find Luke."

Georgia Lee feeds the children, puts on their pajamas, and takes them upstairs to bed. She calls, "Erin, Alex and Brennan are in our daughter's room. Kayleigh's in the guest room where she'll sleep with you. It's time for you to get comfortable now." She brings me coffee.

For the following year our marriage stays touch and go, on and off, lukewarm, cool, then cold, depending on Luke's presence of mind and mood. The only stability in my life are my children and my job teaching. I stubbornly hold on to that hope that somehow, miraculously, we'll find ourselves happily in the middle of that old American Dream: the little white house with red geranium flower boxes, a picket fence, children romping with the collie in the yard, mother in the kitchen baking bread, and daddy every night home for dinner. In the meantime I simply take whatever life, or Luke, has to offer from one day to the next. True, I am intelligent. I know the improbability of dreams. But what do you do when illusions go?

One afternoon I return home from school and find Luke's closet door is ajar. When I look inside, all of his clothes are gone. His shelves in the bathroom are empty, his half of the medicine cabinet wiped clean. It is days before he calls to say that he moved out so that he could "find himself"—the stock phrase of the flower children of the '60s.

In a way, it's a relief. I no longer have to wonder when he'll be home. He's gone. No more anxiety over his moods and over what-should-I-do? I'll continue living as I'm doing anyway.

When money is no longer coming in, except my teacher's salary, I soon see I can't cover all of our expenses. Luke has been gone for several months and has not assumed any financial responsibility. I've left messages at his office, but my calls are not returned. I finally call a lawyer to ask about my options. I'm advised to file for legal separation to ensure a fixed income for us, and Luke will have to pay the legal bill. When Luke does call, he's surprised that I'd seek a lawyer; however, he goes along with the financial settlement debates, finally agreeing with whatever the two lawyers draw up, which primarily is what his lawyer asked for. I'm too depressed to care about money, or even pay attention to details. The legal separation is January 1967.

Several days later, on a late Sunday afternoon, dusk settling in an already gray winter day, the phone rings. It's Luke's mother, Marty. Very seldom does she call, but the two of us have always been on very good terms. I'm somewhat surprised but pleased to hear from her.

Over the years I've grown very fond of Marty who taught me to cook when Luke and I first got married. She took me out to her garden beside the old tobacco barn and showed me how to pick field peas and butter beans and shell them, how to sauté them in a small amount of simmering salt pork until the fatback flavor seeped in and then to pour boiling water over them to cook until they're tender. She showed me how to make bread-and-butter pickles and how to trim the white part of watermelon rind to marinate overnight for pickling in her special sweet and sour syrup for the best watermelon pickle ever.

We spent many afternoons sitting on the back steps shucking corn and scraping kernels off the cobs to freeze. She showed me how to blanch vegetables before freezing them and how to drop homemade dumplings into the broth. Marty would bring a bushel or so of oysters from the beach and drop them on a metal sheet that she put across the outdoor brick fireplace, and we would watch the oysters roast, their shells popping open, the fire crackling underneath. She showed me how to plant flowers and take care of them. I always remember her with food and flowers. Her roses grew large and bright; her azaleas full and heavy. Marty was of the earth.

She asks about the children. She says how sorry she is that our marriage has turned out this way. She says she thinks of me often and prays for us, that she can't understand why Luke does the things he does. She wants me to know how much she cares for me, that she knows in her heart that I'll do the right thing. I tell her how nice it is to hear from her and thank her for calling. There's a pause and she says, "I wanted to call and say I love you."

After we hang up, I feel homesick. Her words and tone of voice are touching. It'd feel so good to sit on her steps again and listen to her simple remedies for plants and babies, bee stings and roses. I miss her.

Later that night Luke calls me. His father has just reached him with the news that his mother shot and killed herself earlier in the evening. After supper she had washed the dishes, gone to their bedroom, stood in front of the mirror of her dresser, put her husband's pistol to her temple, and pulled the trigger. His father had been sitting, reading the Sunday paper, when he heard the gunshot. She'd fallen where she stood. It was January 25th, the fifth anniversary date of her son Paul's death in a car wreck, and Luke's father thinks that's what triggered her suicide. All I can think of is that she called me and that I am probably the last person to speak to her.

The children and I fly home to North Carolina with Luke to attend his mother's funeral. Marty is lying in an open coffin in the living room when we arrive. Her head has been repaired and her face made up so that family and friends can view her. I don't want to look, but a relative has already taken Alex right up to the coffin for her to get a last glimpse of her Grandma McLeod, and I have to hurry to get her before someone else will have her touching the corpse. I know without looking that Alex is horror-struck. I can't stay for a minute in a house that contains a corpse so the children and I stay at Mama's. The McLeod house is never again the same without Marty.

By the middle of February, our divorce becomes final. There are a few people in the courtroom, but Luke does not appear. My lawyer accompanies me to the front, where I hear the judge announce the final decree. I feel as though I've heard my death sentence: so exact, so cold, so final. I'm choked with grief. What do you do when hope is stripped bare? There's a hollow feeling inside, an empty space that will never be filled. My world has ended.

Luke calls that afternoon, after hearing from his lawyer about the final divorce decree. He says, "Erin, I never meant for it to go this far. Not a divorce. We need to do something about it."

I'm too choked to reply. He never calls back.

Chapter 33

The phone rings on a Friday afternoon in April, two months later.

"Hello, Erin," Luke says softly.

My breath catches in my throat as it always does when I hear his voice.

"How are you?" he asks.

"Fine," I lie.

"And the kids?"

"They're fine, too."

He hesitates. "Are you doing anything tonight?"

"No. Nothing's planned."

"Why don't you get a sitter and we'll go out for dinner?"

Why is he asking me out? We haven't spoken since the day of the divorce. He hasn't even called about the children. And I've lied to them again and again, saying Daddy called and wanted to talk to you and says he misses you and he loves you.

"I don't know. I don't ... think that would be wise."

"Why not?"

Yes-no-heart-head—I'm so mixed-up. *What should I do?*

I stutter, "I probably can't get a sitter this late anyway."

"You can try."

"Luke, why are you calling?"

"I miss you. I'd like to see you. We really do need to talk."

"I don't see that ... there's anything to discuss."

"Yes there is. Us. We need to talk about *us*."

Relief, even now, surges through me—but I've been there before, too many times. Yet it's automatic: the tape rewinds, then winds forward again, the lines already written, rehearsed, said, and re-said. The scene keeps going on and on, and I can't change my role.

"Erin, are you still there?"

Before I can answer, Luke takes over. "Look. You get a sitter and I'll call for reservations and get back with you. Okay?"

"All right." The scene has commenced to play.

"Great. Talk to you later."

The children are waiting at the door when he arrives, claim his attention, welcome him like a favorite uncle come home at last. They're all over him and talking at once. When I look at Luke, I know I love him, despite every deceitful, unsavory thing he's ever done.

Brennan's telling his daddy about losing a tooth but he dropped it in the grass so his Mama wrote a letter to the tooth fairy for him, explaining why the tooth couldn't be put under his pillow, and he still got 50 cents. Then he runs to get his new baseball glove, calling at the same time, can Luke catch with him tomorrow? Alex starts describing the routine she's practicing each week for her dance recital and explaining the doctor said she can start wearing glasses. Then Kayleigh joins in with how Racer buried his bone in Mrs. Penrod's flower garden and Brennan painted part of the bricks of our house black but you can't see it unless you get behind the bushes and she skinned her knee.

Later in the Colony Club a golden softness spreads around the table. With dim lights, candle glow, and the plaintive melody of the alto sax drifting across the dance floor, I feel as though I've traveled backwards through a time tunnel, and perhaps we're together again as we're meant to be.

Luke smiles at me, the smile I remember so well. The kind that starts with his eyes and spreads over his face. He reaches over and takes my hand. "Glad you came?"

"Yes. The prime rib is delicious. And the band sounds wonderful."

"And?" His eyes penetrate mine.

"And the company's okay, too." I make an attempt to be light, to keep this date impersonal.

He raises a quizzical eyebrow. Reaching across the table, Luke touches my face, runs a finger down my cheek and across my lips, which open, of course. "I've missed you."

Careful. Careful. Careful, my brain screams. I recognize my eighteen-year-old hormones here now, ready.

"Have you?" I stare back while he talks. He's still good-looking in a most appealing way. Kayleigh has his thick auburn hair and straight nose, Brennan has his sharp jaw and chin, and Alex has his smile and that expansive laugh. Perhaps his hands are his alone—brawny ... and sometimes gentle.

"Hey, are you listening to me?"

"What? Oh ... I'm sorry. I was thinking."

"What were you thinking about?"

"Oh, how handsome you are," I reply in a joking manner.

"Yeah, sure. Now I'm being the serious one, and you don't hear me."

"What did you say?"

"I said I've been doing a lot of thinking. I've had a lot of time to think, and I've really missed you and the kids." He

379

pauses. His green eyes keep searching, trying to read what lies beneath mine. "Have you missed me?"

"Well." I can't lie. "Sort of."

"Erin, I want to come back home."

I'm too stunned to answer.

His eyes hold mine. "You know I never wanted a divorce."

I know I mustn't falter. "Luke, you could've come home. If you'd just moved your clothes back in or contacted me in some way, I wouldn't have gone to a lawyer. You had a choice."

"I know." He presses his lips firmly together, and a muscle flinches in his upper jaw. He looks as if he's about to cry.

I blurt out, "I can't be married to someone who lives in two different places: part-time with me and part-time with another woman."

"I know." He sighs. "I've been unfair to you. I realize now how wrong I was." He looks at me squarely. "I want to make up for it."

I find myself toying with the wine glass and biting my lip. My throat is completely dry. I want this to be true so much, but I'm afraid the way you are when you have stage fright, the big scene approaching and you're not sure of your lines anymore or the way the scene will play.

"What are you suggesting, Luke?"

"I want to move back home." He hesitates, then says, "Start over. Get married again. Everything will be different. I promise."

It's hard to ask, but I have to know. "And what about Rita?"

"It's you I love. She doesn't matter. Believe me."

I want to believe Luke with every inch of my being. Maybe the divorce—the shock that I pursued it and followed through with it—maybe that forced him to realize a few things he hadn't recognized before.

"Luke, don't. Don't do this to me again."

"I love you. I never meant to hurt you." He reaches over and wipes a tear that's spilling down my face. Then holding my chin, he leans across the table and kisses me. "Let's go home."

In the morning I awake with bright sunshine splaying through the curtains and onto the bed. After a long Ohio winter, it's finally spring. I look over at Luke asleep on his stomach with his arm slung over my waist, and I hear his deep, even breathing. I'm content to lie still in the pleasure of having him beside me and watching him sleep.

Suddenly, the door flings open with Alex calling, "Mama." She stops and her eyes widen and she rushes out to the top of the stairs and yells, "Brennan! Kayleigh! Daddy's home!"

Always the first one downstairs on Saturday mornings to turn on his favorite cartoon, Brennan bolts up the stairs three at a time. He rushes into our bedroom with Alex, and the two pile on top of Luke. Soon Kayleigh comes trailing after, giggling and jumping on top of them. Then Luke throws a pillow at Brennan, and Brennan throws a pillow at Alex, who throws one at Kayleigh, who topples over everyone, squealing. I've slipped out of bed to start breakfast.

By mid-morning Luke leaves for his apartment to pack his clothes to move back home. He says it won't take long, but he has to stop by his office to catch up on some paperwork. He promises Brennan he'll be home early enough to catch some balls with his son's new glove. He says that dinner at 5:00 sounds fine to him.

He stops in front of me, pulls me to him, whispers softly, "I love you," and passionately kisses me good-bye.

By 7:00 the children are hungry, and dinner has long lost its flavor after warming on the stove for two hours. Brennan has waited all day outside on the patio with his glove to play catch with his dad. I feed and bathe them, play a game of Battleship, read to Kayleigh, and make excuses to all of us. Finally, I put them to bed. I wait up until midnight and then go to bed, where I'm unable to sleep. Staring at nothing. Waiting for night to change to dawn.

By late Sunday afternoon, Luke hasn't returned or called. I'm sitting on the front steps, waiting for the day to end. Georgia Lee walks over from across the street to sit a while. She knows I'm hurting. I told her Luke was coming back. She tries to console me by saying that Monday will bring a perfectly logical reason.

At the breakfast table Monday when the phone rings, Brennan scrambles from his chair, shouting, "That's Daddy," and grabs the phone. Then he frowns. "It's for you, Mama."

It's Georgia Lee. "Have you seen the morning paper?"

My heart turns to lead. *What possibly can happen next?* "No, I haven't brought in the paper yet."

"Then don't. I'm coming right over."

I rush to meet her at the door without the children.

"I didn't want you to be by yourself when you read the news," she says.

I reach for it, and as I turn the pages, my hands begin trembling, my heart thumping. "Where is it? What is it?"

"On the entertainment page."

I scan the page, stopping when I see Luke's name halfway down the left side: *STARLET WEDS. Local television star Rita Vann became the bride of Lucas McLeod on Sunday afternoon in the home of her manager*

.... The wedding rehearsal was held Saturday at one o'clock followed by a rehearsal luncheon given by ....

"I'm so sorry, Erin."

The print blurs.

"Erin, sit down. I'll see about the kids. Don't worry about them. Just go sit down." Georgia Lee puts her arm around me. "Can I get you anything?"

Slowly I shake my head. "No. I don't need anything."

"I'll get Alex off to school, and I'll take Brennan and Kayleigh home with me."

All day I sit in my gown in the den staring out the window unaware of time.

Alex has gone to her friend Gina's house after school. When she gets home, she bursts into the room. "Mama! Mama! I just saw Daddy on TV at Gina's house with a pretty girl—she had long blonde hair—and Gina's mama said they got married. Did they, Mama?

I reach out for Alex and pull her into my arms, and we sit close together on the sofa.

"Mama, Daddy said he was coming home. Does this mean he's not coming home now? Why did he marry *her*?" Alex's eyes fill with tears that spill down her cheeks. "Mama?"

"I don't know, Alex. I really don't know."

Alex huddles down beside me and cries against my shoulder. We sit until the afternoon is gone and twilight shadows spread across the room. I sit holding her and staring out the window, glad that Georgia Lee's looking after Brennan and Kayleigh today. Though it's April, the March wind's still strong, bending limbs back and forth, back and forth, blowing away the first signs of spring. The sky is gray, and a chill spreads through the house. Ohio's long winter hasn't given up.

Fright keeps me from plunging into deep depression. Divorce is unacceptable and nearly unheard of in most circles in the '50s and early '60s, especially in Oak Glen. It destroys the chance of my children being normal and successful. So says the media, during this heyday of articles about juvenile delinquency caused by broken homes. Every magazine and newspaper documents percentages of doom: hell for a single mother. How can I prevent this? There's no hope for reconciliation, for a marriage with Luke.

Then the world turns upside down. It's May—one month since Luke's wedding. I answer the phone and can almost move my lips in sync with his words. Strangely, he never changes his return-to-me habit or his words, and today Luke's playing his best romantic role. Innumerable times my heart has wanted to say *yes,* yet my head wanted more to say *no.* He's like a demonic force that overpowers me so that I question my own perspective. I wait out his talk. And I feel I'm facing a tidal wave and know I can't swim away fast enough. So I tread in shallow water and wait, watching it crest over, crash, and suck me under. I can't escape.

O-o-ka-ay ... I'll play this game with him. See what it's like with the tables turned. Now *I'm* the other woman. I brush off my depression as if it were a piece of lint on my shoulder. I'm going out on a date with Luke—he'll pay for the sitter for our three children and tell a lie to his new bride. It strikes me as so ludicrous that I catch myself laughing almost hysterically, but I feel a vindictive pleasure luring Luke away from the starlet Rita Vann. I'm flattered in a misdirected way: I always thought I was inadequate, but now I'm becoming as twisted as Luke. Or are we both addicted to illusion?

Then I rationalize (my conscience requires it): our vows in church "for better or worse 'till death" makes me his wife and cancels wife number two. I feel young again living in the moment.

For the first time in years I'm enjoying Luke while he's showering me with attention—and I can call the shots if I want to. We go away together a lot on weekends—at first, usually one a month. I discover being his mistress is a whole lot better than being his wife. First I model outfits in an exclusive shop for him to choose for me—a long black embroidered dress, form-fitting, low in front and with a split up the back—to take to New York to see the new musical hit *Cabaret,* my first Broadway show; another long dress, gold metallic thread on blue with matching evening coat; a cashmere coat with a large mink collar. We go to Miami and attend a jewelry auction; he buys me a ring. We're companionable, talking just about the moment. But he talks to strangers more than I. He talks to the children briefly when I call them twice a day. And Luke calls his Number Two Wife Rita each day and talks to her in front of me. I can't believe that now I find it funny. I'm on the side of the *lie.* I'm on the side of the deceit and the betrayal. I'm on the side of pleasing myself in the moment—as long as I think the children are safe and okay. I've living a role.

As months pass and then a year, I find this game very lacking. I'm weary of the "out on the town" weekends with too much of everything. After all, you can only shop so much, eat so much, drink so much, have sex so much, and talk so much to strangers about nothing. At the end of each time I feel something important is missing. Maybe tomorrow. Perhaps we can sit in some quiet, secluded place, just the two of us, and relax and talk and listen or wear blue jeans and go to a movie and eat popcorn.

Though I'm switching roles, my emotional responses stay. During the week when he brings me home after a night out, I want him to stay; or if he stays part of the night, I want him there in the morning. I crave that missing part to suddenly appear. Then a deep sadness comes over me, and I know I can't continue living this way. This is not me. It's like I'm throwing myself away. At too great a cost. I cannot be all that he wants—he wants too much. And he does not have it in him to give me what I need.

All I feel is despair. Too much time has passed. And the time spent with him makes me more depressed afterward than when he ignored me.

One afternoon "out of the blue," Daddy's words come to me: "Only *you* can lose who you are. Then it's hard to find what's lost." When a child, I had asked him, "*How, Daddy? How do you find it?*" and he replied, "When *you* find the answer, be true to your thoughts, your conscience." *From where did these words come—they just popped into my head?*

Sleep doesn't come. I toss and turn in a nightmare of little brain explosions. Mama's dejected face pops up, and I think of her addiction to not only alcohol and drugs, but also to Preston, her long-term lover. Never, never will I become my mother or have I? With a different addiction. I have to get away from here. A long way away.

But time keeps running away—fall fading to winter, cold as ever, and spring coming late again—I sit staring out at the rain. No change. My future stretches before me as bleak as the day. I cannot cast off this heavy feeling. I know school will be out in May, and I've made no plans. How does anyone start over? Give up your job and your home and take three children to a strange place far away—alone?

I am so depressed I call in sick. Every day I take Alex to school and Brennan and Kayleigh to the nursery. And every day I come home and collapse until late afternoon when I get the children. All day I lie on the sofa, curled up, exhausted from praying then crying then both at the same time, unable to move. I start to doze. For two weeks I yield to this paralysis.

The phone keeps ringing and ringing—I ignore it. I don't want to hear Luke's voice.

Then one day the phone rings.

Alex runs to me. "It's for you, Mama."

"Erin Rose?"

I hear a man's voice. No one calls me that name anymore, not since high school, except Mama or someone from home.

"Yes?" I'm still trying to place that voice. I've heard it before.

"Erin Rose, why don't you come home?" It is like the voice of God reading my mind, booming out.

Before I can reply, he continues. "This is Alan Grayson. We have an opening for an English teacher. And we need you. Won't you come home?"

How does he know where I live and that I'm flexible to move? It's so strange. It's as if he's sensed my despair and is continuing a conversation I was having with myself. Mr. Grayson—superintendent of schools in Oak Glen and Oakland County—I haven't seen since I shook his hand at my high school graduation.

I find myself replying, "All right. I will. I'll come home." I don't hesitate. I don't even think about pros and cons. It's like something outside myself is directing me. Again I affirm: "Yes, I'll come."

Mr. Grayson says, "Good! I'll have Don Wyatt—you know Don—he's principal of the high school now—I'll have Don call you about the particulars. Nice talking with you."

As soon as we hang up, Don Wyatt calls and explains the teaching position: senior English, all college preparatory classes. He says to come by the school to see him whenever I get settled. The job is mine.

I know their word is good.

I flip through the yellow pages for a local realtor, and the first one offers to buy the house for speculation—without a sign in the yard until we move. I call a moving company. Then I call a realtor in Oak Glen to find us a house with my specifications. I type a resignation from my current teaching position.

Within an hour I've taken charge of my life and completely rearranged it. I tell no one until it's time to go.

Chapter 34

Three years have passed since Mama's funeral. One afternoon Alex goes to the cemetery, walks to the O'Donovan lot, and looks for her grandmother's grave. "It's like she hasn't died, but I know she's there ... somewhere under the grass," she says. "Mama, why haven't you ordered a marker?"

I have no answer.

Alex keeps after me from time to time. I say I don't like to go to the cemetery. Then she says she'll order a footstone and take care of the details. "All you'll have to do is pay for it." I promise her I'll take care of it myself.

I drop the subject. And do nothing.

Several more years pass, and Mama has been dead for about five years or so in an unmarked grave. One night I awake with a clear voice in my head, as if it's been taped, that sounds like someone reading poetry. That voice from the realm of dreams is startling, the words puzzling.

I switch on the lamp and reach for a notepad and pen to write the words before the voice fades away: *Years you have been in that unmarked grave that cracks in the still night, Pandora's Box, unfettered horrors and plaguing doubts. No burial mark to ferry you away; you wander restively, hovering near.* As I write the words, the voice starts fading, but my unconscious continues: *By your grave the tall magnolia patiently waits for spring to burst forth*

*white blossoms in the night. Maybe, then, something will
break to make me return to bury you, Mama.*

I put these lines aside, perplexed, feeling creepy. I
haven't read mythology recently. Why would I dream of
Pandora's Box? And why would it become Mama's coffin?
The line about the unmarked grave is certainly true. And
what white flower will burst forth? I file away what I've
written.

During the last few years I've tried to obliterate every
thought about her grave. Then, like a compulsive ritual, I
start returning, circling the cemetery, slowing down near
the magnolia tree where O'Donovan is carved in tall granite.
One day I cut off the motor and sit waiting, car clock ticking
away, afternoon shadows lengthening.

I stare at Daddy's footstone: *Jacob Lewis
O'Donovan, born July 29, 1898; died December 29, 1947.*
My mind drifts to our walks across field and meadow, my
hand in his ... we would walk the path of hickory leaves the
dried sheen of leather crunching beneath our feet and see
old cherry trees and trellising ivy reaching for deep nutrients
from old soil. We'd sit on an old bench, spotting pink-white
hints of spring in the garden. Daddy, my oracle, waits to
answer my unasked questions.

Here in the cemetery life no longer seems defined as
if the souls of the dead breathe beside us. Why can't I
remember crying when Daddy died? Sitting beside him on
the bed, I showed him my dolls and watched him die
smiling, his eyes touching me with love as they rolled back.
He tried with unintelligible words to tell me something.

Alone beside his coffin, I stood and stared at the still
face that looked as if it were sculpted from chalk; I touched
his cold hand, hard like marble, and quickly withdrew mine.
Then I knew he wasn't there. When they rushed me out of

390

the room because I was a child, I understood what they did not. Daddy wasn't there. His hand was warm to me when I touched it with my mind. That was why I hadn't cried.

Years later, though, reaching out in darkness for his hand, I found nothing. I lost that childlike faith, whatever it was, but I longed to touch a hand like his.

Now I try to remember what we talked about, and I remember some words, but mostly I carry with me our silent closeness and so I feel he's beside me.

I look at the nearby patch of earth, my mother's grave. For so long after that bleak January day when I watched her lowered into blackness, I haven't wanted to return. Now I see only flat, hard ground, covered with dry grass trying to turn green. I knew the ground would be unmarked, but I expected to find the grave. Strangely, nothing bears witness to Mama; it is as if Nature, as well as I, has canceled her life.

I wait. Surely if I stand still and wait long enough, I'll feel something ... any feeling will do—remorse, compassion, guilt? A flickering of love? Disgust? Anger ... I wait and still feel nothing. Just those dream words repeating: you wander restively, hovering near ... *No burial mark to ferry you away.*

Then that inner voice whispers silently ... *Don't you see, Mama, I need to find some good in you. And, Mama, I need to feel some love for you. The locked door at Dorothea Dix, the tiny peep square of glass with bars, seeing you go beyond the door and passing down the long hall in the dark brick building on that forlorn hill—I was relieved to leave you there.*

The hate in your eyes when I left you later on that snowy mountaintop in dead of winter at Grace Home, where you stayed for the nuns of God to cure nothing and the call in the night during the blizzard to come get you quick for they could not deal with you with your brain fried. I was glad the roads were closed. You had to stay a little longer out of my sight.

And, Mama, I saw the Memory Verses Booklet they gave you and the scrawled pages you once earmarked but straightened again as if you no longer wanted to turn that page to "You must be born again" or any of the other pages with meaningless phrases for one who never thought of those things—or did you? You did leave one dog-eared page with this line marked: "For to me, to live is Christ, and to die is gain." Did this tell you what to do?

I was glad, Mama. I was glad you were dead. You should never have confessed your ultimate betrayal as my mother. What gave you the right to tell me about your secret sin? Fucking my husband, Mama? How did you expect me to forget? Or to forgive? How can I forgive such treachery? Do you know how much anger I've held inside me?

A gentle breeze murmurs from pines near the edge of the woods next to the family plot. The warm late-afternoon sun casts long shadows behind the O'Donovan monument, and a robin glides down on the unmarked grave. I still wait.

Both your granddaughters tell me to bury you properly with a marker with your name inscribed. Maybe ... someday. Maybe I'll return some spring to see the magnolias in the cemetery blossoming white. Maybe then, Mama, I'll bury you right.

Soon the night train will clack down the railroad track that cuts across the cemetery's backfield, its mournful whistle piercing, prolonged, deep—its primeval cry. Dusk nearing, the air chilled, the shadows deepened, I hurry to leave before the train approaches.

Another five years later, I start having nightmares again, each one the same recurring lucid dream, each one more intense.

Kayleigh asks me to stay with her during the summer in Hickory, where she's moved for a job after college graduation. While she's at work, I have a lot of time on my hands that I spend on reading and reflecting. On impulse, I start writing about my memories, returning time and again to our old house on Church Street and memories of Daddy and Mama. Sometimes I become oblivious of time until Kayleigh comes home. The more I write, the more I concentrate on the past reliving scene by scene, and the more I dream the old nightmare.

Then I'll sit up in bed with my heart thumping so hard, so fast, my rib cage heaving, that I can hardly catch my breath. I flip on the lamp switch and leave the light on for the rest of the night, afraid to go back to sleep.

One weekend Kayleigh leaves town to go to Clemson to see her fiancée. That Saturday night the same nightmare is so intense that when she returns, Kayleigh finds me in bed, afraid to get up lest I see Mama materialize in front of me. By then I've stopped writing and even avoid looking at the closed folder.

The next morning Kayleigh calls a clinical psychologist for an urgent appointment. She had heard of Dr. Jeremy Goldstein's excellent reputation.

Dr. Goldstein takes me through my dream. Mama, bigger than life, is coming after me; I am running from her and can't get away. Trapped, I awake in sweating terror of the darkness. Once I see her looking viciously at me while she burns me with a cigarette. I don't tell him about Mama's betrayal with Luke that must be at the root of the rage and cruel trauma of suicide witnessed by my children.

The doctor points out the figure is not necessarily my mother, but instead my own anger and sheer repressed rage I've projected onto her likeness, perhaps wanting to inflict pain on her. He pauses a minute, looks up at me straight in the eyes, and says, "Erin, you're a 'time-bomb' ticking away under a Southern Belle façade."

"Do you mean I'm chasing myself with that rage?"

Dr. Goldstein stares at me and shrugs his shoulders. "What do you think? Is there something you're angry at yourself about? Anything you've done ... or failed to do?"

That summer I visit Dr. Goldstein several times a week and when I return home to Oak Glen, I drive to Hickory to see him for almost two years. This is by far the best thing I have ever done for myself.

That year I also start working on my Master's degree at night after a long day of teaching, and I sign up for a course called "Myth in Literature," thinking it will be Greek Mythology. Not so. It's a Jungian interpretation of motifs and behavior in literature, focusing on the concept of the shadow found in all of us. We frequently discuss Carl Jung's theory of anima and animus.

After all the reading I do for class, including Jung's *Memories, Dreams and Reflections*, I begin seeing my own life in a different perspective. Ironically, what Dr. Goldstein brings up in our sessions is touched upon during my next graduate class as if someone's coordinating the two. It is uncanny, an unbroken conversation.

Dr. Goldstein asks questions and using what I've learned in class, I do most of the analyzing. He warns me not to lean too much on theory but to follow my own intuition, as valuable as any psychological school of thought.

He says that as long as I awake before the frightening figure reveals itself, I'll keep dreaming since I'm refusing to face it. (I know I haven't been facing many things.) He says to tell myself I will not awake until I face the figure.

I don't think I can. If I fear the dark in my own room, I certainly cannot face the dark in my mind. I can feel the

394

darkness, and I can feel the silence. I can see strange shadows in the room. My mind tells me these are clothes thrown over a chair outlined in moonlight, but still I sense an unknown something in the room, and I want to scream and run, but I'm afraid to get up. How can I stare at something even worse in my head?

Dr. Goldstein doesn't press, but keeps asking, "Don't you think you're ready to look at that figure in your dreams?" Instead, I stop dreaming. I talk about how relieved I am when Mama dies, that I can't be responsible for making her life okay when I'm simply trying to survive. That helpless longing, the raw empty space within that gnaws at you to be filled—I recognize it, and I hate raw need following me around, her shadow swallowing my own shadow.

One day Dr. Goldstein turns to me and asks about her suicide. "Erin, did you do it?"

"*What?*"

"Her suicide. After all, there were no witnesses."

I just stare at him.

"Did you slip away from school during your planning period? You have some free time after lunch, don't you?"

I sit and stare.

"Did you return home and kill your mother? Fake the scene? Clean yourself up from the gunk of the residue?"

I don't answer. I can't. My mouth won't move.

He waits. He keeps waiting. I feel confused like a victim of amnesia. I can't answer. Suddenly I don't know if I did or not. I wanted to be rid of her. I didn't want another day of Kayleigh coming home from school to find her grandmother still in her nightgown lying in a puddle of pee in the bathroom, too drunk to get up on her own. I didn't want another day of looking at the nylon gown with cigarette holes. I didn't want to see her naked arm with burn marks up and down it as if someone had tortured her. And I didn't want another reminder of her hanging around Luke's neck and rubbing against him in rhythm with the music. I was glad she was dead. Was my wish made tangible?

Finally, he speaks. "Erin, you have to admit your part in her death, whatever it was, before you can let her go."

"Sometimes I hated her. I didn't want to have to deal with her."

He waits for me to continue. Like pausing a videotape I remain suspended in a time warp. Gradually I slide back into the present.

"I caused her death just as much as if I'd pulled the trigger ... From the time she came to live with us, I didn't show her love ... I paid doctors instead ... sent her off to others to fix her ... even to Chapel Hill where after a few days doctors dismissed her because of dead brain cells ... then to nuns who made her memorize Bible verses when she needed a personal touch ... someone to care." I break down and cry uncontrollably.

Finally Dr. Goldstein says, "Then admit your part of the blame and let it go. Go on to other things. And don't wait for something to make you get a grave marker; go ahead and do it. A marker with her name beside her grave so you know her body's there. Close the lid and put an end to this part of your past."

As I'm leaving his office, Dr. Goldstein calls, "Erin, remember your Pandora's Box dream? I looked up the myth. I'm sure you recall the last thing she let out of the box."

I pause at the door. "At the moment I can't remember."

"Pandora wanted to see what was in the box so she opened it, and before she could slam the lid down, evil flew out with mischief and sorrow and one good thing—Hope."

I can feel my face lighting up. "I remember that now ... thanks." I pause and look up at him and smile. "Thank you so much, Dr. Goldstein."

One night soon afterwards I dream again but not the usual nightmare. *I know Mama is in the dream, somewhere, though I'm hoping she doesn't appear. She is in the background along with other people. I don't want to see her, but at the same time I will myself to wait. I know she's coming and I tell myself "I am going to face her." Suddenly, she's close to me, and she turns around so I can see her clearly. There is no half-faced monster. It is Mama as I remember her when she was much younger, smiling at me. I walk up to her, put my arms around her, and hear myself say, "I miss you, Mama ... I love you." She vanishes and I awake.*

When I describe this dream to Dr. Goldstein during the next session, he says, "You don't need me anymore, Erin."

I really miss those sessions, and not just his insight and compassion. I had never before expressed myself fully to another person, and because he was a man it was a turning point for me. It is possible now for me to trust a man. He helped transform my nightmare about anger, rage, hate, and guilt into a dream about love.

The marker issue is too complex for me to say why Mama's grave is still unmarked. Perhaps I had not wanted to visualize a grave for which I felt guilty. The repressed rage had made me terribly vindictive. All of a sudden I remember that Mama once said she had a fear of being left in an unmarked, unclaimed grave. I consciously forgot those words until now, but unconsciously, I was avenging her acts of suicide and betrayal with Luke. Somehow I have to forgive and let it go.

I keep waiting for something inside myself to give me a push to order the footstone. I think somehow I'll get a sign, maybe like a burning bush? But staring at her grave never gives me the urge.

Kayleigh keeps insisting, "Mama, you need to bury her properly—give her a name. Don't think about it. Just do it."

I reread the poem I wrote so many years before. The last verse described waiting for a "white blossom" to burst forth in the night. "And then I'll return to bury you, Mama."

One morning that voice wakes me again. "Make your own blossom." This time I'm ready. I ask the local monument company to engrave a picture on a footstone of granite that would match Daddy's old gravestone. I look at their designs, but none will do. I do not want a rose: I want one open magnolia blossom.

I ask an artist friend to draw a simple picture of what I'd imagined. She sketches the blossom on paper for a sculptor to trace as well as an angel holding a mirror for Daddy's footstone because I still think of him as my guardian angel.

At last I stand at my parents' graves. Daddy's angel is abstract with a suggestion of wings: one arm extended down, the hand holding a mirror to remind me of his words: "Look in the mirror, Baby. If you smile, it smiles back." Below Daddy's name and dates is the newly chiseled word *Love*.

Mama's marker will always remind me of my poem that ends "something will break to make me return to bury you, Mama." Beneath her name and dates are chiseled *Peace, Mama*, and on the corner is my friend's drawing of a full magnolia blossom, its petals smoother and lighter than the rest of the granite so that at a distance it appears white.

I stand for a while staring at the markers. Time remains irrelevant in the old cemetery, tucked away from the highway among trees. The sun is setting, and a pronounced stillness settles in. I feel more at peace than I have in a long, long time.

I turn toward the narrow road where my car is parked on the edge of the lot. Near the graves stands a tall magnolia tree, its limbs hanging over the plot, one branch hanging low and pointing toward Mama's grave. There on the branch a large magnolia blooms.

Startled I search the other branches for blooms but see only small, tight cones. There is only one magnolia flower blooming in the cemetery. Out of season. I cry all the way home.

Chapter 35

On Bird Island I sit on a large piece of driftwood and gaze out to sea. The early morning sea is still, except for gentle waves lapping on the shore. Around me a hollow hum, long, prolonged, like a conch shell held to your ear. I close my eyes to this sea-music and relish its rhythms.

Down the beach as far as I can see sand dunes spread with sea oats and grasses. Pelicans, terns, egrets, and blue herons settle and lift up in flight to nearby marshlands. I watch the birds, the way they flap their wings and soar up and away. Though the sun is up, the sea gulls are quiet, still asleep in clusters along the strand, each propped on one leg, the other enfolded underneath, heads turned and tucked into folded wings.

This is my place where I escape, tuck my head between sky and sea, and lose my sense of reality. Like a bird I fly into mists that open to my past, hover at its portal, and relive its images. Lately I do a lot of this—conjuring up the past, seeing again and again the molding of myself.

I live at Sunset Beach now. In June I retired at 58 from Oakland County Schools after teaching for 30 years. That spring I inherited a house here from Uncle Henry.

Every morning I walk two miles from the Sunset Pier to the windblown end of Bird Island to seek words in the old mailbox, a relic of the '70s, nailed to a weather-beaten post on the highest dune, its red flag waving in the ocean breeze. I heard that a lonely widower, who yearned to speak to his wife after she died, built the mailbox. Each day he would place a letter to her in the mailbox or write the letter in a journal he left there. Then others discovered the box and were inspired to share their deepest thoughts. And Kindred Spirit was born.

Its name painted white on each side of the mailbox glows. This holder of dreams pulls at me, drawing me back time and again to read, to think, and to write in the stacked journals.

Through the years after my return to Oak Glen, I visited Sunset often. I'd check the tides table at the pier before I crossed the shallow low tide pool to Bird Island, finding out how long I could stay on the island before high tide; otherwise, I'd be stuck on top of a dune with the sea crashing in fast and high with strong cross currents to cover the island. At the mailbox, I'd sit and read and write.

I reach into the mailbox and pull out a journal in a large Ziploc bag that contains several pens and markers. Other journals are stacked neatly inside. I open the journal and scan pages for signatures at the bottom and names of states of residence. Names appear from all over the United States and Canada, occasionally from places in Europe. Many writers write about God, spiritual matters, the beach, friends, or themselves.

When I read a man's message written in Arabic in one column with the English translation beside it, I am alarmed by his suicidal feelings. Am I the last one to read his thoughts? Does grief over the loss of his wife make him feel that life is not worth living? I close the journal on my lap, secure the journal in the Ziploc bag, and return it to the mailbox. Will the keeper of the Kindred Spirit collect these journals tonight and leave new ones for tomorrow?

I take a deep breath, inhaling the pungent smell of the sea, and hold the refreshing salty air in my lungs. I breathe out slowly and feel myself open up and expand with the landscape. How wonderful to be alive, especially today, on one of those September mornings when the sun rests warm on the skin after a nippy breeze off the water.

At the beach house I walk up the steps to the kitchen and family room and collapse on the sofa. The walk today has exhausted me, muscles sore from weeks of cleaning, painting, unpacking, arranging furniture, and pulling up weeds and vines grown wild. Thankfully, my adult children volunteered to help me move and clean up the old cottage, making it as livable as they could. They move in Mama and Daddy's original and only bed—the bed I was born in. Brennan nails up the "haunted mirror" (no longer bothering me) and the portrait of Tiger (my totem). They are delighted that they now have a place to visit at the beach, yet apprehensive that I'll be living alone in a house in need of so many repairs—the house creaks at night like an old abandoned shrimp boat docked near shore.

That last night before they return home we sit on the wide porch that overlooks the marshes and the old bridge and the canal that runs to Charleston and on to Florida. Sailboats, fishing boats, yachts, and the barges coast up and down this intra-coastal waterway, stopping at the old pontoon swing bridge, waiting for the bridge to creak and crack open and swing its two arms out wide. At night, lights sparkle across the canal, and the headlights of beach traffic crossing to the mainland sprinkles the darkness like fireflies.

With my grandchildren in bed, the rest of us talk, reminisce, and watch moonlight on the marsh, faraway lights blinking. At times like this, I feel my life whole and complete. Yet Alex and Kayleigh keep asking, "Mama, are you sure you want to do this? Live in this old place? Brennan is concerned the beach will be deserted in another month, and the furnace may not work through the winter. And you'll be by yourself."

I assure them I will be fine. I will try it for a year. If I decide to stay, I'll sell my house in Oak Glen and use that money to refurbish the beach house.

After my family returns home I wonder if this is what I want. I'll only know by staying. That can be a long time when winter settles in: tourists gone, shops and restaurants closed, only a few people left on the island, and the strand desolate. Cold winds will hammer at old boards. The pipes may freeze. And the furnace—will it hold?

I look around at the shabbiness, despite the slap of paint in the living area. What was I thinking? Moving here so suddenly? Ordinarily I never do anything on impulse. Uncle Henry died in March. I retired in June. When his estate was settled, I was delighted he willed me his beach house. (He'd always stated he promised Brother Jacob that he'd take care of Baby.) Immediately I made plans to move. I kept remembering all the good times the children and I had at the beach when they were young: running into the surf, jumping waves, collecting seashells. Alex and Kayleigh made ankle bracelets by sewing together the tiny shells with holes, and Brennan caught minnows in the tide pools and under the pier.

Inside, I walk to the wide window. The sea at low tide has drained the marsh leaving early autumn grasses yellow. The air is still. The scene reflects a Van Gogh painting of yellow straw and blue sky. The silence of the cottage is broken by unknown thumps and squeaks of the old house.

I turn on the stereo with the *Hits of Andrew Lloyd Weber*, march to the kitchen, and reach into the refrigerator to make a salad. What should I do this afternoon? What do I *want* to do? Since 16 I've worked my entire life. I remember all the things I've wanted to do with no time to do them. Where do I start?

After lunch, I'll read myself into a quick nap, then dress and go shopping at the mall. There are a couple of gift shops, a bookstore, and a Japanese restaurant where I can eat tonight.

And tomorrow? I'll make a list of what I like to do: read another book, experiment with my new keyboard, knit an afghan, peruse through boxes of journals and folders of my fiction, plant some bulbs for spring, and visit the art gallery and craft shops at Southport.

And the rest of my life? I'm excited about getting to know myself—all of myself, not just the pieces I've acknowledged during the last few years. I can throw away all the labels now. I haven't been a wife for a long time. I'll always be a mother even though the children are grown and gone. I'm no longer a hired teacher, since I retired, but my thoughts and "lectures" pop up at each chance I get. My father's child? Yes—I know he lives in me. My mother's daughter? I used to say "Never!" But I was wrong—our choices were just different. Now I can dig out from old journals the little pieces of paper like enlightened confetti caught up in rushing winds. Perhaps turn them into a book.

Near the pier, darkness has settled. I park around the grassy area where a few cars are parked, indicating some conscientious fishermen are still catching the fish of the day. In a weathered gray gazebo, a young couple snuggles up against the wind. I wonder if my sweater will be warm enough. The sky is clear, filled with stars. The Milky Way arches in a luminous ribbon of sparkles.

I walk down the pier as far as I can. Usually, the only fishermen here are those few fishing for King Mackerel. Tonight I see no one near. At high tide there's crashing of waves. The wind whips my hair back from my face and presses my sweater and pants taut. At the pier's end, I feel a slight swaying as if I'm at sea in a cruiser off to unknown places.

I hear the sound of someone's radio that drifts over the humming of the wind. I close my eyes and start moving to the music, totally oblivious to everything except the music, the wind, and the sea. Time passes. Slowly, I walk down the pier back to my car.

I pull up in front of the beach house. Inside there is no light. In the car I sit looking out at the darkness. I step in circling fog. I feel the stillness of an all-consuming darkness, strange shadows from the trees. I stand in the kitchen and do not touch the wall switch. I want to feel the darkness. Across the family room I stare out the large window that overlooks the marsh. Through the fog curling across the canal, I see spectral lights, unusually bright, of cars passing over the old bridge. The beauty of the night sweeps over me. Darkness cannot consume me anymore. I feel a comforting presence like a huge hand on my back as I walk through the darkness to my bedroom, my body soothed like it's floating in the gentle ripples of sea. I slip under the old quilt on the bed I was born in and sink into sleep.

In early morning I walk to Kindred Spirit and sit on the driftwood and write:

Dear Luke,

The last words you said to me were, "Erin, take care of yourself." I am taking care of myself. I am free.

I realize that neither you nor anyone else can define who I am or grant me happiness. Only I can.

Erin

I fold the letter, put it in an envelope, and slide it into Kindred Spirit.

Author

Patsy Ann Odom

Patsy Ann Odom, a native of Laurinburg, North Carolina, is a former teacher of English at Scotland High School in Laurinburg, NC, and a former instructor of English at the University of North Carolina at Pembroke. She holds a BA in English from the University of North Carolina at Greensboro and an MA in English from the University of North Carolina at Pembroke. She was awarded scholarships to attend Bread Loaf at Middlebury College in Vermont and to attend a Study In Humanities at the University of North Carolina at Chapel Hill. Recently, she has been one of the writers in residence at the Weymouth Center in Southern Pines. She has had work published in *Pembroke Magazine* and *Gravity Hill*.

Cover Artist

Cathy Adams

Cover artist Cathy Adams lives in Salisbury, North Carolina, where she and her husband Frank relocated to be close to their children and grandchildren. Cathy retired from Scotland County Schools after 30 years teaching elementary students in both the regular classroom and in art. As an artist, she enjoys a wide variety of mediums including watercolor, acrylic, silkscreen and block printmaking, pen and ink, pyrography, carving and painting gourds.

To see more of Cathy's artwork, visit https://squareup.com/store/art-happy.